What Gifts We Give

Mark Vedder

Library of Congress Control Number: 2020925776
Vedder, Mark 1965–2102
      What Gifts We Give / Mark Vedder
      285 pp. 1.5 cm
Published in Mechanicsburg, Pennsylvania
ISBN 978-1-941776-36-0

2018
ISBN 978-1-941776-36-0
Publishing rights reserved
by
Mark Vedder
sufferingduckman@gmail.com

To My Son
Ashriel

Contents

Chapter		Page
2	No More Introductions, Please	11
3	Things Really Do Happen	23
4	Not By Land	38
5	I'm Feeling Much Better Now	45
6	Daddy Knows Best	62
7	Not Like That At All	79
8	It's Killing Me.	87
9	Hostess	103
10	Ghosts. They're All Ghosts.	120
11	What are you going to do about it?	135
12	Oh. Right.	142
13	I Tried to Tell You	157
14	Or Does He	170
15	The Other Side	188
16	Knick-Knack Paddywhack	206
17	Under the Sea	221
18	Ship of Fools	241
19	East Wind by Way of West	253
20	Harbor	272

What Gifts We Give

The dream faces pulsing nearer, her heart throbbing in protest, panic; running again forever down that eighteen foot hallway, awake, asleep, through the door and crouched on her knees before the silent form in the overstuffed chair. Grandfather had an unpronounceable nerve disorder that didn't allow him to sleep. Night after night he would sit in the chair, eyes open or shut, becoming part of the moments that passed. Days were not different. No one knew for sure the extent of the disorder, nor how much, if any, sentience he possessed. Below his seated form in the dark she shivered and cried uncontrollably; "I'm sorry, I'm so sorry…" half an hour passed. Shakily to her feet, face wet and sinuses clearing, walked the eighteen feet back to her bedroom, picking up the sheet from the doorway in which it had been dropped. Curled up around a pillow, a long sigh, then peaceful sleep, her heart beating out the measure of each breath.

Mornings she enjoyed for their loneliness. Hopeful sun rays angling through the oddest windows, bare feet on cool wood floors, breakfast as a ritual of choice and patience. No "Hi, how are you? how was your day?" Just yogurt, cantaloupe, and varied musings of class. University was not yet as expected, but no matter; she was unaccustomed to expectations. It was not until in the car that she remembered last night; and even then wondered if it had been a dream. The ritual went back as far as she could remember; the dreams, the hallway —there had been other places, but always the hallway—and the desperate rush… away from…? to…? then shuddering at grandfather's feet, crying. She returned to the highway, to the world, to simpler, more puerile things, began to calculate what stance to take in Medieval History.

*   *   *

He first noticed Jason an early Tuesday morning, barefoot he was, though that was not what had drawn his attention. They were moving Mrs. Kurl's belongings to her new place—rest home actually, he wouldn't have commented on that had you asked—and Cris had the sense of something funny in the air. Mornings didn't normally lend themselves to picking up nuances of this sort, give him a good evening full of quarter-moon light any day for nuances. Jason was handed a computer monitor to carry to Bobbert's pickup. Watching, he couldn't tell if the monitor was made of lead or Styrofoam. Body language was smooth, professional, as if he had practiced taking the monitor from just that position for months on end; Charles handed it to him and began to turn away early, for Jason was exuding an undercurrent of physical confidence, the kind that makes one feel that the job is already as good as done. He walked lightly, naturally; the monitor might have grown out of his hands in youth for the difference it made to him. He watched this Jason, interested. It was the kind of attributes you never see, but more remarkable was the realization that this demeanor would never be noticed by others. He neglected Mrs. Kurl's work for a space and parked himself on a concrete pediment, drawing a quizzical look from Charles, but no matter, he needed to watch.

Driving back with Charles to return the pickup to Bobbert, he realized with a shock that Jason had been watching him even more closely. But he couldn't once remember Jason giving him a second glance, other than the normal conversation. As his mind raced around for clues, he saw the clock; 10:20. They had planned on four hours of moving, and finished in thirty-five minutes. He stifled his urge to say something to Charles and leaned back in the seat, thinking.

*　　*　　*

The luxury of no morning classes, and a dorm room facing Southeast. Cat stretched in the autumn sunbeams and breathed back into semi sleep, some wonderful dream just eluding her consciousness. Brother sun began to insist, and she sat up in a haze of long blond curls. Breakfast first, no; tea first, then breakfast, then… hm. Calculus homework for the evening class. Nothing to prepare for the afternoon's class in Medieval History, they were having discussions this week. Hmm. She wondered what Tera would do today, maybe she'd meet her beforehand and they could talk. Things seemed to be coming to a head in class, but things always seemed to be coming to a head around Tera. Cat was about her height, but looked shorter from the insistent aura of luxury, almost baby-fat like, that surrounded her. She liked to slouch, and could make any position look comfortable; her favorite clothes were cotton sweats and an oversized T-shirt. Tera was *lithe*, quiet, and dark. They both had long hair, but Cat's spilled out in blond curls in every direction. One might think Tera personally arranged each hair every few moments; it was almost magical, the way it served her. Stares became more frequent as they began to spend more time together. The tea was good; peppermint and feverfew began to clear her mind. Tera had told her something… something about wanting to give the Medieval History class something. She had tried to pay attention, but so often, when Tera gets that intense attitude, and speaks so quietly, Cat would wonder if she wanted to be heard at all. In fact, *that* was it, what she had planned to ask her: what was it exactly that she wanted from life. If she could find her for lunch, she'd ask her then. The day arranged, Cat began training a bagel and some cream cheese to perform a breakfast.

*　　*　　*

Jason walked to class, his thoughts his own, even his pace his own. Of those with whom he crossed paths, some stepped out of the path to let him pass, others treated him as if he were invisible. Watching closely, one might have begun to suspect that Jason produced each reaction deliberately, were not that idea almost ridiculous. He carried a worn notebook and nothing else. College. He looked around at the passing buildings with what might have been amusement, perhaps even disdain, yet exuding friendliness nonetheless. Just as his thoughts belonged to himself alone, each encountered person formed their own different picture of who they had just met. Some seemed as though they had received a gift; others became furtive, almost guilty; and still others hardened and became more confident of themselves in this hardness. There was no reaction to this discrepancy in his eyes; the late morning sun and he passed along on their own. He was walking to class.

*   *   *

"…A society," continued the slightly nasal voice, "A society is designated by its *form*. And since these *forms* are constantly evolving, history alone can inform us as to our *place* in the *progression* of these forms." Each emphasized word shrilled up two and one-quarter notes, Cris observed, sometimes two and one-third, but never as high as two and a half. "Now this makes it our *duty* to actively investigate ancient and more recent *forms*, else we have no *context* in which to frame our *description* of the *process* by which we've arrived to where we find ourselves today. So our discussion *so far* in medieval history has been the *only tool* by which we can obtain *intelligent* information as to the *current* state in which we find ourselves." Cris glanced over at Tera. Class had only started two weeks ago, but already she'd earned the position of the person at whom the professor glanced nervously whenever he was making a tenuous point. She wasn't giving any signs, impenetrable features as usual. The professor went on. "In *other* words, we learn the *role* of our society by learning *what* our place is in its evolution." Tera cleared her throat, very quietly, but it was enough. "Yes, Miss McCory, have you some input to this discussion?"

"Yes, I do have a question," her voice was always surprisingly quiet; "You talked last week of the twelve-part function of a society in the larger context of history, and how those twelve parts produce the forms that we still acknowledge today. In essence, then, you were saying that society develops forms from its historically contextual operations, which you called its functions, making function primary. Now you're saying the *form* is primary; do you intend to relegate the roles in society to the manner in which they operate, or is there something else you mean by form?" She got more seconds of silence than her customary half dozen. Yet consistent with her style, she had left him a way out.

"*The form*," he began, already squeaking, "*The form* is unfortunately the *tangible* aspect of society, which makes it far too easy for us to …ahh… *focus* on what is an *effect* rather than, as you say, the *historically contextual* function. But we must remember the *interrelationships* between these ideas, or we lose sight of the *evolutionary process*. Both the *forms* and the *roles* of society can be *interchangeable* in this light…"

She interrupted him. "Oh. So you were saying the forms *of* the functions inform our historic role then?" Cris thought she was letting him off the hook way too easily and looked around to see if anyone else agreed. Cat caught his eye, and he found himself holding hers for an extra moment. She smiled and exuded a small bit of appreciation before they both folded back to the interchange.

"Yes, that's a good way of putting it." He looked relieved, but not in the mood for further discussion. "Let's break into our *own* societies of four or five people each, and compare the religious attitude of last half of the tenth century with the first half of the eleventh. Each group can compose a one-page summary, which you can hand in at the end of class, with your group's names." Cris chuckled to himself… easy out. He noted with disappointment that both Cat and Tera were in a group with already five people, but the kids with whom he settled were okay, and the class passed with a minimum of pain. They even listened to him when he said the only thing he wanted to share, that the rapid building of cathedrals from 950 to 1000 in expectation of Jesus' return was never really abandoned after the turn of the millennium, rather the frantic attitude was seasoned and matured, and subsequently building styles began to explore depths that led directly into the making of the first really magnificent cathedral styles. He compared it to what happens when folks are frantic about something of which they know very little, and how it takes going through the experience of panic before they let go of expectations and begin to initiate the development of the elements of our life. Someone wrote the whole comment down; he felt vaguely pleased.

"I'm heading out for a quick lunch, would you girls like to join me?" He had caught up with them outside the building.

Cat didn't miss a beat; "Oh, so I smile at you in class and now you think you can move in on us, do you?" There was a bemused challenge in her voice. Tera had a vague smile, obviously waiting for his reply.

"Well thank you so much for asking; you seem like people worth moving in on." He was taking a chance, but he didn't want to falter in front of Tera, with whom he felt in danger of momentarily being swatted like a fly. "So… ?"

"I wouldn't mind the company," says Tera quietly; warm smile.

Cat put her hand on her hip and pointed with the other one; "And don't even dream of trying anything buster. You're here as male decoration, nothing else."

"Fair enough. He began to relax. "Though I like to think of it as a male decorated by two females." Tera shot him a sidelong glance but said nothing. Cat tossed her head contemptuously. He decided to ignore her for the moment; she was far too aware of his feelings. Tera also seemed aware, but it was a distant, an accepting awareness. Better get the conversation rolling: "Nice job on our prof, Tera." She made an amused grunt and was silent. The Cat came alive.

"Nice, that was *great!* You had him stuttering like... like, there's no way even the *idiots* in the class didn't see that. What was it, you said something about forms…"

"Right. She corrected him for saying that forms made society."

"Yeah, right. And you totally blew him away by using that stuff he was teaching us last week. Cause remember last week, you made him look like an idiot for not understanding how those twelve steps work?"

"That *was* good. She called him on the carpet for trying to explain with absolutely no clue, what a 'historically contextual function' was. And when he tried to put you on the spot, you explained what it *wasn't*, instead of what it was; but all you really did was take what he had been saying, put it in different words, and ask him if that would be a mistaken way to think about it. *And he agreed!*"

She glanced at him again, slight smile. "That's actually very perceptive." She seemed vaguely embarrassed, but determined to put up with it. Cat was walking in the middle, and Tera noticed that Cat was relaxing as if a hammock were strung between her and Cris, and she were swinging in it. She noticed also that Cris missed almost nothing, yet Cat, whom she was just beginning to know, could care less about noticing anything, she simply exuded in all directions. Introspecting for a moment, she went on. "The question is, where is it all going to go?"

"Um… I was kind of wondering about that too." Cris. "Other than having an enormous amount of fun at the instructors' expense, what exactly do we do here?"

Cat's face was twisted up in a puzzled look. "You guys are worried about that? C'mon, it's *fun*. We're showing that we don't get pushed around, that you have to know something if you're going to teach, that one day we're going to run the whole world."

They both smiled simultaneously at her words. Tera said, "Well at this point he's screwing up his ideas in almost every sentence. The only reason I spoke up today is because he was connecting a wrong thought with the worse idea of the evolution of society, and I didn't want that to pass."

Cris was puzzled. "What do you mean, you don't believe in the evolution of society? We're not progressing?"

Tera sighed. "Yes and no. The books and professors make it sound like we're progressing on every level. I can only think of one way we're progressing, and I haven't found the words for it yet. But the further I go back in history, on every other level, the more I see that we're devolving."

"What? Go back where?"

"Well, have you ever read any ancient literature. I mean either actual Syriac, Egyptian, Hebrew, Sanskrit or a word-for-word translation."

"Um… no…"

"If I were you, I'd hold off my opinion of how far we've progressed until you do."

Cat spoke up. "You mean that? You've really looked into all that stuff?"

Tera sighed. "Not much of the stuff, but yes, some. and the more I look into it, the more I'm convinced." They were passing the diner, Cris motioned them in and waited for Tera to continue. "It's… it's like we're… it's actually like we're really much worse than the book 1984, and we're completely brainwashed. It's hard to describe." The two listeners waited patiently. "It's like we're all asleep, or we all have bags over our heads, and while everything's supposed to be possible, nothing's possible in this *society!*" She raised her voice at this last word, and the other two almost jumped. She went on, animated. "And that's exactly it. We're in the plastic age, the age of materials so wonderful that you can do *anything* with them, and because they makes life so much easier, we do nothing except cheapen life with them. And—whatever we do is only for ourselves… nothing whatsoever is possible to do *in society*. We've been fooled as to what is ease and what is hardship. We've been fooled as to what's *accomplishing* something, and what's treading water. But it's worse than treading water, we're serving giant monsters, collections of idiotic ideas… and we're doing it willingly because, well because we're pretty much a society of serfs. But these monsters are *ideals*, and since there's no more royalty to serve, we serve huge shapeless beasts that hang around like vultures perched on long-deserted thrones." A bit of silence. "I'm sorry, I began to ramble." She smiled. Cris noted the word "began" and wondered how far she could go with this. Glancing at Cat, he saw she wondered the same thing.

"Okay, so how bad is it?" Cat. "Am I brainwashed? Is Cris?"

Wry smile. "We all are. You are, I am, Cris is, we all are. The question is, how does one break out, and how far can one go." Silence for a bit. Cris picked up a menu and started looking it over. Cat was thoughtful.

"*My* grandfather says that everything we have is a gift, like there's different kinds, some are from God, some from people; but that no one can take another step unless someone gives it to them, and they have to accept it too. Like a gift." Tera was thoughtful, looking at her. Cat gave a little shrug. "Well anyway, that's what he says."

Cris laughed appreciatively, noting that Tera had soaked that in. "So that would mean that any time anything happens, it's a gift from somebody."

"Well, anything good," Cat corrected.

"Okay, so in your grandfather's world…" he started.

"Are you ready to order yet, or would you like more time?" The waitress was a townie, not a student. Better service that way, though you had to be nicer.

"Oh, sorry, we hadn't even looked at the menus," smiled Cat.

"Okay, I'll be back in a couple minutes." She swayed off.

"You were saying, Cris?" asked Tera quietly.

"Um… right. Um… I don't quite get it. Like who gives the person who's on top of the pile any gifts?"

Cat was nonplussed. "God, I guess; isn't it like a big pyramid?"

"No, that doesn't make sense… sure, it might be a bit like a pyramid, but even the best person needs stuff from other people. Otherwise society itself would only be for those of us who can't handle perfection. Which would mean that society is necessarily imperfect, and I certainly don't believe that."

"Hm." Cat was thoughtful. Tera broke in with her quiet voice.

"Do you necessarily have to be better than someone to give them something?"

After a moment, Cris started laughing. "Well *there's* a blunder I should have seen coming. So, okay, Cat's grandfather could be right then… but there's got to be more to it." He buried his face in his menu. Cat was already meandering over the greasy plastic-clad words.

"Greek salad," said Tera.

"Nah, chef's salad," returns Cat.

"Yeah right. Blue cheese burger extra rare with fries." Male.

"Greek salad," says Tera, and closes the menu.

"Hot fudge brownie sundae," Cat. Few seconds silence; "Well, you know, I already had lunch…"

Tera smiles. Cris looks out the window. Jason. Freezes. Cat sees Cris freeze, looks. Jason, walking by, smiles slightly at Cat. Tera looks up.

Reality hesitates.

Tera gasps and covers her face. Cris and Cat, alarmed. Tera pulls her knees up around her head, shudders, sobbing uncontrollably for only a long moment. Tera is still. Cris, then Cat look out window, Jason is gone. Cris: "Tera?"

"I'm sorry… I'm so sorry… I… I didn't mean to…" long sigh. She looks up, composed already.

"Tera, you really scared me!" Cat is wide-eyed.

"I'm sorry, I had a… memory… of a dream I had just last night… running to my grandfather's room, he's sick you know… I… I'm sorry, this is bad, let me think."

Silence, thirty seconds. Waitress returns, orders are given in normal voices. Food comes. Curtain closes. After the curtain, thirty more seconds of silence. Audience, if restless, can go to the concession stand.

Chapter 2: No More Introductions, Please

"Do you know him?" Tera's voice was different; not plaintive, but real; scary real. The kind of voice you can't *not* answer.

"Not yet, not really." Cris held the phone like a china doll. "I helped a lady move into an apartment and he was there… we finished a four hour job in… in like thirty-five minutes, and no one realized it… I don't know, I've been watching him like hell, but I know he's been watching me even closer." Silence.

"Let me know if you see him again."

"Okay."

"Wait. Never mind."

"You sure?"

"Yes… yes. Thank you."

"Okay."

"See you in class?"

"Sure."

"K. Bye."

"Bye." He hung up, wondering if he was shaking. Can't tell. As his eyes returned to Cat's, he realized that this was probably the first opportunity he had to be with her without Tera knowing. The phone rang.

"And don't think I don't know that Cat is there." The amusement was back in her voice.

"Go to sleep!" he barked, trying to keep the blush down. Now he had to try to hide that from Cat instead. He put the phone down. She was looking at him.

"She's pretty sharp, isn't she?" Cat was smiling.

Cris laid back on the floor. "What we need is more males around here!" he complained.

Cat rarely missed a step. "Depends on what you mean by "need" I guess.

"Hmph. What I need is Jason. I should go look him up and get his support."

No smile this time. "I think he'll probably find you first."

"I wonder."

Late lunch after Medieval History became a tradition. So much so that Cris found himself at the Slogan Diner alone on a Saturday afternoon. Same waitress though; she must have hellish hours. He'd become addicted to the Blue Cheese Burgers, or the company, or something. Tera had mixed it with the prof several more times, and Cris found himself wishing he was in more classes with her. Cat was always surprising; she connected with him on every level that he tried, and then some; always effortlessly. There was no way to get his mental arms around her. And between Tera and himself there was like a new being created, like an innocent female which Cat had the uncanny ability to embody. But the attention required by classes had begun to shoulder out his normal thinking patterns; this bothered him in some way he couldn't quite finger. Even watching people, his favorite pastime, was becoming a rare luxury. Saturday at the Slogan was a welcome break, he had resisted bringing classwork, and glad for it. The row of ancient Maples across the street were towers of sanity against the backdrop of civilization. He noted that pedestrians felt freer, looked around, relaxed their pace while under those canopies, then hunched back down under the weight of brick and concrete walls with wires randomly zigzagging overhead.

"Thanks for noticing me the other day. I'm not used to it."

Jason was sitting across from him.

"You were affecting everyone. It was hard to miss." In spite of his shock, he found himself responding as if they had been talking for hours.

Wry smile. "Perhaps." He stared out the window. "See that lady?" Across the street, under the maples. Cris had seen her before, she seemed like a street person, very difficult to categorize though, even as such. "She seems very powerful,"

Jason mused. They watched her for a few moments. "Lonely, too. Like someone who can do significant things and has nowhere to do them."

"I'm Cris, by the way. And I know your name is Jason from when you were helping move Mrs. Kurl's stuff."

"Maybe you didn't read this chapter's title. It said 'No More Introductions.'"

"What?"

"Never mind. Private joke." He smiled. "I like that blonde girl you were with, what's her name?"

Cris felt as if he were revealing a personal secret. "Cat."

"Spelled with a K or a C?"

"C."

"Hm." Silence. "You may have a lot in common."

"We're not that alike at all."

"That's not what I meant by a lot in common."

Cris thought about this for a bit. Better turn the conversation. "Have you eaten here before?"

"Nope."

"You gonna order?" This seemed to amuse Jason.

"Um… sure." He picked up Cris's menu and glanced at it. Bit of silence. "Aren't you going to tell me her name?" Cris realized with a shock that he had just been thinking of how to bring up the subject of Tera. Jason was smiling again, he seemed to get amused easily.

Cris bluffed. "I told you her name was Cat."

"Very funny." His eyes, still amused, narrowed and darkened. Cris wondered how exactly he did that. *Okay, I lose this one.*

"Tera. You had quite an affect on her, you know."

"We all have quite an affect on each other, just few of us bother to realize it."

"She started crying." Jason was silent. "She said she was thrown into some nightmare from the night before."

"Tell me *exactly* what she said." Cris found himself on the receiving end of Jason's focused interest; it was intense, and sharp. He found himself talking whether he wanted to or not.

"She said it was a dream she had of running to her grandfather's room. Something about him being sick, too. I think that was all." Jason continued to stare at him for a moment, and then leaned back into his seat with a distant, almost troubled, look in his face.

"Hi Cris. Are you guys ready to order?" The waitress had warmed up nicely over the last few weeks. Jason looked at Cris expectantly.

"I'll have the… "

"…Blue Cheese Burger," she finished for him with a smile. Coffee or Coke today?"

Cris grinned. "Coffee." She glanced at Jason

"Greek salad. Milk. That's all" She snapped her gum and swirled efficiently away.

"Greek salad?" Cris accused.

Jason smiled. "In honor of Tera."

"What exactly did you do to her? And don't skip around the question."

"I… I was going to look into her. She's deep. All the way in. But I stopped, thinking that it might be rude. But I underestimated her; she was quick enough to see me stop, realized what I was about to do, mostly that I *could* do that. I had also underestimated her ability to look into me… it was almost simultaneous… anyway, when she saw me stop and pull back, she went into shock."

"Why?"

"My guess is she's starving for contact, and the combination of me almost contacting her, then pulling back, revived a similar conflict in her life she's with which she's been living for a long time."

"What kind of conflict would be that strong?"

"Hm. If what you told me is true, somebody …noble… and close to her… entrusted her with something. And someone even closer to her took it away again. A very powerful gift. But it's not going to be easy to figure out." A bit of silence. He suddenly seemed amused again. "So. Did I dance around the question?"

"I don't know now. Hey, there's that lady we were talking about!" She was walking slowly by the diner.

"Shall we invite her in for a chat?"

Cris looked at him. "But…"

Jason smiled, began to get up, and paused halfway, and smiled at Cris. "Things really happen, you know." Then he was out on the sidewalk talking to the lady. He seemed for all the world like a little kid, slightly embarrassed, hands in his pockets. She was taking him very seriously, as if she were being asked to the royal ball. The he was bustling around, opening the doors for her, bringing her to the table. "Cris, this is Laura. *Lady* Laura," he smiled at her, "Laura, this is my friend Cris. You'll find him perceptive, unobtrusive, with balanced *emotions*, forward *thoughts*, but often hesitating before he acts. Please, have a seat." She sat where Jason had been, Jason and Cris across from her.

"It's a perfectly disastrous day." She stated firmly.

"Disastrous for whom?" asked Jason, interestedly. She smiled.

"For the sons of disaster. But for us…" She folded her hands under her chin. "What kind of day shall we have?" The waitress brought their food.

"Anything for you, ma'am?"

"English muffin. Toasted. With butter." She sounded for all the world like a lady accustomed to wielding authority. "And a cup of hot tea."

"You got it." The waitress was nonplussed.

"In reply to your question, I myself should like to refrain from proffering a moral assessment of the day until our lady has her tea," stated Jason. She nodded politely and turned her attention to Cris.

"You're in here almost every day. Who are those two girls with you, and why aren't they here today?" Cris winced under the directness of the questions, wondered if he could get used to these kinds of people.

"Um… they're Tera and Cat, we have a Medieval History class together." Laura was nodding, listening. "Tera can… call the professor on the carpet quite well when he's being an idiot, and Cat and I kind of met cause… we liked that." Laura smiled, an intelligent smile that made Cris feel good. He kept going. "I guess if you've seen us you know that Cat and I have a lot in common, and I'd kind of like to… know her better. I mean I really like Tera too, but… well I don't know, I haven't really talked about this, but… I mean, we're just friends now, I wouldn't do anything to screw up the friendships, I really like both those girls…"

"Young man, now you listen to me." The waitress brought her tea and muffin. She pointed the spoon at him. "Those are fine and noble sentiments, but you know what's going to happen when the choice is on your lap and it's either friendship or your silly notion of love? No choice about it. You'll destroy the friendship, and grab for the love. And you know what happens next?" He shook his head. "You focus on each other instead of what you're doing with your lives. Watch this." She picked up the salt and pepper shakers one in each hand and slid them slowly toward his burger. "You're both walking along in life. You're going somewhere. You're going to flavor the burger on that plate. Suddenly you both see each other." She stopped the shakers halfway to his plate. "Then you decide to 'love' each other, lose your focus, and head toward each other." She smacked the two shakers together so hard that Cris thought she might have cracked one. She let them lie on their sides and sat back. "No more goals. No more flavoring the burger. And guess what?" She leaned toward him. "No more love. It's only fun when you're running toward each other, not after you've hit."

"I'd like to interrupt this very excellent dialogue with a toast." It was Jason. "You asked what kind of day we might have. Here's a toast to a day of exploring our ability." Milk, tea, and coffee clinked. Cris was looking at Laura, puzzled.

"So… how do you prevent that from happening?"

"Easy," she said with an offhand air, "share goals." Cris stared at her, trying to figure out what that meant.

"And *is* that so easy." Jason's question sounded like a statement.

She looked up. "Easy *answer* to his question, not easily done. Not anymore."

"Hm." Jason was thoughtful, munching on an olive. For the rest of the meal they talked about her royal status. It turned out that she *was* a Lady, her parents were both English. After they all had parted, Cris realized that Jason had promised to join them next time, although he didn't remember ever actually talking about it. He wondered whether to warn the girls or not. He then wondered if he'd even have the chance.

As it turned out he didn't. Cat was going on and on about her fencing class, she seemed fixated on the importance of the stance one had to maintain. Cris was busy listening, and Tera… well he had learned not to assume *what* Tera was doing. Before he knew it, they were in their familiar booth by the window, and the waitress had already gotten their orders. Cat was staring out the window through the slight drizzle, and asked, "Hey Cris, is that that guy… what's his name; Jason?" He was walking across the street at an angle toward them; one that gave them maximum visibility of him, Cris noticed.

"That's him. I didn't have a chance to tell you that he met me here Saturday for lunch." Tera's eyes flashed across his, but she was silent.

"Really, how was it?" wondered Cat.

"Very… odd. But kind of fun, we invited an old lady off the street to join us. Actually it was pretty surreal. Made me feel like… well, like Jason said to me: 'Things really happen.'" Jason had a relaxed, casual pace; he made no pretense of not coming to join them. That slight smile of his as he nodded to them through the window, and then he was standing inside by their window booth, covered with drizzle. Always before, Cris had to put out effort to notice him, but today he looked like a framed painting. Book bag over his shoulder, it seemed to be black leather, tan jacket over a faded T-shirt, jeans.

"Hi folks. Thought I'd drop by and say hi to Cris." Smile. Pause. "Though I wouldn't mind meeting his exquisitely sculptured friends." The compliment put the Cat on edge, but Tera didn't miss a beat.

"You wouldn't know the half of it," she said quietly, returning his gaze. Cris jumped in quickly.

"Um, Cat, Tera, this is Jason; Jason, these are my friends Cat and Tera. Do you girls mind if he joins us?"

"Sure. Sit down." Cat was suddenly a ball of friendliness, leaning forward to study him across the table once he sat down beside Cris. She flashed a huge grin and looked right in his eyes. "Hi. Jason."

Anyone else in the world, thought Cris, would look awkward doing that. Jason smiled back with a quieter "Hi Cat." He held her gaze for a moment then turned to Tera. "Hello, Tera."

"Good evening Jason." Cris couldn't see past either of their masks as they looked at each other; they could have been assassins or lovers.

"So," said Jason, returning to Cat's glowing friendliness, "is anyone else here a freshman like me?"

"Yup. We all are. I'm doing international studies, I *think* Tera's going to be a history major, though you can never tell with her, and Cris is doing some kind of engineering."

"Chemistry," stated Cris, "not chemical engineering, chemistry."

She tossed her head. "Like I said, some kind of engineering. So Jason. What are you doing?"

"Uh… Physics right now. I guess that would be engineering to you too, wouldn't it."

Tera broke in. "Why physics?"

"Well… actually, I'm working on a bunch of different things, I don't even know if I'm going to 'major' in something. Still figuring it out."

"Well you have to declare a major. Or are you taking 'Undergraduate Studies' for the undecided?"

"No, I told them I'd major in physics. But I'd like to… kind of sketch out a course across all the fields…—except perhaps international studies—" he smiled a tease at Cat, "something that gives me an idea of the whole picture."

"Well, how do you choose what to take? You won't know if it's valuable until after you learn it."

"Yeah, that's a real problem. I'm going to concentrate on the physical sciences right now. But I've made myself a map of all… um, all human endeavors, and I'd like to follow it through all the fields."

"How on earth do you make a map of all human endeavors?" Cris asked, and Cat jumped in.

"Is it like you're going to do one of everything until you cover it all?" The waitress appeared, and Cris noticed that Jason looked genuinely relieved. Walking cold into an established three-way friendship, Jason's aura of invincibility was reduced to almost human. And he seemed uncomfortable talking about himself. After she left, he continued.

"I have kind of a simple way of going about it, really. Everything's a combination of thinking and doing. Like the arts and sciences; art is our composition of understanding, science is our understanding of all composition; doing from thinking, and thinking from what's been done. Philosophy is pure thinking. Trades are pure doing. So those four cover pretty much any human endeavor." There was a pause.

"I'd like to point out that this time you *didn't* answer the question." Cris.

"Yeah. Like if everything is art, science, and whatever, how does that tell you which classes to take?" Cat.

"Actually I could use help with that. Because in every class I take, like for instance physics, I find that somewhere along the line people have discovered a lot of cool stuff, and almost without exception, it's been glossed over, and what we believe today is a lie. In physics the lies expanded with Newton, then Einstein gave them a really bad turn. But there were contemporaries with these men who you can't find in the textbooks who really figured out what was what. So what I have to do in each field is apply the only endeavor that's *not* in that little thinking/doing formula I mentioned."

"History," said Tera.

"Yes, history. I have to study the history of each science." He leaned back. "And that's an enormous amount of busywork."

Cat asked matter-of-factly, "So how do you keep yourself entertained in the meantime?"

Jason smiled. "I guess I'm working on that. So. Cris, why did you pick chemistry?"

"Well… I had always liked the idea of reducing things down to essentials, I though I could actually grapple with things on that level. Which I guess I can, but… it seems that the more basic you get, the more possibilities there are. Like at our level right now, there's maybe ten different significant things I could do in this situation, and after that anything else is just a variation of one of those. But at the molecular level, or especially at the atomic level, it's crazy. Anything can happen. I mean it all happens according to the essential principles, but… it's so much more complex."

"Like when you go back in history, civilization gets more advanced, not less?" asked Tera quietly.

We left them talking at the diner, they are comfortable there, warm from the drizzle of rain and crowds. We moved on, over roofs, fields, a spattering of trees under grey clouds on grey; we came to a lane that wanders back into the woods, and to a door who waits patiently to give his patrons the exchange of in and out. We moved through this door without its service, and the smell of wood smoke grows stronger. The small cabin is dim, and the old man is arranging vegetables on a huge cutting board, the vortex of a small kitchen. We watch him in the well organized clutter, filling the cast iron pot with his work. Firelight flickers cozily at our back, and we stay for a bit.

"Leeks in June. No fresh basil yet, but that's okay. Garlic to invigorate, leave it sit chopped for fifteen minutes before tossing it in. I am tired in my heart, but I think the garlic will remind me. Wake me for the coming cycle. How long has it been?" He glanced at the wall clock. "Four-thirty. Enough time to prepare, and time enough to eat. Monday is always the second of days. My last cycle is over and seasoned, eleven years of days. Four thirty, time enough to begin anew, a fresh cycle calls. How long this time, I wonder." A carrot was becoming diagonal slices. "A day as a thousand years, and a thousand years as a day. The little things we do are bulwarks, our endeavors are bits of ash. Flakes of frost. I am only what I have done, and what I wish to do. Unless I fail to hope. Unless I fail. I fail to see the humor in this as once I did. And just once I did do what I hoped and now my heart is tired. The garlic is ready. Into the pot with you. A tomato is welcome, but just one. And my friends the spices are most welcome. Sage for clarity, dried basil for friendliness, just a touch of ginger, but pour in the mustard seed. No fennel, anise, or caraway seed; they don't know how to keep to themselves. Marjoram to settle things down, paprika to cheer them up. Oregano for substance, and a touch of rosemary to help him. Red pepper to activate, and thyme to… hm, what does thyme do? I see that I'm almost out of thyme. Almost out of time. New cycle coming, must prepare." He was silent for the remainder of the soup's preparation. The soup bubbled and steamed energetically to itself. The fire flickered lower, and he placed more wood in the stone fireplace. We stayed and watched as he ate his meal in silence, and cleaned the bowl. We looked around at the clutter, books predominated. But most presented their titles from shelves, only two were opened on the small table by a stuffed brown leather chair. We mused that a chair like that would cost a small fortune in any store. We noticed that many of the items on his shelves are only ever seen in the houses of the very rich, or in museums. We noticed that everything looked poor, but nothing was. We wondered a bit, and he took his place by the firelight and filled his pipe from a ceramic cruse. The air filled with spices that we did not recognize. He spoke again.

"There is nothing profound about the lower class. We brought these circumstances from the dirt, and now we deny our roots. There is nothing insignificant about history except the fact that we use it to ignore the future. There is nothing we can do about our future that we can't do in the present. We must act, and the first act is patience." Pause. "I have waited a long time. I think… I think that I will go into town." Pause. "Yes, the new cycle may start there. I will go and see." He picked a worn notebook from the shelf, and began writing. We left him then, and returned through the gathering mist that made shapes against the wood like restless spirits.

Chapter 3: Things Really Do Happen

We are not alone, we are not alone, we are not alone, it only seems that way. It seems the way it is, and it is neither what it seems, nor is it different from what it seems. We hope for something more and grope for what we think we believe. We want to love and we want to understand, to be loved and to be understood. We want to be able to want, we want to be able at all. We want to live.

Child person. Do you want to be one with the one you want to be with? Tera wondered if those were lyrics to a song she had heard. Her father had left her some articles on the table that he thought she would like; they were regarding the work of a seventeenth century linguist who had taken the stance that each letter in the ancient languages was a hieroglyph with its own world of meaning. This had run in the teeth of the then developing idea that even the Egyptian hieroglyphics could be translated by relegating each symbol to a letter. She read it with interest. Her father was brilliant, two PhD's from Harvard and a working knowledge of almost any subject. He was reading an abstract on recent applications of chaos theory to gravitational fields in the living room. She went in, sat on the couch, and waited. He finished the page and set it aside.

"Well, what did you think?"

"It makes sense. A lot of sense, actually. They're suggesting that we've completely missed the boat in translating the ancients, which would mean there's a whole world that we already have on our laps waiting to be rediscovered."

He smiled, but his eyes remained distant. "Yes, that's what they're saying. One has to wonder though; it's quite easy to claim such things, but why is there so little development of these sorts of ideas in academic thought, whether historical or current? I'm reminded of the cold fusion fiasco; everyone wants something to be true that's wonderful and new, but when it comes down to brass tacks, nothing happens."

"Perhaps it's the lack of support. This article describes how much these ideas were resisted and ignored by the academics of the time."

"Resistance has always proved, over time, to winnow out the bad ideas, and sharpen the good. Natural selection is a prime example; resistance in the end simply weeds out the less fit."

Something disturbed her about this idea, as it always had. But putting it into words, especially to her father, was another matter. "But we're *thinking* beings, we're different from the rest of nature. An animal's value for life is limited to survival of his species. But we define the *level of civilization* of a society by its value for life. Perhaps these other values that we have, which run against natural selection, are meant to inform us as to our method of dealing with the uniquely *human* frame of thought."

He looked at her interestedly, but a bit coldly. "And what exactly *are* these other values? You've got a bit of a task now, to explain how human endeavors run against natural law."

Her mind felt like it was straining against an enclosing net. She found herself using Jason's ideas almost out of desperation. "Humans endeavor takes advantage, not only of self and environment, but of the relationships between them. Self is simply doing, and environment is simply perceiving; these two make up the entirety of an animal's universe. But we can compose and analyze; these produce art and science. Art is the composition of our analysis, an expression of the values of each generation; and science is the analysis of composition, the study of all things that are, and why. So it's the relationships within existence that we can access which produce the uniquely human endeavors. And neither art nor science have any place in natural selection."

He paused and looked at her for a long moment. Then he picked up his article again. "An interesting idea, though I think that once you've thought through you'll realize that natural selection is a broader force that you're imagining." He resumed reading. She was crestfallen. Whenever her and father had these talks, he always led her through her ideas carefully, and always pointed it out when she had missed something. But she had been so confident that she was on to something really good; her mind raced around trying to figure out what he had seen that she hadn't. No use, and she felt tired. She went to the kitchen, sliced up a peach, and decided to go check on grandfather. The family had been caring for him for several years now, the habit had grown on all of them.

He was seated as usual in his overstuffed chair. "Hi grandpa, how you doing?" she asked cheerfully. She refilled his water glass from the kitchen sink and opened the curtain for the afternoon sun. Then she stopped, shocked. His eyes had lost the perpetual glaze, and he was looking directly at her. There was a deep sadness, almost a horror. He closed his eyes and opened them just as slowly. He had a look of tired relief, like something had just been taken off his shoulders that had been there for ages. "Grandpa?" He made no motion, no sign. She stared at him as pieces of memories from her childhood brushed through her mind. Laughter, dreams, that large figure always there, always providing a strange energy that she took so much for granted that she had never seen it; and his eyes. These were the same eyes again. She remembered a troubled look in his eyes shortly before the nerve disorder had set in; now the troubled look was gone, and there was a great sadness. She realized she had sat down on the floor in front of him, but she was calm, she was there. Looking back later, she realized that one of them had a tear running down the cheek; she didn't know which one; now, she was lost in those eyes. After speaking, she realized that she had just said "Thank you, grandpa" and he closed his eyes. She got up, closed the curtains halfway, and left. There was an afternoon class, and life to encounter. Driving away, she couldn't remember if she had seen her father on the way out or not.

Love isn't something in which you get buried, decided Cris at last. The flurry of emotions he felt around Cat was new, exhilarating and confusing. Thinking long and hard on it, he decided that what was happening was simply them getting to actually know one another. They were different, and there was so much to get to know… no, it's not love. It well may turn into love, but regardless of feelings, this wasn't it. A knock on his dorm door, she was stopping over to walk with him to The Slogan. "Come in." He closed the art history paper on his computer and looked up. *She had cut her hair.* Standing in the doorway, all that usual aura of yellow gone, replaced with… curly waves that wrapped around her head like a gold hood. It was beautiful, but… strange. She grinned and spun around.

"Well? What do you think?"

"It's…" he stopped and walked up to her. She spun around again, obviously enjoying his dumbfoundedness. "It's… it's beautiful, but… why did you do it?" She grinned again.

"Why not? C'mon, let's go." As they walked corridor to the steps and outside, he decided she was having a bit too much fun, but he couldn't take his eyes off her. She was a completely different person. The lazy comfort had turned into flashy radiance, and she was turning even more heads than usual. Finally she relented. "I was thinking about motion, and how whenever I move, it's like I have a blanket around me. Which is real comfortable, but I wanted to be able to snap, to feel free, you know; to feel different."

"But I thought you were so proud of your hair. You carried it so well."

"Well… sure. I mean thank you; but I only had one way of carrying it. I mean, if I have long hair, and it's the only thing I've ever done, I'm kind of… you know; stuck. Limited. I want to have hair that I've earned, not hair that I've simply had all my life."

"So… you might grow it long again?"

"Sure. But it won't be the same thing at all. At least I hope not."

Cris shook his head. "Girls" he said, trying to sound disgusted, but there was no way she was coming off of this high.

"I think I look like Cleopatra" she said, putting a bit of an accent into her voice.

"Sure. And didn't Cleopatra have black hair? She was Egyptian, you know."

"Ah, what do you know about royalty?" she retorted, increasing the accent. An old man, perhaps seventy or seventy-five was approaching and looked at them interestedly.

"How y'doing?" asked Cris politely as they passed.

"Not quite as confused than yourself at present, but enjoying life equally, by the looks of it." The response was immediate and casual. Cris turned and looked at him; he stopped and returned the stare. He stood straight and had strong blue eyes. His face was unreadable. He carried a quiet antiquity about him; he could have just stepped out of any time at all. His jacket was cut to perfection; it seemed to be woven in its present shape. His shirt might have been leather, but Cris had never seen leather clothes that lacked that bulky look. Deerskin perhaps.

"Have you eaten yet? We're heading to the diner." Cris was surprised by his own forwardness.

"No, I don't think I'll join you two just now, thank you for your offer. What are your names, and what year are you each?"

Cat spoke up, using her peculiar ability to shape to any situation. Now she was formal and friendly. "I'm Cat. We're both freshmen. I'm doing International Studies, and Cris here is in Chemistry."

"So you are." He stood there looking at them for a moment. "Let me ask you a question. In what way has your time here at the university changed you?"

Cris tried to clear his mind to answer, but Cat was immediate. "I've found out that when you're with people, either you lock yourself into what you think your personality is to keep your privacy, or you accept them as friends, and open yourself up to something new." She paused. "Also, I'm no longer in awe of people who know a lot. I used to think that being a college professor was the greatest thing, but it's no different than anything else. It's not what you know, it's… it's something else."

Cris jumped in. "It's not so much what you know, but *why* you wanted to know it in the first place. If you were a jerk when you started learning, all the knowledge in the world won't change that, unless *you* do." The man smiled.

"Sounds wise. Now what about you?" he turned his eyes to Cris.

"Um… I feel like I'm still changing so fast that it's hard to get an objective idea about what's happening." He felt kind of stupid bailing out like that.

"Also wise," he said kindly, then paused. "How much would you like to change?"

"That's easy," Cat said, "all the way." The man raised one eyebrow at her, then looked to Cris.

"I'd like… I'd like to at least become what my friends are. More than that, I know, but that's what I'm working on now."

"Ah. So you have friends." The man's eyes took on a glow.

Cris smiled. "Yes… yes we do actually."

"Very good. I'm pleased to have met you kids. I am Tiron Jarome, and I will be pleased to meet you again." He turned slightly to indicate he was finished. Cat responded cheerfully.

"K. Hope we do. Take care."

"Be aware is more like it. But godspeed to both of you." As they walked away, Cris spoke.

"That was rather weird."

"I liked him. He was like, totally cool. And really interesting; everything he said made you think."

"I notice it never stumped you for long."

"Oh, you just think about everything too much."

"And that's a disadvantage?"

"Depending on what you need to think about."

"Well about everything, don't you?"

"I guess that would be true if you never wanted to do anything."

"You're saying that you can't think about something and do it at the same time?"

"Well, maybe you can, but I doubt it. One would have to be pretty mature to do that."

"So now I'm immature."

"Are you?"

"Well sure, but coming from you it sounds like an insult."

Cat tossed her head. "Guys," she said, imitating his earlier tone. They were at The Slogan, where Jason and Tera were waiting. As they walked in the door, someone whistled loudly at Cat, drawing the attention of the whole diner. Jason was grinning. "Did you whistle at me?" she demanded when as they approached the booth.

"Guilty" smiled Jason, and slid down, making room for Cat. "Please. Do me the honor." She sat down, slightly embarrassed. Cris sat across from them with Tera. "I've always believed that there's a time to whistle at beautiful things, and this seemed like a great one." He touched her hair in a few places. "Gorgeous. When did you do this?"

"This morning. Tera convinced me I should go for it."

Jason turned to Tera. "You knew this and didn't tell me?"

Tera shrugged, smiling. "You didn't ask."

Cat shook her head vigorously. "I like it a lot. Even Cris seems to have recovered a bit." She reached across the table and patted him on the head.

"No, I'm just learning to coexist with beings from other dimensions, peaceably. Seems it's my fate to be surrounded by them."

"Hey Cris, tell them about that guy we talked to on the way over."

"Oh, yeah. This guy was looking at us..." Cat interrupted him and took over the story.

"Like he totally made this sharp comment when Cris said hi to him, and we stopped, and he had like these blue eyes that were almost glowing. And he asked us all sorts of questions like what had we learned and how we had changed and if we were going to change any more."

"Yeah, that's what I was about to say myself," muttered Cris wryly.

Tera. "What did he look like?"

"That's what was interesting," Cris explained, "I've never seen clothes like that before. They didn't seem unusual at first, and certainly not flashy, but… well I don't think you could buy clothes like that… anywhere actually. They looked like a combination of top-of-the-line expensive and completely homemade."

Jason was getting interested. "Did he tell you his name?"

"Sure," says Cris, "it was Jerome or Tarome or something like that."

"Wasn't like Tiron his first name?" Cat.

"Yeah, that's right. Tiron Jarome. I remember now. Odd sounding name. Like a combination of Arab and English or something."

"Tiron Jarome…" mused Jason, "Did he ask for your names?"

"Yup," said Cat, "That was the first thing he asked us."

"Did he mention if he intended to meet you again?"

Cris spoke up. "That's what was odd. He said he would meet us again in such a way that seemed to suggest he was going to do something about it. At least that was my impression."

"Yeah, that makes sense," agreed Cat. "He seemed awfully sure of himself. But not proud of it like most professors we see."

Tera was watching Jason's interest in the old man carefully. Cris guessed that she was taking advantage of the situation to figure out what motivated him. With Jason, it was next to impossible to tell if he even *was* motivated. Cris suddenly looked back to Cat to give Tera more room; the pressure of both he and Tera watching Jason at once was producing an even more impenetrable mask than usual. He was conscious that he needed to somehow do something with Cat to celebrate her new looks, but was at a loss as to what to do at the moment. Jason seemed satisfied with the information on the old man. "Tiron Jarome…" he mused. "Let's keep an eye out for this gentleman. How old did he look?"

"About seventy or seventy-five I'd guess," replied Cat, "but he was awfully healthy looking. Almost beautiful in some strange way."

"Hm. That brings me back to the present nicely," started Jason, as he put his arm around Cat, "So, my strange beauty, when's the last time you were on a date you really enjoyed?" It was simultaneously both natural and shockingly sudden. Cat glowed. Cris' heart jumped a beat and he started thinking furiously; all his perceptive range pulled in and focused on the four of them. Tera smiled slightly and leaned back.

"Depends on what you mean by a date," said Cat, tossing her head, her features alive. She now looked excruciatingly pretty to Cris.

"That's easy," said Jason, leaning with his other elbow on the table, making a half circle around her, "Someone asks you to spend time alone with him to find out if you believe in each other. Whoever believes the most in the other wins. The winner gets to say what happens next."

"Oh, so it's a contest?" asked Tera.

Jason smiled over his shoulder to Tera. "A rare luxury of a contest, to be sure." He turned back to Cat. "So. What do you say?"

She put her face close to his. "Are you asking me out on a date?" she demanded.

Jason put on a face of feigned shock. "I wouldn't presume. I merely asking for *permission* to ask you for a date."

"You may ask" stated Cat.

"Thank you," said Jason, and took his arm away. There were a few moments of expectant silence. After they passed, Cris spoke up.

"Well, aren't you going to ask her for a date?"

"Now?" said Jason incredulously, "I've just gotten permission; I wouldn't destroy a priceless moment like this by actually asking. These things take time and planning. And how could I trust myself to ask in a manner befitting the stature of her excellence while still under the influence of her graciousness in allowing herself to entertain the notion of my presence at all?" Cat raised her eyebrows, but said nothing.

Tera spoke up. "So, in other words, you're saying that as of right now, you're chicken."

Jason smiled. "Perhaps a better male than I could cross these particular barriers, but propriety must honor propriety. I wouldn't cross a line this fine for all the secrets of Egypt."

Cris cleared his throat. He felt more formal addressing Cat now than he ever had. "So… Cat. May have permission to ask you for a date?"

She locked eyes with him. "You have permission." Tera's eyes were flashing back and forth across the three. Cris went on.

"You are invited to a date with me tonight to explore our… potential together. A movie of your choice, and dinner afterwards in my dorm. If you so please."

Cat smiled graciously, formally at him. "Thank you very much, Cris, I accept."

Jason leaned back and sighed. "Ah, the bourgeoisie. Ever moving in on the proletarians' hard-earned work. What revolution has ever *not* been characterized by such?" His eyes were smiling in a peculiar way.

"Quite a few, actually," retorted Tera. "So basically, you're saying you're too good to compete properly."

"On the contrary, my dear, I enjoy proper competition sufficiently to engage in nothing else."

Cat was brimming with energy. She leaned over and kissed Jason on the cheek. "Thanks for asking; better luck next time."

*　　*　　*

The dean of Cherell University glanced at the clock. A large man, not fat, but definitely large. The dean of Architecture had seemed quite anxious for him to meet someone. He hoped vaguely that it wasn't another alumni who wanted too much attention for donating too few funds. His time this week was valuable; an unconventional donation had prompted the board to open a new major in time for the coming semester, and things had come down to brass tacks. Environmental Studies, they had decided to call it, and immediately there had been a conflict between the Social Sciences and Engineering as to who got to carry it. A juicy morsel for them both; the board was excited about it and funding was liberal. And there was a great deal of flexibility as to how it would be set up. Too much flexibility, he mused darkly; he had two more positions to fill—not that candidates were wanting—but with too many options as to exactly what these positions should be. Every time something new was on the table, every Tom, Dick, and Harry came out of the woodwork with his own favorite theory as to how it should work. And now that they were down to deadlines it seemed that Tom and Harry had gone home, leaving him to deal with all the Dicks.

"Howard Lawrence here with Mr. Jarome," his speaker squawked cheerfully.

"Let them in, June." He leaned back in his customary position of authority so often used to put pretentious people off their guard. The large walnut doors swung open, and Howard walked in, followed at a distance by an elderly gentleman who seemed to move entirely at his own pace. Howard strode up to the desk and made introductions.

"Jerry, this is Tiron, Tiron, this is Jerry Fitzgerald, the dean of our little university here. Jerry stood up and leaned over his desk to shake hands with the gentleman, who returned the gesture firmly, but without leaning forward in the slightest.

"Is that Latvian, 'Tiron?'" Jerry asked amicably.

The old man's voice was quiet and powerful. "*Tirōn*. Rhymes with 'my own'. Celtic and Belgian combination, actually. I have spent time in Latvia, however." His smile was disarming.

Howard cut in. "Now I know this is unusual, but please, each one of you sit down, and Jerry, I want you to read this over before we go another step farther." He handed Jerry some papers, and motioned Tiron into one of the chairs. Jerry looked at it skeptically, nodded to Howard, and sat down to read. It was

Tiron's resume. Used to rapidly digesting these sorts of things, he scanned through it. Then he stopped and started at the beginning again, reading more carefully. After six minutes of involvement, he looked up.

"Mr. Jarome…" He was interrupted.

"Call me Tiron, please." Smile.

"Yes, Tiron… This is a most… engaging resume." Howard was beaming, as if he had just brought in a rare species of butterfly. Jerry continued. "You have five doctorates, two of which were granted by the universities of… Tufts for your work on genetics, and Boston University for your technical guide to recursive anomalies in optoelectronics. The rest you earned at Oxford in Organic Chemistry, Physics, and Medieval & Ancient Literature. Where did you start your undergraduate work?"

"Yale, mostly. Things weren't quite so complicated back then."

"It says here that you were offered the chair of Physics at Oxford, but turned it down. Why?"

"I had some commitments to follow up that didn't allow the luxury of a professorship. I've had to travel extensively to fill those."

Jerry glanced down, then looked at him with some respect. "You were actually on that expedition in Qatar?"

"Yes I was. Now that it's been so publicized, people forget that we were basically a bunch of stubborn Englishmen traipsing about in a desert in which we had little right to be. The actual discoveries were a bit of a surprise to everyone involved. Were it not for the indefatigableness of our guides and some excellent direction on the part of a few scholars, that is all we would have been."

Howard noticed that Jerry was putting on his best face, the one reserved for the board on especially delicate issues. "Let me ask then, is it true that you lost two-thirds of your party on the way to the site, and several more lives during the excavation?"

Tiron said nothing for a moment, then "Yes. Good friends are hard to come by, and I lost one on that trip. As I said, had not our guides stuck with us, likely none of us would have returned."

"I'm sorry to hear that, I really am," said Jerry. "Where are you living now?"

"I'm in semi-retirement, working on some things for which I've prepared most of my life. I have a small cabin, about twenty-five miles from town here."

Howard spoke up, unable to contain himself. "I was doing research on the cathedrals of the French High Gothic period, and I met Tiron in Lyon, France at a café almost twenty years ago. He was studying something about Lyon's stance during the French revolution, but he knew more about the cathedrals than I thought possible, and as you know, it's a bit of a specialty of mine. He took my name, and promised to look me up some day. I never expected to see his face when he knocked on my office door yesterday afternoon. I knew you'd be pleased to meet him…"

Tiron cut him off. "Jerry, your own work is worth notice, I think. Before accepting your current position, you were dean of Social Sciences here, in which time you published two books on the relationship between the degeneration of political ideals and nationalism."

Jerry seemed embarrassed. "Compared to your…" he looked through the papers; "fifteen publications in… a rather wide range of fields, I'm honored that you've taken the time to check into my works."

"Actually, I took the liberty of reading them not so long ago. It seems to me that you have a third work that wants publishing, this one perhaps zeroing in more upon the elements of society that produce the necessary goals for its continued existence, and how to nurture them without yet knowing precisely what they might be." Jerry looked at him, stunned, for this was exactly what he had been planning to do for some time.

Howard laughed. "Jerry, don't mind him, he did the same thing to me yesterday. Told me exactly what I was planning to do next, and had some excellent suggestions as to how to go about doing it." Jerry leaned back, wondering what to say next, his mind racing as to what position he had to offer. Tiron's voice suddenly became businesslike.

"So let's make our little meeting here of some practical use, shall we?"

"Um… Certainly. Are you open to… considering a position in…" his eyes raced frantically over the resume looking for the most likely clue.

Tiron interrupted him. "You are just opening a new major, Environmental Studies. You've filled three of the five positions, and you likely have more options for the remaining two than you can handle." He waited.

Jerry didn't know whether to feel trapped or relieved. "Yes, that's true."

Tiron handed him a manila envelope. "This represents my analysis of the new major's potential, and my suggestion for how to complete it into a cohesive whole. I've included my opinion as to the two best candidates for the remaining positions—which is only my opinion, mind you—and one of those is myself. There's a full description of the course objectives and methodology, including how the content will interrelate with your current program. I've included an abstract for you to present to the board of directors if you see fit. As I'm sure you understand, this is merely a submission for your consideration; you may ignore it or accept it with no offense taken on my part." Jerry held the folder like a live scorpion. If what Tiron was saying was true, he had just handed him relief from several grueling weeks of work. He looked up. Tiron was smiling. Jerry gathered himself—he hadn't become dean for lack of ability to react—and smiled back.

"Thank you, we will be most happy to take this into consideration. When can I call you with our reaction?"

Tiron stood up. "If I don't hear from you, I'll call you in a few days. Meanwhile, it's been a pleasure to find friendly faces in Cherell." Jerry stood up hastily, and proffered his hand. Tiron shook it graciously, and waited for Howard to pull himself together. Howard eagerly shook Jerry's hand, and followed Tiron out the door. Jerry sat down and sighed; he felt like he had just come through some interrogation. He hit the buzzer. "June, get me Donna on the board of directors." Then he sat silently, staring at the walnut doors that lead to the rest of the university, and wondered whether he were more sea-captain or prisoner, and whether anyone ever thought about these sorts of things.

The sun set into a bath of purple and orange on the far west of town. Jason watched it, sitting on a branch two-thirds of the way up a maple sipping the remains of a bottle of eighteen-year Glenlivet.

Chapter 4: Not By Land

Saturday, Cris found Jason and Laura talking over lunch at the Slogan. They made room for him and Laura smiled warmly. "And how is the Chemist of Perceptions today?" She had a way of making him feel important and dignified just with her smile; he felt as though he were joining a conversation at the senate.

"Pretty good, actually. Cat may be joining us here if she finishes her paper on Kenya. What am I interrupting?"

Jason smiled. "Laura's been educating me as to the best ways to use the media to your own advantage. Kind of interesting, because I had always considered it a useless evil."

"Yes," said Laura, "Folks with integrity, like you boys, often make that mistake. You see…" she was gesturing with her fork again, "For example, what is the most disturbing aspect of today's paper? As a matter of fact, find us today's paper if you would." Cris went since he was on the outside of the bench, and picked up a paper from the counter. Laura spread the first page on the table facing the boys, the *Cherell Sun.* "Now I want you lads to look this over, and tell me what disturbs you the most about it." They read over the various front-page articles.

Jason spoke up first. "The sensationalism. None of the featured stories here are relevant to life, they're just here because they're sensational. We have a car wreck, a flood, a serial killer's appeal, the president vetoing a tax cut, etcetera. The only remotely useful story might be the veto, but when I read through the article, I notice that there's nothing about what the proposed tax cut actually was, or any normal information that would make the story of substance. Just the sensational description of the conflict between the president and congress, and suppositions as to who's ahead. I mean, how much effort or room would it take to print an abstract of what the veto said, or even put it on another page and refer to it."

"Quite true," she responded; "and Cris?"

"The thing that bothers me the most would be the lack of truth or relevance. There *are* things that really affect us every day, much of which we're unaware, but the whole effort of this page is to convince us that these *other* things, stupid things, affect us more, and the important things don't exist. It's not that they don't get their facts right, it's like Jason says, it's that there *are* no facts. Its misdirection, not misinformation."

"Very Good. Now I want you boys to tell me something *good* about this page."

They both thought for a moment. Cris spoke wryly; "It's *effective…*"

Jason grunted. "Yep, that it is. And the style makes one feel as if one is really getting something. They're experts at telling us that they're actually telling us something."

Laura laughed. "Excellent. Now here's the question for you boys: How would you go about being effective, or convincing someone that you're really giving them something? That is, after all, what you've just said was good here." She was obviously brimming with the subject, but pacing herself to the boys' reactions.

Cris and Jason both leaned back, thinking. Cris spoke up. "Well we'd have to start by convincing people that we're telling them something important."

"Mm. And how would you go about doing that?" she asked. The waitress came by and took Cris' order for a blue cheese burger and a coke. She seemed to Cris to be extra friendly on days the boys weren't accompanied by the girls.

Jason answered, "That would be a bit of a trick. Because people get threatened if you tell them that you're going to tell them something real."

"They do."

Jason went on. "It would be easier if we could *show* people what we want to affect them, and tell them what just happened afterwards, in our own words. But with media…"

Cris interrupted him. "We'd have to start with something that people already know or accept. Then tell it in such a way that they think you're telling them something new when in fact you're telling them what they already know about it."

"Or better yet, if it's possible," said Jason, "Have something to do ourselves with the story."

"Which is why reporters try to get as close to the scene as possible. To make it look like it happened to them," continued Cris.

"But that can be an enormous task," said Jason, "how could we find a way to slide ourselves into every situation this paper reports? How would you introduce to the paper-reading society some way of seeing things that was valuable to them and have them accept it?"

"Why don't you just use the system?" asked Laura.

Jason blinked. "What do you mean?"

"Like be a writer for the paper and change things around subtly?" asked Cris.

"Yes, after a manner of speaking. How hard would that be?"

"Well first of all," said Jason, "wouldn't it be… immoral to use something for which you obviously have no respect, to use to get something good across?"

She looked at him. "Do you have respect for the menu here?"

"Well… no, not really."

"Yet you use it to feed yourself."

"Yes… Okay, you have a point. Use the system." He sat back, thinking.

Cris spoke up. "You'd have to know the system inside-out to do that."

She smiled. "You would."

"And you'd have to have some sort of access to it."

"True."

"So basically," said Jason, "you would have had to have done your homework. Prepared."

"Yes" she said. "Nothing good is accomplished without preparation on some part." Cris mentally applied this to his relationship with Cat, and winced. No wonder things had progressed like they had. He looked outside and was rewarded by the sight of her crossing the street in their direction. Jason followed his eyes, and smiled to Laura.

"Cat's coming. I guess you'll get to meet her after all." He said this in such a way that made Cris wonder what they had really been talking about before he came. But Laura just smiled politely, and waited for Cris, who opened the door for Cat, to bring her over and make introductions.

"Cat, this is *Lady* Laura. Laura, this is Cat." Laura smiled and offered her hand, which Cat shook graciously, and sat down on the bench on her side of the table, and sighed happily.

"Got it done. Kenya is now history," she said cheerfully.

"That must feel good," said Jason.

"It does." She noticed the paper on the table. "Were you guys reading something in the paper?"

"They were considering for the first time, its usefulness," remarked Laura.

Cat considered Laura for a moment. "Are you a reporter?" she asked.

"Yes I am, thank you for asking. I do articles for the *Cherell Sun* and a bit of editing."

"What's that like, is it fun?"

"Well, as I was telling the boys, it can be, if one is subtle enough."

Cat smiled. "That sounds like quite a bit of fun."

Jason spoke up. "So you were serious about using the system."

"Of course."

Cris asked, "But what do you try to accomplish?"

Laura smiled. "That, my dear, is what we're here to find out every day. Today, mostly. There's something new that wants doing every day, and it's up to us to find it out. And once we've found it out, it's up to us to pass it on."

"…By using the system…" murmured Jason.

"Makes you a bit uncomfortable, doesn't it Jason?" she interrogated him.

"Um… yes. I don't really like using any system but my own." At this she stared at him for a few seconds, thinking. Then, abruptly, she turned to Cat.

"What is your mother like, dearie?" she asked.

Cat's face took on a distant, dreamy look. "Ah, my mom. I've got the cutest mom in the whole world. She'll totally do anything for anyone, and she worries about everything. Like the wrinkles on her face—not that she has a whole lot of them—are all made from her smiling. Y'know how some people have frown-wrinkles; well hers are smile-wrinkles. And bright, almost innocent eyes. She scolds a lot, but never really gets angry, just concerned. And she likes dad a lot, although she says she doesn't understand him." Cat looked at Laura. "She's not formal or proper like you, I guess; and she would never start a conversation like you do. More like a person who reacts to things. Mostly I think she's just kindhearted."

Laura tilted her head and looked at Cat, who didn't seem to mind at all. Cris noticed that Cat and Laura were naturals together. "Do you get your beauty from her or your father, dear?" she demanded.

"Actually I think I look a lot more like my father than her. Mom's face is sharper than mine, and I don't have her eyes at all. She has like the kindest eyes you've ever seen. But dad blames all my stubbornness on her. Which is funny, because I don't think mom's stubborn at all."

"Are you?" piped in Jason. Cat simply stuck her tongue out at him in reply; Jason nodded as if he had received a royal compliment.

"What's your blood then, dearie?" asked Laura

"Um… Irish, a little German, and Welsh, I think. there's also some American in there that goes way back past the civil war." Cris realized that the whole conversation between the two was composed of things that he had been wanting to ask Cat for some time, but didn't know how. He sat mesmerized, promising himself that next time he had an opportunity, he wouldn't hold back. The conversation continued for almost three-quarters of an hour while outside, an unusually large black crow beat its lazy wings toward Rhoboth Hall where the board of directors was meeting with Jerry in the top floor conference room. It perched on a corner of the building and looked around at its new habitat. Not bad. Universities usually afforded more than the usual perks for a bird of carrion. Below the concrete roof, the board discussed the last choice for a position in Environmental Studies. They had already approved Tiron, and were on the verge of accepting his suggestion for the other position, someone who had already been high on the list. The crow lifted one wing and nibbled vigorously at an itch.

Tera woke suddenly and sat up; the dreams faces were still pulsing in the dark in front of her, but she wasn't backing down; and she wasn't sorry, for once she wasn't sorry. Her head was buzzing and throbbing; too much happening; too many faces, she closed her eyes, found that she was breathing normal, heartbeat normal. She opened her eyes, pulled a sheet around her, walked to the door and opened it a crack. Silence. She slipped into the hallway and walked slowly down the eighteen-foot hallway to grandfather's room. With her hand on the door, she waited for a moment and listened. Then she boldly swung the door open, walked in, and sat cross-legged in front of her grandfather. His face was silhouetted against the streetlight outside the window.

"Good evening Grandpa."

Silence.

"I've missed you, Grandpa; ever since you had to leave us and go into yourself." She let the silence hang between her sentences; it felt like a real conversation that way.

"I've begun to realize that I'm going to have to do something. Not just succeed even, but really do something." Pause. "You told me that once, didn't you?"

"I'm in trouble, aren't I, Grandpa." For all the world it looked like he was nodding his head. Against the half-lit window, it could have been anything. She realized that she had never come here like this before; she was awake, she had walked quietly, deliberately, instead of panic or being overcome with that strange emotion.

"Something bad happened, didn't it." It was more a statement of realization to him than a question. If he nodded that time, there was no indication.

"I always wanted to… do something for you, grandpa. I wanted to give you something. I guess I was pretty foolish. I see a bit of the reality now. You gave me something. And whatever it is, is in danger."

Again, that barely perceptible nod that could have been nothing.

"I… I never thought it meant something to accept, to accept what someone gives you." Pause. "I guess I have to find out what it is, so I can really accept it." Pause. "And if it's in danger, I need to defend it." She sat in silence for six minutes, then stood up and walked to the door.

"Thank you, Grandpa; I'm going to do what I can. No one's taking it from me, whatever it is. Goodnight, Grandpa."

He spoke. "Goodnight Tera." It was that *voice*, the voice she had missed so long. It cut through the dark like a thunderbolt and rolled around her head; she was sure the whole neighborhood had heard it. Her heart pounded against her chest, straining to get out; she for all the world wanted to rush over, embrace him, to have the grandpa she had always known, to have him back. But the sound of her voice from what she had just said was calming her, making her shut the door and release the handle… *This is the code; do not betray him, do not betray yourself, this is the code, this is the time you have together and no more; danger is everywhere, do not betray him nor yourself, do not break the code.* She turned and walked the eighteen feet down the hallway, and entered her room. She sat for a long time on the side of the bed, the faces small and distant now; it seemed they were scared. Curling up on the pillow, she fell into a deep sleep. In the morning the tear stains on the pillow had dried and faded. Truly morning is wonderful, isn't it, my children?

Chapter 5: I'm Feeling Much Better Now

I didn't tell you of his difficulties, nor his nightmares. Nor did I tell you of his apartment. Let us go there now, for Cris is coming over to visit him; Cris has been promised supper, which as you know is a rare luxury while at university.

"Come in. Find a seat and put your butt in it."

The door opened into the main room of the basement apartment. Jason was moving swiftly and expertly over the fully loaded stovetop among three boiling pots and a large skillet. He smiled at Cris. "Or wander around all you like. Nothing's sacred so make yourself at home." Dropping two catfish fillets onto the skillet, he grabbed various vials from a long array of spices. Cris wandered around the living room, which was the other half of the same room separated by a counter. Books were everywhere, filling the limited shelf space and stacked anywhere convenient. Artwork covered the walls; prints, some photographs, and many original pieces; even drawings on the walls themselves. Models of odd shapes and materials were everywhere; on the low table in the middle of the room was a partially constructed round structure of geometric shapes. The pattern was mesmerizing; sticks that looked like an ancient city turned in on itself, growing in a crystalline pattern or perhaps decaying.

"Did you do the artwork?" Cris' mind was spinning; trying to grasp for a foothold. Everything was… everything was something that couldn't be described. The phrase "things really happen" came to mind. Something vague underneath everything seemed almost tragic, but this passed as a fleeting impression that he couldn't find when he focused on the thought.

"Of course not. That;" Jason pointed a long two-pronged meat fork, "…is Bosch's *Garden of Earthly Delights*. He lived a long time before me." Then he was dropping slices of butter into the skillet in hissing clouds of steam.

"I mean the original stuff. Who drew all those?"

"Oh. Yeah, I did most of that. I was going to go into art but it's kind of a luxury; don't know as I'll have time for luxury this time around." Cris was staring at a panoramic painting of a post-nuclear-war urban scene, only about a foot high but five feet wide. Looking closely at the buildings, he saw many of them were composed of such disparate objects as broccoli, cigarettes, electrical cords, books… all grossly out of scale but skillfully woven together. The background was a brilliant red-orange, with strange symbols in the sky. "That's kind of a fun one," Jason remarked as he poured the water from a pot of corn-on-the-cob.

"I don't know if *fun* is the word I'd use," murmured Cris. The painting was crawling with life, but nowhere in it was a sign of any living beings. He shook his head and returned to the spider-like model in the center of the room. "What's this?"

"I don't know yet. I'm hoping to make an abacus out of it."

"For what, Martian calculus?"

"Actually, that's pretty close. C'mon, grub's ready. You gotta serve yourself." He handed Cris a plate. He was reassuringly casual; Cris found himself feeling like he was home. The food was great: Cajun catfish fried in butter, a hot lentil stew that tasted oriental, some kind of thick sauce that melted when put over the corn-on-the-cob, and a rice-pasta with garlic.

"You eat like this every day?"

"Nah. Just when dignitaries visit. Normally I have what I call the Eternal Pot of Stew. You never really finish it, just keep adding things every day. I had to clean it up to make this stuff though."

"Doesn't it rot?"

"Um… would that be so bad? But no, I heat it up afresh every day; that kills most of the maggots." He smiled and leaned back on the couch. Cris noticed that he was eating with chopsticks, left-handed; and that he didn't lean over his plate to eat. The food seemed to waft like a lazy butterfly into his mouth, picture-perfect. He remembered a similar pattern at the Slogan Diner.

"Are you left-handed?"

"You notice quite a bit, don't you? No, I've trained myself to be ambidextrous. Gives me something to do in boring classes and whatnot."

"You *write* left-handed too?"

"Heh. Yes, actually, but like this." He put down his plate, fetched a notebook, and handed it to Cris. The notes were in mirror-writing, from right to left. The next page was in mirror writing *upside-down*. As he leafed through, he saw more variations; flips, twists; it made him dizzy to read it. He turned to one leaf on the right side written in standard format, but each letter was a work of art in itself. An "h" would loop several lines downward, where it formed the backbone of a "d," whose curve shot past forming the following "e"… it was like cursive done in Art Nouveau with either meticulous planning or insanity, it was hard to tell. "That was done with my right hand," explained Jason, "I can relax a bit and have fun that way."

"Um… sure. But why write backwards?"

"Try it sometime. It feels far more natural when using your left hand, and to be truthful, it's much easier. Leonardo di Vinci wrote that way. And when you have hours of dead lecture time to fill, it gives you something interesting to do."

Cris put the notebook down and returned to his catfish. After a few moments of thinking, he said "You're bored most of the time, aren't you?"

Jason didn't look up. Munching into the corn cob, he said, "Kind of depends on what you mean by bored, doesn't it?"

"Like you already know the answers to everything, and you're just killing time getting through life."

"That's quite an accusation."

"It's true, isn't it."

"If it were true, what would I be doing here?"

"I don't know. That's what puzzles me. You obviously don't need this kind of an education. I haven't had any classes with you, but I'll bet you're even harder on your profs than Tera."

Jason grunted. "Most of them aren't worth it." he murmured. He looked up. "But I don't have the knowledge they have. It's useful."

"For what? I mean, for crying out loud, you can write backwards effortlessly, and I've never seen anyone interested in science who could do ten cents worth of art. Every subject that comes up in conversation you always have already covered. You spend most of your time holding back from saying anything and guiding everyone else into discovering the answers. I'll bet even *you* don't have any idea what you know."

"Sounds like you're talking about yourself," said Jason quietly. Cris' mind raced. He was right, almost everything he had just accused Jason of, he felt was true in some way about himself. Then he realized the bait he had taken, and shook his head.

"No. Nice try, but we're talking about you here. What are you hoping to accomplish at university; why are you here?"

Jason carried his plate back to the kitchen, and washed it. "What you're talking about is the subject of understanding versus knowledge. Keep eating, I'll show you." He took a print of Picasso's *Guernica* down from the wall opposite Cris and began to draw on the wall. "Here's you meandering through life." He began to draw a horizontal line. "Then you begin to learn something." He sloped the line up.

"Then you begin to realize that the subject is not just a collection of facts, but you're learning an actual art or science." He looped the slope still up, but backward until it was above the starting point.

"At this point, you're at the *same place* in life you were when you started learning, but much higher. Usually you feel really smart about now. Most people in this condition become college professors or teachers of some sort. But guess what? You still need to integrate the knowledge you've learned into actual life practice. As you do, you'll find that you have to *give up* a lot of the details in order to convert them into life process. For example, when driving a car, you don't go through all twenty steps it took you to make a turn that you did when you first were learning, you simply "go left." That "go left" took you many steps of which you were quite proud when you first knew them; but now they'd just clutter up your mind. So this process of *integration* actually takes you *backwards* because you're dumping what you know." He drew the third segment of the loop, heading backwards and down.

"At this point, once you've given up *knowledge* per se, you begin finally to see the whole picture as it really is. Now you're gaining something new, called *understanding*. This brings you to… exactly where you started." He finished the loop and continued his original straight line. "Now you can go on with life like you were doing, before you wasted all this time.

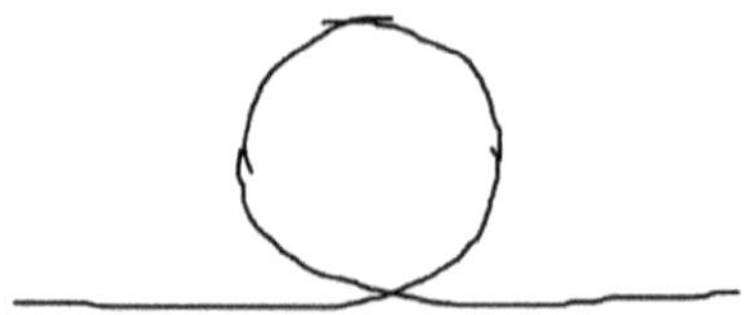

"Then what was the point?" asked Cris, slightly puzzled.

"Easy. To gain understanding."

"But… what's the advantage of understanding over knowledge?"

"Let's start with the disadvantages. Big one is, there's no value to your opinion that's higher than any sincere man on the street. Mind you, I did say sincere. Someone who, out of an honest sense of life and with no silly preconceptions says, "That new building is an eyesore," has 100% as much right to say so as a 50-year old architect who understands every brick of it. But. The architect, if he's gone all the way around the loop, can tell you exactly *why*, in every aspect of architecture, it's an eyesore. The educated professor, on the other hand, is way up here…" Jason pointed to the top of the loop, "and will undoubtedly disagree with both the man on the street *and* the master architect. Why? Because all he has by which to assess the building's worth is knowledge. He sees via a huge collection of *facts*, all of which are useful, but none of which he can *use*, because he's so busy hoarding them. By definition, you can't use something you're keeping, because to *use* means to *use up*. Like spending money; you can't have your cake and wash your face with it too." Jason smiled, enjoying himself. "In other words, you can't understand something you know about."

"So then what's the advantage of understanding, if you've discarded all the facts?"

"Easy. Instead of knowing all sorts of things, like pressing the gas means go, pressing the brake means stop, turning the wheel to the left makes the car go that direction, and so on, you simply *drive*. If you thoroughly understand the subject, you *don't care* to know about it because it's part of you."

"What does this have to do with my question? What are you doing here, and what do you hope to accomplish?" Cris was feeling good about his ability to bring Jason back to the conversation.

"Well… I hope to get through some loops. All the way through." Jason hung *Guernica* back into its space and resumed the couch.

"You hope to understand things."

"Right. But it's a large commitment to start the journey through a loop, because there's nothing worse than knowing part of a subject; being halfway through a loop."

Cris mused this over. "I'll bet you write a book if you ever get through all the subjects you want, called *"All Things."*

"Cute. Anyway I think it's already been written."

"No doubt. But you could do it better I think."

Jason smiled. "I doubt that." His eyes had that faraway look again, then he snapped back. "Like some after-dinner wine?"

"Sure. Knowing you, it's probably some expensive import only available on blue moons."

"Last blue moon I was on, they only had whisky. But I'll let you judge for yourself." He put their dishes in the sink and got out what looked like an antique bottle from the cupboard. Cris noticed that he had cleaned most of the pots and pans while preparing the food, so there was little cleanup left to do. Jason poured two glasses, brought one to Cris, and resumed washing the dishes.

"Hey! This stuff is fizzy like champagne."

"You like it?"

"Hell yeah. Let me see the bottle." Jason handed him the bottle with an amused smile. It was obviously an antique, green tinted. There was no paper label, but the glass itself had raised letters that read "Dr. Simpson's Amazing Bitters." Cris was puzzled. "Is this for real?"

"It's a real bottle if that's what you're asking. But no, it now has wine in it, not bitters. I made the wine from the black raspberries that grew along the fence in the backyard."

"Oh. Now I feel kind of stupid. How did you get it fizzy, do you add carbonation?"

"No, it's simply not done working. If you keep it under pressure while it works, it stays fizzy; that's how they make champagne.

"So you just left the cork in?"

"If I did that, I'd be out one antique bottle. The stuff builds enough pressure to shatter normal containers. You ever see how thick champagne bottles are? But for this batch I left it work almost the whole way, then yes, left the cork in." He finished the dishes, pulled some paraphernalia from a drawer, and made himself comfortable on the couch. "Would you like an after-dinner cigar?"

"You smoke?" Cris was rather surprised.

"Are you asking if know how to enjoy smoking, or if I have a habit that controls me?"

"Oh. Well how often do you smoke?"

"Beats me. Last time was… about two weeks ago, I think. But I went through quite a few cigars in a very short time then. That's like asking me how I often eat avocados. Depends on how I feel and if they're there. I take it that's a 'no' then."

"Um… right. I don't think I could hack a cigar. But that looks more like a cigarette you're rolling."

"Don't let the size fool you." He finished rolling, lit it, and the room filled with the smells of peppermint and vanilla. It was the fist time Cris had really enjoyed the smell of someone smoking since his grandfather's cherry tobacco as a child.

"What's in that?"

"Y'know, tonight you've spent more time asking me about things I'm doing than anything else."

"At least you're not evading as much as you usually do."

"I don't evade much."

"No, what you do is answer a question with a question of your own, and the person soon forgets what they were asking in the first place."

"That's because people are rarely interested in finding something out about me, they really are inquiring as to something about themselves. I simply accommodate them."

"So what's in that?"

"Tobacco, peppermint, clove, and vanilla bean."

"And you mixed it yourself of course."

Jason blew a few smoke rings that hung lazily around his head. "Let's talk about the girls."

"Why?"

"You were planning to bring the subject up before you came in, and I enjoy introducing subjects formally. So. What do you think of the way they get along?"

"I've never seen a relationship as mutually accepting as theirs. Between them they could affect almost anyone in any way they want. And they're as different as…"

"As you and me." Jason smiled.

"Yeah, really. And we don't have that much in common with them either, personality-wise. We're like four oddities that came together."

"Well you're the one that started it. Remember how you told me you took them to lunch the first time?"

"Yeah, that was weird, come to think of it. Cat and I were both attracted to Tera. Then once we started talking, it felt like family. And when you came in, it felt like you had been there the whole time."

Jason blew a large smoke ring that went straight up and crawled along the ceiling. "It makes me wonder who else is in this family that we haven't encountered yet. Doesn't it feel to you like there's some others who are here, but just not yet?"

"You mean like Lady Laura? She's quite a character."

"Yeah, I suppose; although I hadn't thought of her in that light before."

"I guess she'd be like an aunt or something… doesn't quite feel like a mother."

"True. And it seems to me that this kind of family doesn't necessarily have the same parts as what we call a standard family. Although the analogies are interesting…"

"It'd be really cool if we could all take a class together next semester."

"That would. Trouble is, it's dangerous to do that; it's hard to take a class seriously if you're primary motivation is to be with others in it. But I like the idea."

"Well maybe there'll be something that we all have to take anyway; it wouldn't be that hard to arrange our schedules together."

"Okay, I'm open to the idea. More wine?"

"Sure, please. You're not trying to get me inebriated, are you?"

Jason refilled their glasses. "That's something folks can only do to themselves. How patient are you?"

"Patient? You filled my glass right away."

"I was talking of the girls. It is the subject, by the way."

"Oh. Um… patient for…?"

"I think it would be wisest if we avoided pairing off right away."

Cris realized that he had been avoiding thinking of this subject. "You mean we should take it easy on the romance?"

"Not necessarily. But I've noticed that a group, or maybe a family in this case, changes when people begin to pair off."

Cris thought about this. "Y'know, I think you're right. I remember in high school, every time a bunch of people began to get close-knit, it'd be destroyed by romances. But it's really hard to resist that, because the atmosphere of a close-knit group is conducive to guys and girls getting to know each other in ways that otherwise might take years."

"Right. Soap-opera stuff. I believe that while the individual is the most powerful unit, the relationship between two people is *smaller* than their relationship to their society. As such, it can be more intimate, but certainly not more important."

"But… then you're promoting the kind of societies where there's things like arranged marriages; or forbidden ones like in *Romeo and Juliet* can rule."

"That's true. But in most of those cases, the rules are the result of questionable traditions that are enforced. We now have one in which everyone does exactly what they want. If we respect the loose society that we are, we'll think twice before taking personal advantage of relationships that have been built by everyone, or using them up just on one other person."

"So you're basically telling me to go easy on Cat."

"No, I'm saying that if you're interested in her, initiate a pursuit of her on your own, and be cognizant of how it affects your family."

"That actually clears up a few things I've been wondering about. Like that time in the Slogan when I asked her for a date; that wasn't really me, that was… *everyone* putting energy into it." Jason smiled. Cris thought for a second and suddenly exclaimed, "Wait! You set that whole thing up to push me into asking Cat for a date!"

Jason was amused. "Well you wanted to ask her so badly, it seemed a shame not to."

"What a dirty lousy trick! I certainly hope I have the opportunity to return the favor."

"Me too. I think if someone lets themselves that open to a setup, they deserve it."

"So how did I leave myself open?"

"You wanted something."

"…Oh."

"In any situation, the person who wants the most has the least power. That's why people lose when they gamble."

"Well how would one win at gambling?"

"Do it for the challenge, or for some other reason than to get free money."

"Have you tried this?"

Jason smiled. "Always."

"You and your analogies. Just once I'd like to hear you say something that only means one thing on one level."

"Okay. I think you should take Tera on a date. And consider her as seriously as you consider Cat."

"Why?!? Besides, I don't know if I could; she scares me."

"No she doesn't."

"She has that potential."

"She's a girl."

"What's that supposed to mean?"

"You're scared of her because you think of her as a guy; someone who will challenge you with what she knows. But girls don't 'know' things like guys. They *access* their knowledge, while we tend to *hold* it. She'll listen and respect any platform you present."

"She will?"

"Have you ever tried it?"

"No, I figured she was too smart."

"Regardless of how 'smart' she is, if she's a real woman she'll respond to whatever you present without competing."

"Okay. I'm actually going to consider this. But… wouldn't it contradict what we were saying about pairing off?"

"We haven't been pairing off. Things done on the strength of a society never actually achieve that initial footing that begins a true personal relationship."

"So I should ask her out the same way I did Cat; within the structure of our society."

"Exactly. In my opinion, anytime you have an opportunity to enjoy yourself you should take it."

Cris thought a moment. "Cool. This is actually a good distinction we're making; the difference between what we do as individuals and what we do as a family. It opens up quite a few possibilities."

"I think so." Jason got out a deck of cards. "You up for some poker?"

"Why not, we're drinking and smoking, might as well learn to play poker too."

"I have Scrabble if you'd rather."
"No word games on wine. Deal 'em up."

*   *   *

And why wouldn't Cat and Tera be talking, now that the boys were engaged in a frivolous game of cards? They had been hiking back down Buzzard Pass, the state park behind the university; we find them beside the trail reclining on a boulder and watching the sunset arrange the events of the day onto the horizon in those winding colors that sailors use to assess the character of the morrow. Listen carefully, for Cat is talking, and few, even of the wise, understand where the value of her speech is hidden.

"…like I don't mind, he's probably one of the kindest people I've met. It's just difficult to know what motivates him. I mean I don't really know what motivates Cris either …I don't think Cris knows himself, it's like not important to him right now. But Jason lives on motivation; you can see it in his eyes, and it's one of the things he always brings up when someone's talking. He can nail people by understanding what motivates them. I just want to… maybe hand him a magical mirror that he could look into and see his own motivation. He's… *driven*; but not by himself. But it is by himself, it's just like he can't relax and enjoy it. It's like…"

"It's like his understanding is making him hungry."

"Yeah. And the more he understands, the hungrier he gets. And he's not eating, he's starving to death. When he talks to us, he's not using whatever his world is, he's using ours. That's what I meant about him being so kind; I've never met anyone who does that. Whenever you're around him, you feel like you're being handed breakfast every time he looks at you. All nice and prepared perfectly, and you're so glad to get it that you've got it half wolfed down before you think of giving him something back. And then it's too late, he's already got the next meal prepared."

"I wonder what he's hungry for."

"Y'know what I think? I think he understands too much. I mean, we've all seen that there's no subject or person he can't take down to the core instantly… and he only pretends to be thinking about it before he says something; I think he understands so much, even more than he realizes, that he's starving to be understood himself."

Tera turned and looked at her; Cat's eyes were animated with color. Tera sighed. "That's like an impossible task."

"Well it's not like an academic problem. It just takes time and effort. I'll bet he'd spill like a landslide if someone was focused enough to listen. Heck, I'll bet he'd learn things about himself that he thinks he's permanently blocked out. 'Cause people do that, they only think of themselves in ways that they can relate to other people. That's why I don't even try to think of myself anymore, it's not worth the bother."

"You think you could do that?"

"Do what?"

"Get him to talk."

"Well… sure. Anyone could. He's one of us you know; a human being. We keep treating him like some kind of superhuman."

"Yeah. I know I do. And I have all these images of what he could mean to me that just clutter everything up. It's like I can't even get near the real him."

"That's not good you know. You're just feeding his hunger. You're making him into those images instead of letting him be whoever he is. You know that he reads images we have in our heads like an open book."

"How do we know that?"

"Ever notice how everything he says caters to whatever daydreams we're playing with? I notice it with you even more than me. Like I can see when you've had a hard day and you want some place to relax and feel cared-for, and presto, he turns into some kind of protective featherbed that lulls you into all your fairytales. He does it to me all the time too, and it's really hard not to accept it and fall asleep into whatever world he makes. But all it's doing is perpetuating the daydreams; he's doing all the work and getting… basically nothing out of it. But it's always what you *want*; he's like a prisoner to providing us with whatever we want. And it works; I feel so much better afterwards… I've slept on a beautiful featherbed, and the next day I have all this extra energy. But it's just not… I mean, it *is* real, but it's not real for him. He's a professional actor who can actually make his acting into real life, and it's killing him because he doesn't get any time off stage."

"But what does he want?"

"I don't know, but it wouldn't be that hard to find out. You notice how he gets shy when he talks about himself? It means he's still like a little kid in that area, and none of us… adults have taken the time to get to know that child. And it's so simple; he's just waiting for people to do it and no one ever does."

We watch for half a minute of silence. The sun set, leaving behind a battalion of golden-red ambassadors guarding his exit. Tera spoke.

"Do you think you could do that?"

"What do you mean?"

"Do you think you could talk to him?"

"Um… It would take a lot of time. It wouldn't be easy."

"You just said it would be."

"I mean… like with the relationships we all have. Cris is treating me almost like a girlfriend, and everyone is watching you and Jason to see if anything's going to happen."

"Well from what you've just talked about, and it makes a lot of sense, I think we all need a lot more growing before we go pairing off."

"Well… like when we're all together, I don't get Jason at all, but I understand almost everything Cris does. But when we're talking like this, I totally get Jason, and Cris is a mystery. Like there's no way I can anticipate anything Cris is going to do, except when he's actually around."

"Cris has a way of being there without being there. He sees everything. When he talks to me one-on-one, I feel like we have a huge container between us that could hold anything."

"Really? Like I get this consciousness thing going with him… where we're aware of everything about each other so much that no one needs to talk. The thing that I admire about him the most is his ability to wait; it's like his strength; he could wait anyone out, and still have whatever answer they were floundering for all that time. He's probably one of the most patient people… no, he's easily the most patient person I've ever met."

"It's like he's already succeeded, and is simply going through the motions. But not like Jason, who seems to have had it all figured out at birth. Cris is enjoying figuring things out as he goes along."

"Yeah…" Cat's eyes were glowing in the dusk. "I never feel insulted or inferior around Cris no matter how hard he tries to be arrogant. He couldn't be arrogant if he tried. Everything we do, I feel like we're doing it together."

"Agreed. He's like someone you know will always be there… it's easy to forget how special that is, and take him for granted."

Cat grinned. "That's the second time you've used the word 'like' that you're always criticizing me for."

"Well. You ended your sentence with a preposition." Tera always had comebacks for proprietary accusations. Cat shifted on the rock and arched her back into the customary perfect stretch.

"You ready to go? The moon's not up yet, and we've got to be able to see the trail the rest of the way down."

"Yeah. Let me find my bag." Tera pulled her leather pouch from a nook, unscrewed the canteen, drank, and passed it to Cat. A cool wind caressed them. Climbing down the boulder, Tera was thoughtful. "Do you think you could do it then?"

"Do what?"

"Talk to Jason."

Cat stood on the trail and contemplated Tera's silhouette against the sky. "Okay. Actually, yes, I think I'd like to give it a try. But I may need you at some point."

There was some silence, and some intercommunication, the type that occurs between females, audible or otherwise, of which we won't speak here. Had Cris been there, he would have noticed them walking hand-in-hand through the elderberry bushes that lined both sides of the trail. But he himself was humming his way back to the dorm, with a pocketful of poker change, a belly full of catfish, and a head full of wonderful wine.

Chapter 6: Daddy Knows Best

It's funny how things turn out when you turn them out yourself. What you barely believed, becomes a reality, and with it a new reality emerges, itself changing all the priorities. And yet there you are, as it is often believed, in control; but who can know that, far less know themself? For true control starts with self-control.

Finals week at Cherell showed a mixture of intense studying and intense partying by the students. The Medieval History final was a two-hour affair of essay questions. Cris finished his in an hour and a half, and Cat shortly thereafter. They stood by the door watching Tera writing; she was completely engrossed in what she was doing.

"She's probably going to use every available minute," whispered Cat.

"You're right. Let's wait for her at the Slogan."

The air was crisp; winter was wielding his influence even this far south. With their minds whirling around history compositions, they didn't notice Tiron sitting on a bench by the path until they were nearly in front of him. Cat caught the moment with an "Oh, hi…"

He smiled. "Tiron's the name, and you're Cris and Cat. How was the History Exam?" His warmth put them at ease at once. Cat waited for Cris to speak up.

"It was pretty much what we expected. We got ten subjects from which we had to pick four, then write essays on those. Most of the students are still in there, but I guess we put everything we could remember down already."

Cat spoke up: "It's like there's no point in pouring your heart into it, or making any profound points, because our professor would just grade you lower. He's got like a grudge against meaning."

Tiron chuckled. "He's not the only blackbird in this pie with a grudge like that. Well congratulations on learning how much effort to spend. Are you done with finals for the year?"

"I've got one more, and Cris has… two more I think."

"Yup, one in Organic Chemistry, and one in English Lit."

He nodded to them. "Well I won't bother you any further then; enjoy the rest of your studies."

Cat hesitated. "Actually, we're going to catch a late lunch at the Slogan Diner with some friends, if you'd like to join us."

Tiron raised one eyebrow. "Are these the same friends to whom you alluded the last time we spoke?"

"Actually, I think they are," said Cris; "…Tera and Jason. It's not like a big crowd or anything, just the four of us."

"I accept your invitation; I have the time and will be glad to join you." Tiron had a formal quality about him that rubbed off, making one feel important just being around him. The three walked to the Slogan with the tall blue-eyed stranger in the middle. His walk was fluid and confident, and he certainly didn't need the cane he carried, though the flare it gave him was attractive. They both found themselves automatically falling into pace with him. "Will Tera and Jason be there now?" he inquired.

"Um… I think Jason will probably be there, but Tera's still taking the test; she'll probably be another 20 minutes or so."

Tiron cocked his head interestedly at Cat. "Your friend is the Tera McCory in your history class?"

"Well… yes; how may Tera's are there?"

"At this university… there's four. Two are seniors, one is a sophomore who is about to drop out, and one is a freshman who has a peculiar reputation for insight. Her faculty-commentary file is about three inches thick. Professors either hate the girl with their customary academic passion, which can be quite fierce, or they can't say enough good about her."

Cris was becoming intrigued. "How did you know all that? And for that matter, how did you know that we were coming out of a History Final?"

Tiron held the door open for them at the diner. "Plenty of time for questions and answers when we're seated."

Jason was already at the booth by the window with a cup of tea. He tilted his head interestedly when he saw Tiron following Cat and Cris. "Welcome." Tiron nodded and slid in the bench across from Jason. Cris sat by Jason so Cat slid in by Tiron and made introductions.

"Jason, this is Tiron, the man we met halfway through this semester. Tiron, this is Jason; he's in physics."

Tiron grunted. "Actually, he's applied for a triple major in Physics, Mathematics, and History, with minors in English Literature and Linguistics, haven't you?"

"Yes." He returned the gaze steadily, but with no expression on his face.

Tiron smiled. "I thought as much. Jason Sardic, it's a pleasure to meet you. You drive your science professors mad by asking questions that threaten to topple their house of cards. You've won two national awards this semester with your compositions for Creative Writing. Your test scores are all over the board; sometimes you don't even show up for exams, most times you're the top scorer. You've got your advisor scared to death of you, so it's probably just as well that you refuse to consult with him except when you need his signature. And most interestingly… every female professor or teachers' aide that put comments into your file seems hopelessly in love with you. With the exception of Miss Hawley, who is going through a nervous breakdown."

Cat had started laughing during Tiron's description, and she applauded when he finished. "I think I've just learned more about him in the last 30 seconds than the last three months!"

Jason said nothing, sizing Tiron up and soaking in who he was. Cris spoke up. "Okay, let's have it. How do you know all this stuff. Start with how you knew we were in History Class."

"Everything can seem so difficult to people who are unused to doing their homework. When you last spoke with me, you told me that you were freshmen, you told me your names, and you told me your majors. I didn't even have to do any guessing;

there's only six freshman classes holding both a Cris and a Cat…
I did have to consider all the variations on Cat, like Katrinica,
Katherine, Katrina, etcetera; but as it turns out, there was only
one class with a Cat –imagine my delight when I found it spelled
C-a-t—" he flashed a smile at her, "…and a Cris both, holding
your majors. From there it's a simple matter to look up your
classes and schedules."

"And what about Jason and Tera?" Cris turned to Jason, "He
knew all about Tera too."

"Well as it turns out, I'm going to begin a teaching job this
coming semester. And rather than sit on my butt waiting to be
thrown whatever students the system pushes my way, I've taken
the liberty of scanning through the university's files. Tera and
Jason aren't exactly what you would call low-profile students. I
have to admit I was curious if Tera, who turned out to be in your
Medieval History class, was also going to turn out to be the one
you mentioned was one of your friends."

"That's impressive," said Cris; "what kind of class are you
going to be teaching?"

Jason interrupted. "It'll be in Environmental Studies,
probably a class dealing with something like the Theory of Chaos
applied to society."

Tiron laughed. "Very close. And how, if I may ask, did you
come to that conclusion?"

"The dean has been trying to open up Environmental Studies
for some time, and encountering all sorts of political
pandemonium. You are an opportunist who doesn't mind doing
his homework; you probably waltzed into the dean's office and
offered to solve all his problems if he'd just do it your way.
Which the dean would accept, because if there's one thing no
politician can stand, it's work. But you have keen analytical skills,
which would mean you detest environmental studies almost as
much as you detest contemporary sociology; they're both about
as organized as Hong Kong's street life. So I'm guessing you'd try
to organize the whole department in your own way by placing
yourself in a key position. Chaos theory comes in handy there,

because it's the study of patterns, which is organization, but it's *called* just the opposite. So you'd be sitting pretty, doing what you want, and completely disguised from the idiots."

"That's a very bleak picture you paint of Cherell university," smiled Tiron.

"Wait a minute," said Cris, "this means you were sitting on that bench *waiting* for me and Cat."

"Among other things, yes," stated Tiron matter-of-factly.

Cat spoke up. "Is the scenario that Jason just sketched out true? Are you starting a class in… Chaos Theory in Society?"

"That, I'm afraid, was Mr. Sardic being a bit too fanciful, although I do like his reasoning. The class will be called Being and will have three parts; firstly, what is possible to achieve in a real society, secondly, how is that ideal affected by its sociological environment, and thirdly, how is the environment affected by the society. Possibly. I may change it."

"You're going to have a class called 'Being'?" said Cat, "That's so cool."

Cris spoke up. "Was Jason right on that part about waltzing into Jerry's office and taking the job?"

"Let's just say…" he looked at Jason, "…he wasn't entirely wrong." He held his eyes until Jason spoke.

"You're very old." It was said matter-of-factly.

"Am I." Statement, not a question.

Jason didn't falter. "Yes. It's interesting that it doesn't show."

Tiron smiled. "If it does show, it means you're dying; and if you're dying, you can't choose your death." A few moments of silence.

"I suspected that was possible."

"It is. But you don't need to know that now."

"Oh? What *do* I need to know now then?"

"If I told you, it wouldn't take the need away, just redirect it somewhere less tangible."

"Of all the things I may or may not need, tangibility doesn't seem to be one."

Tiron leaned forward ever so slightly. "That would be right, except you don't believe that you yourself are tangible. Everything and everyone else in your environment you touch at will; you have a gift for believing in who someone really is, even if they're not acting that way, or if they don't see it themselves. But while you think you apply that belief to yourself, you don't do it on a day to day basis, because you refuse to allow the day-to-day-*you* be tangible." He spoke with such a combination of kindness, authority, and experience, that Cat and Cris were amazed that Jason dared speak back. Their attention was so fixed on the interchange between the two, that they didn't notice Tera standing at the table until she cleared her throat.

"Tera, welcome," said Cris. "Tiron has been telling us all about you." He got up, and pulled a chair from another table, put it at the end of their booth, ushered Tera into the place he had been sitting, and sat in the chair himself. Tera looked quizzically at Tiron. He proffered his hand.

"Tiron Jarome at your service, Miss McCory."

"Tera." she said, and offered her hand across the table where, instead of shaking it, he kissed it formally, then smiled at her with a twinkle in his eye.

"This is the guy that Cris and I met awhile ago that we told you about," says Cat. "He's starting a new class about society, and I think he's recruiting." Tera raised one eyebrow at Tiron, glancing quickly to Jason, who seemed thoughtful, but certainly not subdued.

Tiron went on. "Tera, I'm afraid you have me at disadvantage. Your friends here have been dragging me through the coals for the last twenty minutes, and it seems I've been forced to tell all my secrets."

"Not exactly," said Cat, "The only things we know are what he told us and what Jason guessed, and he won't even admit that Jason guessed right." Jason shot an appreciative glance to Cat for her support.

Cris spoke up. "He's read all of our academic files, including the teachers' comments, both good and bad." Tera continued to say nothing. She shook her hair to one side, and tilted her chin toward Tiron as if to say, 'Well?' Tiron drew back, smiled, and looked around at the four. All were looking at him with the same voice; expectant, intrigued, yet slightly challenging. He sighed and spoke.

"When you two said you had friends, I didn't expect a full-fledged tetra-psyche. This is quite a treat. And I fully intend to make a presentation to you all, however, I believe if I did it now, the waitress would become impatient." Everyone glanced up, where the waitress was waiting for them to notice her.

"That's twice I've missed my cue here today," muttered Cris to himself.

"You guys ready to order, now that Tera's here?" Their waitress had become like an old friend.

"Sure," said Jason, "I'll have whatever soup you have today."

"It's lentil… it's pretty gross."

"Sounds perfect, Andrea."

"Cris? Blue cheese burger and a coke?" She had a way of telling when he preferred coffee and when he preferred coke.

"Yup."

"Tera? Greek salad?"

"Um… sure, that'll be fine tonight. And water."

"Cat?"

"Chicken Salad and an ice tea."

"And you sir?"

"I'll have the lentil soup like Jason. And hot tea." Tiron's voice wasn't deep, but it resonated with experience; a musical quality.

"K. Thank you." She sauntered off, and the table enjoyed a moment of silence.

Tiron broke it. "What do you suppose the minimum requirements are for a real society?" Cris noticed that it was the second time tonight he had taken the offensive. He vaguely wondered if he could follow through as well as he came on. The question rolled around their minds. Cat spoke up.

"Diversity."

Tera. "A homeland in common."

"…but many things could be a 'homeland,'" interjected Cris, "like there's chess clubs that make up their own society; in that case *chess* would be part of their homeland."

Cat continued; "…or like on the internet, there's a lot of chat-rooms that have mini-societies. Or even a church is a kind of society by itself."

"Maturity," stated Jason.

"Let's see now… we have diversity, a common ground, maturity… anything else?"

"Well what do you mean by a *real* society?" asked Cris; "this university has its own society, but I don't think I could bring myself to consider it a real one."

"Why not?"

"Well, we've got the diversity for sure. But the common ground is different for students and the staff. Most of us students are following our own agendas; we're not necessarily here because we want to be part of whatever is happening here—I mean, I'm sure a lot of students are—but I'm here more like someone in a store buying something. I pay them money, and I get trained in whatever subject I've chosen. And I get to use the university facilities, like the library and the dorms. But the more I see of the professors, the less I like the idea of being part of this all."

"And it's certainly not mature," said Tera.

"What exactly do we mean by mature, then?" asked Tiron.

Jason was examining the contents of his empty teacup. "There's necessary stages in life through which a person goes before becoming an adult. If he doesn't go through them, regardless of how old he is, he's not an adult. It seems to me that societies go through those same stages; only it's easier for a society to become stymied on one stage indefinitely than it is for individuals. Since we have a constant influx and egress of new students, extreme interaction becomes the only means of sustaining a viable fabric of society; otherwise it washes out every time a class graduates. But universities are generally oriented *not* to allow this kind of interaction, far less take advantage of it…" He stopped and leaned back as Andrea brought their food.

"There you go again, stopping the conversation when I come so I can't get in on it," she teased, setting their orders. The table was a bit crowded with five people and Jason moved the condiments rack to the windowsill.

"Thanks, Andrea," he said quietly.

"You're welcome. If you get into anything interesting, wave and I'll join you." As she swayed off, Tiron touched Jason's teacup, and reached in his jacket pocket.

"Before you pour water over that Tetley teabag, try this." He pulled out two teabags and handed one to Jason. "I usually carry my own when in America."

Jason looked genuinely appreciative. "Thank you."

"You're welcome. I think you'll like the blend. A pity the water cools so fast from their pot to the table, we're not likely to get a good steep."

"Are you two going to be like connoisseurs of everything?" complained Cat, "It's bad enough having one of you around."

"At least they're getting along temporarily," smiled Cris.

Tera spoke up. "Jason, what do you mean by interaction? What kind of interaction would it take to solve the problem of maintaining the society of a university?"

"Um… sure, okay. The common ground we have is education. Whether we are just paying for it like Cris says, or whether we're going to be faithful alumni who want to forever remain a part of this society, it's still about education. We're not talking about the maturity of the individual students, we're talking about the maturity of the university as a whole—throughout the years. So we would need a sense of where the university is, how it got here, and where it's to go next. In the normal maturing process, these things should be obvious, but we have the turnover problem. The question then becomes, what actually should change through this process, and what should stay the same."

Cat sipped her ice tea. "Oh, right. I should have thought of that. Maturing means changing, so the key to a university's maturity is how it changes."

"How *what* changes, the information we're learning?" asked Cris, noticing that Cat was one of the only people he knew who looked good drinking from a straw.

Tera cut in. "No, it would have to be the method of learning."

"Exactly," said Jason, with a spoon of lentils poised like a hummingbird before him, "As students are taught, both the professor and the student learn from the process. Some processes work, some don't. Some work at one point in the university's growth, others we're not ready for, regardless of how good they might be."

Cat. "So using the same method year in and year out would effectively stop growth."

Cris. "But that's a huge thing to change. You'd have to catch up new professors, train existing ones, and constantly have meetings with everyone to figure out how to go on."

"Well that's what I meant by extreme interaction. In a dynamic society, you have to be dynamic. In education, you have to educate each other, no exceptions. Imagine: if we did do this, it would become immediately obvious who the deadbeat professors were. Our current system encourages the deadbeats, both students and teachers. The current system encourages universities to be strongholds of the status quo."

"Like our history professor," exclaimed Cat; "he spent the whole semester dancing around real interaction. He'd come up with all sorts of ways for us to interact, but if it started to be like actual back-and-forth instead of play-acting, he'd cut it short."

Cris agreed. "Right; Tera had him so scared by the end of the class that he made whole lessons designed specifically to prevent us from using any information from previous lessons. I think he fudged the last two weeks completely."

"Speaking of which," Jason asked Tera, "how did you deal with him on the final?"

Tera shifted and put down her fork. "He gave us a choice of ten subjects, for four of which we were to write essays. I covered five of them, then made up two questions of my own that tied the whole year together, and wrote two more essays for those."

Cat grinned. "He's gonna freak, you know. Don't you think he might give you a low grade?"

"Nah," said Cris, "he's to scared of her to do that. I think he's just relieved that the class is over."

"He's not going to be very relieved when the dean gets our evaluations," said Tera quietly.

"If he reads them," retorted Cris.

"Yeah, there's always that," she sighed. "But we were talking about what makes an ideal society… where did we get lost?"

Tiron spoke up. "Jason explained his idea of maturity fairly well, I think. I'd like to ask Cat what she meant by diversity."

"Well… a village where everyone's a blacksmith wouldn't operate very well."

Cris laughed. "Now why can't Jason put things that succinctly?"

Jason smiled then turned to Tiron. "How have we done with your question? Have we touched the minimum requirements for a real society?"

"That I believe you have. Touched. Let me ask you this: Do you have a real society right here?"

Everyone was silent for a bit; applying the idea to themselves was different. Tera spoke up.

"I've learned one thing that makes me believe we have. Before meeting these three, all my planning for what to say and what to do were based on myself or my family. But now, for example, when I was taking the history exam, all my ideas are like… like I imagine talking to everyone here about them, and that's the form they take. When I wrote the essays, I wrote them secondly to piss off Professor Hanley, and firstly to read to everyone here when I get the test back. And I didn't feel like they were my ideas, I felt like they were *ours*."

"I would concur with that, for myself," Jason said.

"Yeah, I agree," said Cat, "I even think about it when I get dressed or decide what to eat. It's like… *we're* doing it, not just me."

"In how many ways? How deeply does it go?" Tiron was relentless.

Cris. "Well if you're getting at the idea that we should be changing into each other, I can't really go with that. I mean, we have to be individuals first and foremost. I find myself getting more and more individualistic at the same time that I get along with everyone more. In fact, I don't remember a time in my life that I've felt more strong as an isolated individual."

Tiron's eyes were smiling, almost glowing, but he said nothing, simply nodded.

Jason spoke up. "Why do you ask; what exactly are you proposing that we be?"

Tiron had finished his soup. He sipped his tea and leaned forward. "When you look out there," he said, with a wave of his hand, "when you look out there, you see competition. Fierce, constant, and fake. It makes you feel good to take down a moron or two. But those aren't real feelings. The real…" he looked at them all intently; "the *real* is here. Now. What you do, what you are, and what you give." He leaned back. "The question is: *Can you be here?*"

Cris. "What do you mean by that? You mean like being our whole selves or something?"

"That's part of it. But just being here." His eyes held a somewhat distant amusement.

Jason spoke up "You're talking about how deeply we engage with each other again, aren't you?"

"I'm talking about a society. I'm speaking of relationships that build instead of pass."

"Well please go on," said Tera quietly.

The power of the old man was considerable; the air around him fairly glowed with a peculiar energy. "There is a measure of comfort in taking a position, say a blacksmith in a village, as Cat said. There's also considerable danger; one begins to depend on the security of an established identity. In a village, this can be good to quite some extent." He paused. "Among *friends*, it can be deadly. A society of friends is the strongest society that exists; even a family, which is the root and pattern of societies, fails without friendship. A friend, a true friend, is someone who believes in you. To do that, you must know what it is in which you are believing. So we get to know one another. As we do so, we find as a most *peculiar* phenomena: that distance grows simultaneously. The more familiar we become with someone, the more distant they become. Why?"

"Because there's more to us than who we are," said Jason quietly and firmly.

"Right. Would anyone here accept an upper limit on who they could become?"

Cat spoke for them all. "No, of course not."

"If that then is true, you do your friend a great disservice by getting to know him. You are, in effect, putting him in your mind's box; and it is your appreciation for him *as he is*, which often replaces your actual love for him, that tempts him to stop and maintain those qualities that you appreciate."

"Friendship destroys itself?" asked Cris.

"It can, and it usually does. If we're to build relationships that have no ceiling, we must believe, not in who someone is, but who they *can* be."

Cat. "But you can only see so much of that."

"Well how far do you need to see in order to be here now?"

She thought. "Well... at least past 'now' ...to the next step."

"Right. One step at a time. And how does one see where the next step is?"

Tera. "By having direction."

"And how does one achieve direction?"

Tera again. "By having a goal."

"Excellent. What is it, then, that will give the society itself direction?"

Cris. "Commonality of goals."

Tiron looked at him kindly. Cris realized that he had broken with his habit of always questioning, and given an answer, and that Tiron had noticed and was pleased. "Very good. So what do I mean by *being here*?" There was a few moments of silence. Tera's mind whirled, but she couldn't peg it. She looked at Jason, who took it as a signal to speak up.

"You mean that we need to be intensely aware of every moment, no drawing back; yet that intensity has to come from a consciousness of our goals rather than an emotional high from the moment."

He looked at Jason without expression. "Yes, that's correct. However, you sound like a textbook. Would anyone care to translate?" Cris winced. He had never seen anyone who could be this hard on Jason, yet the harshness seemed to be coming from an ability to appreciate who Jason was.

Cat jumped in. "It seemed clear to me. He's saying that we don't use the moment for our motivation, like telling jokes to keep the atmosphere good and stuff like that. He's saying that the good feelings should already be there because we know what we're doing, and the effort should be poured into basically paying complete attention to everything instead of being lazy, so that whatever growth is waiting to happen can go ahead and happen." Tiron nodded, then proceeded to pull out a pipe, fill it, and light it. A most peculiar smell filled the air; it reminded Cat of home; Tera of being in the mountains, and Cris of being in Jason's apartment. Jason made no motion with his eyes, nor assessment with his thoughts.

"So is that what your class is going to be about?" asked Tera, "Are you going to be teaching what a society is, and how it works?"

"No," said Tiron, pointing his pipe at her, "we're going to *do* it."

"What?"

"I can sit here and teach you something until I'm blue in the face, but unless you've already experienced it, I'm making you liars and myself a hypocrite. What I propose to do in my class, is, as Jason said earlier, interact. We're going to build a society, and do something to our social environment. Furthermore, each of you at this table is invited." He took a puff on his pipe and leaned back. He seemed like someone who had no place in time; he didn't belong in this diner, he didn't belong in America, he didn't belong in this century. Yet at the same time, he fit perfectly; as if the diner belonged to him, America belonged to him, and momentarily you would expect him to pull any century out of his pocket and serve it for tea.

"Thank you for your invitation," said Tera.

"And thanks for the tea," added Jason. A silence descended, the kind that follows a particularly engaging film.

"Having stated my business, and enjoyed a delightful conversation, I'm going to take my leave of you all at this time, if you'd be so kind as to excuse me." He directed this to Cat who slid off the bench for him so he could get out. He dropped a ten on the table. "Here's my contribution to Andrea. And I sincerely hope you four will consider my invitation." He paused and looked at them.

"I think we will," said Jason. Tiron nodded to them, almost a bow, and made his way out the door. Cat and Cris slid into the bench. There was a pause as they looked at each other.

"Whew," breathed Cat, "He is something else!"

Cris. "You guys actually going to consider taking his class?"

Jason. "Well for one, I'm rather curious to see who else he's got coming."

Tera. "Yeah. This is actually quite a proposal."

Cris. "You guys notice the compliment he gave us?"

Cat. "Which one?"

Tera. "He said, 'I can sit here and teach you till I'm blue in the face, but unless you've already experienced it, I'm making you liars and me a hypocrite.'"

Cat. "Oh. He was saying that we're already there. With all that stuff about being a society that he was talking about. He was calling us a successful society."

Jason smiled. "Subtle."

Tera turned to Jason. "I'm not so sure you guys are going to get along very well. I kept expecting you two to start a fistfight or something.

Jason laughed. "I have to say that I genuinely enjoyed him." He shook his head. "But hell, he's one of the most dangerous people I've ever met."

Cris. "How so?"

"It's almost impossible to both contrive a situation and have it work out, and that's what he's proposing to do. The only position from which I can conceive of it working, is the master/apprentice relationship, which I guess is kind of like the kind of professorship he's considering. But if he can pull it off, and it looks like there's a good chance he can, then he's *already* someone who can do pretty much anything he wants, and then some. A person like that does not normally have any wants, which means he's got a pretty powerful agenda. And I don't like entering into a relationship with someone like that, blind. I need to know more about him."

Cris. "Well he sure knew about us."

Tera. "Right. I won't be a bit surprised if I find out he's talked to our advisors already."

Cat murmured under her breath, "Well, I guess daddy knows best," which made Jason chuckle. As they pulled their change together for the meal, Cat picked up the ten from Tiron. "Hey! This is a silver certificate; it's an antique!" They all looked at it.

"Well," said Jason, "I guess we'll leave it for Andrea, she deserves it anyway. I'm heading further into town to pick up some groceries if anyone wants to come along." He glanced at Tera, then the other two. There was an odd moment of hesitation.

Cat smiled and threw her scarf over her shoulder. "I'd love to come along. I haven't chatted with you for a while." Jason looked at her, not surprised, but intrigued.

"Great. See you two tonight maybe?"

Tera smiled. "Maybe."

"Don't go meeting any more old men," laughed Cris. "I've had about all I can handle for now." They piled out into the afternoon sun poking through the overcast here and there, and parted. We leave them now, Cris and Tera, walking calmly, deliberately, almost as newly acquainted with each other, and the other two? They embarked upon the town. Her walk was springy and cheerful with flashes of gold; his quiet, thoughtful, and withdrawn.

Chapter 7: Not Like That At All

No, not like that at all. We had something there, something like the past, but not like it at all. For like and unalike, we fall into reflections of what we do while waiting for our deeds to mature into experience. And how many, how many, ever realize that that's exactly what experience is.

"What was he accusing you of in there?" Cat slowed down her pace and watched Jason.

"Tiron?"

"Yeah. It was like you were resisting some accusation of his."

"You may be right." He walked on in silence. After half a minute, he realized that she was patiently waiting for him to answer. "He was accusing me of being outside the fold of humanity."

She thought about the idea. It certainly had merit of some sort. Jason had never seemed to be part of anything, except possibly their little group. "Do you think that's true?"

"I don't know. I didn't want to think about it yet, I had wanted to get a little further in life before I considered it. Tiron's forcing the issue on me."

She thought some more. "Isn't it impossible to be outside of humanity? I mean, even the rejects and freaks have a part in society; like what would a town be like without the village idiot, or the town drunk?"

He gave her a wry smile. "Nice comparison."

"I didn't mean it like that and you know it. I'm just saying that by definition, no one can really be outside the 'fold' of humanity, whatever that means."

"Hm." He grunted and was silent. Then he asked, "How much do you feel a part of humanity?"

"Um... very much I guess. Except if I think about it too much I get depressed... not really depressed, more like confused, at the insignificance of being one individual among... how many billion? It makes it hard to think realistically about the subject of humanity as a whole."

"Yes, that can be depressing. I can solve that for you if you like."

"Really? How?" She realized suddenly that he had, as usual, switched the conversation to be about her.

"Humanity is a whole, a unit. All of us. We're one living sentient being. And that being, every day, is going through the experience of growth." He paused. "Sometimes you exercise your body, sometimes your mind, sometimes your emotions. Whichever part of yourself is doing the experiencing at any one time is the part that leads the whole body. The whole body responds to that experience, like your mind and your emotions get involved when you're exercising. With Humanity, each new day there is a new issue with which every individual on earth grapples. We all have different facets of the issue, but it's the same issue at any one time. If you ever watch the news about what is happening all over the earth, you'll notice the most amazing coincidences; whether it's war, natural disaster, elections, new music groups, whatever; all of it addresses the same issue, the only difference is that… let's take the example of dignity versus pride. The issue on a certain day is the lesson of learning to accept true dignity without succumbing to pride. Now if I were to ask you for what kind of circumstances would bring that conflict to the forefront in your life, your example would be significantly different than mine. And rather different from a businessman in China, or a monk in Tibet, or a bushman in Australia."

"So we're having different experiences, but all about the same issue."

"Yes."

"But… like, what decides what the issue is every day?"

"It's the process of growth. Mankind isn't evolving; evolution is a conceptual lie of the highest degree, without even having to touch its merits as a theory. Mankind isn't evolving, he's growing." She waited for him to answer the question. "After a baby is weaned, there's no question that the next step is: to get him strong enough to eat more and more substantial foods. As Humanity grows, we learn to become competent in our abilities; the next step of what we're able to do. It's ends up being a very natural process."

"So we all are making mankind grow?"

"In various degrees."

"What do you mean?"

"Do you downhill ski?"

"Sure, I love it. And I'm getting pretty good too."

"Okay. When you were learning how, you probably went through the process of learning to lean forward in your skis instead of backwards."

"Right, that's one of the first things they tried to teach us. Because it's scary to lean forward, it feels like you're going to fall or go too fast. But in order to bite into the snow, and *lead* your turns instead of being led by them, you have to lean forward. You have far more control."

"Right. In your own life, you affect humanity in the measure that you lean forward in your skis."

"Like whoever's trying the hardest is affecting everyone the most?"

"Not really hardest, but smartest. Just like skiing, you have to know where you're going, why, and engage as fully as possible with your facet of the universal issue."

"Wow. That's really cool."

"Yes, that's what I meant by solving the problem of the insignificance of the individual. Every single one of us has full opportunity every day to not only lead the struggle of humanity, but to feel it, and to direct it into the next issue. By being one of the people who lean the farthest into their skis."

"That's so cool! You're right, it changes quite a bit." She was silent as she soaked in the idea. "So is Tiron accusing you of not being part of this process?"

"No. Of being too good at it."

"At understanding that mankind is growing?" She was pleased to get him back on the subject of himself.

"At manipulating it."

That put her to silence again, not sure of the extent to which this was even possible. "What do you mean?"

"I don't have words by which to phrase it to you. You haven't seen me in… in my own world, so everything I might try to say will sound like a fairy tale. Which it very well might be anyway; nothing we do is really solid until we die."

So close and yet so far, she thought. "So because I don't know the language, you won't talk?"

"Because you… well sure, that's close enough."

"Try me."

He looked at her and said nothing for a while. Then, "Have you noticed that it's grown chillier while we've talked?" The late afternoon overcast was complete.

"Um… yes it has."

"Have you noticed how well that fit with our conversation?"

"Well, I didn't notice it, but now that you've mentioned it, you're right."

He said nothing again for a bit. Then, "Okay, let's do it." She looked at him wondering what was expected to happen, but said nothing for fear of interfering with it. He put his arm around her and led her towards a bench across the street. She felt his protective warmth surrounding her like a cloak, his manner had changed inexplicably. "This will take a bit of patience on your part." It sounded like an order to her. He had once again taken control of the conversation, but she had asked specifically for this, so she relaxed and went with it. He sat them down on the bench, crossed his leg, and relaxed, looking around, noticing everything as if he were setting a stage. The combination of chill and warmth made her deliciously comfortable. After two minutes, she leaned her head on his shoulder and relaxed. Pedestrians smiled warmly at them as they passed; cars passed winding through the ad hoc paraphernalia of the college-town. She closed her eyes. After… she didn't know; six or ten minutes, she felt a change in the air, something warm, to which she dreamily opened her eyes. The clouds had broken, and a shaft of sunlight was lighting up their section of town. She got up and looked at him; he had a serious, yet slightly amused look on his face.

"The sun…?" He smiled and didn't reply. His eyes said 'Let's go.' They walked through the sunlight arm in arm to the grocery store in silence. As the automatic doors swung open, she asked, "Did you do that?"

"Now there's the question. Did we stop and rest because we felt the change in the air coming? Did the whole weather pattern reverse itself just because we stopped? Everything in the universe is so interconnected that there's no sure way to trace the pattern of cause and effect."

"But you knew it was going to happen! You practically told me." He smiled. "Can you do that often, I mean, does that happen to you a lot? Like the weather responding to your every mood?"

He sighed, and said quietly, "Always. With everything. Pause here and feel the grocery store before allowing yourself to be engulfed in it." She waited with him, listening to the mixture of noises, smelling the store's atmosphere. "First, find the base. Today is relaxed, yet expectant; they're waiting for the rush that comes in here about 6:00. The workers are enjoying themselves. Next, feel for the interference. It'll feel like a bump or a prickle; focus on whatever triggered it to your senses, and make a note of it. All things communicate with each other, and *in order for something negative to exist in a positive environment, it has to ride the existing negative forces already allowed there by those same positive forces.*" She looked to him, unable to push this new game any further with her senses. He saw that and smiled again. "Probably in that aisle," he pointed at the aisle containing bread and snack foods, "we'll encounter a rather overweight middle-aged lady with grey hair and her face permanently set with frown-wrinkles. She'll try to shove rudeness vibes at us in some way. Over there," he pointed at the back left corner, "there's likely a worker who is trying to get through the day with the minimum of effort, the which is dragging down the mood of everyone around him. C'mon, let's get some groceries." She followed him up the middle aisle where he picked up maple syrup, real of course, and coffee.

"I didn't know you drank coffee."

"I don't, normally, but I do have guests sometimes." As they rounded the aisle into the next, she glanced into the corner he had mentioned, but saw no one behind the counter. Turning around, she nearly ran into an enormous lady with a full grocery cart and three small children. The lady ignored her completely, and the kids were having an argument and blocking their way. Jason walked up to them, then stopped suddenly as if he had seen a live snake on the shelf. "Hey!" All three kids stopped and stared. He pointed at a box of pop tarts. In a voice shaking with amazement, he said "Look at those!" The kids approached, staring at the box. Jason leaned over them and said in a stage whisper, "They're inside of a box!" Then as suddenly as he had started, he resumed walking down the now cleared aisle. Cat caught up with him and grabbed his arm.

"What... what on earth was all that about?"

Jason was chuckling. "A little surrealism never hurt anybody. They'll be talking about that for a while. Probably the first time today that they won't be fighting." She shook her head. This had potential to be fun. They picked up a few more items, fish, lamb chops, cheese, and headed toward the fruits and vegetables. Jason picked up broccoli and asparagus and began sorting through the fruit. "There's never anything ripe. They pump everything with chemicals and hormones, pick it green, and expect us to buy it."

"What were you looking for?"

"Well I'd kind of like some peaches but all they have here is peach-shaped green rocks. Hmph." He stood there thinking. "These look like they were just put out recently, let's see what they did with the old ones." He walked back to the counter in the corner and rang the bell. A blonde kid in his mid-twenties appeared and looked at him expectantly. His name tag said 'Joe.' "Your peaches aren't ripe," stated Jason, as if he were there solely to make conversation. Joe looked at him blankly. "And it's kind of chilly in here too." Joe blinked. "Do you suppose," Jason went on, "that the temperature is kept cool to prevent the peaches from ripening?"

The kid swallowed. "Uh… I suppose so. It's so stuff won't spoil too."

"Ah," said Jason, as if the man had just expounded the meaning of the universe to him. He thought for a moment. "So food *does* spoil in here."

"Um… no, I mean, we take it off the shelf if it gets bad."

Jason looked at him quizzically. "Take *what* off the shelf?"

"Um… the food. Like anything that goes bad we take off the shelf."

"Give me an example. Broccoli?"

"Um… yeah, if it goes bad."

"Peaches?"

"Um, yeah, them too. Peaches…"

Jason interrupted him. "Show me."

"Huh?"

"Show me the peaches you took off the shelf." Joe hesitated. Jason's voice became brisk and commanding. "Hup, hup. Let's go; you don't want to keep the lady waiting all day."

The man looked at Cat for the first time, then stammered, "Th… they're back here. I'll show you." They followed him behind the counter and through the door, where several crates of apples and peaches were lined against a concrete wall. Joe stood there uncertainly.

Jason turned to Cat. "Well, ma'am, what do you think?"

Cat fell into her role immediately. "They'll do. Just one crate though. She pointed to the largest one. "That one."

Joe walked over to the crate. "Um… where do you want me to put it?"

Jason let a bit of exasperation into his voice. "Joe, the lady wants to purchase it. Put a price on it and send it up front." Joe was now certain that this man was a supervisor of some sort.

"But… they're not for sale anymore… I can give them to you for free."

Cat spoke up in a businesslike tone. "I'm *purchasing* them because I need the receipt."

Jason looked at Joe as if he were a two-year-old. "You don't expect her to leave without her *peach* receipt." Joe swallowed. "Now put a price on them and send it up front." He turned and walked out with Cat.

When they were out of sight, she asked him, "Why didn't you let him give them to us for free?"

"I didn't want to go through all that again up front; I really don't have the stomach for it. They're not allowed to give food that's been taken off the shelf to customers, so I figured that this was the easiest way to get some ripe peaches." When they reached the register, he said to the girl, "Include those peaches they brought up for us."

She rang them up and remarked, "Only fifty cents for a crate of peaches?"

"Yup," said Jason, "they're about to go bad."

"Well seems like a good deal," she smiled. Cat took the bag of groceries and Jason put the crate on his shoulder.

"You going to be okay with that?" Cat needn't have said anything; he looked as if he had been carrying them all his life.

"Well, how close was I?" he asked her.

"On?"

"The atmosphere here."

"Um… dead on. What's next?"

"If you don't know, wait and see." They walked out of the store into the chilly air. Cat gasped. The entire sky was clear, and the sun was splattering evening rays on the brick facades of the town.

She took his free hand in hers, and swung it in tune to their steps all the way to his basement apartment; then walked alone slowly, pensively back to her dorm; wondering how his introspective mood had crept its way into her heart.

*   *   *

Chapter 8: It's Killing Me.

The sky was ashen, crisp, and grey;
And passing by, a single rat
Refused to comment much on that.

In between semesters, Jason chose to stay in his apartment for the holidays rather than fly home. Cris and Cat both are spending time with their families, and Tera, of course, lives close by town. The lady Laura is comfortable in her third floor apartment above the laundromat, and Tiron is undoubtedly muttering to himself in his cabin while doing something strange. The girls talked about Jason and Cat's conversation before Cat left; they agreed that she had barely begun to get him to talk. Cris' flight home was immediately after his last exam, so his anticipated interactions with the three, whatever they may have been, were cut short. And yes, all four decided to take Tiron's class. Was there any doubt?

Jason sat in his apartment and looked at nothing in particular. The pot of stew simmered to itself as the minutes ticked by. And the hours. Jason could feel himself breathing in and out, he could hear the creaks of the house as it shifted in the winter winds. He rose finally, scooped out a bowl of stew, ate it slowly, washed the bowl, and resumed his seat. The food felt good in his stomach, but it didn't mask the dead feeling that hovered there, that always hovered there every moment of his life. Nothing. No depression, no elation, no desire; nothing. When with people, he covered the area and became whatever they liked. And it was enjoyable; he would feel what they felt, see what they saw, enjoy what they enjoyed. But once they were gone, there was first a great feeling of relief, then all the other emotions washed away, and the dead area took over, located somewhere around the bottom of his stomach. He didn't know what it was, or who he was for that matter, for it seemed that his sentience was centered in the dead zone. But if that was his sentience, it was a child, one too young or perhaps too damaged to understand what was happening. When he breathed out, he had no desire to breathe back in, and would let his body relax, still. But then his lungs would pressure him with the motivation of panic, and he'd relent and draw in the oxygen, prolonging the irritation called life. His thoughts would sometimes race, other times pool; it made no difference. There was the vague notion somewhere inside him that if he sat motionless for long enough, something inside would heal, and he could, perhaps then, wake up.

The phone rang.

It jarred his whole being. The dead zone spread a flood of foreboding through his stomach. Depression awoke, and his mind recoiled from the irritation of interruption. It would be a person. They would want something from him. He would have to have energy, to be human, to act out another scene. During the scene, he'd have energy and emotions aplenty; but afterwards, when returning into himself, he would feel the irreparable damage done to whatever lived in the dead zone. It was an invitation to more killing of himself via other human beings.

The second ring.

The jarring was dying down, and he began to emerge from within himself and make decisions. He would pick up the phone and talk. He would use a personality. He pulled from memory several personalities, and chose one. Cheerful, a little grave; reserved, but willing to play. It immediately enveloped him, and the dead zone was now out of reach. He picked up the phone.

"Hi, this is Jason." Before she spoke, he knew it was Tera. He had chosen a personality with sharp perceptions.

"Hi Jason, this is Tera; um… we're having a… well, my cousins are visiting for the holidays, and there's going to be a lot of people here tonight, and I wondered if you'd like to come over for supper. If you're not doing anything." Pause. "I can pick you up."

"Well… let me think for a moment. You're not going to put me on the spot in front of your family, are you?"

"Oh, no; nothing like that; I just got this idea five minutes ago; since we're going to have twelve people at the table anyway, I thought you might enjoy getting away for a bit and joining us."

"Well… sure. I'd love to. Are you sure it's no trouble to pick me up?"

"Nope. I'll be right there, in about… in about fifteen minutes. I haven't been there, but Cris pointed out which house it is once. You're in the basement around back, right?"

"Yes. Sure you don't need directions?"

"Yep, I'm sure."

"K. See you then."

The phone was hung up, but the dead zone wouldn't return. He was in that world now, and the night had formed itself, as usual, without him. Perhaps just as well, he mused. Preparations were in order. What does one take to a boisterous family get-together? Hm. We would need cleverness, certainly; a touch of understated humor, willingness to be ignored if the issues in the air weren't sufficiently resolved to sustain a stranger. The people would be educated, probably brimming with something that borders on pride, though you'd be a fool to call them on the carpet for it. What to choose, what to choose… something conducive to wry humor. He went to one of the shelves, picked off a volume of Bertrand Russell, and read his essay, *Why I am not a Christian*. He finished it before Tera arrived, and picked out a fur-lined suede leather jacket that a grateful aunt had once given him. Might as well go in style. Matching scarf, and the door passed an eager knock into the loneliness of his three-room camp. The door opened inward; bad for protection against the wind, but good for making visitors welcome.

"Enter. You're in good time." She came in as if out of a dream. She looked around almost expecting to be in one, and wasn't disappointed. However, she had the presence of mind to say nothing, just look. He went over and turned the stove off, then any lights that weren't already on, he turned on. Guiding her out the door, he shut it behind, testing to make sure it wasn't locked.

"Don't you have a key?"

"Sure, there's a key somewhere. But I like to make people feel welcome."

"That why you left the lights on?"

"Yes."

"Aren't you afraid someone will break in and steal something?"

"Kinda hard to break in when the front door is unlocked. And no, I'm not afraid anyone's going to steal anything. If they want something of mine that badly, they can have it."

"Don't you have anything valuable in there that you'd miss?"

"Nothing that hasn't already been stolen by humanity." She gave him an odd look. "In other words, no, there's nothing in there I would miss that the kind of person who steals would steal." They walked through the windy darkness to her dad's Mercedes. "This your car?"

"No, mine's all parked-in by guests, so I brought dad's. You think I'd drive a Mercedes around?"

"Yes."

"Well you must think awfully highly of me." He said nothing in reply. The car was warm already from the drive over, and after a minute of silence, she turned the music on; it was Mozart's horn concertos. He felt a deep familiar power growing and filling the car. He felt her trying to feel what he thought of the music. They let the music go on, it sounded like it came from forever and could go to there. Finally she commented. "This music makes me feel…"

He interrupted. "…like an old friend is singing to you about the power and continuity of life."

"Yes! Is that what you feel too?"

"Now, yes."

She thought about this. "What do you mean, 'now'?"

He was silent for a few moments. "When I listen to music with someone else present, even if it's a stranger, I don't hear what *I* hear, I hear how they hear it."

She soaked this in for a few moments. Then, "What?"

"Just that."

"Right now you're hearing what I'm hearing, and not anything of yourself."

A moment. Then, "Right."

"Tell me what I'm hearing."

"You're familiar enough with this piece that rather than hearing, you're feeling. This is actually a good recording; usually it's played too fast, which ruins the timelessness of the piece, yet those who play it slowly rarely have a sense of its depth. This piece is paced almost flawlessly; I'm guessing that it's the Philharmonic Orchestra back when Otto Klemperer was conducting."

"I don't know, I'd have to read the label. If you're guessing, you're doing a pretty good job."

"That last series of musical phrases have already set the stage for you. In your mind you're on a moonlit plain, a plateau far from humanity, where you're willing to accept the slow progression we're hearing now as pure profound. You broke our silence when the placing of yourself on the plain was complete. You now feel as if you're safely alone and the music is weaving a tapestry of dignity around you that gives you the power to do anything you wish from a totally relaxed, yet powerful vantage point."

"Okay, that's enough." She glanced over at him, and the car swerved slightly his direction before she corrected it. "Tell me this then: what do you hear when you're alone?" He was silent for a bit, and she broke it before he spoke. "When you hear this by yourself, what do you hear?"

"Sometimes I can't tell whether I'm hearing classical, jazz, or heavy metal. I don't... I don't listen with... labels. And it takes me a long time to hear in such a way that I can communicate. Basically, I don't communicate what I hear in music, it's not worth the time. But I've heard this piece before, the requisite dozen times it takes me to know how to communicate something. When I'm alone, and good music is playing, I hear... light."

"Light?" She was turning into the neighborhood in which her father's house abode.

"That's as best as I can put it. If the music is good enough, it becomes edible light."

"Edible? …please explain what you mean."

"I don't think I can. The next time you watch a sunrise or a sunset, look at the colors in terms of how much you'd like to eat them."

Her analytical nature decided to relinquish the reins. She felt her mind flip around to that rare state that can only be called female. "When do you think I'll get the chance?" The invitation was stated so subtly that it could hardly have been more obvious.

He looked at her. "Easy, as soon as you accept the fact that it will be worth it." He continued watching her, as if her reaction were spelling out the next step.

"But I've always thought that anything like that would be worth it." She was pulling into the car-crowded yard of her father's home.

"Like what?"

"Like…" She turned off the key and looked at him. "Like an opportunity to not just appreciate the mornings, the sunrise, the seasons; but to interact; to have a part of them… to eat." She paused, then proffered, "To be eaten by beauty."

He was still looking at her. "You compose a good bargain. It's a shame you don't know what you're talking about."

The fear of failure washed over her and she spoke angrily without thinking. "That's actually an insult, isn't it?"

He sighed. "Yes. Yes, it is. Shall we go in now and play the game?"

Her head was buzzing. She knew she had been insulted, but she never before had felt so… so challenged. So intrigued. It was as if she had been handed some grand compliment. Damn it all! Why couldn't she get on top of this? She vaguely remembered Cris telling her something… that those with the least amount of desire in any situation had the most power. But her stubborn side was pushing her emotions into action. She swung out of her car door and waited just long enough for him to make his way out of the passenger side, and strode toward the door, forcing him to follow her. With her hand on the doorknob, she realized that this wouldn't work, that she had to walk in strong, on her own energies. In that hesitation, he came up behind her, put his hand on hers on the doorknob, and paused.

"I do love you, Tera."

"You love everybody," she retorted, and opened the door. The atmosphere inside was both a relief and a bother. Everyone there supported her as an individual; Jason would be made into mincemeat if he crossed her. This was her world; he could just damn well follow as best he could. She didn't see his slight, sad smile as he followed her into her domain. The word 'hubbub' was being newly defined for the evening; but the house was brightly lit and spacious for the scene. Three small kids were playing cat-and-mouse through various venues; the bulk of people seemed to hold the living room like children hold an unconforming puppy. The kitchen was emitting the sounds of several busy females; chatter amid clatter. Jason stood in the living room beside the couch, graciously accepting introductions to the verities of kin. Her father's eyes were friendly although businesslike, and Jason's attitude toward him became a quiet observation with a minimum of overtures. Until they met, Tera thought of just how much she wanted Jason to impress her dad; now she watched across the room wishing even harder that her dad would impress Jason. The flurry from the kitchen spilled into the room, announcing that the time had come for each to take a place around the supper scene. The children had a table in the living room apart; the meal was set for conversation, Jason noticed with pleasure. Tera's father took the head, his wife the other end. Jason found himself near her father between a dowdy bearded specimen and a heavyset suited man. Across the table sat Tera and the other women who needed quick access to the kitchen for serving. The meal itself was artwork; one hesitated to ruin the perfectly arranged dishes by actually eating them. A lull of silence fell as everyone seated turned their attention to the host, who cleared his throat dryly, and spoke to the suited man on Jason's left.

"It's not the normal habit here Tom, but if you'd like to say grace for the meal, you may."

Tom looked pleased, if not a little arrogant. "Thank you William." He looked around at everyone's expectant eyes. "Let's bow our heads and give thanks for the food." Most complied; Tera's dad stared forward with a patient look. "Dear heavenly Father," he began with his eyes clenched, "thank you for this wonderful day to enjoy with all our family here and thank you for this wonderful food which loving hands have prepared. Bless this time together with family and friends and may we all be drawn closer to you by the good things you have given us. In Jesus name. Amen." There was a chorus of small amen's, then the hostess took over.

"Everything is edible," she smiled sweetly at the crowd, "pass to your left, and Tera and I will be getting your drinks." She served herself some beet salad, then said quietly to the woman on her left, "serve me just a little bit of everything, except the avocados," and proceeded to offer drink selections to the guests, accompanied by Tera.

"It's hard to believe it's only been a year," stated a dark-haired woman with a Bostonian accent.

"And a good year it's been on my part," replied a tall man with a handle-bar mustache. "Better sales this year than the previous two."

"I envy salesmen," stated a short bald man with a squeaky voice. "You travel the world for free while the rest of us are held prisoner to our jobs or pay through the nose to get anywhere."

"There is that benefit," he agreed. His voice was deep with the undercurrent of a drawl. "But I'd give one of my eye-teeth to have the time to do some serious uninterrupted study."

"What would you take up first?" asked William. Jason felt the opening; Tera's father was likely leading to an arena in which there'd be an argument.

"Entomology," he drawled. "There's more things to be learned from those little critters than with what you could fill a set of encyclopedias. Always wished I had more time to give them than flipping through some books."

"Bugs?" asked a tall blonde lady, "You travel the world and you'd rather be studying bugs?"

He looked at her. "For example," he said, dropping a stuffed mushroom on his plate, "the genders would understand each other a lot better if we knew a little bit more about bugs."

"The genders won't understand each other one whit until they actually want to," muttered the dowdy man to his plate. It went mostly unheard.

"He's right," squeaked the bald man. "Take the spider; it's the ultimate example of a female."

"The spider is not, strictly speaking, an *insect*," said William. "Entomology is the study of insects; a spider is an arachnid."

"Insect, arachnid, it's still a bug," said the blond lady. "And I want to know just exactly how the spider is a perfect example of a female?"

"That should be obvious," replied the tall man. "It builds a web, spends its life catching things that wander into it and devouring them. Including, no, I should say, *especially* its mate." Everyone laughed at this except the blonde lady.

"And I suppose that since it's the *female* spider that does all the work, that that somehow carries over in the analogy."

"Well I reckon it does," he drawled. "Guys can be pretty low-down, but that's because they don't give much of a hoot about anything. It takes a female, on the other hand, to actually plan out *how* to be low-down, and turn it into an art."

The dark-haired Bostonian lady spoke up. "Well then, what 'bug' most closely represents the male? The grasshopper?"

Tom, the stout man, spoke up. "Hey, don't give us a bum rap just because some males are lazy. Most of us work like ants, not grasshoppers."

A quiet girl at William's left said "Yes, to serve the queen," eliciting general laughter.

"I think we're like the beetle," said the squeaky man, "did you know that there's more kinds of beetles than any other insect?"

"And second-most are the butterflies," said the dark-haired lady, "does that mean butterflies are feminine?" This conversation is going nowhere, thought Jason. A familiar hand tapped his shoulder.

"What drink would you like? We have soda, wine, water, grapefruit juice, and later we'll have coffee and tea."

"I'll have wine, Tera, and thank you."

Tom overheard them. "Ahem. Are you twenty-one yet, young man?" he teased.

"Well I'll make you a deal." The table watched them, interestedly. "Have William here, or anyone whom you choose, ask me any question about alcohol. If I answer it correctly, I get my wine; if I miss it, I'll have water instead."

Tom laughed. "You're on. Now who here is an expert on alcohol?" He looked around.

"I'll give him a question," said William. "How many years do they age the single malt scotch that is made by the first legally licensed distillery in Scotland?"

Jason smiled. "That's a trick question. The Glenlivet comes aged both twelve and eighteen years."

"Well I guess the lad gets his drink after all," laughed Tom.

"It was a pretty easy question," said Jason, "The Glenlivet is one of the most well-known scotches around."

The tall man raised one eyebrow. "That was easy, young feller? How about this then; which hard liquor is hallucinogenic?"

"That's actually a myth. The Aztecs call the agave plant, from which tequila is made, *mezcal*. We frequently misspell it as *mescal*, which is the name of a cactus which produces mescaline, from which a popular hallucinogenic is made. But tequila is produced from the Blue Agave cactus, although in recent years it's been contaminated with cane sugar. Legally, they can use up to 49% cane sugar with the agave juice, and still call it tequila."

"Well if that don't beat all," he shook his head. "I'm not asking you any more questions. When a man stands to be corrected by his youngers, it's time to quit talking."

"Hmph," grunted Tom, "I don't know if I'd admit it if I were an expert on alcohol."

"Here we all are picking on the only stranger," remarked the dark-haired lady. "Jason, don't mind us, we're a pretty dysfunctional family."

"Yeah," said Tom, "we're the ones who put the 'fun' in dysfunctional!" and laughed loudly. Everyone else groaned. Jason gave him a slight smile, waiting for the attention to be taken off him again. The soft-spoken girl by William came to the rescue.

"Speaking of family, how's great-uncle Lester doing?" Jason noticed Tera's eyes dart to her father, then quickly away. Hm.

"It's the same as ever," sighed Tera's Mother. "He sits and sits. We take turns caring for him. It's really kind of discouraging. There's no telling how long he'll be in this state; Dr. Jambian tells us that it's likely to last for life."

"Dad has been showing some improvement in the last six weeks," said William, "his heart rate is up, everything's up. Dr. Jambian says that it's an unexpected reversal of symptoms, but he's still showing no signs of recognizing anything or anyone."

"It's such a shame," sighed Tom, "Lester was probably the strongest positive force I've ever met. I always expected him to change the world somehow."

"I wonder if he didn't do that, and we just never noticed," drawled the tall man. "Fact is, if anyone was set up to do so, it was him."

The dark-haired lady spoke quietly but with conviction. "All those millions that he made… he's the only person I know at that level of success who had that combination of hard work and kindness. When I lost my teaching position at MIT, I was heartbroken; it meant I wouldn't be able to complete my doctorate, the one I had been hoping to do on genetics. Although I was hiding it, he noticed my mood at our family reunion, and made me tell him what happened. He just asked me one question:

How hard are you willing to work at your doctorate? I told him I'd never found anything I wanted to work so hard on in my life. The next semester when I went to the registrar to see whether I could work my way through the program with loans, I found that someone had anonymously paid for the entire bill, including an extra semester. I think he admired hard work more than anything."

"Hard work with a heart," said the young girl at William's right. "If you loved what you were doing, he'd sit and listen to you for hours. It's just his listening that encouraged me to cling to what I was really interested in for long enough to get through every other guidance counselor's muddled ideas of what they thought I should go into. I would feel his interest in what I was doing pushing me to where I could begin to really grasp it for myself."

Tom's voice was a tad raucous among the others. "He put you through every school you ever wanted to go through, didn't he William?"

Tera's father gave a tight smile. "Yes, dad wanted me to… take every opportunity that I could take. Even many I didn't necessarily care for that much."

Tom continued. "Well you sure are doing well for yourself for it. Aren't you an expert on just about every subject by now?" It was almost a challenge, from which William didn't flinch.

"I suppose I am," he said, looking Tom in the eye, "with perhaps the exception of your particular area of fascination, the Christian views of the Bible."

"Now don't you two get started," stated the blonde lady matter-of-factly, "we had this conversation already last Christmas. It's Tom's turn to say that the Christian view of the Bible is the only decent way of looking into it, then William starts quoting alternative views, then you both take the conversation to hell in a hand-basket. Let's skip that this year."

Jason spoke up quietly. "What did Lester do for a living?" He saw Tera's eyes flash again, almost looking at him, then purposely swinging away.

Tera's mom answered, "He was an entrepreneur. Poor man only had a sixth grade education, but once he started in business, he just kept making money. Everything he touched turned to gold."

The tall man continued, "He started working at his dad's dry goods store. By the time he took over, it was the largest store in his town, and somehow he kept out the grocery store chains that kept trying to move in. The whole town loved that place. Then when he got Jake to take care of it for him, he started a line of footwear that had the best work boots you could get anywhere. He had an eye for quality, and the will to make it happen. Then I guess he started a few appliance stores, which were quite successful, and after that, he started funding any decent business that he encountered, and like sis says, everything he touched turned to gold."

"Yeah, it's a shame he only had one son," said Tom, apparently still eager to clash with William, who just smiled and didn't take the bait. Tera and her mom began clearing dishes, and conversation floated through the harmless topics of the stock market and deep sea fishing. Jason watched this family with renewed interest, no longer as a collection of odd kin, but as the results of a certain old man's work. *Hm.* Dessert was appropriately impressive, for which the lights were dimmed while flames lept from the plate. When they were excused to the living room, he sat and spoke with Tom, perhaps to keep him from running amok with William, perhaps to upset William with his interest in Tom. He waited patiently for Tera's return to him, which took the better part of an hour while the ladies cleaned up the meal. She had seen him talking to Tom was circling around to enter the conversation unobtrusively but before she got to him, Jason had already arisen and walked into the hallway between the living room and kitchen where he waited for her.

"Do you want to stick around for whatever everyone does, or do you want to head back soon? About half of them will usually play some sort of games on the table, while the rest will have some sort of philosophical discussion or argument in the living room."

"I'd like to meet Lester." He felt her heart jump, but she gave no expression.

"Okay." She turned and led him up the stairs to her grandfather's room. She first knocked gently, then went in. Jason shut the door behind him as he entered. Lester was sitting in his usual chair, the glass of water half-full on the table at his side. "Good evening grandpa. This is my friend Jason, who wanted to meet you." She stepped aside and stood at the foot of the unused bed watching them. Jason stood in front of the old man quiet and expectantly, with no expression on his face.

"Hello, Lester."

The old man was staring straight ahead at nothing. A minute passed, then slowly his head lifted until he was looking directly into Jason's eyes. He spoke, and his voice was soft and powerful. "Good evening, Jason." Tera's found her heart pounding, even though she had prepared herself for the possibility of grandpa speaking again. After looking at Jason for a bit, he continued. "I had hoped that you would find time to come. I wanted to thank you for what you've decided to do." Now Tera was panicking inside, but she made no motion.

"I appreciate that. Have you been waiting long?"

"No. Not that long. Tera had a conversation with her father. I heard your ideas. She got them from someone who could begin to turn the tide for the first time."

Jason sighed and shook his head. "I'm not looking forward to a scene."

"I wasn't either when I was your age. But it happens." He spoke slowly. "Remember that all you ever need to do is be there. For a long time I was there; but there's been quite a gap since I had to step aside. You will do just fine."

"I'll need some help. This is not my arena."

"You've made it your arena by existing. We each have that choice and you've made yours. Besides, you will get the help. It is always there if you accept that it is going to be there. Just mind your place."

"What will you do?"

"I'll be here until the stronghold is secured, then I will rest." He paused for a long moment, then went on. "You are different, Jason, but that doesn't change the fact that you are here. Anywhere you find yourself, be there. If afterwards, you find yourself still apart, then you may go your way. But as long as you have a place, chosen or not, be there."

Jason stared at him for a long time without speaking. Then, "Okay." The old man and Jason's eyes were locked for a long time; Tera felt they were having a conversation by themselves. Finally the old man closed his eyes and did not open them again. Jason turned to Tera. "I'd like to go now." She suddenly realized that she could breathe, the blood rushing from her lungs through her body again. Silently she led him out the door, back down the stairs, and pausing to tell her mother where she was going, they made their way back to the Mercedes. They rode in silence until out of their development, then she pressed 'play' and Mozart's horn concertos filled the air. She couldn't think of or imagine what they had argued about on the way there. Near his apartment, Jason spoke. "I like Lester." She found she couldn't reply; she wondered how it is that one can access so many emotions with so few words. She barely could drive, far less speak. When she pulled up at his house, he said, "Come in, I'll make you some tea." She followed him in, and sat exhausted on the couch while he brewed a strange and warm liquid, which filled her stomach and calmed her mind. The room pulsed in its display of shadow and color; he turned off the lights and sat down beside her with no word. Halfway through her cup, she curled up beside him and put her head on his shoulder; in a few moments she was dreaming, standing on a glowing ember the size of a planet in a shifting atmosphere of spiced shadows. He waited patiently without sleeping until the sky turned silver-grey to make room for dawn. Extracting himself from the couch, he rewarmed the tea, serving it without a word. She pulled herself together, drained the cup, then was standing by the door, looking at him. He smiled, advancing easily to her, and kissed her cheek. She found herself walking through the crisp winter air to the car, then driving through a surreal glow of a grey-orange sunrise. Jason walked to his bedroom where life sometimes allowed him to sleep, and lay down. The night of experiences faded, leaving nothing but the dead zone. The thought of Lester was the last image to burn out, then he allowed his mind to go blank. Damage he felt; he would have felt depression, but where depression might have lodged there was only a hole. Then thoughts washed over him like a flood of desperate lemmings, each seeking only to hasten its own demise. But he noticed he was tired; this would help. Reaching for tiredness, he embraced it, spinning down its vortex into temporary relief. Outside, a large crow worried away at a freshly killed chipmunk against the full-fledged golden strength of dawn. Inside, Jason slept.

Chapter 9: Hostess

```
woman dances. man still born of woman,
and woman of the man;
the seahorse curls his tail
tugging to the bottom
swaying, makes no expression.
```

You should probably know that Tera loaned her car to Jason to pick up Cris. Cat, who has returned already, accompanied him. They found him waiting outside at the passenger pick-up, and Cat was a sweetheart and made Cris ride up front. The music was a mix that Cris had made for just such occasions, which Cat enjoyed and Jason analyzed with occasional quips. Cris had never seen Jason driving before; he observed with pleasure that he always anticipated, bit into curves perfectly, accelerating through them on the inside for tight roads and on the outside for the highway. Cluster melted away around him, even in heavy traffic. His use of the gas was extremely smooth, and except at stop signs and red lights, he never used the brake. Nor did he seem to be paying particular attention to what he was doing; Cris almost interrupted Jason's talk with Cat in the rear view mirror to tell him to watch out for a strip of retread tire that lay on the road but Jason drove around it smoothly, then put his flashers on for a few blinks to warn the drivers behind all without looking away from the rear view mirror. As Cris relaxed, Jason smiled and said to him, "I was just doing that to impress you."

Great, thought Cris, fuming; he's aware of everything *including* my thoughts.

"Oh relax," said Jason, "we have two sides of the brain, and it's possible to use both at once."

"Well what side do you use to drive?"

"Everyone uses their right side to drive, whether they like it or not. Have you ever noticed how hard it is to unwrap a candy bar while you drive?"

"Uh… sure, now that you mention it; it always gives me a problem."

"That's because the act of unwrapping something is too complicated to do consciously. After learning it we relegate the whole process to automation; it becomes a simple pattern which the right brain takes charge of except when it's already engaged in something like driving. The only way to unwrap something well while driving is to think consciously about every step so you don't interfere with what the right side is already doing."

"And the left brain?"

"The left brain is everything that you do consciously. That's why you can have such good conversations when you drive; a proper conversation depends on conscious effort. Meanwhile your pattern side does all the driving unhindered by blundering nuances of conscious help. In contrast people who don't think when they speak have trouble simultaneously driving and holding a conversation. They're trying to fall back on reactionary speaking patterns while the brain is busy using those patterns to drive."

"So a bad driver would be someone that tries to drive consciously?"

"That's the worst kind of bad driver. Next are the ones who learned bad patterns; once you stick a pattern into the right brain, it's twice as much work to change it."

Cat spoke up from the back seat. "But aren't you supposed to be conscious when you drive?"

"You're supposed to pay attention. You do this by being confident of unconscious patterns and ignoring them so that you know what to pay attention to. Confidence is the only center from conscious action works."

"Well I haven't studied this like you guys have; what exactly is the difference between the right side of the brain and the left?"

There was a bit of silence, then Jason spoke up. "Cris here will tell you the classical definition of them, and I'll tell you what actually is happening."

"Why don't we just cut to what actually happens," said Cris wryly.

"Okay. It's amazingly simple. There's a flow of energy between your heart and your brain. Energy flows to your brain from your heart, and back again. Your right brain is the half that uses the energy that flows *from* your heart, and your left brain directs energy *to* your heart."

"That's it?" asked Cris.

"That's all. Once explored, it explains every phenomena that science has managed to figure out so far about the two halves."

"So… pattern recognition is the result getting a thought the heart has just handled."

"Of course. When you *like* something, you like the entire thing, not the collection of pieces that make it up. That's the heart. It sends that wholeness picture to the brain. Have you ever noticed how much easier it is to memorize songs or even poems, than prose?"

"Sure," said Cat, "so you're saying that songs read more easily as a whole unit."

"Well that makes sense," said Cris, "not only are they more of a unit, but they have far more relationships going on, like rhyme and music."

"Yes. But both sides are needed or you're stopping the flow of energy; basically not living."

"Wouldn't that mean that the heart is conscious, in much the same way as the brain is conscious?" asked Cris.

"Yes."

"But… how can you prove that?"

"The heart never validates itself; it depends on the brain for validation. The only way to 'prove' the sentience of the heart is to look at its effect on the brain. And our view of the brain lacks use of the whole brain, which is why the subject seems so novel." They were off the highway now, and on the long winding road that lead to Cherell University, following a Honda Civic being driven five miles per hour under the 45 speed limit.

"Well you could say that about any modern pursuit," said Cris, "intuition isn't treated as valid in scientific method."

"However, if the heart truly is sentient, then the scientific method is a lie."

"Well… sure, that makes sense; but how do you accomplish things without double-checking your work? That's what the scientific method is supposed to cover."

"Easy. By results. We live in the age of copyrights and patents; both are an attempt to replace results with ownership. If you're the only one allowed to make a certain widget, you don't have to worry about someone making a higher quality widget, because you've got a patent. And when your patent runs out, you hurry up and make a different widget, patenting that, and leaving it to the huge department stores and other conglomerations to churn out your expired widgets at even lower quality and lower price. Ownership destroys true competition."

"You sound almost communist there. What's so wrong with owning your house, or your car?"

"I'm sorry; what I meant to say is ownership of ideas. I think we very much should own our possessions, but you can't own an idea. And an idea is proved, not by what it represents, but by what it does: its results."

"And the scientific method doesn't produce results?"

"Only anticipated results. You don't learn anything new from proving what you already anticipated. Or rather I should say that you learn very slowly that way." Cat broke in.

"You guys are way out in left field somewhere. Care to give an example so I have some idea what you're talking about?"

"Sure," said Jason, "Cris, how would you use the scientific method to get that lady ahead of us to speed up?"

"I'd… well one easy way would be to stop her and ask her. That wouldn't really be worth the trouble though, and you'd probably offend her. Hm. You could try driving right on her bumper, but that often irritates people and makes them slow down. I guess you'd have to try different things until something worked. But I sure don't see how you could use intuition to do it."

"The right side of the brain not only handles pattern recognition, but pattern implementation. If all driving is done with the right side, then every driver immediately sizes up every other driver by *recognizing* that person's pattern; kind of like knowing what someone's attitude is by looking at their face. You can transfer the pattern you see in someone else to conscious thought and figure out what to do about it."

"Yeah, but you can't speed up a driver ahead of you."

Jason smiled. "Well, let's see. If she were more aware, I'd do the equal-distance trick to her; that's the process of picking a distance, like 25 feet, from the car ahead of you, and don't vary an inch from it. It's tricky to pull off, but it always speeds people up; once they're at the right speed, you let it go. But it's obvious that she's slightly irritated at life right now, and indulging herself with a bit of self-righteousness, thinking that people should learn not to drive so fast. Notice that when someone has an attitude, they cling to one way of doing things instead of being balanced. In this case it's making her drive too near the left side of the road, except when traffic passes, at which time she takes the far right." Cris and Cat watched; he was right. "Now I've been driving near the center all this while; it's a natural reaction to trying to balance someone out. But she senses me whether she knows it or not; that's pattern recognition. So there's two ways I could handle this; one will speed up yet irritate her and the other will get her to speed up without knowing that she's doing it. I'm going to be nice and not irritate her." Cris and Cat watched as he took a position even further to the left than the Honda. After a bit, it was driving on the line, as if insisting on being the furthest left. Jason maintained a position of about two inches further left than her at all times, matching every slight movement of her car. A pickup truck came at them, and the lady swung over to the far right, with Jason ever so slightly further right. Once it passed, she took her place on the left again, this time not quite as far, and once again Jason mimicked her every move with slight exaggeration. After about one mile of this, she finally was driving in the center of the road. Cris looked at the speedometer; they were traveling 52 miles an hour.

"You did it!" said Cat, "...and she doesn't even know she sped up?"

"Nope. People aren't normally that aware when they drive. What I was doing was showing her that I could have the same exact attitude, only more intense. She tried to prove me wrong until it was no longer worth the trouble. I have the advantage because I'm doing this consciously, and she has no idea what's going on; I don't need to actually have her attitude, simply drive as if I do."

"How would you have driven to irritate her?" asked Cris.

"It's what I call the switchover method. I drive as far left as they are right, and vice versa. The success of that method depends on how skillfully you switch sides as you each cross that invisible line in the center of our lane; it has to be absolutely simultaneous. Done properly, this method drives people crazy and they don't even know why. But they do speed up."

"I want to try this!" exclaimed Cat suddenly.

"Now?"

"Yeah, right now. Pull over and I'll switch you." Jason chuckled and pulled off the road. A few cars passed them as they switched places, then Cat was catching up with them. "Aw, this won't work; there's three of them."

"That's not a problem," said Jason, "Whether driving or starting riots, the more people you have to influence at once, the easier it is. Go ahead and speed up the last car in line."

"K. Should I use the same method you used?"

"Try the equal-distance method. First thing is, you have to find the magic distance at which he's completely uncomfortable having you drive. It's different for everyone, so just kind of feel him out till you find it." At about one and a half car-lengths away, Cat found him alternately speeding up and slowing down to get her to change the distance. "That's it. Now it's just a matter of skill." Her foot fluttered on the gas pedal, trying to maintain the distance. After half a mile she got the hang of it, and was able lock in the distance. Soon the driver ahead of her zoomed up to the bumper of the car ahead of him, who had already been tailgating the pickup he was following for some time. He backed off the pickup, which then slowly began to speed up, until the whole line caught up with the lady in the Honda, who also began to speed up. "See, each driver intuitively knows what it will take to speed up the one ahead of him, whether crowding or backing off. As long as no one but you is conscious of the process, the whole thing runs smoothly."

"This is great! How many methods like this are there?"

"Oh, there's hundreds, but I don't try to know them all. You just sort of feel out whatever you need to do at the time. The amount of unconscious communication between drivers is amazing." They were driving into Cherell; Cat guided the car to Cris' dorm, where they unloaded his things, then headed over to Cat's room, where Tera was to meet them. She was sitting on the bed, reading. She jumped up when they came in."

"Hi Cris, welcome back!" She gave him a warm hug. The four of them stood there looking at each other. Even with the three of them in the car, there had lacked something of the old feeling; now that the magic was back, it was obvious that it had been missing. They looked at each other without talking for a long moment. Tera's quiet confidence had deepened; Cat's radiance had sharpened, and the guys looked like renaissance paintings. Cat finally broke the silence.

"Well, I'm starved."

"Yeah," said Cris, "Let's go reclaim the Slogan."

"I'm ready," said Jason, "I've got a teabag on me."

"Oh, right; *Tiron*," exclaimed Tera; "we've got to figure out what we're doing with his class."

They headed out of the dorm. "I want to compare everyone's schedules," said Cris, "some of us might have other classes together."

"Sure," said Cat, "Soon as I have some food in me."

The diner had changed surprisingly little. Their usual booth was occupied so they sat around a large round table. Andrea was extra friendly and in no time at all they had their food.

"So did Tiron get to your advisors too?" Jason asked everyone.

"Did mine," said Tera.

Cris and Cat both said "yup."

Jason unfolded his schedule and looked it over. "Wednesdays and Fridays at 9:30 for Tiron's 'Being' class. Let's see… anyone else have Greek I?" Okay, how about Middle Eastern History?"

"I have that I think," said Tera, "Is it… lemme see…" she pulled out her schedule. "…Tuesday and Thursday at 4:00?"

"Yep. Cool. That means one of us will be able to flirt with the professor. Okay, probably no one has Topology…"

Cris spoke up. "I was thinking of taking it, but they advised me to get some more calculus classes first."

"K. Organic Chemistry? Sculpture II? Biological Physics?"

"For crying out loud," exclaimed Cat, "How many credits are you taking this semester?"

"Um… 27. But I'll probably drop a class or two once I figure out which one's are worth having and which ones aren't. No harm in signing up for lots of classes; you can always drop some."

"Hm. I should have done that," mused Tera.

"Here's an odd one my advisor recommended that I have after Tiron's class on Tuesdays and Thursdays. Not that I listen to him, but I thought I'd check it out. It's called Nature of Discovery."

"What?" said Cris, "I've got that too. It's a new class; my advisor recommend it also."

"Wait a minute," said Cat. She put down her fork and rummaged for her schedule. "Yep. I've got it too." Everyone looked at Tera. She slowly shook her head up and down. Cris pounded his fist on the table.

"Tiron! He manipulated *two* classes this semester." Jason leaned back in his seat and chuckled.

Tera raised her eyebrows. "He's pretty good. This one was completely unexpected."

"Well what do we do," said Cat, "do we throw it back in his face and drop it, or keep it?"

"It'd be kind of a shame not to check it out," said Cris.

Jason. "Sure. Let's check it out. We have two weeks to decide whether to drop it or not."

As they went through the rest of their classes, they found no more in common. Cris had noticed someone watching them from another table; he sat alone eating a large bowl of salad. Cris nodded to him in a friendly manner and received a solemn nod back.

"Quite a specimen, isn't he?" said Tera, without looking over at him.

"I'll say," said Cris; "he's got the build of a football player."

Cat. "Who are you guys talking about?"

Jason. "The kid with a goatee behind me. He's been watching us for some time."

Cris. "How can you tell? He's behind you."

"He was here when we came in, scanning everyone. When he saw us, he stopped looking over everyone else and relaxed in his seat as if he found what he had been looking for. Since then, judging from what I can see of his reflection in the coffee machine behind the counter, he's been watching us for some reason."

"That's why I'm the only one who didn't notice him," said Cat with a smile, "he's in front of me and the coffee machine's behind me." As she spoke, the man got up from his table and approached them.

"Excuse me… are any of you guys in Tiron Jerome's new class this semester?"

"We all are," smiled Cat, "pull up a chair and join us."

"Well, I have a salad over at the other table…"

"Bring it over," said Tera, "There's plenty of room here."

"Okay, thank you; I will." He was over six feet tall, and looked about 250 pounds of solid muscle. There was a formality about him that would have bordered on ridiculous if it hadn't been so sincere. He brought his briefcase and salad over, and sat in the empty chair between Jason and Cris. "My name's John," he smiled.

Cat spoke up. "You're sitting between Jason and Cris. This is Tera, and I'm Cat."

"Pleased to meet you all."

"So I take it Tiron recruited you too?" asked Cris.

John nodded. "Yup. I asked him what kind of people he was planning to have in the class, and he told me I could find you four here most afternoons."

"Hmph," said Tera, "makes me feel like having all of us show up in his living room some day."

"He's certainly got me intrigued," said John, "he showed up at rugby practice one day and asked me to consider taking his class. It gives me the credits I need, so I figured why not."

"Did he say why he picked you?" asked Tera.

"No he didn't. That's why I was curious as to who else he'd have. I'd kind of like to know what he's up to before I dive into it."

"Well what's your major?" asked Jason, "what about you would he have singled out?"

"I'm in Hotel Management right now, but I think I'm going to switch over to sports medicine. My grades are okay, but not super great."

"Hm." Jason was thoughtful. "You said you play rugby; do you play any other sports?"

"Well I actually came here on a football scholarship. But I had… some differences with the coach, and quit football altogether…"

Cat interrupted him. "You're John Krisner! You were the first sophomore quarterback the school's had, and you quit because of some fight you had with the coach."

John blushed. "Yes, that's me. Now I have to pay for my own education; I lost the scholarship."

"What was the fight about?" asked Cris.

"Um… it wasn't really a fight… let's just say it was politics."

"Politics?" asked Jason.

"I'd rather not go into the details," said John, "let's just say that if you were a boxer and you found out that you'd have to throw a match whenever you were told to, that you might think again about your profession. I was in football because I love the strategy; but if there's one thing I have no stomach at all for, it's someone else calling the shots who isn't part of the field."

"And rugby's not political?" asked Cris.

"No, it's small enough that no one has anything to gain by manipulating the game. And I find the kind of teamwork that rugby requires to be more to my liking anyway."

"Interesting," mused Tera, "Tiron picked you out for your integrity."

John shrugged. "That might be it. We talked about teamwork for a long time; he listened to all my ideas, and seemed to understand me even when I couldn't clearly say what I was thinking."

"Do you know of anyone else who's going to be in our class?" asked Cat.

"There's some girl named Mary who I know from anthropology last year. She had all the guys drooling over her, but I've never seen her with a boyfriend. I never got to know her real well; she seemed to me to have a wound up ball of bitterness inside that she couldn't let out. But she always put on quite a show of being a friendly airhead though, so I don't think anyone else noticed it. But what about you guys? Why did Tiron pick each of you, and how do you know one another?"

They looked at each other, then Cat spoke up. "I think he picked us *because* we know one another. One of the first things he asked Cris and I was whether we had any friends. Then he sat with us over at that booth one day and talked the whole time about groups and how they interact."

"I think you're right," said Jason, "he's after the interaction we have. I don't know that any of us are that spectacular by ourselves."

"That's not what he said," stated John, "he told me that you four were the strongest in your respective fields. Only that's not the way he phrased it… let's see… he said that two of you were setting a new social standard for the university, or something along those lines, and the other two were using undergraduate studies to do what amounts to doctorate work. Now I'm curious who fits into what category."

Cris smiled. "I believe he's referring to Cat and myself as the social standards, and Jason and Tera as the doctorates. I like the sound of that..." he turned to Tera; "Good evening Dr. McCory."

Tera stuck her tongue out at him. "Good evening Big Cool Social Man on Campus."

"Did I tell you people that you could fraternize?" Andrea was standing over them with a fake stern look.

"We invited him over in the hopes of combining each table's service so we'd get things on time," quipped Jason.

"Yeah right," she retorted, "The only things you don't get on time around here are the jokes."

"If that was another one, I don't get it yet," said Cris with a straight face.

"You never will," she said, "does anyone need anything right now?"

"More hot water for tea, please," said Jason.

"Okay. Cris, you want more coffee?"

"Sure."

"And a refill on my iced tea," said Cat.

"Okay." She turned to leave, then half-turned back and pointed at Jason. "And don't think I don't see you sneaking your own teabags into here." Jason spread his hands out in a gesture of innocence and she swished away with her usual efficient demeanor.

"I take it you guys know her," said John.

"As well as one can know a waitress, I suppose," said Cris. "Back onto your classes; would you by any chance have a class called Nature of Discovery that comes right after Tiron's class?"

John looked puzzled. "I don't think so." He rummaged through his briefcase and pulled out a schedule. "Nope. Next class I have is Trig on Wednesdays at 4:00. But I still have to add some credits; my schedule isn't complete. Why do you ask about that class?"

Cris hesitated, then said, "No reason. Just thinking of any other classes we might have together."

"Well let's see your schedule," said John, "There might be one." He compared his schedule with Cris, then with the rest, but there were no crossovers other than *Being*. The five talked together for a long time, trading stories of conflicts and accomplishments from the previous semester. John turned out to be as solid in personality as he was in body; listening to every statement that was offered to him with the greatest of dignity; eager to delve into anything of depth; almost childlike in his straightforward and friendly manner.

When they left the diner, Jason walked alone to a tall stone building near the center of campus. On the third floor, he entered a large office and stood before the desk of the dean's secretary. The name plaque said June Donnavin. After a few moments, she stopped typing on her computer and looked up.

"Yes?" she asked without a smile.

"Hi June. My name's Jason, and I don't have an appointment. I'd like to ask Jerry a quick question about one of his new professors."

"Absolutely not," she said without hesitation, "we're buried here at the beginning of each semester, and Jerry has given me an iron-clad policy of appointments only."

Jason held her gaze for a few moments, then spoke. "Please. It'll only take a few seconds." He smiled.

She sighed. "I'm sorry, I'd really like to help you, but there's nothing I could do even if wanted to. Jerry can be quite a bear about this sort of thing." She put her hand under her chin and returned his gaze.

"I see. Well thanks for your help, I'll come back when he has time for an appointment." He turned and left too quickly for her to reply, and left her a bit torn on whether to feel successful or guilty. He walked the stairs to the first floor lobby and dialed a number. The phone on June's desk rang.

"Dean Fitzgerald's office." He heard by her voice that she had decided to feel successful.

"Good afternoon," he said in a businesslike tone, "I'm a second-semester freshman, and I'd like to make a two to five minute appointment with Dean Fitzgerald."

"Okay, I'll have to check with him to see if he has time. When were you wanting to see him?"

"The best time would be right now, I could be there in about five to ten minutes. But I'll work around his schedule."

"That would… well if you want to come in right now, let me ask him. Hold on." There was a long pause. "Yes, he could see you briefly in about ten minutes. What is your name please?"

"Mr. Sardic."

"Okay, Mr. Sardic; Jerry will see you in about ten minutes."

"Thank you." He hung up the phone and walked outside. Half a dozen crows were circling around the damp winter lawn of the quad. He watched their antics in the late afternoon sun for a few minutes, then returned to the third floor office. Walking in, he stood as before in front of June's desk. She looked up, and immediately a stern expression covered her face.

"It's not going to do you any good to ask again," she stated firmly.

He smiled. "No, I heard you the first time. But that's not what I'm here for this time."

"Well?"

"My name is Jason Sardic, and I have an appointment with Jerry in…" he looked at the clock on the wall. "…one minute." She blinked twice with no expression. Jason looked back at her, friendly but not smiling. She took her gaze away, and hit the intercom.

"Jason Sardic here to see you."

"Send him in."

She motioned toward his door without looking at him. Inside the double walnut doors he found a large comfortable room done in dark wood. He winced at the placement of the dean's desk: directly across the room facing the door. *So the man loves authority and is a glutton for confrontations.* The path from the door to the desk was set up to disarm visitors; Jason strolled along it, taking his time. Jerry waited until he had reached the desk before rising to offer his hand, which Jason shook firmly, looking him in the eye for the first time. "It's good to see you, Professor Fitzgerald. My name's Jason Sardic."

"Hello, Jason. And please call me Jerry. What can I do for you?"

Jason remained standing as Jerry sat down. "You've just hired a new Professor named Tiron Jarome. I'll be taking his first class, to which I'm rather looking forward. I've come to you because I'm curious about both his qualifications and background." A worried look flickered across Jerry's face. "No, nothing negative; I've met him and have nothing but admiration for the man. He is, however, very unusual. So I thought I'd drop by and ask you what you can tell me about him that might help me understand where he's coming from. It's purely… personal. I'd like to get to know him, but I don't want to presume on his time without knowing first what I'm doing." Jason smiled, and the dean relaxed.

"Well I'm glad you stopped by. Not too many people take the time to get to know their professors, and I will agree with you, this is a most unusual man." The dean's relief was making him talkative. "Truth to tell, I've only met him twice; once when Howard Lawrence in our architecture program introduced him to me, and once to congratulate him on successfully obtaining the position for which he asked. But he has a most impressive resume; five or six doctorates I believe, and he's traveled extensively."

Jason almost had to interrupt to speak. "So he specifically asked for the position in which you've placed him?"

"Are you kidding? He wrote the whole program for me. I'm telling you, that man is one hard-working and well-educated man. But tell you what. You're going to get a lot further talking to Howard than me; they seem to be good friends. Howard has his resume on file—I'm sure we have it here too, but you understand that anything in this office is classified information that I'm not allowed to release. You'll get the same exact thing, and probably a lot more by talking to Howard. Here, let me look up Howard's office number for you…" he began to rummage through the cabinet drawer on his desk."

"Don't bother, June should have that information, shouldn't she?"

"Uh… yes, yes she does."

"I don't want to take all your time; I'll ask her on the way out." The dean sat back up, and Jason smiled. "I think she likes me."

Jerry smiled back. "She can be a character when she wants. But is there anything else I can do for you?"

"No, thank you very much This will get me started." He shook the dean's hand again, and started toward the door, then turned. "One more thing. When Tiron wrote the program for you, did he give you any suggestions as to other professors and their positions?"

The question was so sudden that Jerry answered before he realized that there might be some reason to hold back. "Yes, he was quite good about it. And the board followed his suggestion too, which surprised me; they usually like to pick over good ideas until they're threadbare."

Jason laughed with the dean and continued out, making sure the door was open so that June could hear the terms on which they parted. "Thanks Jerry." Walking by her desk, he said, "Jerry said you might be able to direct me to Howard Lawrence's office.

"Certainly," she said, very proper and businesslike this time. She directed him to the building and the office, then sat there after he left, thinking that after all was said and done, she liked this student. She chuckled and shook her head, returning to work. Jason continued on to visit Howard, who was kind enough to copy Tiron's resume for him. Returning home with the resume, he reflected that he'd already learned all he wanted to know from Jerry. Hostess indeed.

Chapter 10: Ghosts. They're All Ghosts.

And they don't seem to know it. So much so that one's dreams become more real than trudging about among them. Are you then a ghost? Am I? Does it even matter? At times, and these are quite real times, all that matters are the dreams; those worlds which, barring the limits we put on them, exist in realms deeper and more solid than the petty circumstances that pretend to rule these shadows we call lives. Life indeed.

Jason woke on such a morning. *Why get out of bed?* Because it's what you've always done. *You didn't answer the question.* There is no answer. *No right answer, you probably meant.* Just get out of bed. *Why?* You know as well as I do, that to ask that, is a luxury, and you deserve no luxuries. *So dessert has nothing to do with it either?* C'mon, get up; the sun's poking around in odd corners, you want him to get in trouble? *Sure, lay that on my doorstep; put me in charge of trouble.* I didn't; you accepted that a long time ago. *Speaking of time, why don't you get lost and come back when I feel like getting up?* Because no one sells ice skates in hell; I'd get bored. *This, coming from someone who has nothing better to do than try to wake someone else out of reality and into mediocrity?* If you're that sentient already, I've succeeded. *Why don't you go find a nice hornet's nest to play with?* It's winter; they're all sleeping. *Thank you! that was exactly my point.* C'mon, I'll make you some tea. *You mean you'll watch me make some tea.* I'm not going to quibble over details. *Too late to avoid quibbles; you've already woken me.*

He rose and stretched as the day stretched out before him. Brush teeth and shower seemed to be nearest on that road, and he complied as best as one can comply when circumstance demands that one hop through hoops like an unwitting circus dog. The tea was good, however, and he looked farther down the day's highway. Seemed like it was a good day for Tiron's class. The way it seemed turned out to be the way it was.

He looked powerful and very much in his element, standing in front of a classroom of new students. The variety was remarkable. There were twenty-two students; seniors to freshmen, intelligent to seemingly clueless, and the largest stretch: female to male. Cris glanced around infrequently and rapidly; too many people there caught his glance with like understanding. Jason had chosen a seat in the front row on the far right. Cris, Tera, and Cat had spread themselves out through the room. John came in late, and took a seat near the back, after nodding formally to Cris. Cris had a sense of the smallness of his world, of everything he knew, and wondered if it were about to drown, or be torn apart. Cat was eager and it showed. Tera was silent and reticent. But they were drowned in the overwhelming combination of personalities in the room. Tiron spoke, and as he did, the personalities congealed into a respectful whole.

"Welcome to *Being*," he said, his voice echoing with that musical quality; only now it had a resonant dignity that required no second-guessing to apprehend. He wrote 'Being' in barely recognizable characters on the board; they looked more like hieroglyphics. "This class will be in three parts." He turned and face the class. "Firstly: What is possible to achieve in a real society." He paused for a few moments. Cris realized that both slow and sharp students could connect with his timing. "The second of the triad will address how that ideal, the idea of what is possible; how that *ideal* is affected by its sociological environment." Pause. "Lastly, we will undertake a project together to understand how our environment, in turn, is affected by a real society." He turned and wrote some words on the board. "This is a Latin expression. Does anyone know what it means?" There was a long pause, then a redheaded girl near the front raised her hand. "Yes, Rachel?"

"What have we been given, that we have not received?"

"Very good. You preserved the inherent ambiguity of the original. Class, this is Rachel Wainstead, a senior in Religious Studies. I will introduce each one of you as you make yourselves available for being identified. Otherwise, we're simply a collection of faces and names, and I believe, since you've all been here for more than one semester with the exception of Susan Marasta," he indicated a quiet girl in the front row, "you've had ample opportunity to experience that. Now someone please tell me why I've written this on the board as the first statement of this course." In the long silence that ensued, Tera thought to herself, 'Not bad. My Latin's good, but not that good.'

A voice broke the silence without a raised hand. "Because you're bored." Jason. Several heads snapped to his position in the front right at the apparent affront.

"This is Jason Sardic, whom you will all get to know to quite some extent," said Tiron without hesitating a beat. "He has just started a good tradition which we will continue from here on: it is not necessary to raise your hand when answering a question." He paused for a moment, then turned to Jason. "Aside from a possible pun referring to the blackboard, I believe it falls on you to explain your reply." All heads turned to Jason.

"You're introducing the course, but at the same time, you're embarking upon the first step, which you just told us, is: 'What is possible to achieve in a real society?' Achievements are always led by an individual, yet you wrote an expression on the board which negates the individual and makes him dependent on those who have given him everything. Obviously you don't believe that, because you said 'a real society,' not 'a society.' So it appears that you're introducing the idea that we have received everything that we are, so that you can get on to the fact that in a real society, every individual has his place *purely in his being an individual.* Earned, not given; deserved, not apportioned. And I suspect that you're going to define a 'real' society as being made up of such individuals."

"Almost right, as usual, Mr. Sardic. But judging from the faces around you, your thought pattern is a tad… direct." He looked around. "I'd like to appoint a permanent translator for what remains of the semester, who will state your ideas in a properly ambulatory fashion, which I think will communicate much more effectively. This…" he indicated a girl just behind and to the left of Jason, "…is Mary Sendik, a sophomore in Fashion Design, who will restate what Jason just said for the benefit of all of us." Everyone turned to Mary, who hesitated, then spoke lightly.

"He said that you'd like to talk about individual achievements, but first you'd like to get rid of the idea that we are made of what people have made us." She looked confident and calm, but Cris detected a protected angst that made him wonder if this was the same Mary of whom John had spoken in the diner. She certainly had the looks.

"A good job, Mary, thank you. We're still not quite on the mark, however, so while I'd like to retain you for the job of translating Mr. Sardic's comments for the semester, let's call on someone who's been accustomed to dealing with him for some time now. This is simply, 'Cat'," he waved to her place near the back on the left, "who will put his comments even more succinctly."

Cat squirmed for a moment before replying. "He says you can't give a real person anything that he hasn't earned. And he's suggesting that you feel that way as well."

"Ah. We're getting closer. Jason, was that what you were saying?"

"No."

"Thank you for your honesty. What, then, would be different?"

"I agree with the content of Mary and Cat's remarks; however, they implied that I have presumed to impute what *you* feel at this time, which I hope I haven't done. I was simply saying that you can't have a real society without individuals, but you can have individuals without a real society."

Tiron turned and wrote another expression on the board under the Latin. "Rachel, would you be so kind as to translate this expression for us?"

"Um… it's Hebrew. 'Separation is for a man, desire, and by it he thoroughly investigates wisdom."

"I think we can do a bit better. The invitation is open to the class."

The lanky lad with glasses in front of Cat spoke up. "A man who wants to pursue selfishness confuses true judgment."

Tiron thought for a moment. "Let's keep at it. We're still not there. And this is Francois Lyons, a junior in Electrical Engineering."

"I like to be called Frank," he stated bluntly.

"Quite good, Frank it is. Another go at translating, anyone?"

Tera felt herself speaking up in spite of her reticence. "A man separates himself because of his desire, and entangles with all sound wisdom."

"Excellent," said Tiron, "this is a difficult quote to translate. Class, this is Tera, a freshman in History." He smiled at her and gave the class a chance to look. She held herself with her customary calm dignity. "So then Jason, explain how this statement answers your comment."

Jason didn't hesitate for a moment. "I brought up the subject of the individual prematurely, when you had intended to arrive at it after first considering what it is that makes an individual. You're addressing this by pointing out that anyone who separates himself, if motivated by his own desires, becomes subject to those desires; and as a result, adopts an attitude of polarity with society, and as a result of *that*, polarity with the kind of wisdom that society provides."

"Mary?" said Tiron expectantly.

"Um… he just said that you're getting us back on the subject by warning us what kind of attitude is produced by shortcutting it, and simultaneously warning *him* not to get caught in that attitude."

"So then," continued Tiron, "let's take it from here and discuss *how* one becomes an individual without falling prey to one's own desires." He leaned against his desk and looked around. A kid beside Tera near the middle of the room raised his hand. "Yes, Joshua. Before you speak, everyone, this is Joshua

Mainsted, a junior pursuing a double major Sociology and Psychology."

"Is it improper to *want* to be an individual? That's seems to very much be what you're suggesting."

"I think… that it isn't necessary to raise your hand when asking questions either," said Tiron. "We'll continue to try it. Now. What could there possibly be *improper* about wanting to be an individual?" There was a bit of silence. "Let's start with the question, Is a person, at birth, an individual?" After a moment, a chorus of agreement met his question. "Well then?"

A girl in front at the far left answered. "You'd be wanting something that you already have."

"Yes," said Tiron, "and what can we surmise about someone who wants something they already have?"

She went on. "That you no longer believe you really have it. It would be a kind of insecurity."

Joshua spoke up again. "But if you've *lost* that sense of being an individual, there's nothing wrong with trying to capture it again."

Cat spoke up; "nothing *wrong*, no; but that doesn't change the fact you want something you already have."

"Well then," pursued Joshua, "what's the poor guy who's lost sight of his individuality supposed to do? Just float along without trying to get it back?"

The girl in the front corner replied; "Anytime anyone has a problem, there's ways to solve it and there's ways to make it worse. We're just saying that *wanting* to be an individual is a way to make it worse."

"This is Holly Boyer," interjected Tiron quietly, "she's a freshman in Architecture. But go on."

Joshua exclaimed, "then how *would* you suggest that someone who's lost sight of their individuality regain it?"

A student in the far back right spoke up in a slow voice. "That depends on whether your *treating* the problem or *solving* it. Most treatments in psychology *and* medicine are simply methods of perpetuating the problem by addressing the symptoms.

Anytime you want to actually *solve* something, you ignore the symptoms and address the solution. In this case, you'd have to tell our patient very clearly that he *is* an individual, and show him how to act like it. Then he quits trying to achieve *individuality*, and begins to put into practice that he is one."

"This is our second Jason, Jason Thomas," interjected Tiron quietly, "a senior in Premed."

"You don't sound like you embrace medicine's ideals very much," retorted Joshua.

Jason just smiled back at him. "Y'all kin call me *Jason Two* if you want. Are you disagreeing with what I said, Joshua?"

Joshua's confidence seemed untouched. "Well I don't think you can just make a blanket statement about how psychology and medicine approach curing. It depends on the individual carrying it out."

"I disagree," said Holly, "he wasn't talking about the individuals within the professions, he was talking about the attitude of the profession itself. You can't solve the problems of a society by appealing to how individuals should act in it; you have to address the society as a society."

"Holly, write that last statement you made on the board," said Tiron quietly, "the rest of you may continue the discussion if you wish."

Joshua was thoughtful, almost disturbed, but held his tongue. Rachel spoke up. "If you don't mind me asking, is Jason, um… Jason number one, who we're talking about here? Has he lost his sense of being an individual?"

"Let's go to Cris for that," said Tiron, "this is Cris-without-an-'h,' a freshman in Chemistry, who will vouch for Jason." Cris was sitting on the far left, about halfway back.

He would very much have preferred not to be put on the spot. After a touch of silence while he wondered what to do, he simply said, "Jason has the strongest sense of being an individual of any person I've ever met. In fact, I have the impression that it's stronger than any person near my age that I'll ever meet."

"Then how did he get us on this subject?" asked Rachel. Cris noticed that her hair was a *very* unusual shade of deep red. In spite of its vibrancy it seemed quite natural.

"Jason," projected Tiron, "is in the habit of jump-starting new situations. His comments have rarely to do with anything of himself, merely what he considers to be what is upcoming in any scenario. I would advise the class to take advantage of this fact lest he himself reap all the benefits."

"I don't know," piped up a new voice; a front row blonde in front of Tera, "he looks kind of cute to me." Cris realized with a shock that the class itself was pulling together to equalize Jason's aura.

Rachel jumped on the opportunity. "Cute but lonely. I bet he thinks he's never met a girl who he considered his equal." Tiron had an odd smile on his face, and let the class continue. John, from way in the back spoke up.

"We've been talking about individuals within a society; Cris said that Jason was the ultimate individual. It looks to me that you girls are either attracted or threatened by that," then he smiled. There were chuckles throughout the class; the blow was strong and straightforward. Cris looked back at John, surprised at how strong his poise of dignity could be when used in a crowd.

Tiron spoke up, and when he did, everyone expected him to turn the conversation. But he simply stated quietly, "Our blonde commentator is Lisa McDowell, a junior in finances." There was a moment or two of silence. Frank broke the silence.

"I'd like to know why you had Holly write 'You can't solve the problems of a society by appealing to how individuals should act in it; you have to address the society as a society' on the board, and what it has to do what you were trying to teach us."

"What was I 'trying' to teach you?" asked Tiron quietly.

"Well… I couldn't know that, because you haven't taught it to us yet," stated Frank.

"That would contradict what Jason Two said about starting with the solution, wouldn't it?" asked Tiron. There was another bit of silence, then Jason spoke again.

"Discernment."

"Of what?" asked Tiron, not looking at Jason, but continuing to consider the class.

"Discernment is *between* things," said Jason, "so you mean 'between what and what?'"

Tiron was silent and continued to look at the class.

After hesitating, Cris spoke up; he hated to see Jason fielding so much. "So far we've discerned between true individuality and a society-made individual. What we haven't looked at is either a true society or a… I guess a society that just exists because there happens to be a group of people there."

"Okay, I didn't mean *trying* to teach us," said Frank, "so is what you're getting at is something like what a true society is?" His chutzpah was undamaged.

"Your English is appropriately atrocious for your major," piped up a new voice two seats behind Jason. The tall expensively but comfortably dressed lad addressed Tiron, "I believe Frank meant to ask this: Is it now time to turn our attention to the consideration of the construct of a true society?" He faced the class. "And by the way, I'm Charles Andowski. I'm a senior in journalism."

"Are you taking on the job of correcting our English then?" asked the girl behind him.

"Well no, just when it goes beyond the point of no return."

"And you're the best judge of that?" she pressed.

Charles threw up his hands in a mock gesture of giving up. "Hey, if anyone else wants the job, they're welcome to it. I could then spend more time sorting my postcard collection."

She smiled and patted him on the back. "I'm sure you'll do a fine job. Just be nice to us."

The cute blonde girl in front of Tera asked, "do you really have a postcard collection?"

"Lisa, you have a penchant for dignifying the irrelevant," grinned Charles, "yes, about 5,000 of them. I specialize in nineteenth-century French, but that's only about a third of my collection. I have probably the most complete Baltic and Slavic selection in America."

"The young lady behind Charles is Allison Howell, a senior in Education; Special Education being her area of expertise," said Tiron. Cris noticed that he gave no body language reaction whatsoever to the conversation regardless of which direction it turned.

"Special Education covers both retardation *and* gifted areas," stated Allison.

Jason Two behind her spoke up, "they're not all that different, are they?"

"No, actually they're not. In the final analysis, I find that they're both far more straightforward than what we consider standard education."

"You mean, 'what we consider standard education *to be*,'" said Charles with a touch of humor in his voice.

"It was implied. One excellent thing I've learned from my studies is that what you *imply* has far more impact than anything you teach explicitly."

"Amen to that," spoke up a kid from the second row behind Tera, "I read that less than 30% of any given conversation is words and meaning; the rest is body language and implications." He paused. "Um… my name's Jerald Kadid, and I'm in meteorology. A sophomore."

Jerald the katydid, Tera absently thought to herself.

John spoke up from the back again. "Let's get back to the subject. I believe Frank was asking Tiron if he was going to teach us about the construct of a true society." He looked to Tiron expectantly.

"Yes, thank you John," said Tiron, still leaning casually on his desk, "John is in Sports Medicine and Nutrition; you may know him as the famous sophomore quarterback, most missed player since he quit last semester." John kept a straight face as everyone turned around to look at him, but inside he squirmed from the attention on himself directly. He was sure that his face was reddening, and mercifully, Tiron went on. "Yes, although we *certainly* aren't done with the individual." He glanced at Jason with a slight smile. "But first I think it would be proper to explain how you are being graded. I will be employing a pass/fail system on a *daily* basis." He paused. "Let's start with class discussions. You will receive an 'A' whenever you voluntarily speak up. If, in my opinion, a subject passes for which you have the best input in the class and you *don't* speak up, you will receive an 'F'. If you speak up, and fail to make your point, you will also receive an 'F'. It doesn't matter whether your point is correct or incorrect, it is simply incumbent on you to make it. In the event that you make your point, you will receive an 'A'." Cris noticed the half dozen people in the room who hadn't spoken up were suddenly very attentive. One of them, a short brunette behind Jason, immediately asked,

"Um… do you want us to write down what we say so you can keep track?"

Tiron looked at her. "I'll do my job, and you do yours." Then he smiled. "Class, this is Miss DuChamp, a senior in Mechanical Engineering."

"My first name's Bethany," she said quietly.

"Very good, Bethany, that got you an 'A'."

A nervous looking boy beside Jason blurted out, "But how are we supposed to know when it's proper to speak up?"

"This is William Target, a senior in History." He turned to William. "I *am* here to teach you, you know. I'll be guiding you throughout the process. For example, Jason?" He looked at Jason expectantly, who almost seemed to have a pained look on his face but replied after a moment,

"That's an ingenious way to grade."

Tiron smiled and turned back to the class. "Thank you, Jason, you get an 'A'."

"Wait a minute," said Lisa, "How does he get an 'A' from just complimenting you?"

Jason Two drawled from the back of the class, "Because he's the only one in here trying to double-think Tiron, and apparently found that there were no flaws in the plan. Otherwise he would have said so, in order to avoid an 'F'." He looked up at Tiron. "Do I get an 'A' for that?"

"Wait and see when it's posted next class," replied Tiron. "Let's move along. There will be several projects we undertake, some individually, most socially. You will also be graded pass/fail on these projects. If one person in your group fails, the entire group fails. You will have ample opportunity to make up for failure by redoing the project; however you may not take time from new projects to work on old. Does everyone agree to this plan?" There was silence and a general nodding of heads. He waited an extra moment. "Good. Since, in addition to it being my grading method, I have your agreement, you are all now legally entered into a contract whereby you have no grounds by which to disagree once it's implemented." He smiled.

"He's right," said a boy in the back middle beside John, "I'm going into law, I should know. He's changed it from a school contract into a verbal contract between us and himself."

"Thank you, Phil," said Tiron, "Phil Mupp is planning on transferring to Harvard for law next year, so his time will be valuable to him." He looked around. "Let's see... who haven't we introduced yet..."

"I'm Jude Astor," the red-haired boy beside Cat said cheerfully, "I'm a sophomore in Chemical Engineering."

"Just like Cris!" replied Cat.

"Um... no, I think Cris said he was in Chemistry—I'm in Chemical Engineering; they're different."

Cat rolled her eyes, "Oh sure, that's what he says too." The class laughed and Cris' face reddened slightly. The lad in front of Jude waved his hand.

"And I'm Mike Moyer. I'm a freshman in architecture like Holly." He spoke with an odd lisp that made it sound as if he had come off a nearby farm. Which, incidentally, he had. The last two introduced themselves, Heth Rejul in the back row, a Mathematics junior, and Susan Marasta reintroduced herself from the front row middle, as a freshman in interior design.

"Your assignment," stated Tiron in a voice that sounded entirely too casual for the subject, "has two parts. First, pick out one example from history of a successful government under weak leadership and explain why it worked. This will be under 200 words and posted on the board before the commencement of class. Second, compose a single sentence to be read to the class that summarizes what the personality of this entire body of students would be if you were not in it."

"But that's impossible," blurted out Joshua. Tiron's gaze rested on him.

"At least one successful approach has been discussed today. The course will not be about parroting information. And you can make this as difficult or simple as you choose. There are benefits to both." The class considered this in silence. Tiron glanced out the window. "With all this sunlight available to us, I think we'll break for the day. I'll be looking forward to your presentations Friday." He took his place behind the desk and began making notes. After a few moments, the class began to mill out with an air of intrigue unfurling into the campus air; a few students gathered around his desk for questions. Cris and Tera met outside and waited for the other two—Jason was talking to 'Jason Two' and Cat was chatting with Rachel, the impulse to do so primarily being admiration for the peculiar red shade of her hair. Girls are like that.

The professor for Nature of Discovery beamed at the incoming students like a proud owner at a prize dog show. He was short and mostly bald with thin sharp features. Looking around at the class, Cris noticed a half dozen students from Being… Lisa the cute blonde, the red haired Jude, Mary with whom Cat had been talking, Allison, Mike Moyer, and Heth, a dark quiet girl who looked like she might be from India. Altogether, ten of the thirty-six students were from Tiron's class.

"I am Professor Leonard Deon, and this is Nature of Discovery," he began in a voice that was surprisingly eloquent. "I would advise any of you who took this class hoping for an easy

'A' or to satisfy a requirement, do yourselves a service by leaving now." Nobody seemed apt to interrupt his dramatic pause by leaving. "Or," he smiled, "you can always drop the class later in the privacy of your advisor's office."

"Most of you think you are at University to learn. While that certainly will be the case here, consider it a minor part of this class. We are here to *do*." Cris noticed by the breaks in his commanding scan of the class that he seemed especially taken with Tera, sitting in her usual second row left-of-center-seat. "Many of you have heard of the Scientific Method and think you understand what it is. I am here to tell you that you do not have the slightest idea what the Scientific Method is. Many of you here use the term 'genius'. I am here to tell you that you do not have the slightest idea of what 'genius' is, nor how it is employed to advance progress. We will explore the Scientific Method until you manage to actually use it. And we will understand genius so thoroughly that anyone who leaves this class and does something idiotic could only be called an idiot." There was a twitter of nervous laughter in the room

"This class is part of Environmental Studies. As such, you will be expected to have an impact on your environment. As of this moment your environment is Cherell University and this town. The impact you are required to make will be, among other things, physical and lasting. Until the midterm your learning will principally be academic. One half of your grade will come from the midterm. The second half of this semester will be the implementation of what you have learned, and the second half of your grade. Failure of either half will result in failure of the course." He smiled disarmingly, "As will failure of both halves." In the ensuing laughter Cris realized that the professor dampened down each point with humor. He noted that neither Tera nor Jason were giving any kind of reaction, and decided against craning his neck around to see what Cat was thinking.

Professor Deon dug right in with a history of the Scientific Method, and Cris didn't have to turn around to know that Cat's attention was wandering. However, he mused by the way the professor kept glancing at Tera when bringing in humor that they might be in some sort of repeat of Medieval History. The class ended with a staggering number of books required to be purchased, and the students dutifully filed out of the room. Jason had stood first, and casually watched them go by, while Cris and Cat hung back to see what he was doing. They were just catching up with Tera when Mary Sendik approached and put her hand on Jason's arm to pause him. Cris and Cat were not sure whether to continue on, but it didn't seem to matter.

"You have sight," said Mary slowly and deliberately. Jason said nothing, just stood there looking at her. She held his gaze without flinching while Tera slowly joined them. Mary glanced around and let go of Jason's arm. "My grandmother warned me about people like you." Everyone laughed, but Tera noticed that both Mary and Jason took the comment seriously.

Cat broke in, "Mary, we're meeting later at the Slogan if you'd like to join us…"

Mary looked at her like she was waking from a dream. "Um… yes, that would be nice… but not today; I've got things to do. But okay, next time you go let me know and I'll be there. Thanks." She smiled and hurried off.

"What on earth was that about?" exclaimed Tera. Jason had the odd mixture of a smile and a distant sadness.

"Hm. I haven't lived that long yet," said Jason, "But I have learned one thing. No one ever accuses you of something that they don't have themselves." He shook his head. "That's enough for one chapter. Let's figure out what we're doing with Leonard and go have fun."

It turns out that the campus bookstore had to do for fun, and Jason was right; that's enough for one chapter.

Chapter 11: What are you going to do about it?

Perhaps Jason had a fleeting thought of a Chinese official deciding that it might not be in the nation's best interests to keep stomping out tradition; for whatever reason we find him in his apartment painting on a grey canvas hung opposite the kitchen, humming. He is, of course, using grey paint, albeit a different shade from the canvas. The door, of course, bursts open. Jason, of course, does not turn around.

"Hi Cat. Your tea is by the stove. Lavender with a bit of Sassafras. At least sip it a bit, I made it fresh for you." Cat shut the door firmly, stared at him for a moment, went over to the stove and took a sip of tea and put the cup down.

"You. Me. Slogan Diner. Right now."

Jason looked at her. "You sure?"

"Now."

Jason sighed. "Okay. Let me at least get my teabags." He grabbed a knapsack, put in a book and some teabags, and headed out the door with his military escort following.

"You left your bedroom light off."

He looked back. "Oh. Well these things have a way of reversing themselves."

"I don't want to hear it. Go." She walked with him in determined silence while he resisted the temptation to ask for clear weather and enjoyed the spatters of rain that the wind whipped around them. The diner was almost empty at this late hour, and she said nothing until he had taken his first sip of tea. Arms crossed, elbows on the table, leaning forward with piercing eyes, she looked like the world's deadliest, but cutest, interrogator. "What can you do?"

He looked at her for a long moment. There really wasn't a way out of this one.

She spoke slowly and deliberately. "No bullshit. What can you do?"

He waited until she knew that he wouldn't lie. "I don't know." It wasn't a statement of helplessness, nor a statement of ignorance, it was simply a statement. The reaction was inevitable either way.

"Bullshit! You can do anything you want! You probably made it windy and cold on the way over here! You can probably fly! ...can you fly?"

"I don't know. I haven't in recent memory, if that's what you're asking."

"No, that's not what I'm asking and you know it very well! What—can—you—do?" A familiar shape in her periphery cleared its throat. Lady Laura.

"I hope I'm not late dearies." Normally Jason would have jumped up until Laura was seated, but he waited for Cat, who dropped her head in her arms, then immediately recovered.

"Lady Laura… welcome… Um, I respect you a lot, but you can't let him get out of this one. He's got to answer the question."

"No problem dear, I won't interfere one bit. Maybe I'll help. Jason, you *do* have one or two of those teabags about you I hope?" She settled in beside Cat and Andrea brought her over some hot water, only rolling her eyes a bit.

Cat kept her eyes on Jason. "What can you do?"

This time it almost sounded like a confession. "Anything I want." Cat stared at him for a minute, her mind racing.

"He did answer the question dear," stated Laura.

"No he's not done. Okay, Jason, What—do—you—want?"

Now it seemed there was a fire behind Jason's eyes, one that smoldered without emotion.

"Nothing." It was raw, and it was the truth. Cat realized that it was what she had been looking for without knowing that it was what she was looking for. It made no sense at all, and yet somehow, this was the answer. After a few moments she realized that her mouth was open and shut it determinedly. But she couldn't think of anything to say. Finally her mind began to work and she said softly, "But… that can't be true." She looked to Lady Laura for any kind of help, suddenly glad of her presence.

"If you squeeze a tube of toothpaste, you're probably going to get toothpaste out of it dear. You've got him pinned down and he's got no reason to talk like that if it isn't true. Let's just take him at his word." She cocked her head at Jason. "Now do you think you *could* want something?"

He thought for a bit. "Um… sure."

"Okay then," Laura smiled at Cat, "so he's not a monster. So what *are* you, Jason?" *I'm being tag-teamed.*

"I… don't… know."

"You can't leave us hanging! You have to know!" Cat wasn't sure why she felt this was so important.

"I'm… sorry… I… don't… know."

"You can't say you don't want anything! You mean you don't want Tera as a friend? You don't want any friends? You don't want to be here? You don't want to live?"

It was Jason's turn to be at a loss. He started to form a word, but nothing came out. Finally Laura put her head next to Cat's like they were sharing a secret. "It looks like we're not the ones left hanging. If what he says is true, he's the one that's hanging."

"Hanging in what sense?"

Laura snorted. "In every sense of the word that I can think of right now." She straightened up. "That being said, let's have a bit of the word game Hangman." She got out a pencil and drew the spaces for an eleven-letter word, and the beginnings of a hanging scaffold. "Now who is going to guess the first letter?"

"E?" asked Cat, not sure what she was doing. Laura began to write an 'e' in the second space, when Jason spoke up quietly.

"The word is 'Restitution'."

"Exactly!" chirped Laura triumphantly, "You see dear? He's easy."

"Easy? He just did something impossible."

"Really. Well tell me, what did he just do?"

"He did that thing where it looks like he can do anything."

"Well you can't very easily get the toothpaste back in the tube. What did he just say about what he can or can't do?"

"Um… that he can do anything he wants."

"And what did he say about what he wants?"

"Um… that he doesn't want anything."

"Exactly!" Laura leaned back with a satisfied smile. Cat looked back and forth between Jason and Laura trying to somehow make this work.

"Cat." Jason seemed resigned, though not diminished. "You and Laura made me want to do that. Otherwise I couldn't have done it." Cat's jaw dropped slightly, then she put her head down on her arms for the second time. When she looked up again, she saw for the first time in Jason's eyes what was so obvious that it had gone completely unnoticed: pure vulnerability. "I'm sorry." He managed a wry smile.

"Does… it hurt?" she asked.

Pause. "Yes."

"But… What do you do when you're alone?"

Jason's face held no expression as he gathered his thoughts, when Laura interrupted; "Enough of this!" she exclaimed, "Master Sardik, I have no patience for theater unless it's on a stage and there's a playbill in my pocket. You have, I trust, something of substance to offer our little tête-à-tête?"

Jason smiled brightly and reached for his backpack. "Indeed, I've brought you a gift."

She raised her chin. "Well let's see it then young man."

He pulled out an ancient-looking book and held it out to Lady Laura with both hands. She took it respectfully, began to look through it, and looked up with her eyes shining. "This is Isaac Pitman's shorthand New Testament from 1849! Jason—this is a treasure!"

He was smiling like a little boy again. "I was hoping you'd like it."

"Like it! Where on earth did you get this?"

"I was helping a lady move her stuff, and it was part of a library of her father's that she no longer wanted. She let me have a pile of his books."

"What is it... a New Testament?" asked Cat.

"Isaac Pitman was one of the inventors of shorthand," said Laura, caressing the pages, "One of the first works he did to popularize his method was a New Testament. This must be a first printing!"

"But Jason, does that mean that you knew Laura would be here?"

Jason smiled and shrugged. "Just in case." She noticed that for once she was no longer disturbed by the sudden personality change, or what seemed like one.

"Thank you Jason, I will reward this gift by mentioning you in one of my articles." Both girls laughed at the sudden glare the comment elicited from him. "Now you kids run along; having all the toothpaste squeezed out can be tiring, and besides, I came here to discuss things with Andrea."

"Our waitress?" asked Cat.

"Yes of course. She watches the town and I write about the town. It's a very practical arrangement. Now scoot along, and let me enjoy my gift in peace."

Walking back in the dark, Cat enjoyed the silence until her thoughts settled down into a single sentence, which she didn't mind verbalizing at all. "So everything you said, this means we need each other, doesn't it?"

"That makes sense. But I wouldn't use the word 'need', it's too ...I don't know; limiting."

"How would you put it?"

"It means that we love one another."

"Ah." She walked on in silence for a bit. "That sure expands the word 'love'."

"Yes. Yes it does."

Her mind was picking up on the possibilities. "This means we could..."

"Stop right there. I'm not a slot machine."

"Yes but… it's like there's no limits; there's nothing we can't do if…" she paused, looking for the right words.

"…If we believe in each other."

"Yes! that's the only limit. If you don't want, and you don't do what I want, only what *I* make *you* want, then…"

Jason chuckled. "Then it gets really complicated." They were walking down the gravel drive to the back door that led to his basement apartment.

"Whoa," she said, stopping them both. "Look." The only light on in his apartment was the bedroom; all the others that had been left on were out.

"Well," he mused, "I didn't expect *all* the lights to be reversed." Walking to the door, they could hear muffled laughter from within. He motioned her to be quiet and silently swung open the door.

"Check this one out!" It was Cris' voice from the bedroom. *"Mr Hafer has failed to take notice of the unusual two-three beat dripping from the broken gutter, save that he loses his train of thought every fourth stanza, and repeats the word 'derivative' to restore himself. Memo to self: must check alternating rhythm patterns with induced psychosis in left-brain-subjected bipeds."*

This was followed by howls of laughter, then Tera's voice; "Look at this drawing of Professor Deon!"

Cris again. "That's grotesque. He looks like an eighteenth-century preacher on crack."

"I know. Turn it upside-down."

Howls of laughter again. "It's a perfect drawing of a baboon's butt!"

Jason motioned Cat forward, and she swung the door open with a booming "What's going on here?", eliciting an unusual and most satisfying shriek out of Tera.

"Oh rats, we were going to surprise you," Cris said sheepishly.

"Yeah, we were going to turn all the lights out and see if we could surprise Jason, but we found his class notes in here and couldn't stop reading them.

Jason actually looked embarrassed. "Um, they're not exactly…"

"Not exactly class notes?" exclaimed Tera, "I should think not. Is this what you spend all your time doing?"

"No, sometimes I get sequestered by gorgeous chicks who make me give away rare volumes from my library."

Cris. "What? What on earth have you two been doing?"

Cat plopped down between them on the bed, right on top of the spread out notes. "He said that he loves me," she said dreamily.

"Really," said Tera, "Tell us *exactly* what he said."

Cat sat up, "He said that like he can do anything but it doesn't matter and like if I want something that doesn't matter either but if I make him want something then he can do anything again but he only does it if we make him but we can't cause it's gotta be him and… um… he's hanging like in a hangman's noose only he didn't say that, Laura did, and when we make it happen, that's love. Oh, and he might have flown but it was a long time ago. He didn't really answer that one." She turned to Jason. "Did you really fly?"

Jason grimaced. "Okay, yes. Anything else while you're holding the gun?"

"Whoa, whoa!" said Cris, "I want to hear about every bit of this, and not in blondese. Turn the rest of the lights on; no one's going anywhere till this is recorded!"

"In shorthand," said Cat, "like the Bible."

Tera was fully intrigued. "Cris is right; let's have a blow-by-blow."

Jason looked everyone over. "Okay, okay. But only if we have some wine."

Tera raised one eyebrow. "Bring it on, mister."

Chapter 12: Oh. Right.

The class assembled in Tiron's room to a message on the board: "Please continue in the seats first chosen for the remainder of this class" which caused a few chuckles and a few more grumbles. Tiron looked over the row posted assignments on the side wall, picked two down, and when the expectant silence settled on the students, stated without fanfare, "The assignments still posted have failed to pass. You may resubmit them for a passing grade so long as it does not interfere with your work on future assignments." He looked up and waited.

Amid the chorus of dismay that swept the class, Jason and John looked at each other. John shrugged and said, "Okay, I'll go first." He carried his sizable bulk lightly to the front and addressed the class. "Tiron said last time that if we had something to offer and failed to do so, we would be given a failure for that omission. Because Jason and I have had our projects pass, it looks like we have to explain why. I don't know what Jason did; here's what I did." He hesitated a moment, then asked Tiron, "May I just read my paper?"

"Certainly," said Tiron.

John seemed to unconsciously pull confidence from reading his own work. "A successful society is one in which every member operates to the fullest of its own capacity using his own unique abilities while simultaneously contributing to the whole in an indispensable manner. A strong leader is one who advantages such a society by taking it into new circumstances forcing it to grow and transform. Thus a weak leader seeks to maintain the status quo, causing the society to atrophy through disuse of ability, and this in direct proportion to the previous strength of these abilities. For this reason I choose the founding and governing of the Commonwealth of Pennsylvania by William Penn. As the largest non-royal landowner in the civilized world, he implemented a radically different government designed to protect a larger proportion of men than had been attempted in recent history, and succeeded. He then failed to utilize either this society or its individual members; rather, he allowed mismanagement to foster and even attempted to give the property back to the crown on several occasions. As such, one of the strongest and most innovative societies of the New World became progressively subject to a variety of constraining laws which characterize the limits found in Pennsylvanian to this day."

He handed the paper back to Tiron, shrugged, and said, "Well there it is. I'm not sure why it passed, but I'm sure glad it did."

As he made his way back to his desk, Tiron stood and said, "Well done, John; whether or not we agree with your point, you filled the requirements of the assignment. Those of you who like to count might notice that John used precisely 199 words."

"Well you said *under* 200 words," John replied, "but are you going to say why mine passed?"

"That will become quite plain very shortly," said Tiron with a smile. "Jason, as much as you or the rest of us might find it distasteful, I would like you to follow John's example of presentation." He handed Jason his paper, who sat there for a moment before getting up and facing the class.

"You did not define successful. You did not define weak. This is not an assignment because assignments have clearly defined parameters."

The class gasped. "That's so rude!" exclaimed Allison.

"Yes," said Tiron, "in the three years that you have studied education Allison, protocol has generally frowned upon this approach. However, in this particular he was right. I used parameters which I did not define which means that in reality there were no parameters. Every paper still posted uses definitions for a 'successful society' or a 'weak leader' using assumptions that are not stated, or at best, partially stated. John chose to clearly define for himself those terms which I purposefully left undefined, which then gives him the right to make an example using them. Jason, in contrast, chose to point out the obvious discrepancy in the assignment. Which approach do you think worked the best?"

Tera's quiet voice popped up. "You just did it again. Define 'best'."

Tiron nodded. "Very good. I trust that those of you who wish to resubmit the assignment will have little trouble. And now let us start in the back with Mr. Thomas, who many of you know as 'Jason Two', and proceed with the second assignment."

Jason stood up with the relaxed awkwardness that made him likable. "Without yours truly, this class, while overall less sarcastic, could not be trusted to competently perform a cricothyroidotomy." He looked up at the blank expressions, then pretended to stab himself in the neck with his pencil.

"Oh," said Cat, "That's the track-anomy thingy where you stab someone who's choking."

"Are you certain of your facts, Jason?" asked Tiron.

"Yup. The only other person in here with medical training is John, and I checked with him before I wrote this. He said he kind of knew how to do one, but would have to brush up."

"Very good. Miss Rejul?"

Heth stood up shyly. "If I were not in this class, its personality would be more vibrant, more outgoing, and possibly less comprehensive."

This raised a few eyebrows, but Tiron simply said, "Thank you Miss Rejul. Mr Krisner?"

John stood up. "Without me, the personality of this class would be dynamic, friendly, comfortable, and interactive."

Joshua spoke up; "Wait, you're saying that you make it less so?"

John grinned. "Nope. I'm saying that the class is that way whether I'm here or not."

"Clever Mr Krisner," said Tiron, "Phil Mupp?" Cris noted that he had started from the back and was making his way forward, and wondered if he would use this to have Jason go last.

"Without me, the personality of this class would be Blunderful!"

"That's not a word!" exclaimed Charles from the middle right.

Phil did a play of being shocked. "And in journalism you never use a creative word? It means the class would have a wonderful time while blundering more without the participation of an attorney."

"Yeah, you and Lewis Carroll. Lawyers aren't supposed to be poets."

"Hah! And I should listen to a journalist who doesn't know that his own national anthem was written by a lawyer?"

"Thank you Phil," said Tiron, "Mister Astor?"

Jude stood up. "I would summarize the personality of this class if I were not in it as inquisitive, enthusiastic, and a bit directionless."

"Miss Ambrose?" Cris's mind buzzed… *Ambrose?* As Cat stood up, he realized with a shock that he had never heard, or thought to ask about, Cat's last name. But she was already speaking.

"This body of students would be more formal, energetic, and lonelier without me." She looked around and Joshua from the center of the room winked at her, which elicited her sticking her tongue out at him.

Joshua grinned, "I sure know I'd be lonelier!"

"You'll get your chance to make your case Mr. Mainsted," said Tiron, "Mr. Lyons?"

Francois in front of Cat stood up. "Without myself, this class would have an energy overload likely leading to a misphased isolation arc."

After a moment Jerold spoke up and said, "I think he's saying that we'd have our circuits crossed."

"Right. We'll look to you for the position you seem to be volunteering for Frank," said Tiron. He nodded to Mike beside him, "Mr. Moyer?"

"Um… this body of students would be great and probably more impulsive without me."

The next two seats were empty, and Tiron looked to Allison at the far right "Miss Howell?"

"If I were not in this class," said Allison, "its actions and attitudes would be centralized more powerfully, but take less advantage of the fringe elements."

"Thank you Miss Howell. Mr. Andowski?"

Charles took his time standing up, struck a dramatic pose, and began orating like a Shakespearean actor. "The totality of character, the spheres of singularity and intercourse, yea! the very interchange of granular articulation, how it must needs languish; how it suffers inconsolably; how discards that bright expectancy which holds the anxious soul to its but scarcely realized destination, blindly groping in the midday aggregation of bewilderment, but for the solace of the fact that I, your humble servant, *I* am here."

The red-haired Rachel raised an eyebrow. "Really."

"I'm glad he said a *single sentence*," commented Phil from the back. Charles made an exaggerated bow and sat down.

Tiron smiled and moved on. "Mr. Mainsted?"

Joshua stood up and cleared his throat with a glance at Charles. "The sociological impact of my absence, though of course not noticed under the implied terms of the circumstances of that absence, would likely result in a body of students slightly more oriented toward a peculiar type of hive-mind that so often results from being motivated to agree without knowing what the terms of agreement are to be."

"Very good, Joshua. Mr. Kadid?"

Jerold stood up a bit nervously. "Taking a wild guess at what the class would be like without me, I'd have to say that they would be smart, enthusiastic, and better at interacting."

"Hm. Don't sell yourself short, Jerold. Mr. Ianoff?"

Cris winced at hearing his last name, which he also liked to go without. He stood up as casually as he could, walked to the door and left the room, shutting it behind him. He then began counting down from sixty, while listening intently to whatever he could hear through the door. Inside, Lisa in the front row said, "Does that mean he doesn't want to go?"

"He did go," quipped John.

Holly from the front left said, "Jason, you know him; what's he doing?" Jason just smiled and shrugged. Tiron waited patiently until Cris reentered and was by his seat again.

"The personality of this body of students would be very much just like that," he said, and sat down.

"That's cheating!" exclaimed Jude from the back.

Tiron simply smiled and moved to the next row up. "Miss McCory?"

Cris was feeling a bit clever and looked forward to whatever Tera would say. To his surprise, she looked a bit flustered and crestfallen. "I… actually didn't come up with anything," she admitted, "I guess you'll have to fail me on this assignment, but however much I thought about it, I just drew a blank."

"You can always make up an assignment at a later time," said Tiron, "Miss Wainstead?"

Rachel stood up, red hair practically glowing. "Without yours truly, this 'entire body of students', as Tiron put it, would be focused, enthusiastic, and diligent."

"We're less focused with you here?" quizzed Holly from the front.

"Yeah, she's quite a distraction," drawled Jason Two from the back, eliciting laughter and the hint of a blush from Rachel.

"Miss Sendik?"

Mary stood up. "Without me, this class would be much as it is, but more dangerous," she stated in her quiet deadpan manner and sat again.

"Does that mean you're safe?" asked Frank.

"Not necessarily." She turned around to hold his gaze for a moment, then Tiron went on.

"Miss DuChamp?"

Bethany stood up and stated, "The personality of this class if I were not in it would be absolutely lovely. Whether it would be different or not is entirely up to you."

"Mr. Sardic?"

Jason stood up. "The personality of this entire body of students if I were not in it would be less hypocritical." This drew a lot of quizzical looks, but Tiron simply went on.

"Mr. Target?"

William stood up. "If I were not in this class, I don't have the slightest idea what its personality would be, but I know that it would have less of a sense of continuity of development necessary to progress without creating repetitive loops."

"Thank you Mr. Target. Miss Marasta?" Susan stood up timidly. "If I were not in this class, the personality would likely be just as outgoing and friendly, but perhaps less comprehensively experienced."

"That's like what Heth said," interjected Charles from the middle right.

Allison behind him added, "I guess they're going to broaden our minds somehow."

"Miss McDower?"

Lisa stood up and smiled. "If for some strange reason I were not here, the class would struggle along valiantly, though somewhat poorer for the absence." Mike Moyer let out an involuntary snort from four seats behind her, for which he was immediately sorry as the ripple of laughter was directed at him. Tiron finished up with Holly in the front left corner.

"Miss Boyer."

"If I were not in this class, it would probably be smarter and more sophisticated, but with less of a sense of life."

"Thank you everyone," said Tiron, "Now Miss Rejul, would you be so kind as to verbalize the difficulty which had to be overcome in order to complete this assignment?"

"Is it complete?" interrupted Frank, "I mean, did we all pass? Like, except for Tera?"

Tiron raised one eyebrow at him. "Let's address that first. Miss McCory, as your resubmission of the assignment would you like to be responsible for grading the rest of the class?"

Tera looked up and cocked her head slightly. "Okay."

"You may proceed."

Tera stood up straight and looked slowly around the collection of expectant eyes trained on her. Finally she stated, "They all pass except for Jude's."

Jude clenched his red hair in both hands. "Why me!?"

"The assignment was specific to the personality of the entire body of students. One of the elements you mentioned was 'directionless'. But the direction of a class is not in the realm of its own personality; it belongs in the realm of the Professor."

"Is she right? Do I fail this assignment because of what she said?"

Tiron: "It doesn't matter if she is 'right' or not; she was given the responsibility to grade the class, and she has done so. Consider yourselves graded. Now, Miss Rejul?"

Heth looked like she was unsure of whether to stand or not, but remained seated. "The difficulty was that ostensibly we were describing everyone else, but the only way to do so was by revealing what we thought was special about ourselves."

"Yeah," said Jason Two behind her, "We had the choice between bragging and putting everyone else down, or being popular by degrading ourselves. It's a catch-22."

"I have a question," piped up Cat from her back left corner, "You said we would be learning what is possible in a real society; how does this do that?"

"Go ahead, Heth," said Tiron.

"Well… I would guess that what Tiron is doing is distinguishing between a typical society and a real society. Typically people want to get along, and one of the first things to disappear are individual traits to brag about or be ashamed of." Her confidence seemed to grow as she spoke. "But in actual practice this becomes finding polite ways to ignore strengths and weaknesses. If instead, we laid all our strengths and weaknesses out on the table it would be a lot more real, though I would guess it could be a lot more uncomfortable. We need to find a way of dealing with that discomfort."

Holly interjected from the opposite corner, "That's tough. It's like being totally exposed."

"And what is it about being totally exposed that makes it tough?" asked Tiron. "Susan?"

Susan squirmed a bit under the attention. "Um… there's things that are private, and there's things that we're willing to share. Being exposed blurs the line between them. It makes it hard to have any dignity because people might define you by your weaknesses."

"Quite," said Tiron. "And who can balance this out by stating the advantage to the individual of having their weaknesses exposed?"

Mike Moyer raised his hand, quickly lowering it as he remembered that it wasn't necessary. "Um… if people think you have a weakness and you overcome it, they admire you for it. It's like a way to impress people."

Phil spoke up from the back, "Yeah but pool sharks use that all the time to win games. Act like you're not as good as you are and fleece the suckers."

John beside him said, "It's a question of honesty. People who don't mind faking things can impress everyone around them more easily. I've heard that liars make excellent leaders."

"Correct," said Tiron, "So who can tell us what is the motivation for honesty in any society?"

There was a bit of silence, then Jason spoke up from his front corner. "There are two things that everyone longs for: love and understanding. We want to love and we want to be loved. We want to understand and we want to be understood. These are also the only two things we can take with us after we die. The motivation for being honest in our approach to others is inversely proportional to how much we think we can gain love or understanding on our own."

Mary Sendik was wondering why Tiron was looking pointedly at her until she remembered that she was Jason's designated interpreter. "I believe he's saying that if we feel like we're like part of a crew on a ship where everyone's job is necessary and together we make one working unit, we're motivated to be honest with everyone. But if we think we can operate without depending on anyone else, we have no reason to share."

"Is that an accurate assessment of what you said Jason?" asked Tiron.

"Yes."

"Very good. Then what are the necessary parameters for the setting up of an ideal society?"

Jude spoke up from beside Cat in the back corner. "You'd need to figure out what everyone's place is, where their strengths are best used, and put it together like a puzzle."

Jason Two drawled from the other back corner, "That could take forever. Half the time we don't even know what our own strengths are until we're in a situation that requires them."

"You asked the question backwards again," stated Tera quietly. Tiron raised one eyebrow at her and she went on. "You said "setting up" of an ideal society, which implies that someone is doing the setting up. That's impossible. Leaders have been trying to do just that for thousands of years with no lasting success; all it does is lead to various forms of class conflict. Historically the most successful societies have either been a monarchy in which the king was absolute and had very good advisors, or loose tribal cultures in which one's place was individually earned without being hampered by an outside set of rules. Everything else was simply a construct, and no matter how well the construct was set up, it eventually collapsed of its own weight."

"I thought kings were bad," retorted Holly from the front corner, "Wasn't the whole reason for the… um… Magna Carta to limit the misuse of royal power?"

Cris couldn't help jumping in. "Good or bad, I think Tera's saying that a strong Monarchy can be a very *successful* form of government. The trouble is that they tend to be family-based, and the way families run, it's traditionally difficult to get two good kings in a row. It mixes two very different ideas, government relations and family relations."

William Target broke in from beside Jason, "Well isn't that what why we set up the presidency in America? To eliminate the royalty problem?"

Tera began to say something but was interrupted by Frank sitting between Cris and Cat; "Sure, but look at the results. Virtually every president we've elected has had close blood ties to the royal family in England. And once a family gets wedged into the power structure, it has all the tools it need to stay there."

"That's kind of the whole point," said Rachel, "I think what Tera was getting at was that a government of the people, by the people, and for the people is still a government. By definition it's not 'we the people' no matter how much we're involved."

"Miss McCory, you had begun to say something." Tiron's powerful but soft-spoken voice slipped in and out of the discussion almost unnoticed.

"Yes, I was going to ask about the elephant in the room. It's obvious that you, at some point, are going to want this class to materialize into some form of an ideal society. Given that fact, will you be tending toward a monarchy, a tribal culture, or another structure?"

Tiron stood still for a few moments, almost as if he hadn't heard her. Then sauntered over to his desk, sat down, and looked over the class. "I will answer your question in a moment Miss McCory. And since you have asked a very specific question, you will get a very specific answer. But first let us review. What are the three parts of this class that I announced at the beginning of our first session?"

Bethany DuChamp behind Jason was rustling through her notes. "You said that the first part would be what is possible to achieve in a real society, the second part would be how that ideal, the idea of what is possible, is affected by its sociological environment, and the third part would be... um... to undertake a project together to understand how our environment, in turn, is affected by a real society."

"Yes. And how much of these objectives have been achieved to date?"

"We don't have the slightest idea," retorted Holly, "we don't know what's possible, we don't even know if there *is* an ideal, and how do we know what our environment is?"

The usually quiet Heth spoke up from the back of Jason's row. "If we focus, not on what has been said, but who is saying it and how, we might already have those answers."

Charles two seats ahead of her turned around, "For once I have absolutely no idea what you just said."

"Holly used the word *we*," said Heth.

"Oh..." said Cat, and stopped. Everyone turned around to look at her.

"Well?" asked Rachel.

"Um... we wouldn't use the word 'we' if we weren't already operating as a unit."

Rachel blinked. "Oh. Right." She turned around to Tiron. "Is that what you were getting at?"

"Ending a sentence in a preposition," muttered Charles in a sing-song voice.

Tiron smiled, "That is certainly part of it. Mr. Krisner, could you summarize for us the precise difference between being merely a collection of people and being a group that can use the word *us*?"

John thought for a moment. "Self-realization."

"Very good. Now Mr. Mainsted, be so kind as to explain the relationship between self-realization and what is possible to be accomplished by that self."

Joshua folded his arms and thought for a while. Finally he shrugged and said, "I have no idea. Potentially, anything is possible as long as nobody's stopping you."

"Keep going Mr. Mainsted. What are the potential sources of limitation?"

"Well... they would either come from inside, like not believing in ourselves, or they would be forced on us from some kind of outside resistance."

Tiron leaned back comfortably in his chair. "We'll avail ourselves of Jason for the next question. Mr. Sardik, explain the difference between the resources needed to address both inside resistance and outside resistance, and put it on the board for us."

Jason went to the board with a more impenetrable mask than usual. Facing the class, he clipped out his phrases with a deliberate pause between each one. "A balance between inner strength and outer strength is rare. The requisite abilities are diametrically opposed. Inner cohesion requires love, belief, and openness to the future. It's like the yolk of an egg." He wrote *Trust* on the left. "Outer cohesion requires experience, knowledge, and stamina. It's like the shell of an egg." He wrote *Purpose* on the right. "Between the two is the albumen, the white of the egg. It is designed not so much to keep the yolk and the shell apart, but to keep them apart *comfortably*." He wrote *Enjoyment* in the middle and faced the class. "The secret to maintaining inner strength and outer strength is the albumen." He gave a smile that Cris thought was a perfect parody of Tiron's, and sat down.

Tiron looked at Mary. "Miss Sendik?"

Mary started to speak, but Tiron interrupted her. "On the board, Miss Sendik." She made her way to Jason's words, faced the class, began to speak but changed her mind and turned to the board. Above Jason's words she drew a large egg holding a yolk with arrows inside pointing from the yolk to the shell and from the shell to the yolk.

Turning back to the class, she said quietly, "The object of being a yolk is to grow to get outside the shell someday, not just keep existing as a protected object. Similarly, the object of the shell is to protect the yolk, not itself, until then. Neither exists to simply be itself. Trust exists to strengthen purpose, just as purpose exists to nurture trust. In other words, the *roles* of each are opposite from their *identities*. When we accept that fact, we are flexible enough to take a punch and strong enough to resist one."

"Succinct and salient Miss Sendik, thank you," said Tiron. He stood up and leaned forward with both fists on the desk. "Now. Shall we institute a monarchy, a tribal culture, or another structure?"

After some silence, John spoke up from the back. "Well we kind of already have both."

"Yeah. We do," said Holly.

"And since a monarchy and a tribal culture are opposites, we also have 'another structure'," said Charles, "So really we have all three."

Tiron straightened up and began slowly pacing. "Then by your own admission you are halfway through the expectations for this course. We have yet to see the complete environmental effect because we have not yet tested ourselves in a larger society. This could be done in small steps, but it is my judgment that this particular..." he paused, turning his head a bit to the side, "...*organism* is ready to act. The last part of this course is to undertake a project that will educate you with the experience of seeing how society reacts to you." He went to the board and wrote "The Giving" on it. "The manner in which we will proceed is the giving of a gift to this university. Your assignment for next class is to determine what that gift will be." He looked at them with a straight face but a smile in his eyes. "Dismissed."

As the somewhat bewildered class began leaving the building, Charles caught up with Cris and Jason and elbowed them to a spot of muddy grass off the path. "Well?" asked Charles with a grin.

"Go on." said Jason. He had that same impenetrable look Cris had seen at the chalkboard.

"Okay, you know as well as I do that it's going to be you and me who decide in the end what this great 'gift' has to be. Let's take the bull by the horns and save ourselves the trouble of pretending that the democratic process is anything but a myth."

"That's so rude!" said Cat as she and Tera were just catching up to them.

Holly had overheard too. "Yeah, what are the rest of us, chopped liver?"

Jason smiled. "Let's meet and figure it out at the gazebo in the corner of the Quad in about an hour and a half. Some of us have Nature of Discovery right now with Professor Deon.

"Some of you?" queried Charles, "like who?"

"Um… Tera and I, Cris, Cat, Mary, Allison, Lisa, Heth, and Mike.

"And Jude," interjected Tera.

"Oh yes, Jude. Whoever can make it afterwards, have them meet us there." Jason smiled, "After all, Charles, you're the naturally born leader."

"Yeah, and the rest of us are just a pie for him to slice up any way he deems fit," said Cat with a snort.

Charles grinned. "I didn't mean to offend any slices of the great American pie;" he smiled grandly at Cat, "especially this particular slice."

"That's *Miss* American pie to you buster," she retorted.

We will skip the attendance of Leonard Deon's class as it was grueling, exasperating, and would likely make us wince. Let us instead go directly to the gazebo where the late afternoon air is just beginning to cool, and the cicadas are engaging in a not unpleasant background cacophony.

Chapter 13: I Tried to Tell You

"No, no; it is not that I am different from everyone else; it is that everyone else is pretending to be different from me." —*the Last Hierophant*

Charles was smiling —*not unlike a sideshow barker* thought Tera as the four friends and eight classmates converged on his expectant group, effectively doubling its size. A few more friends and curious passer-by's were hanging around the gazebo, which was large enough to hold about a dozen people, making for a colorfully eclectic crowd. Tera noticed that Jason had assumed a casual, almost lazy, demeanor. She knew him well enough to know that this meant he was anything but.

He spoke quickly and quietly to Cris, "Take the stage and summarize to everyone why we're here. I need to talk to Charles. If you get stuck, call on Charles as the organizer, but no more; he'll be ready," and slipped off to the side. Cris felt like he'd just been pushed out of a plane without a parachute, but Tera nudged him and Cat grabbed his hand.

"All three of us together," said Cat. They joined Charles on the gazebo just as he saw Jason signaling to him from the edge of the crowd and left them to the spotlight.

Cris looked around at the suddenly expectant faces. "I don't feel like a speaker," he muttered, "I feel like a midwife."

"Go with that," urged Tera.

Cris winced and cleared his throat. "I hope everyone remembers their Lamaze training," he started. There were a few belated chuckles by those who got it.

"I didn't mean *literally*," hissed Tera. Cris grinned and gave an exaggerated shrug.

"Okay, what I mean is we're going to be doing something new, and it can be as big as we want it to be, though if the analogy to having a baby holds, we may not have as much control as we think." He looked and felt a bit awkward, which was exactly what everyone needed to put them at ease.

Meanwhile, Jason was rapidly firing suggestions to Charles, though they sounded more like orders. "Put John and Rachel in charge; she's comfortable in the spotlight, easy on the eyes, and competent. He gives everything a sense of dignity and paces things. Call for ideas from the guys with egos first like Phil, Jude, and Joshua; that will keep them from retreating to the shadows. Follow up with the girls who don't prioritize attractiveness; this will pull the ones that do forward. Always be on the lookout for someone who isn't engaging and prod them. Don't put down bad ideas or you'll waste time in conflict; accept everything then move on; the good ideas will have a life of their own. But watch out for the position of Detractor; one individual always steps into it; face it head-on every time or it will grow. Use humor. Remember, you're a conductor, not a general. Now go."

Charles put his hands on his hips. "Um… if I'm the conductor, what does that make you? Oh. Right. The composer."

Jason smiled, "Who knows? If the gloves fit, step in the ring. Let's do this."

As Charles joined the trio on the gazebo, Allison was saying "…so don't we need to establish some sort of protocols to insure we're doing more than just taking the average of everyone's ideas?"

"We'll need to pick some kind of leaders whether we like it or not," began Tera, and was interrupted by Charles.

"…And just in time, I have an excellent suggestion for us all. We need someone who is dignified," he struck a serious pose, "experienced," he polished his nails on his shirt, "outgoing," he spread his arms wide, "personable," he grinned, "and beautiful," he finished up with a hand on his hip and a wrist against his forehead.

"And I suppose you're that person?" asked Holly.

"Moi? Thank you, I had no idea you thought so highly of me. I was merely submitting some candidates for everyone's consideration. Ladies and gentlemen, I submit to you…" he paused dramatically, "John and Rachel! C'mon up here so we can all look at you."

John had been, whether by accident or intent, standing close to Rachel and was thoroughly shocked by the sudden attention. Rachel took it in stride as if she had been expecting it all along. She grabbed John's hand and pulled him to the gazebo. "Let's go, Big Leader, your adoring crowds await!"

Even Cris was taken aback by the smoothness of the switch, though Tera's eyes darted rapidly through the crowd to Jason and caught a rare smile. She and Cris backed away to lean against the rail, but Cat greeted John and Rachel each with a big hug and held their hands up high, spinning them in a slow circle. "Long live the King and Queen!" she announced, eliciting a laughing cheer from everyone.

John, somewhat recovered by now, raised his hand and said, "Uh… shouldn't we put this to a vote? We're not the only ones qualified to be… wait, what *is* it we're supposed to be?"

"Excellent idea," said Charles, "Everyone here who votes to herewith coronate, without delay, King John and Queen Rachel as coregents of this class, signify by shouting *Yes!*" A roar of 'Yes!' filled the grassy quad, attracting a few more passers. "If any person has an objection to this ceremony, let him object now!" The expectant silence was unbroken. "Then let the ceremony commence! I call on our procurator of jurisprudence, Phil Mupp, to implement the ceremony of coronation."

Phil was quick on his feet and took the stage while Cris and Tera made room. Tera noticed Jason saying something to Mike, who dashed across the quad and started climbing a tangled oak tree. Then Jason was at their side. "Cris, fast as you can, go in the far entrance of Gingery Hall. There's a janitor's closet down the stairs on the left, it's unlocked. Behind the sink with a bunch of broom handles there's a golf club handle with no head. Bring it."

"Wait, how do you know this? And what's it for?"

"We can't have a coronation without a scepter. And I explore. Go!" He turned to Tera. "Do you think you could get any of the girls to give up their scarves? I don't see anything else we can use for crowns."

"*Girls?*" said Tera with one raised eyebrow, "Perhaps instead I could ask some of the *ladies?*"

"Um, good, great. Sorry, I never know what to call chicks." He was gone before she could retort, saying something to Phil and handing him a notebook.

Phil waved a hand with two fingers raised for silence. "Before presenting the articles of coronation, let us confirm the bylaws of the Kingdom." He held up the notebook. "This is the Book of Law which will regulate, govern, and be the final arbitration of all decisions made by both the Coregents and subjects."

"Isn't that Jason's notebook?" inquired Jude, "You want us all to do what he says?"

"I do indeed. Jude, would you please come up here and read the Royal Law so that its subjects may ratify or amend the edicts as they see fit?"

Jude strode up, took the notebook, and flipped through it. "It's blank!" He held it open for everyone to see. "It's completely blank!"

Phil took the notebook. "Indeed it is, which makes our ratification far more significant." Holding it high, he asked, "Do the subjects of this kingdom agree to honor, uphold, and abide by these rules, regulations, and edicts as the supreme Law of the Land?" He was rewarded with another rousing 'Yes!' He cleared his throat, "Then please respond by saying 'We do.'"

"*We do!*"

He turned to John and Rachel. "Do your majesties agree to honor, uphold, abide by, and execute these laws through prosperity and adversity, to the best of your abilities?"

"We do," they exclaimed in unison, though Rachel muttered to John, "I think we just signed our lives away."

Phil saw both Mike and Cris running back in the distance. "I see that the articles of coronation are coming," he announced, "Are the crowns… er, royal mantles prepared?" Mary Sendik and Heth Rejul handed up to him each of their scarves.

"This is silk, and Heth's is cashmere," said Mary, "They should be appropriate."

"Their royal majesties thank you for your gracious gifts offered willingly. Will the king and queen please kneel?"

"Why are they kneeling?" asked William, "Aren't they in charge?"

"They are kneeling in respect to the position being bestowed upon them, not to any secular or religious authority. A king or a queen is as much a subject of their position as their subjects are to them."

William wasn't satisfied. "Don't you mean that their subjects *and* the king and queen are subject to the royal position?"

"No. A subject *of* the crown cannot be subject *to* the crown; only the representative of the crown, the king or queen, can be subject to the crown itself, or every subject would be a king. Without a king or a queen to represent the crown, the subjects have no allegiance. Their allegiance is to the king or queen, or any other position granted *by* the crown." Phil was obviously enjoying himself.

Jerold spoke up, "Then who gives the crown itself its authority?"

Phil held up the notebook again. "Two things; this is the supreme law of the land, known variously in all governments as the Law of God, the Constitution, or simply 'the law'; historically its archetype is 'the word'. It stands alone as an authority needing no ratification. The second thing is all of us," he motioned around to the crowd, "who are sovereign *individuals*. Like the law, a sovereign individual stands alone on his own authority needing no ratification by a government. When a relationship for mutual benefit, historically called a *covenant*, is made between sovereign individuals and sovereign law, a new position is created to uphold the interests of both parties. These;" he motioned to John and Rachel who were kneeling, "are being coronated to govern in conformity to the best interests of both parties."

"So what's that make us then?" asked Lisa, who was attempting to put freshly curled blonde hair into a ponytail. *Wish I could still do that*, mused Cat.

"That makes you *both* sovereign individuals *and* subjects of the crown, also called *citizens*. It is a little known fact that no rights as a sovereign individual are given up by entering into the contractual relationship of subject or citizen. *Obligations* to fulfill contractual agreements can be enforced, but only as far as they do not infringe upon the *persona* of the sovereign individual."

Tera spoke up from behind him, "Then how do you explain how this happens in every culture? And America is certainly no exception."

"Simple," said Phil, "When the sovereign individual wishes his monarch or government to go beyond its role as Arbitrator of the Covenant and assume a role that serves his individual interests, he, by law, has relinquished his individual sovereignty and become what is known as an *asset of the state*, because their interests are now common. The historic word for this is *slave*. Likewise if the Law of the Land wishes the government or monarch to go beyond its role as Arbitrator of the Covenant and assume a role that extends its influence, the Law of the Land relinquishes its sovereignty over the land and becomes an *asset of the state*. The historic word for the result is *war*." He looked around at his blinking audience while Mike and Cris took the opportunity to hand him the golf club handle from the janitors' closet and the hornets' nest that Mike had disentangled from the tree.

Frank fired off one more question. "What about the king and the queen? Do they retain sovereign individual identities?"

"Excellent question," said Phil, turning toward Rachel and John. "When a physical sovereign individual assumes the position of arbitration, he or she is *crowned*, which comes from the idea of being *anointed*, which means *taking on the respective interests of*. So their *person*, including physical bodies, are treated with special respect as the *incarnation* of the relationship between the people and the law. So they can use the word *we* with full authority, meaning either *we the people* or *we the laws* as they see fit. But their sovereign identities as individuals remains intact so long as they have the discipline never to use an aspect of one position to advantage the other."

"They don't teach you all of this in your lawyer classes, or do they?" asked Jason Two.

Phil grinned. "No, you've got to do a lot of digging. Plus, I had a long discussion with Tera about the history of monarchies the other day."

Tera used this as an excuse to leave the gazebo and join Jason. "How did you know the nest didn't have hornets in it?"

"I kept dousing it with whiskey over a couple weeks at night while they were asleep. They finally decided to move and built a new nest over by Rhoboth Hall."

"You followed them?"

"No. But I do look up once in a while."

Phil was putting the hornets' nest in John's hands. "Receive this orb, plucked from the tree of education, knowing that the entire hornets' nest is vested to your care." As John gingerly took it, Phil whispered, *"You hold it in your right hand."* He then handed the golf club handle to Rachel, saying "Receive this scepter of justice and mercy; may it improve your swing," then whispered, *"in your left hand."* He stepped back and picked up the scarves. "Please rise for your oath." Placing the cashmere scarf on John, he asked, "Is your majesty willing to take the oath?"

"Uh… sure," said John.

"We are willing," hissed Phil.

"We are willing!" said John in a loud voice.

Phil placed the silk scarf over Rachel, which in fact looked terrific on her. "Is your majesty willing to take the oath?"

"We are willing!"

"Take this book in your hand," he handed them the notebook, *"Your free one,"* he whispered. "Do you solemnly promise to govern the heretofore unnamed assembly of individuals before you according to their customs?" *"We solemnly promise to do so,"* he whispered again.

"We solemnly promise to do so!"

"Will you with all your power execute your appointment in justice and mercy? *We will.*"

"We will!"

"Will you to the utmost of your power carry out this Book of Law and all that is written herein? Will you support, defend, and regulate both letter and tenor of this Law and all representatives authorized by it? *We will.*"

"We will!"

Phil turned to the audience. "I present to you their majesties King John and Queen Rachel.

Cat immediately shouted, "Long live Queen Rachel and King John!"

"Long live Queen Rachel and King John!" echoed everyone with a shout, followed by enthusiastic applause from the now sizable crowd.

Cris muttered to Cat, "You got the order reversed."

"Sucks to be slow, doesn't it?" she smiled triumphantly.

"Be it known that the privilege of being a subject of this kingdom extends to all loyal to the king and queen, whether initially in our class or not," announced Phil, when he was pulled aside by Rachel.

"Kindly announce that our persons will hold court regarding the purpose of this gathering. Now."

"Their majesties will now hold court for the purpose of facilitating the occasion upon which we gather," he announced, "And *my* job is done!"

As he left the gazebo, Charles moved to Jason's side and said, "Did we just create a kingdom?"

"In record time. By the book."

"This is crazy. It's like, the more control you give away, the more you have."

Jason smiled. "I tried to tell you."

"Yeah, well try it a little more overtly next time."

King John opened up a discussion for ideas of what to give the university. Rachel appointed Bethany DuChamp as Scribe of the Court since she had been writing everything down anyway.

Ideas came in like a swarm of locusts, but the king and queen seemed to have a natural knack for keeping things on an even keel. Cat and Cris found Tera and Jason watching the process and Cat asked Jason, "Shouldn't you be giving some advice to help out? There's some pretty weird ideas being thrown around."

"No, the energy is high right now. Once this wave passes there'll be a motivational lull. That's when advice will be useful."

"I guess Tiron's accusation of you could be true," said Cat.

"Maybe. That's probably what we're here to find out. Meanwhile, I promised Mary Sendik that I'd have dinner with her."

"Hm… Sendik and Sardic, sounds like a promising combination," teased Tera, producing Jason's customary wry smile. He made his way over to Mary, and they made their way to the *Copper Frog*. The scenario seems a bit curious, so let's join them.

"I didn't mean to be unkindly dramatic to you," we find her saying, "but I know you can take it."

"It's actually refreshing." They have their dinner already before them, and the restaurant is quiet enough to converse without artificial emphasis, "…though initially alarming. I don't know you well enough to tell what you plan to do with your abilities."

"I don't think any of us know that," she remarked.

"Tiron does."

She paused her fork in the air and thought. "Okay. I'll give you that." She let the silence hang and went on eating, much like a cat playing with an especially clever rodent. Jason decided not to match his eating style to hers and enjoyed his food on his own terms. Eventually she locked his eyes in her singular stare again. "I know you." Then she shook her head and looked away with her chin resting on her fork hand. "That's not what I meant," she entrapped his eyes again. "I know *of* you."

He enjoyed the power of her stare. "Go on."

"I know what someone like you can do. I know what someone like you *must* do. My grandmother told me about it because she once watched one."

"One what?"

"One of you."

"Oh." He thought about this. "How long did she get to watch?"

She smiled her dangerous smile. "A long time."

"Until...?"

"Until he destroyed everything."

"Ah." They were silent again for a few minutes. Today she had worn her dark hair in two braids; she seemed to enjoy using a variety of appearances and certainly had the looks to carry it off. He finally broke the silence.

"You're waiting for me to say that it's unfair to characterize what he did that way."

"Yes."

"Hm." A bit more silence. "It's unfair to characterize what he did that way."

"I know. That's what worries me."

Jason said quietly, "You don't ever want to end up on his side."

Fire seemed to flash from her dark eyes and she came alive. "It's unfair! People like that shouldn't exist! I *know* power!" A peal of thunder shook the *Copper Frog*, or else a stack of beer kegs fell over upstairs, it didn't seem to matter which. "I *know* what makes people tick! I *know* how to wind a room around my little finger! But you... You..." Her eyes became moist and she spoke in almost a broken voice, "You don't know anything. You're hardly a child. But you can walk in and take it all away. And you don't even know what you're doing." She resumed eating without looking at him. Finally she looked up and said, "You're such an idiot." They ate in silence until she had finished torturing the last of her food.

"That's everything, then." He asked the question as a statement.

She looked up with a bright smile. "Yep. Sorry about that, I tried to tell you before. Your turn."

He sighed. "Let's order dessert first. Here's the menu, I doubt there are live scorpions on it though, so you may have to settle for fire ants."

She flashed him a winning smile. "Death by Chocolate will do just fine."

Her smile had not taken the tension out of the air. He waited until she had taken her first bite of chocolate mousse, and sat back, looking at her. "It's too late."

"I knew it!" She jumped to her feet with both fists on the table, spilling her chair on the floor and stared at him breathing hard. A waiter rushed over, straightened up her chair, and quickly made himself scarce. Jason leaned forward and looked up at her.

"But I am not him and you are not your grandmother. Sit down." She sat. "Your grandmother watched him, she did not help him. He was faced with two impossible tasks, neither of which could be done without destroying the other. He was given up to the wolves, and everyone he trusted made sure that there would be failure and it would be his fault no matter what happened."

"You don't know..."

"I don't need to know what he did. And despite what you think happened, answer me this one question: Did he fully accomplish both tasks?"

"Yes, but..."

"The defense rests."

She was settling down a bit, though the staff was certainly not taking any chances. Their wine was refilled quickly and quietly. After a while her smile reappeared, this time a more sincere one. "Okay. Any clue how long? It's not like I anointed you king over me."

"Well according to your grandmother, until I destroy everything. In lieu of that, how about to the end of the semester?"

"That's banally literal."

"And has a pleasantly banal finality about it. Truce?"

She looked at him intently. "Do you *know* what a truce is?

"Yes."

"Very well. Consider it a done deal." She tossed her head. "I guess I've been a bit emotive."

He smiled. "Saves time. You were prevented from using your airhead persona in Tiron's class. Have you picked out a suitable replacement?"

"Oh don't remind me! Humans are so… agh, there's no word for it."

"Human?"

"Yes, humans are so *human.* Do you dance with the elementals?"

"No. And I'm not going to tell you what to do or not to do, so don't try to tease me into it."

"I always know what to do." She paused, thinking. "At least until tonight. Or a few nights ago when…"

"When you decided what you thought you were going to do with me."

"Yep. And now that we're working together, I don't even have to do that." Her smile this time was impenetrable. "I'd like to make amends for my …behavior tonight."

"Your gift is my debt."

"Oh, don't be like that. There's plenty of goodness to go around." She stood up, leaned over and gave him a kiss on the cheek. "You said you'd cover dinner. Thank you. Be nice to the staff so that I don't have to come back and do something nasty to them." She gave a most delightful laugh and sauntered out the door. The visibly relieved staff brought him the bill and he tipped on the high side. Making his way in the dark toward his waiting basement, he cut through a patch of brush, stopped suddenly, looked up, and cocked his ear. Yes, it was the sound he thought he heard, but it didn't belong *there.*

"You want me to come up and get you, don't you?" The kitten mewed again, and Jason found himself hopping out of a tree in the dark into a thorn bush with a kitten in his shirt.

Examining it in the light of his living room, he found it to be male, all black *of course*, and no injuries. "Okay, little one, but no promises. I'm out of milk, so I'll have to go out for some. Pee in the toilet if you have to go." He checked the refrigerator and there was a fresh half gallon of milk with a sticky-note on it that read, "For my friend".

"Does that mean you or me?" he asked the kitten.

Falling asleep with a purring kitten wrapped around his neck, he muttered, "Some evenings actually deserve the designation *weird*."

Chapter 14: Or Does He

Tera emerged from sleep with her usual efficiency and soon headed downstairs where her father was sitting at his customary end of the table with his chair at an uncustomary angle. There was an open paper on the table, and she could see from his demeanor that she was to read it. She approached and leaned over the paper. Then she sat down. It was immediately obvious which article had gotten his attention.

Birth of an American Kingdom

An event has transpired in our little town yesterday that could alter the course of history. Or it could merely pass as a brief but unusual movement by students enraptured by new ideals. In either case, there is now a full-fledged Kingdom residing (primarily) within the confines of Cherell University. King John (Krisner) and Queen Rachel (Wainstead) were officially coronated at a ceremony held in the northwest corner of the Quad, commencing at 4:48 p.m. in accordance with all requisite laws and with full ceremony. Tradition was honored by the presentation of the Orb of Dominion and the Scepter of Justice and Mercy. The Book of the Law of the Kingdom was duly held in hand by the Co-Regents during the swearing of the Oath, and is now held in trust by the appointed Scribe of the Court, Bethany DuChamp. Ratification of the coronation was unanimous both before and after the coronation by what are now the Subjects of the Crown. Following a brief but jubilant celebration, the court was immediately opened for a discussion of the business at hand, which appeared to concern what the business at hand was to be.

To this reporter's knowledge, no event of this kind has occurred on American soil since its birth as a Republic. While the US Constitution expressly forbids the United States from granting any title of nobility (Article 1, Section 9, Clause 8), and citizens naturalized from other countries must renounce all titles of nobility (USC Section 1448,

Subsection (b)), there is no precedence for the rise of nobility *within America itself,* so long as it is not granted by the government or by a Foreign State.

No name has yet been forthcoming for this Kingdom, nor have the contents of its Book of Law been proffered for our scrutiny. Many questions have been raised, not the least of which is: *What are their intentions?* So that the *unaffiliated* citizens in this town might be better informed as to the status of their new neighbors, a partial list is given below of those who have chosen to be Subjects of the Crown. Whatever its future, this reporter looks forward to a mutually beneficial relationship with the new Kingdom, and wishes King John and Queen Rachel a long and prosperous reign.

The rest of the article was a list of everyone in her class, but then it went on. Altogether there were fifty-one names on the list. Tera realized her mouth had dropped open, quickly closed it, and looked up at her father.

"First question," he said dryly, then separated each word with a pause; "What is in that book?"

"It's blank!" she exclaimed, "There's nothing… how did they get this information? What are they talking about?"

Her father pointed to the head of the article. "It was written by 'Laura', who is *Lady* Laura Elizabeth Arundell-Windsor. Her writing is *always* accurate. Do you have any idea what you've done?"

"We set up a kingdom to help organize the class. It was spur-of-the-moment! For crying out loud, the scepter is a broken golf club, and like I said, the Law of the Kingdom is a blank notebook!"

He buried his face in his hands for a moment. "Nothing like this is ever 'spur-of-the-moment'. The article says 'in accordance with all requisite laws and with full ceremony'. There's only one person I know who has done enough research to make something like this work." He lowered his head and raised his eyebrows. "You."

"I didn't… it wasn't even my idea! The whole thing just came together spontaneously! Someone…" she avoided naming Cat, "…said 'Long live the king and queen', then someone else picked it up and called on Phil who's studying law and knew the right things to say, then…"

"Stop there," he interrupted her, and sat thinking. "So you honestly don't know whose idea it was."

She thought rapidly, and decided that she really didn't. "No."

He was silent for a bit. "I will find out then." He rose and pushed his chair back in.

"Why?"

"Let me give you *one* example. What exactly was said when his and her 'majesty' swore fealty to the 'blank notebook' as you've called it?"

"Um… he asked if they would use all their power to carry out the Book of Law and everything in it."

"Exact wording, please."

"Um… let me think. 'Will you to the utmost of your power carry out this Book of Law and all that is written herein?' Yes, that was it exactly."

"I thought so. Do you realize that 'all that is written herein' includes not only 'all that is already written herein', but 'anything that ever *will be* written herein'?"

"Oh…"

"Do you realize that if I, for one, can anticipate the full implications of what is happening, that many others who have far more influence than me are going to take it a lot more seriously?"

"But…"

"I am going to nip this in the bud. I want you to go to these royal mock-ups and their herd and renounce your allegiance immediately."

She felt her face flush and her ears started ringing. Suddenly she was in a daze but everything was in excruciatingly sharp focus; she felt like she was seeing everything from another room. She watched herself slowly stand up and face her father with chin held high. "I am a subject of the Kingdom, loyal to King John and Queen Rachel. I will not renounce!" She watched herself turn on her heel and ascend the stairs with a straight back and forward gaze. A movement in the corner of her eye broke the spell; Lester had raised a finger in greeting as she passed his room. She leaned against his doorway, nearly collapsing.

"Well done." His quiet voice carried a surge of energy that filled her. "Be strong." He pause for a bit as if he were trying to remember something. ". . .Jason. . ."

"I know," she said, and groped through the waves to her room to bury her face in the pillow until the roar subsided into a background murmur. She composed herself and sat up. *Well. I guess I'll be a few minutes late for class.*

Jason resisted the temptation to take Lester with him to class. He was being trained to ride on Jason's shoulder, but had not yet grasped the implications of distance, and would leap at random times, obliging Jason to catch him in midair. He *had*, fortunately, understood how a box of loose dirt was to be used, allowing Jason to give him the run of the apartment. Nearing campus, Jason spotted a news truck at the filling station that was obviously from out of town. The pudgy fellow filling the tank looked less than conversant, so Jason headed went in and got in line behind the driver, who bought a pack of Kents. Jason got the same, and joined him on the walkway having a smoke.

"Ah, a Kent man," the driver remarked, "not too many of us around."

Jason smiled and looked around. "That your truck?"

"Yup. She gets around."

"You must be here for some big news. What happened, a cat get stuck in a tree somewhere?"

The driver scoffed. "Nah, we're headin' back. Story fell through."

"Well that must suck." They watched the pudgy guy putting away the pump.

"Tell ya though. I been in the business long enough to know a hush-up when I see one. Come here to do a story on some politics the kids were gettin' into, editor was all gung-ho on it, then he calls and says to get back pronto."

"Huh. Sounds like he got leaned on."

"Well. I ain't sayin' anything, but when you've been around awhile..." he trailed off.

"You might be back. The players change in politics, but it's always the same game," Jason smiled and turned to go.

"Yeah, ain't that the truth. You take care now."

"Yup. See you around."

Cris heard someone call his name on the way to Calculus; he turned to see Jason Thomas hurrying toward him. "Wait up, did you see the paper today?"

"Which one?"

"Cherell Sun. Here, check it out," he opened Laura's article to Cris, who soaked it in.

"Whaaat?" He looked up. "We're famous already."

"That's not all of it. Jude heard from his advisor that there's a meeting this afternoon with a bunch of the bigwigs about this... he's going to try to find out what they're so worked up about. William Target—y'know, senior in history sits by Jason—went to talk to Tiron but he wasn't in his office. And I talked to Holly and she says her advisor asked her to come in for a 'chat'; she'll tell us if she finds out what's going on."

"Well... okay, has anyone talked to the king or the queen about this?"

"John's in class right now. I'm meeting him and Rachel and Bethany in half an hour with whoever else shows up in Berkely Center. We've got to do something about this... can you make it?"

"Not that soon, I'm headed over to Calculus and that's an hour and a half. Let me think for a moment... have you talked to Phil?"

"Not yet."

"Okay, check with him, but if there's a storm coming, consider meeting in another location, either off campus or in

174

someone's dorm. If the staff is trying to make an issue out of this, they'll start with trying to divide between us being students of the university and subjects of the kingdom. Use of the student center for kingdom business is one of the first objections they'll use to shut us down."

"But there's political rallies and meetings there all the time."

Cris smiled, "Yes, there's a contradiction. But those kinds of gatherings are provocative and exclusive. The kingdom is non-threatening and *inclusive*. Trust me, they're not going to let university grounds be used for something they can't control."

"That kind of makes sense. But aren't dorm rooms university property?"

"Yeah, that's why I said ask Phil. There ought to be something legally protected about our 'domiciles' that falls out of their jurisdiction. I'll catch up with you after class and see what you guys have figured out."

"See if you can get in touch with Tera or Jason, I haven't seen them yet."

"You got it. Don't you have class today?"

Jason grinned. "We don't attend classes in Premed; we just walk around looking important."

Cris smiled and turned to go, "Well I'm a bit late now; keep looking important."

Cat drifted through the quilted shade and sunlight of overhead leaves feeling particularly invigorated. She had just sat through some class, though if asked which one she might have had to think for a while to remember. The luxury of just *being* had been growing on her. At some point she noticed that she wasn't walking alone, and found that Heth's almost invisible gait was matching her own. As neither had anything in particular to say, they enjoyed the morning sun spilling over the mismatched architectural anomalies of the college and the thousand little moods of the students crawling like ants between them.

"Fancy an early lunch?" asked Heth.

"I would. Let's go to..."

"...the Slogan," finished Heth for her, "I see you guys there a lot."

"I wonder what the king is doing tonight?" remarked Cat as they headed into town.

"That's from Camelot. I liked *C'est Moi.*"

"Was that a musical or a movie?"

"Both, eventually."

"Musicals are fun..."

"Yes, you don't have to take either the plot or the music seriously. They're relaxing."

"Is there any music you have to take seriously?"

Heth glanced sidelong at Cat. "I think it's difficult in this era."

"This decade?"

"No, the last few hundred years."

"That sounds like something Tera would say."

"And she'd be right."

"So what, you just like classical?"

"No, classical has just as many of the same kinds of problems. Plus what I *like* is a totally different subject. Me liking something doesn't make it music."

"What makes music music? Most people would say it's entirely subjective."

"That's the sour grapes argument."

"I don't follow."

"If you don't take the time to explore literature or even to learn to read well, you can make a good argument that Dr. Seuss books are the best ones ever written. If you get are backed into a corner for that opinion, you can simply claim that he's the best according to your taste. The fact that you have never bothered to read anything else makes your argument disingenuous.

"Hm. Y'know, you could apply that same argument to people's stances on morality."

"That sounds like something Cris would say."

Cat laughed. They were just entering the Slogan and Heth picked out seats away from the window. Cat settled in sideways with her feet across the bench. "So you're saying that music and art are more than just taste."

"Yes, that's it."

"But I thought you were in mathematics. That's not exactly art."

"Actually, it is. When you step back and look at the world holistically, everything operates using the same principles."

"Which are what?"

Heth smiled. "You want me to just lay out the principles of every discipline and natural system like they're so many pieces of candy?"

Cat put her menu down. "Yes, please."

Heth looked at an imaginary watch on her wrist. "Let's see, how many years do we have..."

Cat interrupted, "First tell me why you went into mathematics."

"Um... okay; because it's not a real science; it's an application."

"But... most people would say mathematics is the scientific ideal."

"And most people would be wrong."

"What about a 'mathematical proof'? Isn't that the gold standard of science?"

"It would be if there were such a thing. In order to make a mathematical model of something, you have to choose parameters. It's those chosen parameters that determine the outcome, not the mathematical process.

"So it's just what assumptions you use?"

Heth made a wry face, then laughed. "Has anyone told you yet that you have a habit of making really complex things seem simple and obvious?"

"Um, yeah I get that a lot from the others."

"You're like Beethoven." She shook her head. "Anyway... so all you can prove with a mathematical proof is that you chose parameters that would work for the solution you wanted. Which is more or less exactly what you just said; the assumptions."

"Okay, I get that. So how does it explain why you went into mathematics?"

"Because once you stop pretending that math is anything different from the keys on a piano, you can use it the way it's meant to be used..."

"...as an art!" Cat interrupted.

"Exactly." Heth leaned forward. "Things like calculus and topography aren't great truths that need studied; they're just different palettes to make whatever painting you want. One palette has globs of oil paint on it and another has gobs of acrylic."

"So if you don't like the way topography works, you can just change the assumptions and make it work the way *you* want it to."

"It's so easy to talk to you."

"So what does this have to do with the ...candy principles... or whatever we were talking about?"

"Well, say with music; if you change your basic assumptions, it helps to know how music works. If you make the assumption that dissonance between notes is beautiful and relaxing, you might have trouble maintaining an audience."

"Good morning, what can I get you today?" Andrea's shift hadn't started yet, but the dark lad who took their order had a winning smile.

"Chicken salad, ranch dressing," beamed Cat.

"Chicken salad, vinegar," said Heth, "and whatever soup you've got."

"It's French onion."

"Ooh. Get me some too," said Cat.

"And to drink?"

"Water."

"Water."

"Thank you ladies," he sauntered off.

"We're *ladies*?" asked Heth.

"Well, if the shoe fits..."

"I would have preferred *princesses*."

"We'll arrange that. Now you have to tell me exactly what makes music music."

"Okay, you asked for it. The three dimensions of music are rhythm, melody, and harmony."

"That's it? Those are the pieces you put together?"

"They're not pieces. *All* of a musical composition has rhythm, *all* of it has melody, and *all* of it has harmony. You can't 'add' say, melody, or take it away; it's always there in every part."

"So if you can't do anything about them, how do they matter?"

"Creativity and art are in the relationships between them."

Cat thought for a moment. "That sounds big. But what if someone *does* take away the melody? Say you have a symphony that just plays one note for half an hour."

"It's still melody. A very monotonous and probably irritating melody, but a melody nonetheless. Look at it this way: light that we see can be split into red, green, and blue just like paint can be mixed into any color with red, yellow, and blue. If we filtered out all the blue light in this room we would just see things in shades of green, yellow, and red. But the reality that we see would still be defined by the absence of the blue light; filtering it out doesn't get rid of the fact that it's real; it just demonstrates how much it is a part of the other two because a complete picture is impossible without it."

"Oh. That's like something Cris said to me about if your brother dies. You can't really say that you don't have a brother because his absence still affects you; he said that yes you still have a brother, just a dead one."

"That's a macabre way to put it, but yes. So the first step in any discipline is to learn what the basic principles are, and the next step the relations between them. If you set up three filters to make white light and used the paint-mixing three instead of the light-mixing three, you'd never get it right."

"So how do you get the basic principles of *every* discipline out of these? Like mathematics probably isn't based on red, green, and blue."

"Easy. The principles—I call them *dimensions*—of every subject are always different, but they also interact in the same way in each case."

"That's kind of nuts. Doesn't that make it too easy? Boiling everything down to three ...dimensions?"

"Actually it makes it much deeper, just more organized. In architecture they have a saying that 'Form follows function'. What they don't seem to have realized yet is that aesthetics also follows function, because 'function' is the *source* member of the three dimensions of architecture."

"So one of them is the source... what are the other two?"

"The second one is the tangible one; it's what you actually see; I call it *manifestation*. In architecture it would be the form, because that's what you actually touch and see."

"And the third?"

"It's the active force that ties everything together and makes it work. In architecture it's the aesthetics, both how you appreciate it and how you use it. Appreciating the *form* is what most people think of when they say aesthetics; how it looks to them or how much they like it. But just as important is appreciating of the *function*; how they use it, how fun or easy it is to use."

"So transfer these over to music."

"Sure. *Rhythm* is the source member, *harmony*—what you hear at any one moment—is the tangible member, and *melody* is the active force member."

"Oh. So most song writers start with a tune—a melody—and treat it like source and try to make a rhythm and some harmonies from it..."

"...they're working backwards and creating all kinds of problems for themselves, yes."

"And this happens in mathematics too?"

"Every single discipline."

Their waiter was back and efficiently set out salads, soup, and water. As he finished with Heth he said, "I hope everything is to your liking your highness," smiled, and sauntered off again.

"He's got good ears," muttered Heth, a bit embarrassed for once.

"Maybe he's looking to marry into a position of prestige."

Heth sniffed. "He may submit an application to the Minister of Relationships for consideration."

"What you were saying about composing music…?"

"Oh. Before you go on, the *composition* of music has different dimensions than music itself."

"Yes, that's what was confusing me. Because when you write a song, you're not starting with the rhythm, you're starting with the reason you want the song. Wouldn't that be like the source dimension."

"Yes."

"Doesn't that get confusing?"

"Only if we make it confusing. Since the dimensions are there whether we like it or not, it's pretty much up to us to screw them up. Which we're very good at doing."

"What are the dimensions of mathematics then?"

"It depends on which branch you're talking about. Most people mean numbers when they say mathematics, and the dimensions of numbers are amount, order, and cycle."

"Amount I get, but order and cycle?"

"Fifteen is ordered fifth in the second cycle of ten. We count to ten, start over with another cycle of ten, and when we get to its fifth part, we're at fifteen. Fifteen is the amount, fifth is the order, and the second ten is the cycle. The fun thing about dimensions is that any two give you the other one."

"I have an aversion to math, so let me skip to something completely unrelated. What about… like anatomy?"

"Nervous system, cardiovascular system, and organ systems."

"Ocean navigation."

"Position, distance, and direction. Any two of those will allow you to calculate the other one."

Cat blinked, "You're like totally on top of these. Have you taken courses in all these subjects?"

Heth rolled her eyes and said nothing for a bit. "I was going to. In my naiveté I actually prepared a doctoral dissertation on the subject. I got slapped down so fast… I'm starting to think that may be why Tiron tapped me."

"Slapped down? But isn't this approach like the key to understanding a subject?"

"It should be. But I was all excited about my own ideas and didn't do my homework thoroughly enough. I should have started with my own subject."

"Um… what would you call the study of how to study things?"

"That's the conflict. The dimensions of learning a subject are understanding, knowledge, and wisdom. But the dimensions of *teaching* a subject—far less getting *paid* to teach a subject—or even setting up an institution to *perpetuate* teaching like what a university does—are rather different. Suffice it to say that it is the job of academia to systematically hide, destroy, or confuse the principles of every subject."

"Oh." Cat had finished her salad and the soup was finally cool enough to enjoy. "That sounds like… either you're insane or they are."

"Right," said Heth wryly, "guess which one they chose."

"But… I know it must be a huge subject, but can you summarize why anyone would want to hide a method of understanding a subject?"

"Sure. Because unlearning a method is more painful than being free."

"So once you've learned one way of doing things…

"…you almost never unlearn it. Look at driving. Once someone learns how to drive, they can keep driving for the next fifty years and their driving doesn't improve one iota. After the first six months or so, no one's driving ever improves unless they take special courses or something."

"But we do get better at things the more we do them."

"Coach Vince Lombardi once said, 'Practice does not make perfect; only perfect practice makes perfect.' Anyone can do the same thing over and over. To learn, you have to do it in a new way every time you do it. And to do something new, you have to discard any *methods* that you have learned."

"So a university…

"…teaches methods. And defends them to the death. You can add all the knowledge in the world to a subject, but if you don't improve on the methods, all you're doing is handing more bricks to someone treading water."

"Oh. And if you discard all your methods, you wouldn't have anything to teach."

"Well you've still got the knowledge. That can be piled up ad infinitum. And the wisdom of how to apply it is largely controlled by the market. You don't have a choice but to find a way to make the knowledge work. What falls through the cracks is the understanding."

"Which is supposed to be the source of the other two."

"You got it." Heth leaned back. "So on the one hand, if you're *really* going to learn, you have virtually no competition because no one else is doing it. On the other hand, anyone who finds out what you're up to is going to move heaven and earth to stop you."

"Yeah. It's not so much *what* you're doing that's a threat to them, it's the fact that you *are* doing it."

"Right. And if you're the kind of person who is going to keep going anyway, it's the fact that you *exist* that gets resented."

"So… where does that leave you? Why mathematics?"

"Every system has to be protected and controlled." Heth had a bemused smile that made her look slightly feral. "When you find out that most sciences are built on a house of cards, it's a simple matter to find the bottom card and pull it out. Like pulling back the curtain in the Wizard of Oz."

"You're saying that mathematics is a house of cards?"

"Yes. The things they say are impossible or extremely difficult aren't in the slightest. They're only difficult when the methods of mathematics taught in universities are used. Academia has manufactured a way of approaching numbers that makes it impossible to see, say, the pattern in the decimals of pi. All they have to do is make sure that everyone uses this method, and they can use these 'impossible' algorithms to protect their securities."

"It's really that easy?"

"No, of course not. You still have to do your homework, and since no one is going to help you, you've got to be pretty dedicated. Basically you have to reinvent the wheel and rediscover fire to find out what fire really is, or how a wheel really works. But once you get started it kind of snowballs."

"I suppose it would be intrusive for me to ask you how far you've gotten."

Heth smiled her feral smile again. "Far enough to have fun. A *lot* of fun. Not the kind that seems to be approaching our table though."

Allison Howell and Jerold Kadid were making their way toward the girls looking somewhat concerned. "They've got French onion soup today!" Cat announced cheerfully.

"Hop in," said Heth, sliding over. Jerold sat down nervously by Heth, and Allison slid in with Cat.

"Have you heard what's going on?" asked Allison.

"Not unless the Pentagon has announced that Iran is an imminent threat again," she smiled, "Tera says you can set your watch by it. So what's going on?"

"My professor in Atmospheric Thermodynamics pulled me aside," blurted out Jerold, "and grilled me on the kingdom. I had no idea what to say to him; he seemed upset. Then I got a call from someone in the dean's office I never heard of, and *they* gave me the same third degree."

"And I don't have to tell you how political it is in Education," said Allison, "My advisor is looking for me right now." She grimaced and looked around, "I kind of told her I'd be here, so you've been warned."

Heth said quietly, "Well..."

"We've got to do something!" said Jerold, "It's like everyone's going crazy... sorry for interrupting you Heth."

Heth smiled. "Have you thought about ordering some French onion soup?"

Jerold looked at her confusedly. "But..."

"It's really good," chirped in Cat, "Try some. Are you hungry?"

"Yes, but..."

"Okay." Cat waved to the waiter who was already on his way over.

"We are honored to have you at our humble diner, my name is Jimmy. What can I get for you?"

"I may have to go soon, nothing for me," said Allison.

"Jerold will have some of your French onion soup," said Cat, "and he wants a cherry coke."

"Very good." He directed his attention at Heth. "And anything else for your..." he hesitated at the word *highness*.

Heth lifted her chin. "That will be all for now Jimmy."

"What's going on with him and Heth?" asked Allison as Jimmy sauntered away.

Cat leaned back in her customary perfect stretch. "Ah, spring... the time when flowers bloom and the heart turns to loftier ideals." She relaxed and crossed her arms on the table. "I think he's hoping to marry up."

"He's got quite the mischievous streak," muttered Allison. "So what are we going to do about the kingdom?"

"I think Cat has an action plan that we can all participate in quite effectively," stated Heth.

"Oh good, let's hear it,"

Cat looked at Jerold and Allison complacently. "We do absolutely nothing."

"We give up?" asked Jerold.

"No, that's doing something. If they want us to panic, we don't. If they want us to defend ourselves, we don't. If they want to turn it into a chess game, we don't play."

Heth spoke up. "In order for them to accomplish whatever it is they're doing—which is unlikely to be supportive—they have to get us either to participate or resist. Then they own the kingdom."

"And it's not theirs," stated Cat.

"But we can't stand by while they figure out how to destroy us," exclaimed Jerold.

"To destroy us, they need our participation," said Cat.

"Which is disingenuous," continued Heth, "because they have no part in the kingdom. We don't need their permission or approval. If they can convince us that we do, we're allowing someone else to dictate the terms of our freely chosen 'covenant' as Phil called it. They either need to approach us with a covenant of their own, or accept the terms of ours."

"Tera says that this is exactly what's been happening between state rights and federal authority in America since even before we were a country," mused Cat.

"Ah, I think I see," said Allison, "If they want to change the kingdom they should join. If they want to challenge it, they need their own kingdom. Everything else is incidental."

"But what do we do in the meantime?" asked Jerold as Jimmy brought his soup.

"We eat our soup," said Cat cheerfully, "and whatever else we want to do."

"But I don't know if I can take much more pressure like this."

Heth spoke up, "Rain is good for everyone; if you don't like getting wet while it's raining, don't hide inside, carry an umbrella."

"Is that supposed to be some kind of mystical analogy? Because I don't think I get it," complained Jerold.

Allison jumped up, "There's my advisor waving to me outside. Thanks for the advice, I'll pass it on." She hurried out the door to join a frazzled lady who seemed to be doing her best to look concerned.

"Right," said Jerold, "So where do I get an umbrella?"

Heth shrugged and looked at Cat. "Know where to get an umbrella?"

"Hm. That gives me an idea. Neither of you have seen Jason's apartment yet, have you?"

Heth shook her head slowly, interested. Jerold said, "Jason One, the kid who seems like he's going to start a fight with Tiron at any given moment?"

"Yes, him. Why don't you both come over tonight? I'll give you directions."

"You're inviting us to *his* place?" asked Heth.

"Of course. I'm his social secretary," grinned Cat.

"As of when?"

"As of right now. Don't worry, his door is always open, and I mean *always*."

"Even in winter?" asked Jerold.

"Well, I meant it's always unlocked, and there is no possible way to surprise him. He's probably setting up for us all right now."

"Heck, if you're sure it's okay, sounds like fun," said Jerold.

"*Heck?*" said Cat, "Sounds like you've been hanging around with Mike Moyer."

"I like a challenge," smiled Heth, turning a bit feral again.

In a small cabin smelling of old books and new spices, Tiron leafed through a characteristically gaudy self-help paperback and chuckled. "All well and good if one forgets that water flows downhill. Those wishing to gain by being willing to be fooled are doomed to be plucked when ripe. What does one do when the orchard is overripe? The 'short con' I suppose. Substitute resources for time from the long con." He looked slowly around at the structural elements of his cabin. "Seems this could be duplicated. Time to play with banks and attorneys. Hm. I may need a scarecrow."

Chapter 15: The Other Side

Cris had accompanied Tera home, ostensibly to pick up a fan she was giving him to use in his dorm room; in actuality because once he saw the state she was in he grilled her and got the story of her confrontation with her dad. He insisted she use him to get a breathing space until she got her feet back under her. They needn't have worried; upon arrival it was quickly apparent that William was out.

"Well," quipped Cris, "it looks like I'm the only one in your fan club tonight."

"I've been waiting all night for you to crack that stupid pun. C'mon it's upstairs; you have the rare honor of seeing my room." She led the way up the stairs and into her room."

"Um… impressive lair. Who was that in the room at the end of the hall?"

"Thank you. That's Lester my grandad."

"Yeah, you told me about him. I think he was signaling as we passed; I could have sworn he moved his hand."

"Oh." She stood thinking for a moment. "Okay, here, take the fan; let's go see. I'll introduce you, though he may not respond." He followed her into Lester's room. "Hi grandpa, this is Cris…" Lester was moving his right hand back and forth in a peculiar way.

"I'm new here," muttered Cris to Tera, "but it looks to me like he wants to write something."

"It does." Tera snatched up a pad and pencil from the rolltop and carefully placed them in Lester's hands. He was staring straight ahead at nothing in particular, but his hand moved with almost painful deliberation, writing one slow letter after another, then he relaxed completely with the pad on his lap and the pencil slipping to the floor. Cris picked up the pencil and looked at the notepad with Tera.

It read, "**TWO DAYS + one. SEE BARI then.**" Tera's mouth slowly opened as she looked at it.

"I take it this means something to you?"

"Um… yes, or maybe; Grandpa can you say anything right now?" She may as well have been addressing the chair for all the response she got. "Uh, Cris let's go. Let me… no, put this in your pocket. The whole pad. Here, let me put the pencil back. Um… is there anywhere we can go?" She was getting more flustered by the moment. "Go sit on the top of the stairs and tell me if dad comes home. I need to call someone… who should I call…"

"Tera! Slow down," he held her by the shoulders and looked into her eyes. "Let's go outside right now and take a nice slow walk around this ritzy neighborhood of yours while you get your head together."

She looked at him and took a breath. "Okay."

It was more than a block along sidewalks decorated with shadows of leaves thrown by streetlamps before she spoke.

"In two days it's my nineteenth birthday. 'Bari' is short for 'barrister' Lester's nickname for Tony Steller, one of his attorneys."

"One of?"

"Yes. Tony handles his will."

Cris stopped. "Oh."

"There's more."

"And there's a bench at the end of this block. Let's go sit."

He sat leaning back with his arms along the top of the bench while she leaned forward and rocked back and forth. "I wish I could figure it all out. Let me see the note again." He handed her the pad and she stared at the letters trying to comprehend all the implications. "I guess it doesn't hurt to just ramble, it's not like it's going to make a difference. Or maybe it will, I just don't know. Okay, did Jason tell you about our family get-together over the holidays?"

"You both did. Sounds to me like you fill the house with baking soda and vinegar and see what happens when you shake it."

"Exactly. Any idea what would keep such different people coming back every year when any way you cut them, the one half can't stand the other?"

"Well... from what I hear, mostly respect for Lester. He was kind of the family patron, wasn't he?"

"Not *was*. Is."

"But he's not... what do you call it? ...legally competent right now, is he?"

"He set up a trust while his mind was still sound. That's how Uncle Tom keeps his Bible ministry afloat. That's how Aunt Sylvia—not my real aunt but that's what I call her—funds her stem cell research lab in Cambridge. That's how Andy keeps an edge in sales... I could go on."

"And ...your dad?"

Tera grimaced. "Yes. Dad makes good money as a professor and consultant, but we live like we do because he's in charge of the trust fund. For now."

"For now?"

"No one knows what's in Lester's will except Tony. Lester chose him because he knows how to keep his mouth shut; besides they go way way back. All anyone knows is that the trust will be finalized when the will is read. Lester told everyone plainly that once he was gone, everyone was on their own."

"Oh." The note was starting to look rather ominous.

"There's more."

"I'm scared to hear it." Cris thought for a bit. "But even more scared of not hearing it. Go on."

"One year ago, grandpa had a lot more clarity. Two days before my birthday, he asked me to sit down, then he just stared at me for a long time. I though he was having one of his episodes. Then he said, 'I'm not giving you your birthday gift this year, even though you're eighteen. You're not ready for it yet.' Then suddenly he smiled this great big smile and said, 'I'm going to be so proud of you!' And that was it. I never had the slightest idea what he meant."

"Did you get a birthday present from him that year?"

"No. First time ever. Even mom and dad were puzzled but they chalked it up to his condition."

"Are you... his only granddaughter?"

"By blood, yes. The family's kind of a large collection of different kinds of relationships."

"And now this."

"It's scary. I don't know what it means. Everything that I can think of that it *might* mean is even scarier, to quote you."

Cris' practical side was recovering. "All right, let's go one step at a time. We can kind of assume that when he wrote 'TWO DAYS' that somewhere in there he knows very well that it's your birthday in two days."

"It's hard to believe, but if we go with that..."

"Let's just assume that for now and forget about the implications. Next he writes in lower case, '+ one'. The obvious meaning is three days from now, the day after your birthday. Don't think about any implications, let's just look at what he wrote."

"That's hard to do."

"Well I'm here with you now and you're probably not eager to show this around so *use* me while I'm here. Next he writes in capitals, 'SEE BARI', and in case you're wondering when or why, he writes in lower case letters, 'then.' That matches the lower case of the '+ one'.

"I'm supposed to talk to Tony three days from now."

"Yes. That's the simple practical instruction you can draw from this."

She shuddered and he instinctively put his arm around her. "But this could mean that... I mean, no one's allowed to look at his will until..."

"He didn't write 'Look at my will.' He wrote 'SEE BARI'. That's all you have to do, and that's all you can do. Everything else is completely out of your hands."

She slumped forward with her face in her hands. "Yeah. Yeah I guess it is."

They sat there in silence until he began to feel a bit awkward. "Well… Cat is taking Jerold and Heth over to Jason's tonight. Do you want to join them?"

"No… I just… Take me home, Cris."

He led her back through the neighborhood's incandescent shadows and guided her up the walk to her door, and waited. She finally sighed, straightened her shoulders, and looked at him from shadowed eyes. "Thank you Cris." He turned and left without a word as she walked into her house as if it were for the first time. Her father glanced up from the table and seemed about to say something, then stopped. She smiled at him and headed toward her bed, leaving his quizzical expression unanswered.

On the other side of town Jason was just pouring from a pot of tea into four cups when the door burst open with Cat yelling, "Surprise!" Heth and Jerold gingerly followed her in. She put one hand on her hip and waved at the tea cups, "Toldja guys. No way to surprise him."

"Welcome," said Jason, "refreshments are served."

"Tea?" asked Jerold incredulously.

Heth sniffed the air, "It's Nilgiri tea, Jerold dear; one of the highest altitude grown teas in the world. Doesn't cloud and doesn't get bitter. Very thoughtful Jason."

"It's *tea*," complained Jerold.

"House rules dude," said Jason, "There's Budweiser in the fridge. But you gotta drink your tea first."

"I drink that cup of tea and I can have beer?"

"All you want."

Jerold strode over, picked up his tea, and started to drink it. "Hot!" he sputtered, spilling half of it down his shirt to Cat's delight.

"I brought Jerold over to teach us all manners," she explained.

"Manners?" smiled Jason, "I was all geared up to talk about meteorology."

Jerold grabbed the opportunity to recover; "Okay, smarty, I got you on this one. Tell me one thing I don't know about the weather."

Jason put the tea pot down and put on a thoughtful expression. Cat spoke in a stage whisper to Jerold, "Don't let him fool you, he's just pretending to think."

Jason ignored Cat and continued, "Why is it that when two typhoons or hurricanes are in proximity, in every recorded case they have moved toward each other when positioned north-south, and away from each other when positioned east-west?" He looked at Jerold's furrowed brow. "Or haven't they noticed that in meteorology yet?"

"There better be beers in there," said Jerold, taking another sip of his tea.

Heth had picked up her tea and was holding it with both hands under her nose as she walked around looking at everything in the apartment. "This is wonderful," she exclaimed.

Cat plopped into the only easy chair. "Keep complimenting him. I want to see him blush."

"Before things get totally out of control," said Jason, "I would like to know: To what do I owe the honor and pleasure of this visit?"

There was a moment of silence then Heth turned to Jason and said, "Music."

"Music?" Jason tilted his head, interested.

"And architecture!" exclaimed Cat, "Heth was explaining music to me when we got on to architecture as an example, then like other things like navigation and anatomy and playing cards with math, or building houses out of them..."

"Slow down!" said Jerold, "start with just one thing." He drained his tea and made a beeline for the refrigerator. "You *do* have Budweiser!" he exclaimed happily, "Now I can listen to anything. As long as it's one at a time."

Cat glanced at Heth, then went on. "Okay, she was saying there's dimensions to everything that are always different but there's always three of them and no matter what subject it is they work the same way…"

Heth cleared her throat, "So do you remember what we said the three dimensions of architecture were?"

"Form, function, and um… prettiness."

"*Aesthetics*," said Heth, "both how it looks *and* how well it works."

"Right, prettiness," said Cat, "because it should look pretty and work pretty well."

"Okay," said Jason, "dimensional correspondences across disciplines. Were you distinguishing between inherent properties and compositional protocols?"

"Huh?" choired Jerold and Cat simultaneously.

"You know, dimensions of things that you *study* as opposed to dimensions of things that you *make*."

Cat glanced at Heth, whose face had gone completely feral. Her eyes were slits with dark flashes, and her lips were slightly parted showing two perfectly formed cuspids. "So Jason. You consider yourself competent to discuss the mathematical properties of concepts?"

"I've looked into them." He smiled brightly and innocently, which didn't fool Cat. She was relieved to see that Heth wasn't disarmed in the slightest. "Though I like to think of them as the *geometrical* properties of concepts." He smiled again. "I like to draw things."

"Oh boy," said Jerold. He opened the fridge, took out two more beers, and headed for the far corner of the room where he sat down by the bedroom door. "What are you doing?" asked Cat.

"Jerold's rule No. 2 for surviving duels. Don't stand between the dueling parties."

"What's rule No. 1?"

"Don't *be* one of the dueling parties."

"I have some Russian-grip foils in the bedroom," said Jason brightly, "or would you prefer a Rajput sabre?"

"He's parried the drawing cut," stated Heth, stepping forward and tilting her head slightly, "let's see how he handles the twisting thrust. Name the four-system of music."

"Theme, range, resonance, composition in that order."

"Sound doesn't have to have a theme," objected Jerold.

"Sound, noise, voice, speech, tone, and music are all different realms with their own sets of concepts," said Jason. "The trick to understanding the distinctions is to clarify your purpose for making them."

"Wait! Slow down!" exclaimed Cat, "I thought there had to be exactly three dimensions, not four."

"She asked about the directions of music, not the dimensions. There's always three dimensions which are all about capacity and have no fixed center. And there's always four directions which are completely centric and emerge from the central concept."

"I call them core dynamics," said Heth.

"Yes, that works well. I use 'directions' for the geometrical approach. How far have you gotten with exploring subjects?"

"How far have *you*?"

"I'm not sure; I've kind of internalized the structure, so it's not that difficult to roll them off."

"Mechanics then. What are the dimensions?"

"Mechanics like gears and levers, or like motors?"

"Both."

"Gears and levers and moving things, the dimensions are Stroke, Position, and Timing. Energy systems like motors the dimensions are Magnetism, Motion, and Electricity." He turned to Cat, "When we're talking about physical systems, it's easier to see that each dimension always lies at a right angle to the other two. It's like a Cartesian coordinate system."

"Hey, I understand that one!" said Jerold, "Electricity is produced at a right angle to the magnetic field the wire is moving through, but the motion itself has to be at a right angle to both the magnetic field and the direction of electricity."

"Is that like what you said that any two give you the other one Heth?" asked Cat.

"Yes," said Heth, "only it's a bit more complex. In Jerold's example, the magnetism could be north pole or south pole. The electricity could be moving up the wire or down the wire. The motion could be from right to left or from left to right. Each of the three dimensions has two opposite faces."

"You've considered dimensional polarization!", said Jason, "Can you apply that to music for us?" When she hesitated, he said, "You know, the two opposite sides of Rhythm, Harmony, and Melody; and how to distinguish them."

"I *could*," she stated dryly, "if I had any confidence that you would be able to comprehend."

"We might."

"It requires the ability to do recursive thinking."

"My favorite kind," said Jason. He put on a serious face and said to Jerold, "*Recursive* is when you swear twice at your longhand writing." Cat groaned and threw her cup at Jason who plucked it neatly out of the air and set it in the sink.

"He always does that," she complained to Jerold, who was suddenly occupied with something behind him.

"Look what I found!" he exclaimed triumphantly as he held up the kitten.

"You have a cat?" said Heth in surprise, "Maybe you're not so bad after all." Cat was off her chair and in the corner immediately.

"Lemme see, lemme see. What's his name Jason?"

"Lester."

"Lester? Like Tera's grandfather?"

"No, Tera's grandfather is bigger. He's more like Lester the kitten. In fact, he *is* Lester the kitten." Cat looked around for something else to throw at Jason, but had to console herself with cuddling Lester, who seemed to think that her hair was alive and needed to be captured at any cost.

"Where'd you get him?" asked Heth.

"He was trapped in a tree by a witch who tried to entrap me but had to settle for dropping me into a thorn bush."

"Ah. That explains the color. And the reason you made Nilgiri tea; to hide the smell of the litterbox."

"Yep. It's in the bedroom, where Lester was until Jerold leaned against the door."

"I'll take the blame," said Jerold, "as long as I get the beer."

"If you are quite finished anthropomorphizing with Lester, I believe the incomparable Heth has the floor," stated Jason. "You were about to demonstrate a recursive investigation into the polarity of musical dimensions. Please continue."

Heth stared at him for a while as if not sure whether to speak or not. Finally she smiled and said, "Okay." She sat down on the couch and settled her tea beside her. Jason grabbed the teapot, refilled her cup, returned to his station leaning on the kitchen counter, and waited. "All right, I'll just dive right in. We think of rhythm as the pace of music that sets up a structure of time and emphasis. To understand any more clearly we need to see how rhythm itself is produced." She paused.

"Like find the parts of rhythm?" asked Cat helpfully.

"Just the opposite. It's no use to keep finding smaller and smaller parts of things, because if we don't know what a thing is to begin with, we'll be even more confused when it's all divvied up into smaller pieces. What we do is re-form our definition of rhythm from somewhere completely unrelated. For that we go to the other dimensions of music." She looked at Jason then Jerold.

"We're listening," said Jerold, toasting her with his Budweiser.

"The two opposite elements that make up Rhythm are pace and emphasis. Pace is constant and pervasive, emphasis is specific and momentary. The two opposite elements that make up Melody are tune and variation. The tune is the basic musical path, and variation is anything else you happen to want to do on that path. The two opposite elements of Harmony are expectation and satisfaction. Some harmonies lift up the theme, and others put it to rest. You don't need to remember all these right now," she glanced at Jason, "except for you," she smiled at the other two, "just know that we now have six completely different ideas to deal with."

"I can remember the number six," said Cat brightly.

"Me too. Yay six!" chorused Jerold.

"Okay, let's see what would happen if Harmony itself had a Melody. Think about it for a moment. You would be listening for a kind of song made from harmonies, not notes."

"Sure," said Jerold, "that's like the chords that a guitar plays."

"Perfect. And as the guitarist steps through the chords—assuming he's not the lead guitarist playing the tune—he is setting the pace for the whole song, right?"

"Riiight…" said Cat, "So?"

"Well, didn't we say that 'pace' was one of the two elements of Rhythm?"

"Whoa there!" exclaimed Jerold, "What did you just do? You twisted it all around."

"Be patient, I'm going to do it again. Let's start over. What if the entire tune of the song—the Melody—made one big giant harmony by itself."

"You mean like the feeling you get when you think of the whole song, like when you remember a song you like but can't remember which one it is?" inquired Cat.

"Exactly. If the entire Melody made one big harmony, that would be that feeling you get when the song hits you. You could call it that song's specific emphasis."

"Sure, why not?"

"Didn't we say that 'emphasis' was the other one of the two elements of Rhythm?"

Jerold shook his head violently then banged it on the wall. "I don't think I like where this is going!"

"Jason dear, would you do the honors please?" said Heth sweetly.

"As you wish. Rhythm is composed of pace and emphasis. Pace is the Melody of Harmony, and emphasis is the Harmony of the Melody."

"You know what's whacked out?" asked Jerold, "I totally understand this right now, but I can guarantee that five minutes from now I'll have no idea what you just said."

"Do another one!" said Cat, "Can you do that with Harmony?" Jerold groaned and opened his second beer. "Don't you want to Jerold?"

"Yes I do actually want to hear this. I just know that I'm going to end up with a headache at some point."

"Uh-huh. And that will have nothing to do with the beer I'm sure."

"The beer is the only thing keeping me sane right now." He toasted Heth again, "Do go on."

"Okay. Let's suppose that the Rhythm has its own tune; it's own Melody."

"That's like the base player," said Jerold.

"Right. What kind of story is the bass player telling?"

"That's hard to put in words," mused Cat. Lester was leaning backwards out of her arms with his paws outstretched. "It kind of gets you in the mood, but it's not the tune..."

"It gets you ready for the tune; sets up the stage," said Jerold.

"Prepares the range of the theme," said Jason.

"Shush you! That's cheating!" Heth jabbed her finger toward Jason. "Staying on subject, we could say that it sets your expectations. Now drop that idea and consider a new one. Most tunes repeat with lines, verses, and choruses. Why?"

"That's just the way it works," said Cat, "There needs to be some sort of continuity so you know where to start and stop and all that." Lester was now more than halfway spilled out her arms, and didn't seem concerned in the slightest.

"Right. So the Melody has its own Rhythm, which is all about satisfying the requirements of the song. Jason?"

Jason smiled, "Harmony is composed of expectation and satisfaction. Expectation is the Melody of the Rhythm and satisfaction is the Rhythm of the Melody."

Jerold clenched his eyes, "Don't do the third one... I know this; you're going to explain how Melody is composed of ...um, tune and variation; and that tune is the Harmony of the Rhythm and variation is the Rhythm of the Harmony." He looked up, "Did I get it right?"

"Yes, if we work that one out, that's what we'll find." Lester slid backwards out of Cat's arms, landed awkwardly on the floor, and sat up looking at her reproachfully.

"It's your own fault, Lester," she said, "I'm not going to keep scooping you in."

"He wanted you to catch him," said Jason, "Watch." He whistled two quick notes and Lester cocked his head, then dashed over to the kitchen, up the stool, and on to Jason's shoulder. Jason rolled a piece of paper into a small ball and flicked it into the air with his thumb, which Lester sprung after. Jason's hand whipped out and caught him in mid-flight, and placed him back on his shoulder. "He's got 'fly' down pat. We're still working on 'land'."

"Kind of like you?" said Heth with one raised eyebrow.

"Touché."

Jerold was applauding slowly, "Encore, encore."

"The encore is when he uses his litterbox. You'll know when."

Cat turned to Jason excitedly, "This is what we were talking about yesterday; it's like a whole different way of learning. Heth says it's almost impossible to teach this way."

"I should think so," said Jerold, "but actually, why not? Once you work it out, doesn't it clarify everything? Like a super-satisfying song sounds great the first time you hear it, but you get tired of it quickly. And a song with a lot of drama and expectation doesn't sound great the first time, but it grows on you. Couldn't you use this to figure out how to balance the ...um ...the satisfaction and expectation stuff?"

"Yes, you could," said Heth, "but it's not so much analysis, it's learning a whole new way to think."

"As a rule of thumb," said Jason, "we take the exact opposite approach to the one that works. Concepts are counter-intuitive to linear thinking. Suppose you have three issues and a problem with one of them. Our approach is to concentrate on the problem issue, when it's actually best to concentrate on the other two and allow them to work out their changes in the problem area." Lester climbed down and began to explore the counter. "Like Lester. He wants Cat to hold him again, so he's going to explore every other avenue first."

"C'mon you, all you had to do is ask;" Cat got up and grabbed Lester, who immediately commenced attacking her hair. She settled into her chair and asked Heth, "Is this why you hit so much resistance?"

Heth nodded. "It's even woven into our language. The accepted way of defining anything—especially in academia—is by ascription through analysis, which turns into description. Think of dictionaries. But the only way to properly understand anything is by seeing how it exists in relation to everything around it; this becomes an associative approach and is much more powerful..."

"...providing you know *which* things associated with it are to have *which* relationships," continued Jason, "Otherwise it's just a guessing game."

"And when you encounter someone who is fixated on their area of expertise, they do not react kindly to someone pointing out that there's a whole structure of relationships that they are completely ignorant of."

"And they *really* get riled if you suggest that it's the same structure of relationships that works in every system," said Jason.

"Wait a sec," said Jerold, "are you saying that you can do this with any subject?"

"Sure," said Jason, "want to hear mathematics laid out by its real principles instead of those silly rules they teach?"

"No!" exclaimed Jerold, "My head would burst. I just need to know that it's possible." He turned to Heth. "Before I start this third beer, I need to know why you had us memorize 'six'." He turned to Cat. "See? I remembered."

She stuck her tongue out at him, "I did too. Okay, Heth, what's up with six?"

Heth glanced at Jason, who shrugged and waved her on. "Okay, when I asked Jason for the four dynamics of music to see if he was just bluffing..."

"...I was," inserted Jason.

"...which he wasn't, *Mister Deflection*, ...he said 'theme, range, resonance, composition'. An easy way to think of the four dynamics is four stages. The pattern is always: the Source, the Distribution, the Organization, and the Sink."

"The sink?" asked Jerold, "Like the kitchen sink?"

"Where it's headed. If you're going to use a kitchen sink, think of the drain."

"I can do drains," said Jerold, "go on."

"For an apple, you have the source bud, the distribution into a flower, the organization into fruit, and the final destination into the seed. That makes it easy to think about. In reality, all four dynamics are operating simultaneously, so it's a bit deeper than that example."

"In a musical composition," continued Jason, "the Theme is the source of every aspect of the song. The range defines the extent to which the musical elements are distributed throughout the song. The resonance of all the parts together organize the song, and the final composition is the goal toward which every part of the music is headed."

"That actually sounds super simple," remarked Cat.

"It is," said Heth, "Now let's do a very simple math exercise. How many relationships are possible between those four dynamics?"

"I know this!" exclaimed Jerold, "There's six. Theme-range, theme-resonance, theme-that last one, range-resonance, range-that last one, and resonance-that last one."

"Composition?" said Cat.

"Yeah. Composition is that one that's the last one."

"Good," said Heth, "now if you count up each of the polar sides of the three dimensions, how many elements do you have?"

"Six," said Cat and Jerold.

"Jason?"

"It must be nice to have your own narrator on beck-and-call." He took a deep breath, then stopped. "You don't really want me to do them all, do you?"

"Give us two examples."

"Okay. The theme, or *bud* as Heth said, spreads out via the range. This relationship is pure expectation, or as we pointed out earlier, the Melody of the Rhythm. Oppositely, the resonance of all the parts working together folds into the composition, the final product. This relationship is pure satisfaction, or as we pointed out earlier, the Rhythm of the Melody."

"Okay, you officially lost me," said Jerold, "I'm getting that everything's folding together, but I can't keep track at this point."

"It's easier if you draw it..." started Jason.

"You don't need to follow the details," said Heth, "you can work them out on your own. The key is..."

Cat's eyes were shining, "I get it! The *dynamics* and *dimensions* are independent structures, but they fit together in one particular way and produce each other!" Lester had fallen asleep in her lap and was beginning another slow slide.

"Exactly," said Heth, "amen." She looked at Jason. "Unless you wanted to extrapolate for an hour?"

"Not me," said Jason, "I've just forgotten everything we're talking about," which elicited a sarcastic grunt out of Cat.

"And you can do this with math and physics?" asked Jerold. Heth just smiled her feral smile and said nothing. "Hell, what do we need college for then?"

"They've got knowledge," said Jason, "lots of it. But knowledge just weighs you down if you don't have a structure to put it in."

"Okay. Wow. And here I thought we came here to talk about the kingdom. This kind of makes the conflict seem a lot smaller."

"And other parts a lot larger," said Cat, "I'm trying to see if all of this would mean anything for the kingdom, and the only thing I can think of is how important it is to have all of our relationships put together properly."

"Well, the theme was given by Tiron with his assignment to make a gift for the university," said Jason, "once we got together to figure out what the final composition was to be, we spontaneously expanded the range by making a kingdom. I think if we're looking at this in stages, it's time to see how everything and everyone resonates together before the composition can show itself."

"So that's why we couldn't make a decision on what to do right away," said Cat, "we didn't know the range and we hadn't resonated together. But that's all music stuff... what would other dynamics be—like the four dynamics of architecture?"

Jason glanced at Heth and said, "Program, context, concept, resolution."

"You use such inspecific terms," remarked Heth.

"*Unspecific*," said Jerold, "*inspecific* isn't a word."

"It is now," retorted Heth.

"So what would the four dynamics be for... um, what we're doing?"

"Beats me," smiled Jason.

"Oh, c'mon; you reel these things off like your ABC's. You can figure it out."

"*Heth* maybe can figure it out. Do you think we could have gone into these subjects without her?"

"Oh..." said Cat, suddenly remembering how Jason used the expectations of people around him. "That's..."

"It's okay," said Heth, "but I do think we should call it a night. I need to at any rate. Besides, I never internalize more than one subject at a time. It prevents shortcutting."

"Internalize?" asked Cat.

"You kind of have to *become* the subject and feel how the relationships wriggle around inside you."

"Like tapeworms!" said Jerold. He was holding his last empty beer can above him, possibly hoping that more would spontaneously pour out.

Cat got up and positioned the unresponsive black ball of fur on the chair. "You're ready to go Jerold. Let's get you out of here before you start singing."

"I can sing," said Jerold, "*Ninety-nine bottles of...*"

"Enough!" ordered Cat, and guided him to the door. "Thanks for the tea and beer, Jason. See you in Tiron's class tomorrow."

"Yeah Jason, thanks for the umbrella," yelled Jerold from outside.

Jason stopped Heth at the door, "One moment." He waited for Cat and Jerold to get partway up the walk. "Have you done the primes?" She held her face in a completely impenetrable mask and said nothing. He scanned her face for a long moment. "I thought so. Did you go the mathematical route or the geometrical one?"

"I started with just numbers but I had to set them in a geometrical matrix."

"Hm. I started with just the geometry, but I had to make a mathematical system to connect it." He paused. "I guess there's not a lot more to say then."

"No. There isn't."

He smiled. "Goodnight Heth, thanks for visiting."

She blinked once slowly, held his eyes for a moment, turned and joined the others, where Jerold was saying to Cat, "I didn't think duels were supposed to end in a draw."

"They're not," said Cat, "I don't think this one is over."

Chapter 16: Knick-Knack Paddywhack

Tiron was oddly missing as the class settled into their seats. John and Rachel had decided to wear their 'royal mantle' scarves, and everyone seemed to be on high alert. Jude finally exclaimed in a loud voice, "University rules are that if the professor is more than fifteen minutes late, we can leave."

Susan Marasta in the middle front row turned to Rachel behind her and waved to John in the back, "Your majesties, I think there's a note on the board."

Rachel went up to the small sticky on the board and read it aloud. "It says, 'Field Trip. 1618 Willow Lane'." She turned to the class, "Does anyone know where that is?"

"Yes," said Tera, "it's on the edge of town by the river. It's about a half-hour's walk from here."

John strode to the front of the room and conferred with Rachel, then motioned Bethany to join them. She soon turned to the class and announced, "The king and the queen are of the opinion that we would be well advised to walk to this address, um ...forthwith."

Charles hopped up, "Then forthwith let us go henceforth!" and the class filed out into the bright morning sunlight and across town. John and Rachel had confirmed Cat's sentiment that there was no need to defend themselves, though most of the talk on the way was taken up by sharing stories of passive-aggressive harassment from the university. Cris noticed that John and Rachel seemed to thrive on the threat of conflict, and noted with pleasure that their confidence was catching. The road became more remote as it followed the river upstream until the announcement was made by the king near the head of the line, "This is it. Let's pull together before we go in."

They were at a large stone cottage, quite run down but still maintaining its dignity beneath the sheets of vines that covered its face. The slate roof still had most of its shingles, and the huge wooden door was still intact, though a twisting tree grew out of one window, and some time in the past a Ford truck had given up the ghost by the drive, and looked like it hosted an unpredictable variety of tenants. The king and the queen stood on the enormous stone slab before the entrance with the class in a semicircle around them. King John pounded loudly on the door, which opened slowly to present the figure of Tiron standing almost proudly before them. "Welcome, your excellencies."

The inside was laid out in one large room which stretched to a balcony in the back overlooking the river and its gorge. The left side of the room hosted a large fireplace with smaller rooms behind it, and the right a large winding staircase that led to an upper story which wrapped around the main room. *This was obviously built for people who did more than huddle in front of a telly all evening,* thought Cris. The scents of must and decay were somewhat obviated by a most intriguing mixture of aromas soon discovered to be a scattering of incense sticks burning throughout. "Explore," said Tiron, "and we will convene on the deck in fifteen minutes. John, Rachel, and Phil, you three join me there early, say in seven minutes." The class broke up in every direction; Cris found himself in the large kitchen whose space radiated from a brick oven set into the wall it shared with the Great Room's fireplace. The once majestic pantries were filled with newspapers and mostly unrecognizable junk; William Target, Frank Lyons, and Jude Astor were going through every drawer and cupboard looking for anything of interest. He wandered back into the Great Room where Jason was sliding down the banister. He did a little hop at the bottom and landed on his feet near Cris.

"The attic has a window. C'mon, lets find the well." He was out the door in a moment, and Cris followed after, catching up to him working his way through the underbrush on the kitchen side of the house. "This way's slightly uphill, so the well should be on this side."

"Why, what's usually downhill?"

"The drain field for the sewer, silly. This place was built in the mid 1800's, so that's where the outhouses would have been until it was upgraded. Ah, here we go. Help me out, we've only got ten minutes." He began digging through a round mound of weeds, loosening the dirt by rooting up plants and scraping the mound away. Cris joined him, and they soon uncovered a large kidney-shaped slab of slate. "Okay, take that side and slide it off carefully. We don't want to crack it." The slate scraped loudly as they exposed a black gaping hole lined with stone that disappeared into the ground. Jason rooted through his knapsack for a penlight and they both peered in. "Only twelve or thirteen feet. Well, here we go." Before Cris knew what was happening, Jason had clambered down the well like a spider, dropping the last few feet with a *shluck* sound into the mud at the bottom.

"I hope you don't expect me to come down there with you."

"There's hardly room. And this should take less than two minutes." Cris watched as Jason began scooping the mud into a heap on one side, holding the penlight in his teeth.

"Did you find it yet?" The voice over Cris' shoulder made him jump. It was Mary Sendik.

"Not yet," came Jason's voice, "but there's only about eight inches of mud."

"What's he looking for?" Cris was suddenly aware of how dirty he was.

"The silver dollar, silly."

"Got it!" came Jason's triumphant voice, "lemme check the rest of the floor."

"Why on earth would a silver dollar be at the bottom of an abandoned well?"

"Humans are so forgetful," said Mary with a smile, "silver kills germs, which is where the belief comes from that you need a silver bullet to kill someone infected by wolf fever."

"You're telling me that because you know about werewolves, you knew that there would be a silver dollar at the bottom of this well."

"People always threw a silver dollar into a well when it was dug as a blessing and to keep the water pure. They would drop one into a milk bottle for the same reason, which is why the old milk bottles' mouths were so wide."

"And you know this how?"

"There are ways to pass on memories so that they don't die when the body dies."

Cris was relieved to see the relatively normal figure of Jason climbing out the well. "Got three of them," he grinned, "They used two large rocks for the base; one of these was wedged in the crack, and two were together at the side." He handed the coins to Mary, "What do you think?"

She spit on the surfaces and carefully wiped them clean. "Okay, we've got an 1839 Grobecht Dollar, an 1851 Seated Liberty, and this one is smaller… oh my." She looked up. "1797 Draped Bust half dollar."

"Is that valuable?" asked Cris.

"Depending on the exact condition, it could be worth as much as this house."

"Great," said Jason, "That should help with repairs, if that's Tiron's plan. Help me get the cover back on."

"You know," said Mary as they scraped the slate back into place, "There's *three* of them..."

"We have a truce," said Jason.

"I know. But your code is so..."

"It works," said Jason abruptly. "You can present these to the appropriate party once we figure out who that turns out to be. Let's get back before they start without us."

When they joined the others on the porch, Charles called out, "Hey Jason! When Tiron said 'Explore' he meant the house, not the septic tank!" He was covered with mud from his knees down and the rest of him wasn't doing too much better. He fielded the laughter good-naturedly and leaned against the rail with Cris, who was glad for the distraction of a much dirtier victim.

Tiron spoke up, "Have you found something for us, Mr. Sardic?"

Jason shrugged, "That depends on who 'us' is."

"Very well." He looked around at the class, "You have presented me with a multifaceted opportunity. It appears that a kingdom has been born. While the kingdom was generated largely from the circumstances of an assignment given to this class over which I preside, it is its own entity and as such I have no say in its affairs except by..." he glanced at Phil, "...*treaty*. So today I have presented to your Sovereigns the terms of a treaty which may facilitate an advantageous relationship. However, that is not the business at hand, as I am the professor of this class, not of the kingdom. Toward the goal of keeping those with overlapping interests—which at present includes all of you—working for mutual advantage, I will now relinquish class time to Queen Rachel and King John."

Rachel stepped forward. "If you think that was complicated, hold on to your hats. Tiron has proposed two different treaties. The first one is a pact of non-aggression between the kingdom and the class."

"But if we're all in both, that doesn't make sense," piped up Lisa McDowell.

"It means basically that the Kingdom and its subjects may not take action detrimental to the purposes of the class—which is under Tiron's control—and neither the students of the class nor Tiron may take action detrimental to the purposes of the Kingdom," she smiled, "which is under *my* control," she reached up and patted John on the head, "and our beloved king."

John spoke, "This treaty has been ratified and signed by both us and Tiron, and has been entered into the Book of the Law."

Jude spoke up, "Is there anything else we should know about in this mysterious book?"

Rachel. "The Book of the Law is kept by the Scribe of the Court, Bethany DuChamp. Bethany?"

Bethany looked up from her writing, "A copy of the Book of the Law," she waved a notebook, "is available at all times to be read by any subject of the Kingdom."

"The second treaty," continued Rachel, "is under consideration. We would appoint a select number of interested individuals to the board of directors for an LLC whose function it is to maintain the affairs of a property held in a separate trust designed for five-year incremental use by the kingdom." She looked around at the puzzled faces. "Phil, you better take over."

"Sure," grinned Phil. "Okay, we need to organize a company. This company will be in charge of the affairs of the *palace* which the kingdom may utilize at its discretion."

"Palace?" asked Charles, "what palace?"

"You're standing in it."

"Oh. And who owns the company… the LLC?"

"Shares of ownership of the LLC are distributed 40% between the board of directors and 60% by the trust who holds the deed."

"We don't hold the deed on our own palace? Why not?" pursued Charles.

"Simple. If you do not actually own something, it can not be taken away from you. And since the LLC is running the palace and not the Kingdom, no one can attack the Kingdom for anything that happens here. But since the treaty between the company that owns the trust, which Tiron is representing today, and the Kingdom, which John and Rachel are representing, stipulates that the board of directors for the LLC be chosen from subjects of the Kingdom, control of the palace cannot be undermined by outside forces. And since the LLC, not the trust that holds the deed, controls all operations with a five-year renewal clause, the Kingdom is protected against interference for five-year intervals from even the deed-holder."

Frank Lyons asked, "What does the trust get out of giving this place over to a bunch of crazy college kids?"

Phil gestured around, "Do you think we're going to use it in this condition? The trust gets a free fix-up, and we get a free palace."

"I assume the LLC will have a bank account?" asked Jason.

"That's the first thing I'm going to set up, if their majesties deem the treaty advisable."

John said, "We have decided to apprise the subjects of the Kingdom before ratifying the treaty. Are there any objections or more questions?"

"Yes," said Jude, "Who is going to want to go through all the work involved with being on the board of directors for the LLC?"

Phil smiled, "Offices of the board of directors are paid positions."

"Paid by whom?"

"A discretionary fund is set up with increasing increments deposited into the LLC's account upon review and approval of how well the last increment was used. It is assumed that a five-acre property with an operating structure in good condition is more than capable of generating its own revenue if properly managed, but will need startup assistance. The initial increment deposited will be forty thousand dollars." A wave of murmurs swept the class. "Trust me, that's not enough to fix the place up properly. But it's certainly enough for a solid start."

"We would like to make a decision immediately," said Rachel. "Ultimately it will be your king and queen who decide. However, let's hear it in yea's and nay's. All those in any way opposed or hesitant to the treaty, say 'nay' now." There was some shuffling of feet, but no one spoke up. "All those in favor of moving forward at present, say 'yea'." An enthusiastic 'Yea!' spilled out into the gorge. "Very well. Holly and Mike, you're in architecture, and Susan you're an interior designer; we would very much like your proposals as soon as a board of directors is assembled. Frank, if electrical engineering includes wiring for old buildings, we need you too. Phil is handling the legal work, and we'll convene later this afternoon to figure out how to best set up the LLC and what else everyone has to offer. Anyone who can, plan on being back here sometime after six, and this includes members of the Kingdom who aren't in this class. And please bring some lanterns or candles. Tiron?"

Tiron came over and shook hands with Rachel and John. "The treaty is made," he said. "We can add signatures once Phil has put together the rest of the paperwork."

"How soon will the bank account be set up?" asked Jason.

"By tomorrow it will be operational," said Phil, "It will take a bit more to register the company, get an EIN, and all those details. Why do you keep asking about it?"

Jason nodded to Mary, who walked over to Phil, looked at Tiron, and held out her hand with the three coins in it. "I see your forty thousand and raise you fifty-five," she said, "that's my rough estimate of the worth these three coins." She paused dramatically as they looked them over. "I had Jason fetch them from the bottom of the well for me."

"She stumbled onto us *after* we found the well," said Cris.

"Either way," she smiled, "it looks like your majesties may need a treasurer. And maybe guards."

"I think it's time to hand the class time back to Tiron," stated John, "We've got more than enough to deal with for now." He nodded to Tiron and stepped back.

"Very well," said Tiron, "I trust everyone is ready for today's assignment?" He looked around at the apprehensive faces. "Your assignment is: Continue on. And don't forget that each of these assignments is pass/fail." He glanced at the sun, "We'll break a half an hour early for those who have classes scheduled immediately after this one." Cris noted that his glance at the sun was as natural as another person's glance at their watch would be. The students began to mill around excitedly, and Heth conferred briefly with John, who then made another announcement.

"I don't know if it's by design or not, but we have no one in this class in computer science. Does anyone know if we have a computer expert in the extended kingdom?"

Holly Boyer spoke up, "My boyfriend is a total hacker freak. He's going to get himself in serious trouble if he keeps it up."

"Good. If you would be so kind as to introduce him to Heth and Jason at your earliest convenience." Jason's head snapped over to look at Heth, who had on her feral smile again.

Professor Leonard Deon's class had turned into a kind of antithesis of Tiron's. They were discussing the conflict between Leibniz and Newton over the discovery of calculus and Cris had long given up trying to think of something relevant to add. He did notice that the professor was being extra careful in some odd way; he even smiled at a remark that Jason made, something Cris had never seen him do. When class was finally over, he noticed that Leonard had invited Jude to go somewhere with him, and made a mental note to ask him what it was about later.

He might have paid more attention. Jude was led to Rhoboth Hall where Leonard showed him into a conference room where half a dozen faculty were gathered. He recognized Jerry Fitzgerald the dean and Professor Huwait from his materials science class, but most of the rest were new to him. Leonard ushered him into a seat, and the conversation paused as Jude realized that he was somehow the center of attention. Finally Jerry cleared his throat and said, "Thanks for coming by; you're Jude Astor I believe."

"Yes… am I in trouble?"

Jerry laughed disarmingly. "Of course not, Jude. We've been looking over your records and I must say… you show a lot of potential. A lot of potential." He paused, seeming not quite to know how to go on.

"You have a very solid and practical approach to problems," interjected Professor Huwait, "and we like to encourage this sort of approach, you being in your sophomore year and all."

The figure at the head of the table cleared his throat a bit impatiently. "Jude, let me introduce myself; I am William McCory. You have shown yourself to be a practical person who does not get bamboozled easily, which is why we've called you here."

"Wait… 'McCory'; are you Tera's father?"

He smiled dryly. "Yes. We would like to talk to you about this 'kingdom' movement."

"It's nothing that should cause alarm," reassured a squeaky voice at his right, "it's just that sometimes the students get themselves into situations that have unintended consequences, and it's our job to anticipate these things and protect them."

Jerry chimed in, "What we're trying to do is prevent a lot of ...unnecessary conflict that could balloon into a disaster by acting decisively now while there's still opportunity."

Jude leaned back. "You're going to try to take down the kingdom?" he asked incredulously.

"No, no..." began several faculty at once, interrupted by William's 'Yes.' The table fell silent.

William went on. "Jude, this is much larger and more dangerous than you can imagine, or would be expected to imagine. Movements start at universities. Kingdoms are unAmerican, both culturally and legally. Cherell could lose funding. Thousands of students could be affected. Even you could find yourself disgraced and on the street. All because of a miscellaneous game some students came up with on a whim." He paused for effect. "Now it looks like this began without Professor Jerome's knowledge, but it also looks like he may decide to encourage it. Everything is in flux right now. We were going to approach him, but his friend Howard here tells us that would have the opposite effect, and looking at his record we are inclined to believe him. That leads us to you as the most straightforward way of finding a solution."

"But what can I do? If anything, I'm like the dissenting voice in the class; I doubt they'll listen to me."

Professor Huwait interjected, "Think of this as an extracurricular project. A successful disarming of what could be a bad situation will be appreciated across the board, and count very positively toward consideration of your ...potential, as we said."

"My potential?"

"Well, I know you're looking very closely at that fellowship when you finish your studies next year."

"Oh."

William resumed, "It's simple. You do a good thing that saves the university a great deal of trouble, and the university is rather inclined to do good things for you. You will have proved yourself ahead of time."

"I see."

Jerry leaned forward, "So, can we count on you help us with what is threatening to become a problem?"

Jude thought for a bit, then smiled. "Certainly, it would be an honor." Jerry seemed visibly relieved, and William took it up immediately.

"I thought we could count on your maturity. Now here's the problem: we don't know what the current plans of the kingdom are, and you probably do. If we're going to nip this in the bud, we need to quickly and quietly divert all this extra energy into useful studies that lead to successful lives, not fantasies. Do you know what they're planning?"

"They have no plans right now. Oh, wait, we're making a palace."

"A *what?*"

"A palace. Converting an old house. At 1618 Willow Lane down by the river."

William spoke to the lady to his left, "Write that down. Talk to the bank. Buy it out from under them if you have to."

"I don't think you'll get very far fighting them on that; I'm no expert but it sounds like they've got an iron-clad deal. Tiron's helping them with it. In fact, I think he owns the trust that is providing it."

"I knew it!" Howard slapped his hand on the table. "If Tiron's set his mind to something, there's no way to stop him. How much would you like to bet the trust is under the jurisdiction of the Cayman Islands?"

William placed his fingertips together and looked at Jude. "Okay. We move on to what's next. We know that John Krisner and Rachel Wainstead are the ostensible king and queen. Shall we simply remove them?"

"I don't think… wait, let me think about this." He closed his eyes and thought about everything that had gone on. "You don't want to just remove Tiron?"

"That solution is fraught with unpleasant consequences," said William, "there is no guarantee that it would solve things, and we would prefer to end things more quietly."

Jude thought some more, then leaned forward. "Okay. The kingdom was spontaneous, as you say, and it doesn't really have any plans, so there's really no plans to thwart. They're operating on excitement and naiveté. Phil Mupp is providing the legal expertise, but he's no leader. John and Rachel were made king and queen, but if you get rid of them, there's plenty of replacements. Charles Andowski is a leader, but he's not really calling the shots. Okay, I think I've got it. There's this group of four kids that work together like they've known each other all their lives. Cat Ambrose, your daughter Tera, Cris Ianoff, and Jason Sardic. Cat seems totally innocent, like a dumb blonde, but she's always with them. Everybody likes her. Cris is quiet, but people go to him for advice. Your daughter seems to be an expert on everything; she even helps Phil Mupp. But Jason… Jason is the one you want."

"I would concur with that assessment," said Leonard, "I have those four in my class. Their seats are spread out because it makes them more effective; they work together insidiously, often in direct opposition to the direction in which I am guiding the class. I have had a growing suspicion that their actions were cooperative."

"Yeah and that's just the tip of the iceberg. Trust me: break those four and you break the kingdom."

William stated in a kind tone, "We will only do what is necessary to protect our students. Your insight is useful. As we proceed with whatever course is best, we will need someone to help facilitate the process so as to minimize harm and maximize effect. I trust that you will be available for consulting?"

"Of course."

Jerry spoke up, "Well it looks like we have some tough decisions to make. Jude, we'll let you go, you must be very busy with your studies. The university thanks you for your help and understanding."

"Glad to be of assistance." He got up and left amid a friendly chorus of 'bye Jude' from the group.

Leonard muttered, "Give a dog a bone..."

"...And he eats for a day," continued Jerry, "that's what bones are for." He turned to William. "So what do you think; do we remove Jason?"

"No," said William, "If we take him out the kingdom is gutted but intact. We have to do something that affects everyone. If this group is operating on fun and fantasy, we need to make it aware of how serious life is."

"You want to expel all four? Even your daughter?"

"If necessary. But that would be much too direct; we don't need martyrs. An army missing half its men is far more dangerous than an army with half its men wounded. Jason definitely needs dealt with. But we need to strike at its sense of innocence. Lancey, get me everything you have on those four; I think I know what direction to take."

That evening the activity at Willow Lane was in full swing as breathtakingly ambitious ideas were considered seriously. However we are not going there tonight; instead we will find the laundromat in town, and enter the door beside it that leads to the apartments above. Going up the narrow stairs all the way to the third floor (surprisingly few of them squeak), we find that someone else has done likewise a bit ago, and is inside having a conversation with Lady Laura.

"Absolutely not," Lady Laura is saying, "Your intentions are noble, your concerns are quite justified, but one does not write a story about something that has not yet happened. It is meddlesome."

We find that her visitor is Lancey. "Then tell me, what would you do in these circumstances? I don't feel that I can just sit around and do nothing."

Laura looked at her. "Tell me, exactly what is your job?"

"Um… Liaison Secretary for the dean. It's a fancy title that means I do whatever June doesn't want to do."

"Does it keep you busy?"

"Of course, all the time."

"Then that's what you do. You're not drinking your tea."

Lancey dutifully took a sip. "Don't you want to help?"

Lady Laura snorted, "Help is a meaningless word these days; too often it means interference. If these kids have attracted that much focused political attention, I should think that someone ought to be helping the faculty. By the sounds of it they are downright desperate. Would you like to know what kind of help is needed by almost every single person I've ever met?"

"Yes, what?"

"A good swift kick in the butt. It does wonders."

Lancey sighed, "I just don't know what to do."

"Hmph. You climbed six flights of stairs to speak with me. That is a lot of work for someone who absolutely refuses to take anything I say seriously."

"So you're saying I should just keep doing my job and help William and Jerry and the rest of them destroy some innocent kids."

"Yes, that is one thing. What else?"

"Well, if I'm to take you seriously, I should find this Jason, come up behind him, and give him a good swift kick in the butt. If I want to help him."

"Yes, that is one more thing."

"Do you mean kick in the butt figuratively?"

"I most certainly do not. People use that phrase all the time figuratively. I have found that there is no substitute for an actual physical kick in the butt. Hard enough to hurt. The harder the better."

"Okay," said Lancey, "I'm going to take you seriously, because I do want to help, and I have a great deal of respect for your opinion. Now you said 'one thing' then you said 'one more thing', which makes me think there's 'one last thing' because you always use your words carefully. What else can I do?"

Laura broke into one of her rare smiles. "You *listened* dearie. What a pleasure. Tell your husband Ronnie that you deserve an extra kiss." She got up and began to gather up the dishes. "The last thing is also to keep doing what you have already done: in this particular case, *keep me informed.*"

"That's… that's what I wanted to do. Thank you Laura, I feel better if I know you're informed."

"And *I* like to be informed. Thank *you* Lancey."

Lancey walked down the stairs feeling like something had been lifted from her shoulders. "And all I have to do is keep Laura informed." She paused holding the rail like a live snake for a moment. "And give Jason a good swift kick in the butt. Laura's probably up there chuckling over this."

Which indeed she was.

Chapter 17: Under the Sea

—Womankind

Wednesday morning found Holly Boyer sleepily watching her boyfriend Mitch hunched over a keyboard with a double espresso, fielding rapid instructions from two tea-wielding angels on his shoulders… or rather seated on each side of his dorm desk. Heth and Jason were working their way through a pot of tea Jason had brought over while they watched Mitch's genius unfold.

"Have I mentioned yet that you two are absolutely completely out of your minds?" Mitch muttered.

"That's the seventh time so far," called out Holly from her perch on a pile of pillows.

"The coordinates have to be flexible enough to allow for the same amount of decimal corrections as the length of the prime," said Jason, "unless Heth has a shortcut for the vector relationships."

"I swear you treat everything like a wobbly gas gauge," complained Heth, "whatever made you pursue the range of distance between the primes instead of going for pinpoint accuracy?

"Accuracy only provides one answer. I wanted to identify the common character of all the results that fell into a particular range. Knowing the general character allows me to make a quick estimate of the answer by eye without using a program."

"Like that would ever be possible in anyone's universe," muttered Mitch, "Okay, one matrix for values set up without values. How the hell am I supposed to put in the relationships between the values without knowing what they are?"

"Easy," said Heth, "we'll tell you."

"You're going to provide the answers for problems and have me set them up before we have any idea what the problems are?"

"Sure," said Jason, taking another sip of tea, "It's a lot easier that way."

There was a tap on the door, and Jude stuck his head in. "Hey guys, John told me I could find you here. I've heard something you should know about." He looked at Mitch and the computer. "Whatcha doin' here?"

"They're frustrating the hell out me is what they're doing," complained Mitch. He leaned back and looked at Jude. "Some emergency in that kingdom you guys got?"

Jude looked over his shoulder and shut the door behind him. "Word is that a special meeting of the student government board is convening today. I think the staff dug up dirt and are going to use it as an excuse to do something to . . .whoever they dug up dirt on. The board is meeting in conference room 2F in Rhoboth hall at 3:00 today."

"If that's like a pre-hearing, anyone is allowed to attend," said Holly, "I sat through that one where they suspended those frat boys last semester for hazing a kid almost to death."

"The university likes to use a peer group to initially assess the situation," mused Jason, "where did you hear about this?"

"I've got a friend on the board," explained Jude, "I'm trying to tell as many people in the kingdom as I can find."

"This may have to wait," remarked Jason to Mitch, "why don't I come with you Jude?"

"Um… it's probably quicker if we split up so we can get the news to everyone we can. I'm headed over to meet with Mary Sendik next, she has a morning class."

"Okay, that makes sense," said Jason, "and if you see Mary, tell her that I said you're like a messenger of the gods going against the tide." He looked at Jude's puzzled expression. "She'll understand what I mean. Can you remember that?"

"Sure, messenger of the gods going against the tide. Okay, see you guys later. Long live the kingdom!" he disappeared out the door, and Jason leaned back thinking.

"What on earth did you tell him?" demanded Mitch.

"Think about it Mitch," said Holly from her pillows, "The messenger of the gods was Mercury."

"Oh. Mercury... in retrograde. You guys are devious. Why tell him that?"

"It appears that we have a Judas," mused Jason.

"That was my assessment," agreed Heth, "but to what extent?"

"I only asked to go with him to confirm that he couldn't allow that. He lied about everything except the time and place. Which means he was sent by the faculty to round everyone up. Which means they want a public spectacle. Which means whatever they're going to do is as good as already done. Which means we need to finish this project in the next few hours."

"See?" complained Mitch, "No matter what happens, I have to work harder."

Mary and Joshua listened to Jude's message without much reaction until he passed on Jason's message. "He said *what?*" she asked, bemused.

"Uh… said to tell you that I was like a messenger of the gods going against the tide."

"Oh that's so sweet. Three o'clock at Rhoboth Hall, eh?"

"Yeah, room 2F."

"Oh I don't think the room is going to matter so much. Thank you so much Jude, do let everyone know."

Once he had run off, Joshua said to her, "You've got that look again like the cat that just ate the canary. And what's up with Jude, he seemed off."

"My dear," she said taking his hand, "you said you were interested in the old ways. Today you're going to learn something about pest control. Care to help me redirect the muroid population?"

"Depends. What do we have to do?"

"We'll need two rats from the pet store and a bag of charcoal biscuits from the hardware store, enough for five separate fires that will burn for half an hour. Maybe some plates or hubcaps or something for the fires and some lighter fluid to get them started... and a blender."

"Burning rat mush does *not* sound appetizing."

"No... it isn't. But it's effective. And I finally get to have a little fun. Besides we're not *burning* rats, we're *smoking* them."

"You *will* explain this—to me at least. Everyone else can be mystified if you like."

"I love your sense of individuality. Let's go, we have to time this just right." As they headed for town she explained, "Jason's message was that this is a set-up; Jude's helping the faculty to do something horrid. And of course Jason will walk right into it, but armed. And if he can walk in armed, so can we."

"Are you planning to do a spell or something? Wing of bat and all that?"

"Wouldn't that be fun? But I think that would be bending the truce I have with Jason a bit too far. What we're doing is very simple: no creature, from humans to insects, can stand the smell of its own species burning. It produces an irrational panic to get away."

"You're going to stink up Rhoboth Hall with burning rats?"

"No darling. *We* are going to stink up every building *except* Rhoboth Hall that is within crawling distance."

The next knock on the door actually made Heth jump. After a few expectant moments Mitch got up and opened it. A tall gentleman with a goatee inquired, "Is Jason Sardic here?" Mitch opened the door wider to show the visitor to Jason.

"Gary," exclaimed Jason, "what on earth are you doing here?" He turned to Heth and Holly, "It's my advisor."

"Uh, Jason I have a summons here for your appearance before the student government board today at 3:00. Any conflicting classes—in fact, all classes—are suspended pending the outcome. Uh, would you like to come out and discuss it with me?"

"No Gary, that won't be necessary. Pass in the hot contraband and I'll look it over."

"I can't do that; I have to hand these directly to you."

Jason made a great show of struggling to get up and limping to the door where he took the papers from Gary. "Care to tell me what the crux of this little game is?"

"Well I'd prefer not to discuss it in public..."

"Public? You mean an attempted suspension without forewarning in front of the board and anyone else who wants to come is *private*? Are you going to ask people to hold a handkerchief over their ears at the moment of execution?" He took the papers and started looking through them.

"Jason, don't be like that. There's no reason to jump to conclusions..."

"I get it," Jason interrupted, "They're trumping up that test in structural engineering from last semester," he looked up at Gary, "Is that the best they could find? What about the classes that I simply quit attending out of boredom; I would have thought they counted for something."

"There weren't enough of them to... No! don't try that kind of passive-aggressive confrontation, I know how you can be. This is a very serious matter and should be dealt with by..."

"Right, right, by your terms not mine. Well Gary, I know how much you dislike confrontation; kudos on showing some backbone by delivering these. You can breathe easy now, the confrontation is over," and he shut the door on Gary, forcing him to step back. Gary was saying something through the door, but Jason ignored him and resumed his seat lightly.

"Oh my goodness," exclaimed Holly, "they're going after *you* Jason."

"Well at least they picked someone who would enjoy it." Jason's mouth had on a peculiar smile involving mainly the left side.

"I've already had one crucifixion and that was enough," said Heth, "though I have to admit I'm a bit jealous."

Mitch was trying to comprehend what had just occurred. "You guys are for real. I thought he was after me for sure! Jason, what on earth did you do?"

"He exists," said Heth; "That's usually enough."

"C'mon, what do the papers say?" demanded Holly.

"They say that I cheated on the structural engineering midterm last semester." He still had on his half-smile. "I was distracted that day and forgot to get a few wrong to make them happy. Hm. They could make this work depending on how desperate they are."

"What should we do? Is there someone you can get help from?" asked Holly.

"I'm not in the habit of looking for help. Let's finish this up."

"Maybe you should be," muttered Heth. "Okay, we incorporated your entirely unnecessary adjustment for range. Let's give it a whirl. Mitch, what's the largest number this program will handle right now for biprimes?"

"The low millions if you want immediate verification. It'll take me a few minutes to tie in the dynamic array. Then we can do hundred-digit numbers easily. Let's test what we have."

"Okay," said Jason, "set the range at two, as tight as it will go. Low millions will put your square root around 1,500 so start there." A few keystrokes by Mitch, and the screen read: '2,214,143 = 1,487 x 1,489'.

Mitch sat back and whistled. Heth jumped in, "C'mon keep going. Widen the range a bit." A moment later the screen read: '2,330,023 = 1,459 x 1,597'. "Widen the range way out and drop to something about half that value." The screen now read: '1,234,561 = 211 x 5,851'. "Now test it for prime evaluation; put the range at one." The screen showed: '2,330,047 Prime'.

Mitch jumped out of his seat with his hands high in the air yelling, "Whoo-Ha! We did it!"

"You guys are all nuts," said Holly, "*What* did you do?"

Mitch turned and exclaimed, "We just factored for primes and semi-primes without factoring!"

"You did something without doing it. What's that supposed to mean?"

Mitch jumped on the bed, hugged Holly, rolled over, and held her flailing above him by the waist. "These crazy idiots just showed me how to do the impossible. This can change everything!"

"Ahem," said Heth, "We have an agreement Mitch. You signed in blood, or the next best thing. And we've still have a lot of work to do." He set Holly down and sat up grinning.

"Okay," demanded a rather disheveled Holly, "you're happy; I get it. Will someone please tell me what you've done?"

"It's like this… should I tell her?" he asked Jason and Heth.

"Give her a summary, and let's keep going," said Jason.

"Okay, it's all about cryptography. If you want to know the factors of 12, it's easy; 2, 3, 4, and 6. But if you want to know the factors of a number that's fifty digits long, it can take years to calculate because you have a crazy amount of calculations to do. So when they protect information, they take two massive prime numbers—ones with no factors—and multiply them together so that the big number only has two factors. It would take years to find the two keys, the two primes that made it. And the two keys are all that's needed to get into the system. Almost every cryptography system is based on this." He grinned again, "It was untouchable until now."

"Um, okay. I don't suppose you guys want to tell me how?"

"Easy," said Heth, "calculate the requisite vector to produce paired integers that balance on the square root. You already have the number with it's own unique vector. Use it to determine the other vectors; they're the only ones that can be related."

"People are taught that numbers are points on a line," said Jason. "They're not. Every number is a huge three-dimensional construct that has specific relationships to every other number. We simply start with those relationships instead of with the numbers."

"Okay. Wouldn't those constructs get too big to handle with a fifty-digit number?"

"That's the beauty of it," said Heth; "the larger a number is, the simpler the construct."

"That means *one* would be the largest most complicated number."

"Exactly. Can we get going now Mitch?"

"What about zero?" continued Holly.

"Zero is a crutch for people who can't think," said Jason, "You guys can probably take it from here, right? I think I'd like to figure out how to prepare for my trial or whatever this fiasco they have planned turns out to be."

"Sure, we got it," said Heth, "You better get going. We'll be at Rhoboth Hall to support you."

He turned at the door and addressed Mitch, "You know that if we've figured this out, that others have too. And *that* means there's already an efficient procedure set in place to deal with this contingency. And since we've never heard of these 'others', I don't think you need me to tell you that discretion is somewhat mandatory."

"What's he mean?" Holly asked Mitch.

"It means," said Mitch, "if you're in charge of security for the nation and can either get rid of the protection for every business, bank, and governmental secret, or get rid of a few meddling students; you'll probably *not* choose to lose the banks."

After hearing the news of the 3:00 board review, Tera immediately looked for John and Rachel and found them in the Quad with a dozen or more students talking at the gazebo. "Tera!" yelled Rachel when she got close, "I'm so glad you're here. You heard?"

"Yes," said Tera, "Does anyone know actual details?"

"Just the rumors," stated John, "It smells like a set-up to me." Cris was standing between them slowly twirling the hornets' nest.

"We got out the Orb of Dominion," he said, "William Target said we should learn a history lesson from it." Tera raised one eyebrow at William.

"Well let's hear it, William," declared Rachel, "What does an empty hornets' nest have to teach us about a planned lynching?"

"Not much," chuckled William, "I just wanted to see it again." He looked around at the expectant faces and relented; "Okay, yes it looks like we're dealing with a lynching of some sort. And like a swarm of hornets, it's almost impossible to defend against enemies buzzing you from every side. So you have two choices: stay away from them, or find their place of safety and attack it. This..." he pointed to the nest, "is the swarm's place of safety. And this..." he pointed at the hole in the bottom, "is the only way in or out. Now we're dealing with one thing rather than a thousand."

"What are you suggesting, that we stay away, or that we attack the entrance?" asked John.

"I suggest that we do both because historically, single-track minds have never won battles. They're after the kingdom and they're trying to lure us into some kind of spectacle that they control. I submit to the court... if this is one," he said, looking around, "that your majesties put as much physical and emotional distance between yourselves and the 3:00 meeting. Go continue our palace project and don't let anything distract you. If they found a way of interfering with the palace, they would have done that first, so it's a fairly good bet that they haven't."

"In other words," said Charles, "strengthen our strengths rather than pouring our resources into fighting a battle of their choosing."

John though for a moment. "What about those who want to be there? Or what about the option of finding the nest entrance and attacking the weak spot?"

Frank added, "And what *is* their weak spot?"

William turned to Tera. "Well?"

She thought to herself, *'Why me?'* but said, "Approval. Whether it's the football team's popularity, student applications, funding, or accreditation; everything that goes in or out of this university has to go through approval."

"Yuck," remarked Jerold, "that's like pure politics; nothing but dirty fighting. Why can't the entrance be a swordfight or something?"

"There are two keys to political fighting," stated Charles, "One, know what to hide and what to make public, as well as when to do so. Two, know how to strategically switch allegiances at a moment's notice and force others to do the same."

"That's insidious," said William, "I'm staying faaar away from you."

King John stood up. "This is good: it gives everyone a clear choice of which strategy to take. Those who can stomach politics by all means attend their meeting. Those who wish to get on with life, the queen and I will be continuing the project of establishing the palace."

"Hm. When and what to hide and make public..." mused Rachel, "That gives me an idea." She shot a knowing look at the king, who nodded solemnly without changing his expression. The group was breaking up when Tera saw Allison hurrying toward them looking rather stressed.

"Have you seen Cat?" asked Tera.

"I was going to ask you that. She isn't answering her phone and her dorm room is locked. We were supposed to do lunch."

Cris was with them immediately. "Did it seem to you like she was in her room?" he demanded.

"That's the thing. I didn't hear anything, but ...you know how you get the feeling that someone's there even if you don't know for sure? That's what it was like." Cris took off like a shot towards her dorm. "Wow. I didn't know he could run that fast. Should we follow him?"

"Let's find Jason first. I think he's with Heth and Holly's boyfriend."

Jason was, in fact, heading that direction, though not yet in sight, discussing things with himself as usual. *All this and we still have Tera's birthday to deal with.* So deal with it, why didn't you prepare ahead of time? *She's hiding something that's important to her, and it's throwing me off.* Okay, genius, why don't you just ask her? *Before or after I'm expelled?* Whine, whine, it's not as if you weren't expecting it. *Sure, but not as a political move to hurt others.* That's what you do, isn't it? Leave a path of destruction in your wake? *I'm hoping to mitigate that somehow.* Well you've got a whole class and your friends involved. The way you're going you might as well start stealing candy from old ladies in front of buses. *Oh knock it off. We just need to get the king and queen out of harms way and isolate the damages.* And you think you can do this alone. *It's kind of in the definition of 'isolate' isn't it?*

A sudden jolt of pain rocked Jason's whole body, interrupting a promising repartee. He turned around to see a well-dressed lady hurrying away from him and doing a not-quite-successful job at maintaining her dignity.

She just kicked me in the butt. He gathered his wits, still wincing from the pain. *Better sit down.* He found a bench and settled gingerly into it. *Wow. I think I needed that.* He sat there letting all his plans and concerns subside with the pain. A walkingstick slowly made its way up the oak beside him. He let his thoughts and feelings float out in all directions. *Hm. Something's wrong with Cat.* He resisted the usual impulse to jump up and do something about it. The sun was doing his last stretch of the climb towards noon, and the walkingstick had disappeared into the branches. *Well there it is then. I'll go talk to Tiron first.*

Holly was leaning on Mitch's shoulders, looking at the screen with Heth. "So you could reroute the mail going to the governor's office to here?"

"Yes," said Mitch gleefully, "but once it gets sorted by a human at the post office on this end, they might notice that something is wrong. But first test: successful!" He looked at her hopefully. "As my designated psychologist of pleasure, perhaps you could procure a celebratory cup of coffee? I've been empty for fifteen minutes."

"I'll have to consult with my inner child to see if I feel like it," she retorted.

"Let's leave the mail alone for now," said Heth, "No one's got much of a reason to hack the Post Office, so hopefully you haven't thrown up any flags. Let's go directly to the APA."

"Is that a state or national accreditation organization?" muttered Mitch, when an insistent knock rattled the door. "Come in!" he called out, complaining to Holly, "Here I am working on the biggest secret since the invention of the computer, and this place turns into Grand Central."

Cris came in and immediately demanded, "Did you get it?"

Heth said hesitantly, "Yes… we're getting there…"

"Good. Stop what you're doing. I need your help right now."

"Yo, what's wrong, dude?" said Mitch, "take a chill pill."

"Later. Mitch, can you access restricted files in a computer that's not hooked up to the internet?"

"You asking if I can get past a password?"

"Is that the only way?"

"Of course not. If you know what directory the files are in, just section off the whole directory, bring it back here and crack it at our leisure. That's not even ten minutes' work if you have access to the computer. That's not usually the problem."

"What's usually the problem?"

"When you go to use whatever you got. Without permission, anything you copied is a crime."

"What if the computer *is* hooked up to the internet."

"Same deal. I can get it, but you're asking for trouble. A *lot* of trouble."

Cris thought for a moment. "Suppose we get permission, but still don't want anyone to be able to tell that we did it?"

"Piece of cake unless they log keystrokes. Even then, you've bought a few days."

"Okay, I think I've got it. Can you remotely make a file look like it's accidentally deleted?"

"Mitch could make your screen crawl across the desk and give you a kiss if he wanted to," remarked Holly. The others looked at her. She shrugged, "Well he practically did that to mine in English Lit."

"Cris, what on earth are you up to?" asked Heth, "What's so terribly important?"

"I'll explain on the way. Heth, you can help."

Leonard Deon was attempting to ignore a particularly insistent fly when Heth knocked on his open office door. "Heth! How nice to see you, please come in. What can I do for you?"

"Thank you. I'm sort of embarrassed to bother you with this, but I have some questions about the assignment you gave us on Maxwell's editing of Cavendish's work ...if you're not too busy."

"Of course not, delighted my dear, delighted. Have a seat." She settled in just as there came another knock on the door by Cris. "Cris, welcome! Don't tell me you're here for a chat also?"

"Well I was, but I can come back later..."

"Nonsense, my boy, come in and sit down. You can help with the discussion. Where were we? Maxwell?"

"Yes," said Heth, "Do you remember that paper I submitted on Newton? The next-to-last paragraph, I just wish I could remember what it was..."

"One second, I'll pull it up for you. Here it is. Very nicely written, by the way; while I don't agree with your argument for an entirely different approach than Newton *or* Leibniz, you covered the issues rather thoroughly. Let's see... the next to the last paragraph, one moment..." He suddenly started hitting keys with a puzzled look on his face. "I don't understand," he muttered.

"What happened?" asked Heth.

"The whole paper disappeared. It looks like the file is corrupted."

"I'm pretty good with computers," offered Cris, "describe it to me."

"It looks like there's a background program running that... here, come take a look." Cris watched over Professor Deon's shoulder as he searched through the files trying to find Heth's paper. "See, that's where it just was, and now there's something called 'debuts' in its place. Oddest thing. And nothing happens when I click on it."

"Oh, I've seen that before," said Cris, trying to sound casual, "you've got the 'debuts' worm. It's nasty, but easy to get rid of." He went back and sat down.

"Wait a minute, get back here! Show me how to get rid of it."

"Oh, you can do it easily yourself, do you know how to start a powershell script from DOS?"

"I most certainly do not. How long does it take?"

Cris shrugged. "I could do it in five or six minutes. Is this the first file you've lost?"

"Yes, I've never seen this happen before."

"That means it just activated. You probably should shut your computer down for the day until someone from IT can get a look at it."

"But you said you knew how to fix it."

"Sure, but I'm not going to get into trouble. I'd probably need all kind of permissions to do that."

Leonard stood up. "I hereby give you permission to fix this computer. That's all you need." Cris started to get up, then hesitated. "Please?" implored Leonard.

"Okay, let's get rid of it." He hopped up and sat down in Professor Deon's chair and started typing.

"Sorry about this," Leonard said to Heth, "It looks like our discussion is put off for a few minutes."

"Do you have the hard copy of my paper anywhere?" asked Heth, "If I could see that one paragraph, I'd know exactly what I was going to ask you about."

"Sure, they're in the filing cabinet in the classroom. Why don't we take a walk on down there while Cris is working his magic?"

"Wait a sec!" exclaimed Cris, "I've got to check a bunch of these files. Do I have your permission to access the system folder to check for clones?"

"For crying out loud, Cris; you have permission to access any folder you want for any reason you want. Let's go my dear, before he asks us to do his typing for him." As they disappeared down the hall, Mitch slipped in and hopped into his chair. Less than a minute later he slipped back out, and Cris took a seat waiting for them to return, which wasn't for almost ten minutes. Heth had gotten Leonard explaining things a mile a minute, and they stood in the door talking for so long that Cris wondered if he'd ever get back to his computer. Finally Leonard turned to his desk and said, "Let's see how Cris did with his magic fingers." The 'lost' paper was up on screen, and everything else was working normally. "Thank you Cris. I really did not relish losing the rest of the day waiting for those geeks from IT to get to this."

"Sure thing. I've actually got to run now, but if I'm around and something else needs tweaked, just let me know."

"I'll go with Cris, professor," said Heth sweetly, "Thank you *so* much for rounding out the picture."

"That's what I'm here for," chuckled Leonard. "A good day to you both." As they left, he mopped his brow and thought to himself, *It's such a shame… but all is fair, as they say.*

Jason glided silently through the cacophony of strange plants that crowded Tiron's walkway. As he approached the door, it slid open before him and Tiron waved him in. "Welcome, Jason."

"Thank you kindly." He entered and soaked in the dim cabin silently.

"You made good time; the fish isn't done yet. How did you travel?"

"Hitchhiked." He sniffed. "That's native trout. You catch those?"

"Yes. There's a stream ten minutes northwest of here that hasn't been invaded by the stock trout they throw in for the fishermen." He handed Jason a cup of tea and a small hand-rolled cigar. "You weren't going to come at first, then you changed your mind rather quickly. What happened?"

"I got a good swift kick in the butt." Tiron raised one eyebrow at him. "Yes, quite literally. It still hurts."

"Oldest cure in the book," smiled Tiron, "Don't worry, I had nothing to do with it, but it's good to have you here."

Jason sat down and sipped his tea. Most of the artwork on the walls he did not recognize, but a particular painting got him to spring out of his chair and go examine it. "This is..."

"Yes. Van Gogh. *The Painter on His Way to Work*. I never tire of the colors." Jason stared at him pointedly. "Well if anyone asks, I let them think it's a very close reproduction. I don't need the German Chancellor knocking on my door." He winked, "I keep it covered for most visitors."

Jason stopped before another painting for a long while. A beautiful nude woman was kneeling on freshly tilled soil, bent almost backwards by the attack of an enormous hornet. "The lines are ...exquisite," Jason said softly, "I've never seen anything like it. Who is the artist?"

"My own," said Tiron, "Have a seat, the fish is ready." He set two dishes out while Jason sat down, still staring at the painting.

"But if you painted that… that means that..."

"It must be refreshing for you to find out that there is more to me than you thought." Tiron stated cheerfully. He paused, raised his hands in the air, and said "God, thank you for the food," and sat down catty-corner to Jason, "Let us eat. Have you questions, or shall I just talk?"

"I came to listen."

"Well we need to start somewhere. Give it a shot."

"Jude?"

"There is always a Judas in every true society. Not for his own sake, which is never very pretty, but to see how the society will successfully deal with him."

"Don't you mean *if* the society will successfully deal with him?"

"No. A true society always succeeds."

Jason looked at him interestedly. "There's times that I admire your faith in your subject."

"Then convert that admiration to confidence and use it."

"Hm." He took a bite of the trout which was perfect. "I suppose you know what's bothering Tera."

"Yes, and you have a few surprises ahead of you."

"Any advice?"

"Between you and her? Only a fool would offer that kind of advice. But between your affairs and her affairs? The same advice. Courage."

Jason smiled and continued with the trout which was irresistible. "Is this going to a repetitious answer?"

"Maybe."

"I suppose you know about the summons I received today."

Tiron raised his eyebrows. "Had not the slightest idea. Do elaborate." Jason pulled the folded papers from his back pocket and handed them to Tiron. He looked them over and broke into a laugh that rolled around the small cabin, then handed them back to Jason. "That is rich," he chuckled, "What are you going to do with it?"

"I hadn't decided. Any advice?"

"Not really. Have fun, I guess."

"It sounds like you're not taking this much more seriously than I am."

"Is there any reason to?"

"It may involve my friends. And it's an obvious intimidation tactic pointed at the kingdom."

"That is true. But as long as decorum and propriety are maintained in the face of just the opposite, there is not really a lot of damage that can be done."

"Even to you?"

"That's a curious remark to cloak as a question. Why do you ask?"

"Because the first time you talked to me about something you thought was important to me, you leaned forward instead of backward. This means it affects you equally."

"Perceptive. But..." he leaned slightly forward, "is there any other way?"

"You're touching on some rather large issues."

"Name one."

"The contradiction between puppeteer and guide."

"That," said Tiron leaning back, "is again a matter of protocol and propriety. Did you know..." he paused for a few moments, "that virtually every difficulty or apparent contradiction can be traced back to simple ignorance of protocol, and the failure to distinguish between the ones we pretend to know?"

"Like the silly 'This statement is not true' puzzle which has been put on a pedestal?"

"That is a weak example, but apt. The fact remains that there is only one contradiction in the universe, and that is existence."

"Existence itself."

"Yes."

"You're going to say that in order for the universe to exist, there has to be a reason for it to exist, and by definition the reason for existence is greater than the existence itself, because the universe can be wiped out and started over without denting the reason."

"So far so good."

"Yet if the universe is *worth* making, then its very existence must somehow equalize itself with the reason for existing, else it immediately ceases to exist by dint of its own comparative insignificance."

"Pleasantly succinct. Some have used copious volumes of parchment to proceed this far. Go on."

"So by definition, if the universe is worth making, a separate potential for its full significance would have been made concomitantly, not as part of the universe, which is impossible by definition, but as a separate reality lying beside it."

"Proceed."

Jason thought for a moment. "So there is a reality of which we know nothing lying right beside us. It is not existence, but must be experienced through existence in order to demonstrate its presence."

"The gracefulness of your storyline is fading," said Tiron, "but you have much of the idea. Now there are protocols to *this* existence. Birds generally stick to the air, and fish generally stick to the water."

"And in that separate reality?"

"Completely different protocols."

"Ah."

"What you do," stated Tiron matter-of-factly, though Jason noticed that he was being very careful to make himself clear, "is *station* yourself in that other reality."

"Leave existence?"

"No, not at all. Everything we do must be here in existence; we have little choice. But our existence protocols do not apply to that other reality. The protocols of that *other* reality, however, apply to *both*."

"Oh." Jason felt the rare pleasure sweep over him of receiving a new idea without having had to wrestle it to the ground himself.

"And *that* is why if someone slaps you, you are perfectly justified in slapping them back in *this* existence..."

"But stationed in a separate reality, you can turn the other cheek."

"Correct. And choice itself has its own set of protocols which are some of the most haunting and intriguing..." The phone rang gently from under a pile of papers. "That's odd." Tiron looked at the phone like it was a strange animal. "I didn't anticipate that at all." He picked up the phone, "Professor Jerome here. Yes. ...Certainly. ...I'm rather sorry to hear that. ...Certainly, my time is at your disposal. ...Leave a message if I am not in, and I will contact you as soon as I am. ...Yes. ..." He looked at the receiver, then hung up the phone.

"They hung up on you?"

"Yes, yes they did."

"Who was it, if I may ask?"

"Mr. and Mrs. Ambrose. They're flying out."

"*Cat's* parents?"

"Yes. Correction: they *have* flown out. That call was from the airport." He glanced at the sunbeams coming in the west window. "If you are going to get to your expulsion on time, I had best drive you. Shall we?"

"But what did they want?"

"They did not say. However, they were quite upset, and demanded to see me at my earliest convenience."

"That could only mean..."

"Jason. Suppositions before the time lead to artificial defenses. Let us deal with circumstances as we encounter them rather than build defensive houses of cards that collapse from lack of full disclosure."

"Yes sir." He turned before stepping out the door, and took one last look at the brushstrokes of the wasp and the woman. "There's a companion painting to that."

"Perceptive."

"You haven't painted it yet."

"I told you why in our first conversation."

Jason thought for a moment "Oh."

Tiron picked up his cane. "Some things are exactly what they are. It can be rather nice."

"I didn't think I'd ever hear you use that word."

"A parochially aural treat, I'm sure. Have you been getting along with Mary?"

"Yes, though it was touch-and-go there for a bit. What is it that she lacks that she seems to think she can get from me?"

"Empathy."

Chapter 18: Ship of Fools

Jason sat with his advisor at the defendant's table in the front of the room which had been set up like a court. Nine members of the board faced him with varying masks of solemnity. He sized them up one at a time like a man counting the twists in the hangman's rope. Behind him some fifty students were gathered on folding chairs with more wandering in every minute. About half of Tiron's class had come, and on the way in he had been a little surprised to see Lady Laura seated in the back with her notepad. There was no sign of Heth or Mitch, but Cris and Tera were near the front, their faces unreadable. Tiron had dropped him off and continued on to meet Cat's parents; Cat herself was nowhere to be seen. Gary was fidgeting nervously with his tie, and Jason realized that the poor man was stressed uncomfortably close to the breaking point. *Must remember to be nice to him*, he mused faintly, but he was feeling anything but nice at this point. Jerry was sitting with a group of faculty on the far right, ostensibly to observe and record the proceedings.

One of the nine, a somewhat chunky girl with short blond hair stood up and waited for the room to quiet. "This is a preliminary hearing," she read from a document, "of Jason Sardic by his peers," she waved to the nine at the front, "all of us his fellow students, to review the evidence and make a recommendation to the faculty." She paused dramatically. "Jason Sardic has been accused of cheating. The alleged act was taken during his first semester here during the midterm test of the Structural Engineering class taught by Professor Wesley Kunz, who is here with us today. This hearing is informal," she smiled at the audience, "—so you don't have to call me 'your honor'. The decision that results from today's findings will factor heavily in the course that the faculty will pursue. Our longest standing board member, David Dobroski—" an older-looking student with a neatly trimmed beard seated in the center waved his hand "—will preside in this review."

David stood up and looked around. "Thank you Deborah. Let's proceed. Jason, how do you plead?"

"Unconvincingly, generally;" stated Jason, "I'm not terribly adept at pleading." A ripple of laughter swept the room, which David ignored.

"What the court, or rather the *board* in this case, needs from you at this time is a declaration of innocent or guilty so that we may proceed accordingly."

"Very well," said Jason turning to his advisor, "What do you think I should plead?"

"If you're guilty, you should plead guilty," muttered Gary, not looking up.

"My advisor thinks I should plead guilty," stated Jason in a clear loud voice. "And judging from the merits of his past advice, I should like to plead innocent." Another twitter of laughter bubbled in the background, which David again ignored.

"Thank you. We would like to present as evidence, a copy of the test in question." He brought a stapled bunch of papers over to Jason and set in front of him. "Do you recognize this as a copy of your test?"

Jason leafed through it, "Yes, it's a copy of *most of* my midterm from Structural Engineering last semester."

"Most of?"

"Yes, there's two pages missing." David looked over at Wesley with a questioning look, then went over to confer with him. They traded copies, and David brought over the original test.

"Is this the actual test that you took that day with all the pages?"

Jason looked it over. "Yes."

"Are you sure? There are no pages missing?"

"No, they're all here. You probably didn't copy them because they were blank. But I had drawn a bowl of fruit on the back of one, and you neglected to copy that. That's how I remembered that they were missing."

"A bowl of *fruit?*"

"Yes, the girl in front of me had her hair done up fancy, and it looked like a bowl of fruit, so I drew it." He held up a page to David, "Here in the corner."

"So you had the time during a midterm examination of a highly technical subject to draw a *bowl of fruit*."

"Yes."

"Thank you. Would you read for the board, please, the score you received on the test."

"Sure. 100%." He shrugged. "There weren't any bonus questions."

"And how did this compare with the other students' scores?"

"I don't know. If I recall correctly, I don't think I attended class the next week."

"Why not?"

"I was studying."

"Obviously you weren't studying structural engineering."

"Obviously not. It's a simplistic course."

"Would it surprise you to learn that the next highest score in the class was 33%?"

"A little. I had expected them to come in closer to 50%."

"And you want us to believe that you somehow pulled off 100% when the other students without exception were struggling to understand the material."

"Yes."

"And this does not strike you as suspicious in any way?"

"Are you saying that you want *me* to plead guilty because Wesley Kunz can't teach?" Cris realized with a shock that Jason was deliberately antagonizing everyone in his field of vision. *What's his end game?* he mused.

"And if Wesley Kunz, a fully tenured professor in an accredited university course 'can't teach' as you say, exactly how did you succeed in achieving 100% on his test?"

"Easy. I didn't listen to him." He turned to Wesley and said cheerfully, "You may have noticed." At the side of the room June was leaning over Jerry, "Sir, I just received a call from the American Psychology Association. We've lost accreditation for our School Psychology department. Do you want to call them back now?"

"Um… after this, June, after this." He wrote it down on his pad, and turned back to the hearing, which was going better than he expected.

"I would like to call Robert Niles for testimony at this time," announced David. A quiet looking lad took the other defendant table which was empty and waited. "Robert, do you recognize Jason here?" asked David.

"Yes. He sat beside me in Structural Engineering."

"Can you please tell us briefly from your perspective Jason's behavior the day of the test?"

"Yes. Um, he filled in all the answers quickly; it didn't look like he read them very closely. In about fifteen minutes he was done. He sat there doing nothing for a minute, said something about how difficult it was to raise honeybees, and left."

"Raise honeybees?"

"Yes, that's what I heard him say."

"It's much more difficult than it seems at first blush," offered Jason. Another ripple of laughter.

June tapped Jerry again. "Sir, I'm sorry but you should know this. The APA called back and apologized; they said it was some sort of computer glitch on their end. However, our Theater school lost *their* accreditation, followed by the practitioner program for our Orthotic and Prosthetic department."

Jerry looked at her strangely. "June, that's impossible. These are all completely different agencies. What's going on?"

"I don't know sir. Do you want me to get them on the phone?"

"After this June. Which departments?"

"Theater, then Orthotic and Prosthetics."

He jotted them down. "Keep me posted."

"Yes sir."

"Let's talk about these blank sheets that we neglected to copy the first time," David was addressing Wesley. "What was the purpose of providing them with the test?"

"Those were to show their work so that I could evaluate how the student arrived at his conclusions," stated Wesley.

"And were you able to evaluate Jason's conclusions on his perfectly answered test?"

"No."

"And why is that?"

"There was no work shown. Just answers."

"Objection!" cried Jason, "Wait, am I allowed to say 'objection'?"

"Yes, Jason, to what that Professor Kunz has just said do you object?"

"I would like to draw your attention to problem fourteen. Perhaps you or Wesley could read the last phrase in that problem."

David flipped through the pages and read, "Clearly show each step toward the solution using the method outlined in the textbook."

"Thank you," said Jason, "and could you please tell us whether you see all the requisite steps written down by me for problem fourteen as outlined in the textbook?"

"They appear to be there, yes. As well as the word 'outdated' inserted before the word 'method'."

"But that's the only problem he showed work for!" exclaimed Wesley.

"And it's the only problem that asked us to do so," said Jason.

June was back. "Let me guess," said Jerry, "They both called back and said it was computer glitches."

"I'm afraid not sir. I don't understand this. Our predoctoral internship programs in Professional Psychology have lost their accreditation. A minute later it was the baccalaureate and graduate programs in Information Technology."

Jerry groaned and wrote them down. "Please tell me some good news soon," he pleaded.

David was doing his wrap-up, "It is the opinion of Professor Wesley Kunz as well as many others of the staff that this is a clear-cut case of cheating. It is not humanly possible to solve the problems given in the fifteen minutes that Jason actually spent on the test without prior knowledge of the answers. Professor Kunz, could you have answered each test question accurately without foreknowledge in fifteen minutes?"

"No."

"No surprise there," said Jason brightly, sending another ripple of laughter through the audience.

"Before this board considers what recommendation it will deliver to the faculty, is there anything further you would like to offer in your defense, Jason?"

"Yes, I would like to call Bradley Swenton for a few brief questions."

As Brad was making his way forward from the back of the audience, June tapped Jerry's shoulder again. "Lay it on me June."

"Well… our Professional Psychology program turned out to be a computer glitch on their end. They apologized and said this never has happened before. However… we lost accreditation for Teachers Education." Jerry groaned, wrote it down, and turned to Jason questioning Bradley Swenton.

"Bradley, could you tell us where you were during the midterm, please?"

"Yes, taking the test in the room with you and everyone else."

"And do you remember where you were that evening, say around seven-thirty?"

"Sure. I was at your place hanging out. I remember because you made chocolate chip cookies."

"And do you remember how the chocolate chip cookies tasted?"

"You've got to be kidding me. Those were some of the best chocolate chip cookies I've had in my life."

"Thank you." He addressed the nine members of the board, "The defense rests."

"We will confer together and present our finding to the faculty," announced David amid the laughter of the students, "I would like to personally comment to Jason that if you don't take this hearing very seriously, we are hardly expected to believe that you take cheating very seriously. We will reconvene in five minutes for our next case. Dismissed."

"Next case?" said Jason to Gary, "What next case?" Gary said something unintelligible and walked quickly out of the room with his head down.

Jerry glanced down at his notes and felt his heart sink to the bottom of his stomach. He was an experienced politician whose job it was to be able to quickly and accurately assess threats to his well-being from a distance. He had written down:

School Psychology
Theater
Orthotics and Prosthetics
Professional Psychology
Information Technology
Teacher Education

...and even his eye couldn't miss the line-up of first letters: S T O P   I T. He looked around in a panic for anyone watching him closely, but found nothing. His mind raced, assessing the full implications of the threat and what it would take to deliver a message in that manner. Three national agencies and three state agencies had been hit simultaneously in perfect order; he couldn't even imagine the amount of money that would require. He wisely decided that perhaps he would sit out the second half of this hearing after all.

Jason had been trying to make his way around the crowd, most of which wanted to talk to him, when a strange hush spread through the room. Cat and her advisor were heading up to the defendant table, and it was patently obvious that Cat had been crying. She held her head down and looked at no one.

Deborah stood up and did her preamble, only this time it was "Cat Ambrose has been accused of plagiarism." Jason felt his heart pounding; this was not an attempt to intimidate someone who could defend themselves, this was the wholesale sacrifice of a lamb. Out of the corner of his eye he saw Tiron enter with two people who could only have been her parents. And David was being relentless.

"Is this a copy of the paper you handed in to Professor Leonard Deon on the scientific method?"

"Yes… I think so."

"Speak up please."

"Yes, I think so."

"Well it either is or it isn't. Would you please look it over and tell us."

"Yes it is."

"I would like to draw your attention to the entirety of page three which continues for two lines on page four. Do you recognize it?"

Cat stared at it for a while. "Um, I thought I put that in quotes..." she flipped to the back, "with a reference in the back."

"Do you see any quote marks around that section, or a reference in the back?" demanded David.

"No." Cat put her head down, and her advisor patted her reassuringly on the shoulder.

"Professor Deon, is this the paper that was submitted to you by Cat Ambrose?"

"Yes it is." Jason noticed that Leonard was an expert at choosing which expression was needed and maintaining it.

"And what is it about the section in question that caught your attention?"

"Well it seemed to have some very familiar insights that were well-phrased. Then I recognized it from the 1914 book *Pasteur* by Albert Keim and Louis Lumet, and realized that she had lifted wholesale from their writings and presented it as her own. While a *newspaper* might get away with this from time to time, in an academic setting..." he shook his head as if at a loss for words.

David turned to Cat, "Do you have anything to say for yourself?"

"I… thought I put in quotes. I wasn't trying to pass it off as mine. Professor Deon likes us to have lots of references, so I used it." She put her head down in her arms again.

"Is there anything more the defense would like to present before the board reviews this?" asked David.

Cris was seeing red at the edges of his eye. He darted up to Cat's advisor and hissed in her ear, "My name is Cris Ianoff. Call me as a witness or I will rip your head from off your shoulders right here." Cat looked up in a daze, wondering what was going on.

"The defense would like to call ...Cris Ianoff," her advisor said shakily.

"Very well," said David, "Are you Cris Ianoff?"

"I am."

"Are you here as a character witness?"

"Yes. But not for Cat. For Professor Deon."

"Proceed."

Cris handed a sheet of paper to David, and took a copy over to Leonard. "Tell me, Professor Deon, is this an accurate printout of the files holding student assignments on your computer?"

Leonard looked at it surprised, then cleared his throat, "May it please the board to know that this is inadmissible. And illegal. These are copies of my professional records taken without my permission."

Cris picked up a pocket recorder and held it in the air for the board to hear and hit 'play'. The professor's voice crackled out of the recorder, "Cris; you have permission to access any folder you want for any reason you want."

"Did you or did you not say that to me today Professor Deon?"

"Yes, but… the 'debuts' virus…"

"'Debuts' has an anagram which is 'busted'. I would like to draw the attention of the board to the two files named Ambrose; they are near the top. I would especially like to draw your attention to the entirely different time stamps on each of those files. The first matches when the assignment was handed in by the class, as well as the date on Cat's paper. The second, which is the copy you just handed her, dates to *yesterday*. They are of identical size, because they are *almost* identical." He pulled out another pair of papers, handed one to David, and took one over to Cat. "Cat Ambrose, do you recognize this paper?"

She flipped through it. "It's my paper. Look! The quotes are right there where I thought they were." She flipped to the back. "And there it is, '*Pasteur* by Albert Keim and Louis Lumet'. I *knew* I put that in there."

"That is my character witness for Professor Deon. Someone who will alter original work to hang an innocent student for political gain!"

"You have no right!" shouted Leonard, jumping to his feet.

"No right to protect the innocent while being accused by liars?"

"You're time is up, Cris," said David "And I must say that you are out of order."

Cris relaxed and looked around. His voice came out dangerously soft and low. "Out of order? I don't care. You can discipline me. You can kick me out. You can strip yourselves naked and roll around in the grass crooning *Yankee Doodle* for all I care. But see that girl?" he pointed to Cat. "That girl is sacred. You do not touch her. You do not think about her. You do not even deserve to apologize to her for your trumped-up lies. If you even breathe wrong in her direction I will make it my personal business to expose every miserable little secret in every one of your miserable lives. You are a pathetic Ship of Fools! Hang me if you want to." He stared at each of them in turn. "But. You. Leave. Her. Alone."

Cris felt four heartbeats of silent fury pulse in his ears then an entire roomful of students stood up and burst into applause. David threw his arms up helplessly and sat down. Leonard's mouth was open but no sound was coming out.

And Cat burst out of her seat and buried her head in Cris' chest.

When Jason finally made it out of a side door, Mrs. Ambrose was giving Cris an endless hug and Mr. Ambrose looked like he was going to choke on something. Tiron and Lady Laura were nowhere to be seen, and it looked like Tera had also left.

"Strange feeling to be part of a victory that you didn't orchestrate, isn't it?" said a familiar voice. Mary was floating a small rock about six inches above her hand and smiling slyly.

"Is that a trick or are you really doing that?" asked Jason, genuinely curious.

"I'm channeling the energy in the room. I've only been able to do this twice before."

"That's very nice. Try not to freak anyone out with it."

"*Jason*," she said reproachfully, "That what I *do*."

"I have noticed a little more spring in your step. Do I detect Joshua in that extra bounce?"

"A woman never reveals potential pacts, only sealed ones."

Jason approached and looked at the floating rock from every side. "May I?"

"Be my guest." He slipped hand just above hers and the rock followed his as he pulled it away, flipping over once in the air. "Jason! You're a natural. Let me teach you to..."

"Thank you kindly but no." He moved his hand under hers and again the rock flipped and remained hovering above hers. "Just on special occasions."

"Like this," she purred, moving her hand in slow circles. "Come, let me show you something."

"The circus is over isn't it?"

"Not by a long shot. You've only seen the second floor. Come." She led him around the building where a crowd of faculty were huddled a safe distance from the main entrance looking in. "C'mon, they're of little consequence. I want you to see this." She walked with Jason right through the middle of them with her hovering rock and stopped at the entrance. At first Jason thought the lights were flickering, but then realized that the floor was alive. Rats were darting here and there aimlessly; not just a dozen or two, but hoards and hoards of rats.

Jason looked at Mary in amazement. "It's beautiful," he said softly.

"Isn't it? I'd give them… oh, at least three days to clean that up. And they'll never walk down a dark hall alone again." She gave one of her delightfully musical laughs.

As much as I'd like to end the chapter there, we must see to Tera, who has just entered her front door. William was sitting at the table with an odd expression on his face. "Nice birthday present dad," she shot at him, and started for her room.

"Tera." She turned and looked at him. The odd expression was still there. Suddenly the realization hit her and her world began to collapse into itself. She crumpled on to the floor, barely hearing her father's words before she sank into darkness:

"Lester is dead."

Chapter 19: East Wind by Way of West

Tera lay wrapt in a blanket on the couch when she came to. Her mother was cooling her forehead with a damp washcloth. "She's awake dear."

William came over and looked down at her. "Welcome back. How do you feel?"

"Just fine. Weak for some reason." She looked up at her father, "You're in trouble you know. Lady Laura was at that student board fiasco today."

Her mother looked at William then back at her, "Tera, it's Thursday morning."

"Oh my goodness!" she tried to get up but her mother pushed her back down.

"Rest Teri darling. The funeral's today. I know you'll want to be there." 'Teri' was a nickname her mother had used when she was much younger.

"What time is it?"

"Six forty-five. You have several hours to prepare, so there's no hurry. I'm so glad to see you awake little Teri!" her mother gave her a gentle hug and headed for the kitchen.

"Mom, if you're getting Alzheimer's I need to know ahead of time," she called out.

"No chance of that," her mom retorted, "I have to take care of William."

She looked at her dad. "So did you get the paper yet?"

"No. I'll get it now." There was a knock on the door before he got there; he opened it and said, "Good morning Jason. I assume you're here to see Tera?"

"Good morning William, here's your paper. No sir, I'm here to see you." *Odd*, thought Tera, *calling him by his first name and then saying 'sir'*. William cocked his head, unsure of what to say. "I would like to have a brief discussion with you in private if you are open to one," said Jason.

"I am always open to discourse," said William, "I trust this will be of a civil nature?"

"Most. I have but a single question and it requires little other than a yes or no answer."

"Come in. We can talk in my study." William felt as if he was leading a coiled viper through his home. His mind raced over all the issues that Jason might confront him on, but could settle on no fixed point around which to prepare a defense. He gave the morning paper to Tera, and brought Jason to his private study—his sacred space as he like to think of it—and shut the door.

"Handsome study," remarked Jason.

"Thank you." He took his glasses off, gave them a quick polish, and put them back on. "Well Jason, a great many things are happening. You are aware that Lester's funeral is today at one?"

"Yes, thank you. Is the attendance open?"

"That was Lester's wish. There will be a memorial service next week for friends and relatives who have some distance to travel. However, his instructions were to be buried the day following his passing." There was a moment of silence, then William said, "I must admit that I'm a bit curious as to what between us could be summarized so neatly so as to fit into a yes or no question."

"It is a matter of protocol. My culture—and perhaps yours—provides for a hierarchy of safeguards when it comes to matters of ceremony. It has come to my attention that a continued relationship with your daughter may very well result in my decision to make her my wife. If and when that decision is made, I cannot proceed without having previously obtained your permission."

"You came here to ask me for my daughter's hand in marriage."

"I did and I am."

"This was the last thing on earth I anticipated you wanting to discuss with me."

"I trust it satisfies your hope of civility."

William chuckled and leaned back to look at the ceiling. "You know, Jason, it's nice to be a father."

"It's an envious position."

William smiled wryly. "It's an impossible position." He looked at Jason for a while. "Yes."

"Thank you. I am honored."

"Do you have… plans as to when you might 'make this decision' as you put it?"

"None at all. I wanted to cover my bases first."

"Hm. I think I like that about you. Hm. So you didn't come here to talk about your expulsion at all."

"I don't see any need. We could discuss it over a drink sometime, if you were so inclined."

"I may be at some point, I may be. You know, Jason, we might be able to interact like human beings after all." Jason gave a careful smile, then they both burst out laughing. "Dear me," said William scratching his head, "are you wanting me to keep this a secret from my daughter?"

"That is entirely up to you."

"Well I don't see any reason to ruin the surprise, if it ever happens. Besides, it will be interesting to have something in the air that only you and I know about."

As they joined Tera she looked at them strangely. There was absolutely no reason that they should be getting along, but neither had the guarded body language she expected though she knew that Jason could portray what he wished. "Look at this;" she showed them the paper, "Lady Laura came through, but you won't believe what she wrote."

Our Own Royal Wedding

A trip to England or Morocco will not be necessary for those of our unique town wishing to attend a royal wedding. Queen Rachel Wainstead has just announced her engagement to King John Krisner of the local Kingdom which has garnered so much attention of late.

The date for the wedding is pending at this time, however their majesties have assured this reporter that the wedding reception will be open to the public. Preparations are already underway to convert a facility appropriate to the occasion, which her Majesty says "must be able to address the multivarious requirements of both subjects of the Crown and attending citizens." When questioned further as to the location of said facility, her majesty replied enigmatically, "At the palace, of course."

The wedding promises to be a once-in-a-lifetime event with all the pomp, circumstance, and controversy one could hope for. This reporter will faithfully provide details as they are forthcoming, taking care to distinguish between the personal, civil, and royal aspects of Cherell's own regnal event. May the king and the queen find providence in preparations, as well as the requisite fellowship to make this event truly majestic.

"She didn't say a single word about the student government hearing yesterday even though she was there," mused Tera.

"Clever, clever lady;" said William, "I see she's as wily as ever. She seems to approve of your little kingdom, even if only to secure her position as the consummate insider."

"Yes, about the kingdom..." began Tera.

"Not today," interrupted William, "today belongs to Lester. We will have ample opportunity to discuss… that subject when things have settled down a bit."

Her mother was bringing her a small package. "Speaking of unexpected oddities, this arrived for you yesterday. No return address; it looks like it was dropped into a mailbox downtown." She handed it to Tera. "Perhaps it's a birthday present from a secret admirer."

As Tera took the package and began to open it, Jason began to go. "No, no; stay. You can all share this part of my birthday since I slept through most of it." Inside the package was a ring box wrapped in a sheet of parchment which had one large letter scripted by hand: 'L'. "It's from Lester," she said excitedly. The box exposed a gold ring with a quaintly sculpted knot. Looking closely she could see the word 'Before' engraved on the left side of the knot, and the word 'After' engraved on the right. It was, of course, a perfect fit. As it was passed around, she noted Jason's look of understanding.

"I'll be getting along now," he said casually, "I hope to see you at the ceremony Mr. and Mrs McCory."

"Call me Fiona, Jason," said her mother with a bright smile.

As he headed to the door, Tera got unsteadily to her feet. "Let me see you out. I need to ask you something." She closed the door behind them and stood in the long shadow that that morning sun threw over the front walkway with Jason. "You know what the 'Before' and 'After' on my ring mean. Would you care to share?"

He looked at her for a bit as if deciding whether to speak or not. Finally he said, "Tera, you know far more than me, and you're holding back, which is fine; you probably have very good reasons. But you realize that I always find things out whether I want to or not; it just happens. Is that the way you want this to unfold?"

She looked away. "I… want to tell you everything, but I just can't right now. I don't mind what you find out… go ahead. I just can't talk about it yet… everything's up in the air and I don't know what to think. And anything you can tell me about the ring would be helpful."

"Okay. Well two things are obvious. The package came from town, which means Lester has someone there taking care of at least some of his affairs. The little I know about Lester indicates that it would be someone who is taking care of *all* his affairs. The fact that it arrived on your birthday tells me that more than just his passing was anticipated." He paused. "And the look on your face tells me that you already know this much."

"Yes."

"Well if I got a ring prepared for a specific time that had a specific message on it, I would listen to that message."

"What… what is the message?"

"Tera, the gift was time-specific, and insinuates that you have something to do. There's only one immediate event to which the ring can refer to, and that is his funeral. Whatever it is that you are to do, you need to do it 'Before not After' the funeral."

"Oh. 'knot' means 'Before *not* After'. That's the message in the ring?"

"I'm sure it means much more; Lester was a complex person. But that much is so plain that I'll be surprised if your parents don't catch on."

"Wow. Thank you Jason. I need to…"

"You need to get into town before the funeral. And I need to figure out just what you're up to unless you decide to tell me first." He smiled, "But for now I need to rally the troops for a funeral. Nice chatting with you, mystery girl."

Eight thirty found Cat knocking on Tiron's office door which he rarely used except immediately before and after class. He was in, and she found herself sitting comfortably before him with whatever she had come to say completely missing from her memory and somehow unperturbed by this fact.

"Did you hear about the rat infestation in Rhoboth Hall?" she said suddenly.

He chuckled. "Yes, Miss Sendik's contribution." He leaned backwards. "You will be gratified to know that the faculty is withdrawing any charges of plagiarism. An official apology has already been drafted up for your parents."

"Oh. That seems like it was so long ago. But it was only yesterday. Everything is changing so fast." There was a bit of comfortable silence. "Why did you want Mary in the class? I guess I could ask you that about anyone, but she's like a wild card. I would say 'dangerous' but it's a kind of dangerous that is easier to avoid than embrace."

"You might call it a weakness on my part. I knew her grandmother."

"You did? Does she know this?"

"No, and it's likely better that way. I doubt if what she has heard of me was put kindly."

"Did you do something ...bad?"

"Sometimes we are placed into an impossible situation, one designed to hurt us no matter what we choose to do. The trouble with creating situations designed to hurt someone is that if they do not go as anticipated, the creators of the situation get hurt instead. And the results that unfold can last generations."

"So you were in a catch-22 and found a way out."

"Yes."

"It's funny. It's like there's an unwritten law that we have to do what people expect us to do, whether success or failure doesn't matter, so long as it fits within their expectations."

"Yes. Step outside that circle and you are guaranteed to offend most everyone."

"Is that why Jason's so careful not to do anything he wants? Or even want things?"

"That's part of it."

"Could you tell me the rest of it?"

There was another knock on the door. "Enter, your excellency," said Tiron.

Rachel came in and saw Cat. "Oh good, you're here. We wanted advice from someone outside the kingdom on what to do with Jason."

"Jason? What did he do?"

"Before you get into that," said Tiron, "Congratulations on the timing of your announcement."

"Announcement?" asked Cat, "What announcement?"

Rachel took the seat beside Cat. "You didn't see the paper yet." She grinned then recovered with a noble look. "The king and the queen have announced their engagement."

"Rachel! That's wonderful! Congratulations!" Cat was out of her seat embracing Rachel.

"The timing was impeccable," smiled Tiron. "As to Jason, whatever you decide to do, I will not have those sorts of kingdom affairs conducted during class time."

"Do?" asked Cat, "Am I the only one who has no idea what's going on?"

Rachel sighed. "It all started with Jude. We confronted him; Allison, Charles, Frank, John and I. Oh, Lisa was there too. He confessed everything and agreed with us that his standing as a subject of the kingdom should be revoked." She looked at Cat. "He was passing information about the kingdom to the faculty when they were deciding how to try to destroy it. That's partly why they attacked you."

"Oh." She thought for a bit. "What's that got to do with Jason?"

Rachel sighed again. "We had a long discussion afterwards. Jude was dangerous in a bad way. But Jason is even more dangerous in a good way. For the health of the kingdom, we are thinking of asking him to renounce his position as a subject of the kingdom also."

"What?!? But I thought we were all in this together! You can't discard Jason like a dirty rag!"

"Cat, think about it. You were rescued by Cris. But Jason just antagonized them when he could have defended himself. He could have asked for a re-test right there and then; you know he would have aced it. But he's out on a limb sawing it off behind him… and as long as he's associated with the kingdom, we could all fall together. Nobody wants to betray Jason, but as long as he's a subject, everything he does is associated with us."

"You can't..." started Cat.

"What about a treaty?" interrupted Tiron.

"What do you mean?" asked Rachel.

"You will note that the kingdom is moving forward quite well with the two treaties it currently has. Jason has played an integral part in the formation and health of the kingdom up until now. When one relationship is too dangerous to keep, rather than merely discarding it you might find it useful to transform it into another relationship."

"Make a treaty with Jason?"

"Yes. There may be a special relationship with him that can advantage both parties."

"Wow," said Rachel, "I never thought of something like that. Thank you."

"Stop it!" exclaimed Cat, "You can't do that. It's *Jason*! He's one of us!"

Rachel raised her eyebrows. "Is he, Cat?"

"Well… I don't know." She looked imploringly at Tiron, "Help?"

Tiron said nothing for a bit, then he began speaking so softly that the girls had to lean forward to catch his words. "The problem with Jason is that he is normal." He held each of the girls' eyes in turn. "Somewhere deep down you know that it's perfectly normal to do what he does. On a base level that makes you feel inadequate for not being able to do what he does. So you try to make him into someone special in order to hide that fact. He is not special. He is normal. What is he supposed to say 'Thank you for treating me like an idol to cover for your own inadequacies?' What is he supposed to do, embrace the limits that everyone else embraces in order to fit in?" He paused. "The question is not whether he is one of you or not, the question is whether you are one of him. And given the choice, people generally choose fraternity over normalcy."

Cat looked up at him from a lowered head. "That really stings."

"Because it's true," said Rachel, "but right now we have to deal with facts, and it's the job of the king and queen to protect the kingdom. If it's a choice between Jason and the kingdom, we don't really have a choice."

"One of the advantages of life," said Tiron much more casually, "is that our decisions rarely affect matters one way or the other. Someone who is prone to screwing things up will continue to screw things up regardless of how many good decisions he makes, and someone who knows how to succeed will likely succeed in spite of making bad decisions every time. Come, let us get to class."

Jason, perhaps following his advisor's advice, had neglected to attend Tiron's class and was sitting in his basement apartment dialing a number in Texas. *Time to put my Entomology studies to the test.*

"Medical and Institutional Direct," said the crisp voice, "this is Verona, how may I direct your call?"

"Is that name purposefully an acronym for 'maid', Verona?" asked Jason.

"Yes sir, our director insists on a service-based approach to all our clients. How may I direct your call?"

"I'm looking for Andy. Name's Jason. See if he's got five minutes to talk to an old friend about Phasmatodia relationships."

"I'm sorry, what kind of relationships?"

"Phas-ma-toe-dee-ah. He'll understand."

"One moment sir."

A minute later, the familiar drawl from Tera's Christmas party came on the line. "Who the sam hill wants to discuss walking-stick mating rituals with me? I only know two Jasons; one is dead and the other is just a kid, so I'm guessing this is the kid."

"Yes, hello Andy. I thought I could snag your interest with a mating ritual that lasts over a month."

"You're Tera's friend, right? I may see you in a few days, I'll be coming up for Lester's viewing."

"That would be nice. In the short time I knew Lester I learned to respect everything about him. I guess William will be taking care of the farm from now on."

"Oh I wouldn't be too sure about that. Won't know until the fat lady sings, as they say."

That's a tease to see if you're prodding. Better back off and circle around. "I was hoping we might do lunch while you're up this way. I know Tera would enjoy it."

"I'd like that. But you're inviting me without asking Tera first?"

"Well she's a girl and I'm a guy. I tend to like the entomological approach in which the guy does all the planning and the girl does all the follow-through."

Andy laughed, "I thought you were sweet on her. Is this some ploy of yours that I'm getting roped into?"

"Maybe it is. But I can promise you'll get a good meal and possibly a good conversation out of it."

"Well I'm game if you are. How's she doing?"

Give a little and see what he does with it. "She dropped into a dead faint when she heard the news. Plus she's being all mysterious; took off into town by herself for no reason and missed a good class."

"Smart little vixen. She's probably talking to Bari. I wish her all the luck in the world; without Lester half her world is gone."

"Seems that way. Who's Bari?"

"Oh, that's Tony Stellar, Lester's attorney. He handles all of Lester's affairs. Everyone calls him Bari."

"Sounds complicated. Hopefully everyone will be settled down by the time you get up here."

"Sure, I'll give you a ring once I'm in town. Gotta run now Jason, unless I can interest you in some medical supplies."

"I'll let you go. Nice chatting with you Andy."

Jason sat engulfed in thought for a long while. *So close and yet so far. Best wait a bit.* He stared at the grey-on-grey painting he had been working on, but he kept seeing the image of the beautiful woman and the wasp.

As the Mercedes crept from the overloaded parking lot up the hill into sight of the graveside, Fiona exclaimed, "Oh dear, there seems to be something else going on today."

"Or maybe not," said William. The entire hill was filled with people of every description; it appeared that half the town was there. He drove as close as he could and parked by the side of the road. As they walked the rest of the way the crowd silently and respectfully parted for them.

"William, this is a little scary," whispered Fiona.

"Yes," he agreed, "Dad is just as imposing in death as he was in life." Despite the respect he was getting from being Lester's only son, he felt incidental to the crowd's focus, which had organized into groups in the shape of pie slices pointing inward. As they drew closer he saw empty space left around the grave site for thirty feet in every direction. The only person in that space was the black stiletto form of Tera standing alone with a bouquet of flowers in her arms. The slice of pie behind her was composed of students, most of whom were subjects of the kingdom, more than fifty strong.

He approached the raised podium on the opposite side of the grave from Tera and climbed the five stairs alone, leaving Fiona looking up at him expectantly. From this vantage he could see the extent of the crowd and a wave of apprehension to which he was entirely unaccustomed crept over him. Clearing his throat, he opened the speech he had prepared and looked at the words, which suddenly seemed puerile and artificial. Looking around for a familiar anchor he found nothing until he saw the confident form of Fiona looking up at him. He folded the speech into his pocket, abandoned the podium, and joined her on the ground holding her hands before him. "Together?"

"Together," she smiled. Arm in arm they ascended the podium, generating a spatter of applause.

"It was my father's request that his family be given space to express themselves," he said in a clear voice that carried easily. "All of you—" he gestured to the crowd, "have expressed more by being here than I could say. Lester McCory was a great man who lived a full life and left behind a full legacy." He paused, inexplicably at a loss for words again, and Fiona immediately stepped in to rescue him.

"Lester was wonderful, and we honor him today." Her voice resonated with reassurance. "We would like to open the podium to anyone who has words to offer, after his granddaughter Tera, if she wishes to speak." She led William back to the ground, and he walked to the edge of the crowd, both wishing he had said more and thankful that he had not.

All eyes were on the motionless Tera, when Cris realized that not only was she not moving, but that she *could* not move. As soon as the thought crossed his mind he was also aware of Jason's figure by her side speaking to her.

"It's just like the dream," he was saying to her in a low voice, "It's time to go to him."

"When I drop the flowers into the grave, it's over." Her faint voice came from far away. "He will be gone. It's just me." The picture clicked in Jason's mind and he realized what she was shouldering.

"It is as it must be," he said, "Yes, you are alone. But you have friends and you have me. We can be alone together." He changed his tone to match her distant one, "It was eighteen feet to his room… it is eighteen feet to his coffin. Eighteen feet. Go to him." She did not realize that she was walking until she was looking down at the coffin. She spread her arms and the flowers scattered like lost chicks. As she slowly looked up, clarity returned and her mind sharpened into focus. She took to the podium and looked around. *Such a small crowd.* Pulling a sheet of parchment from the velvet of her dress, she read in a clear voice which carried with gentle authority:

"My grandfather asked me to read this to you." William and Fiona looked at each other with the same question in their eyes. "My friends. With many of you I have had fellowship, and many others I have known well. All of you are here today to say goodbye to me, and I as well say goodbye to you. Together we have laughed and cried and together shared the thousands of things that are given to mortals to do. The issues we faced, each in our own respective abilities and strengths, do not pass with my passing. Face them well, for one day you will be with me looking back, as I am. Mortal life is a temporary affair at best, but a most beautiful one that can never be forgotten or made insignificant however far into eternity we traverse. While you are here, be here fully. Live. Love. Create. Sing. Dance. And most of all, enjoy fellowship with each other as passengers on a train which passes this landscape but once. I will never forget one of you. You are here to honor me; for that I thank you. I am gone, but you can still do something most invaluable for me. You can live. Goodbye my friends."

As Tera made her way down from the podium, the strains of 'Danny Boy' started up from musicians scattered artfully through the crowd, thanks to some careful planning from the kingdom. The crowd was inclined to sing along, and Tera found herself standing among friends with Jason's arm around her shoulders. "You were right, I finally figured it out," he said in her ear. "You might have told me and saved us both a great deal of stress."

"I thought I had to do it alone," she said.

"Well no more," he said, nodding to Cat, who came and replaced him as her support. A line of speakers was already forming at the podium, and Tera felt herself beginning to relax for the first time in days. Looking around, she saw that Jason was already gone.

As Jason stormed into the law office, the secretary looked up, smiled, and went back to her work. "*Odd*," thought Jason, yet strode across the plush carpet straight past her and knocked on the office door. After a few moments it was opened by a fully bearded and thoroughly bald gentleman who peered down at Jason through bifocals. "Master Sardik, I presume."

This was the last thing Jason had expected, but he didn't skip a beat. "And you are Attorney Steller, I would likewise presume."

"Call me Tony. That is, if I may call you Jason. Come in, we've been expecting you. And I must say you swallow your surprise admirably. Let us see how well you maintain that." He led Jason into a dimly lit yet magnificently furnished office suite hanging with a thick fog of fresh cigar smoke and motioned to a chair centered around a small table set with several large tomes and three ashtrays. In the second chair sat Tiron Jarome. Jason froze.

When the eternal split-second had worn off, Jason spoke crisply. "I came here to tell you that we have a common issue to discuss. It appears that you have prevent-, uh, precluded me."

"I know the classical meaning of 'prevented' young man," said Tony, "you don't have to tone yourself down in this room. Yes, we have anticipated you in two out of three of the senses of the word."

Jason slowly took his seat and looked around. He was in a room that would make any museum envious. He had considered himself fairly adept at dating antiques, but this was overwhelming. From the sextant pointing out the window to the quipi knotwork draped over the *Erdapfel*—Jason wondered if it was one of the original German globes and decided that it probably was—there was not a thing in the room that a trained eye could easily skip over, and more than half the items in the room were completely unrecognizable to him. He picked up the cigar from the ashtray, smelled it, and was not disappointed. He clipped the end neatly, lit it, and leaned back. After a minute of silence in which he decided that the others were enjoying themselves too much, he raised an eyebrow at Tony.

"Andy's drawl has a way of masking his analytical genius. It's taken down many a competitor."

Half the pieces of the puzzle fell together in Jason's mind. Of course. Andy saw through his phone call. And the only person he would be interested in warning would be Tony.

"First things first," continued Tony, "I have a proposal for you."

He waited for Jason who finally said, "It's your nickel."

"Indeed. You did some work last semester with the energy transformations involved between diatomic hydrogen gas and its elusive atomic state. From what I can gather, you dropped that investigation altogether once you realized the implications."

"Yes, the barrage of misinformation was one of the first things that alerted me to a lot of buried technology in plain sight. Any of the elements under Carbon can be used, but Hydrogen would be the natural choice because of its charge-to-mass ratio." He paused. "This isn't the type of research that anyone smiles on, unless you have some very interesting connections."

"That does not concern me; this is not an Old Boys' Club or anything of the sort. You are being given this offer because I personally have a vested interest in seeing it come to fruition shortly. Furthermore, the results have enough promise to justify an investment. This particular project has been on the back burner for several decades, waiting for the proper confluence of circumstances."

"Such as finding someone dedicated enough to do it and naive enough to agree your terms?"

"Yes. Consider yourself nominated Knave of Naiveté for now." He chuckled, "Do you know how long students like you last at a university? A semester, sometimes two before they quit out of disgust. You are overripe for picking."

Jason took a slow drag on his cigar. "I suddenly feel typical. And common."

"Save your sarcasm for when you are around people who won't get it. The offer is this: a certain university with which I am associated would be willing to consider your proposal for doctoral research on the subject. Acceptance would allow you to finish your education and add some useful letters to your name while honoring the obligation to your patron by producing a finished working model." He looked over his glasses at Jason. "Which I would expect in less than two years."

"Would this 'certain university' allow me to locate the research here in Cherell?"

"As long as it is not on university grounds. There are some relationships which would be healthy for all parties to sever."

Jason looked at Tony for a long while. "I would like to consult with Tiron if you don't mind."

"Consult away." Tony rose from his chair, "I will fetch a splash of cognac."

"As long as it's not Hennessey," said Jason, eliciting a raised eyebrow and a grunt from Tony. He turned to Tiron, who seemed to be lost in his own thoughts, and a good two-thirds of the way down his cigar. Once Tony was out of earshot, Jason asked, "The second painting?"

"Hm. Yes, I was just considering that. It may be time to begin it."

"I see." They sat in silence until three glasses of cognac were placed on the table and Tony was settled back in. "My consultant and I are of the opinion that a contract of this nature would be worth considering," stated Jason briskly.

"It is already drawn up. Pick up your copy from Adeline on the way out and look it over at your leisure." He swirled his cognac and held it under his nose.

"What about the conflict of interest inherent in the fact that this will help my personal circumstances?"

"It does not matter. The fantasy of helping people the way it is commonly envisioned is largely a myth. A person who creates is going to create come hell or high water; he can not be stopped. The only way to get in his way is to try to help. Most great producers who have contributed to the human treasury were in dire straits all of their lives. If they had not been, humanity may have been the poorer for the results."

"Thank you for the cognac. I can't join you in a drink until I state the business for which I've come."

Tony smiled. "It is now your nickel."

"The possibility has come to my attention that Tera McCory is about to be immersed in a measure of responsibility that will alter her position and could severely affect her well-being."

"That is not the kind of information that *any* professional attorney would be inclined to dignify with a comment."

"Correct. It is a mere remote possibility, which only has significance when aligned with yet another remote possibility. Together, however, these produce a situation in which the anticipation of breach of contract would trump the current potential of breach of confidentiality."

"I will entertain your remarks one step further."

"Tera is her own individual, but her well-being is a civil asset in which I have a vested interest."

"How vested?"

"One hundred percent."

"Did you follow the protocols, young man?"

"I have William's permission."

"I see." He peered through his cognac, then took a sip. "I may be inclined to take up these matters—should they turn out to be relevant—with the affected party. If such a discussion occurs, what relationship would best describe the role you propose?"

"Silent prolocutor."

"Hmph. You have apparently been thumbing through a law dictionary. However, you were wise to apprise me at this particular junction. In fact, I believe we may just be able to save a great deal of unnecessary time and bother, a fact to which I will toast." He held his glass out, and Jason clinked his own on it and took a sip, then looked up with surprise.

"You're kidding me. This is Louis XIII."

Tiron smiled triumphantly at Tony, who rolled his eyes and handed him a crumpled five dollar bill. "We had a bet," explained Tiron, "you just won me five dollars." He turned to Tony. "If all the heavy business dealings are quite finished, I'd like to ask you just how many of these 'ripe to pick' students you have patronized over the years."

"About a dozen. They can be difficult to locate." He looked at Jason, "And do not even entertain the thought of asking me about Heth. If that girl does not go underground fast, she is not going to be alive much longer. That is a simple fact of life."

"There *is* an interested party," said Tiron.

"Well they had better be very interested," stated Tony, "she is a hot potato with no indication of cooling off any time soon." He looked at Jason kindly. "I suppose you have realized by now that a life of integrity is a life alone."

"The thought had occurred to me."

Tony shrugged. "It appears to be the way of things. Do you see it any differently Tiron?"

"Anthony, I would have to agree just as far as your way of phrasing it. It appears to be the way of things."

"I can see that with societies and organizations," said Jason. "but what about friends?"

"Ah. Friends. Yes, that is the one monkey wrench in the way of things."

As Tiron and Jason walked back to the university, Jason asked, "Tell me again, why you were there?"

"Anthony engaged me to arbitrate. You have an adversarial side with which he had little interest in engaging."

"Ah. There are a lot of new elements to process."

"The east wind brings new things, the west wind destroys old things. I would say we have an east wind by way of west."

As they passed the laundromat Jason was suddenly reminded of Heth. "Who is this 'interested party'?"

"You of course. But I was not about to tell that to Anthony."

Harbor

Tera and Cat stood in the newly stoned driveway. The palace improvements had progressed at a breathtaking pace. Under the direction of Mike and Holly, a tower matching the original construction was rising above the roof to overlook the gorge. The town zoning board was being remarkably lenient, due in part to the fact that the Historical Society had been trying to get someone to restore the building for years and partly because both Lady Laura and Fiona were long-standing members of the zoning board. A constant stream of students eager to help made the cleanup and bulk work melt away.

"Let's go in and see what they decided," said Tera. Cat nodded and they entered and climbed the curving staircase to the temporary conference room that had been set up for royal affairs. A small crowd of students were waiting outside the room.

Bethany opened the door, looking relieved. "They've come to an agreement. C'mon in." Tera and Cat filed in with the others, where King John, Queen Rachel, Phil, Charles, and Jason Thomas were gathered around a table, looking somewhat disheveled. When everyone had settled in, Phil made the announcements.

"This proposal is announced for consideration by their majesties to all interested subjects on the matter of a treaty between the Kingdom and Jason Sardic. First: that the position of Palace Curator be established separate from the Kingdom, and that Jason in his person hold this position. Second: that the attic space in its entirety, excepting the portion allotted for the tower, be consecrated for use at the sole discretion of the Palace Curator. Third, that this position be honored for a five-year period with allowance made for equitable discharge or breach of treaty in accordance with standard arbitration practice. Fourth, that funds be set aside appropriately proportioned to the duties of the Palace Curator for care and upkeep of the palace and grounds as the changing nature of the duties warrant. Fifth, that the Palace Curator holds the authority to dismiss from palace grounds any persons of his choosing, overruled only by their Majesties the King or the Queen and any designated representative thereof. Sixth..." Phil cleared his throat, "...that subjects of the Kingdom be nice to his cat."

The last condition of the treaty produced snorts of laughter. Rachel spoke up. "This was pared down from several pages you guys. In a nutshell, the kingdom gets a live-in caretaker, and Jason gets... um... people to be nice to his cat. Plus he has to throw out the drunk or disorderly and shovel the walks in winter."

"Cat, you're the one dissenting voice in all this," said King John, "what do you think?"

She shook her head. "I've heard all the arguments, and they make sense. And Jason agrees with you. I just... I don't think it's right. Jason was one of us. I don't care what we do to make everyone happy, it will never be right for me." She looked up. "If you have heard and recorded my objections, I will support the decisions made by your majesties one hundred percent."

"Bethany, have you got all that?" asked John.

"Word for word your majesty."

"Very well then. Are we all in agreement to ratify this treaty between the kingdom and Jason Sardic?"

"Yes" chorused the voices of the subjects.

"I declare the treaty ratified. Phil, you will pass on the six articles as written to Jason?"

"Gladly, your majesty."

"I can take them to him," offered Tera, "I'm going to visit Heth with him at the hospice tonight."

"Thank you," said Phil, "and if there's anyone who can get her out of that coma, it's you and Jason. I know she's unresponsive, but tell her we all miss her."

"I'll do that."

These words were still ringing in her ears when she picked up Jason at his apartment. Driving the forty miles out to the hospice, he was oddly quiet at first. Finally he said, "Tera, there were things that you couldn't tell me, and there are still things that we have not told each other. I trust that you know I am perfectly content with that."

"As am I. But I do want to tell you a few things… they are just so big that I'm not sure where to start."

"Say what you wish. And please realize that I'm in the same position."

"That's kind of expected. I'd like to tell you about what's going to happen tomorrow night after the viewing."

"What makes you think that I don't already know?"

She looked at him. "Don't try that. Nobody knows except myself and one attorney."

"Anthony is discrete. My insights come from Lester, not Bari."

Tera slammed on the brakes, pulled over to the side, and stared at him. He was giving her no expression at all to go on. "Okay Jason. I don't know… I don't know what to think of you." She buried her face in her hands, then composed herself and stared straight forward. "Please tell me what you know," she said in a low even voice.

"Lester apportioned out an appropriate inheritance to your parents. The bulk of his fortune, however, has been given into your care and its use is under your sole discretion, including the trust stipends that have supported your extended family. This freaks you out. Yesterday you privately made the decision to continue the disbursements as they have been going for the last several years. You made this decision after looking at the fund and realizing that it would not significantly depreciate for some time. You have given yourself space to mature and think about all the ramifications. The only decision that you have not yet made is exactly how to express this tomorrow when Tony reads the will. Shall I go on?"

"Yes."

"Tony has told you that he is authorized to conceal the fact that you are the prime benefactor. If you decide to do this, William will fight him on it, and eventually prevail; at most Tony can buy you about six months. The only question you are actually facing is whether you wish to have a showdown with your father now in front of the family, or later when it will hurt him even more. Shall I go on?"

"Yes."

"There are a number of things that you do not know, which you need to know in order to make a wise decision. You would like to know them now so that you can properly decide what to say tomorrow night. The fact is that you are going to have to make a decision without knowing them. There is one thing that you *do* know but have shoved into the back your mind, which would clarify everything and make your decision easy. Shall I tell you what you have purposefully forgotten?"

"Yes… yes, please."

"Lester planned exactly this."

She slammed the palm of her hand into the steering wheel repeatedly then rested her forehead against it. "Why?"

"Because whatever issue he was facing was deemed important enough to take this step. He chose you."

"But that first night when he talked to you… he said something about you stepping in… "

"That is what I'm doing."

"But I thought you would… do more."

"I may. That's in the arena of things we don't know yet. What you know is that he entrusted you with his funerary message and a ring which says 'Before not After'."

She sat in silence for some time, then started up the car and continued their journey. After a while she hit 'play' and Bach's cello suites filled the car with ancient energy.

The hospice was nestled in a grove of pines that extended up and over the mountain. As they pulled into the lot, Jason turned down the music and said, "Are you ready to find out one of my secrets?"

"I don't know. Sure."

"Let's go see Heth first."

The receptionist checked through the records for some time, then asked them for identification. "We need to show identification to visit her?" asked Tera.

"There's only three people on the visitor's list ma'am," explained the receptionist, "Jason Sardic, Tera McCory, and Reyansh Laghari." Tera looked quizzically at Jason, but handed over her license. The receptionist walked them down a long hall and unlocked a private room for them. Tera walked over to the bed, and looked at Jason.

"This is..."

"Sssh," he made a motion to be quiet, then joined her at the bedside, talking in a quiet voice. "I explained to Reyansh that his daughter would get much better care here than her previous institution."

"But who is this?"

He looked at her innocently. "The plaque on the headboard says 'Heth Rejul'. That should be plain to anyone looking for her. Come, let's get some coffee and talk outside." The vending machine faithfully spit out some brown colored liquid, and Jason led Tera to a picnic table behind the hospice set nicely among the pines.

She sat down beside him and glared at him. "Okay, spill it."

"Well, when Mitch heard about Heth's 'accident' he assumed the worst and destroyed all of our work. So he's safe for now, because there's no way for him to duplicate it without our help. But Heth gathered too much attention; it's fairly well-known what she is capable of."

"You faked her death."

"Better; we faked her coma. Anyone who needs proof that she's out the picture can go look in that room, where a real girl in a real coma is getting superlative care. It wasn't hard to find someone who looked like her with only one living relative."

"But then she's..."

"...right here," said a familiar voice behind them.

Tera stopped herself from yelling 'Heth!' just in time, and instead gave her a long hug. "I don't believe you guys."

"We had little choice," said Heth, looking somewhat embarrassed.

"I trust your new accommodations are satisfactory?" asked Jason.

"They're perfect. And I would love to show you my work, after all, we have a duel to finish... but for now discretion is best."

"In good time. The kingdom sends its unwitting regards. You are missed."

"Hm. I must visit some time. I'm actually enjoying building my own little world out in... wherever I happen to be staying." She grinned at Tera.

"So this was your secret?" Tera asked Jason.

"One of them. Lots more to come."

"I'm... I'm flattered that you trusted me as the only other visitor."

"Think carefully about it," said Heth giving her a kiss on the cheek, "Gotta run now. Peace to all."

On the ride back Tera broke the silence with a slap on the dashboard. "Jason."

"Yes?"

"Seeing Heth like that... I don't know what it is, but I'm realizing that everything I've been stressed about has to do with things built up in the past."

"Meaning?"

"It's all irrelevant. It's all stuff that's already happened. There's so many new things coming... Jason, it doesn't matter! Whatever I say tomorrow is just dealing with stuff that's already happened." She looked over at him. "I feel like I'm waking out of a bad dream." He smiled and said nothing, not wanting to interfere with new mood. For the rest of the trip home she babbled like a little girl about plans and possibilities. When Jason reached his bed that night, the dreaming grabbed and pulled him in, and he slept far into the morning.

*   *   *

Cat awoke from a long involved landscape which faded as fast as she tried to remember it. She sat up and looked out the window. What day was it? She remembered Tera excitedly telling about how the showdown with her family had gone down. How long ago was that? The forms outside her window seemed to be drawings in a comic and her dorm looked like an old movie. She sat and stared, waiting for normalcy to return, but nothing happened. Slowly she prepared herself some cereal and cream, wondering what kind of foreign world she had wandered into.

Jason awoke feeling like he was the only figure on a large blank canvas. He waited for his usual dialogue to commence, but apparently he wasn't talking to himself today. As his thoughts crystallized, he realized that everything had stopped happening. No impressions were calling for attention, no signals were impinging on him at all. He looked at his hand and saw it as a strange intricate object. He sat and thought. This was new. New. Ah. When things are new, do something new. He reached for the phone and dialed Tiron.

"Good morning Jason."

"Good morning Tiron. I'm ready."

"Go with God."

"I will. Thank you. Have you begun the painting?"

"I was just getting out the brushes."

"Ah. Goodbye for now."

"Likewise."

Cris awoke thinking that someone had blocked the window and turned off the electricity, until he realized that his eyes were still shut. *Strange.* He rubbed his eyes and looked around. Clutter. Everything his eye fell on looked untidy and unkempt. He was filled with a sudden desire to throw everything out the window, to peel the cracks off the floor and flush them down the toilet. *What is wrong with me?* He had a longing for something clean, a place with no complications, no mess at all. *Maybe a shower will help.* But even standing under the running water he felt trapped, constrained. He dried himself off and got dressed, wishing he had a single clean sheet to wear instead of these ridiculous pieces of colored clothing. The phone rang.

"Cris?"

"Cat!" he suddenly felt a burst of relief, as if cleanness itself were spilling from her voice and enveloping him from the phone.

"Cris, something's going on. I don't know what it is. I feel strange."

"Keep talking, I do too. Wait, better yet, meet me in the quad, it's halfway between us."

"K. Be right there."

Tera awoke with the urgency of something that needed to be done, but she just couldn't remember what it was. A dream perhaps? No, it was something really important. She went through the motions of her morning rituals, but the urgency kept growing. *Did I forget a class? No, am I supposed to meet someone or tell someone something?* After a very distracted breakfast she found herself in Lester's room continuing the progression of organizing and packing his items. It seemed to smooth out the sense of urgency, but only somewhat. Near the bottom of a drawer she came to a vinyl packet holding old family photographs. It cracked apart from age and disuse when opened, and she lost herself for a few minutes in the scenes of the faded pictures. The last two were stuck together; as she peeled them apart she found an old faded note. Carefully opening it, she read in unmistakable handwriting: "Go to Buzzard Pass. Stand on the outcrop of rock at the crest and look East along the ridge. You will see a tall Sycamore tree in the distance, it has lighter bark than the others. On the far side of the tree you will find a path that descends slightly along the ridge. Follow it for about one-quarter mile. It is 9:14. You can get there in half an hour. Go now. —J" She looked up at the clock; it was 9:14. She mentally kicked herself when she realized that the first thought that entered her head was *What am I going to wear?*

The evening crickets were already starting when Cat and Cris wandered on to the newly-renovated deck of the palace. The date of John and Rachel's wedding had been set, and more than just the subjects of the kingdom now had an interest in improving the site of the town's 'royal wedding'. The strangeness of the morning had sent them wandering in every direction; while they could not explain the mood, they had shared it by rediscovering the world around them. They watched the evening shadows grow longer in contented silence until something occurred to Cat.

"Cris?"

"Yes?"

"You know all this… strangeness today? And like right now?"

"Yes."

"I think it might be love."

He said nothing; there was nothing more to be said. After some time the figure of Jason circled around and stood before them. The tops of the trees were catching the last of the sunlight and his figure was cut out in crisp shadows.

"Hey."

"Hey."

"I'd like to introduce you to someone."

Cat turned around but there was no one there but Tera. "Okay, who?"

"I'd like to *introduce* you to someone." Something in his voice made them both stand up. He walked over to Tera, took her by the hand and stood her before them.

"Cat. Cris. I'd like to introduce you to my fiancé, Tera McCory."

There is a cottage outside of town where an old hand paints a new masterpiece. There is a laundromat in the town, above which lives a lady who uses the protocols of nobility without serving them. There is a diner in the town where a young waitress enjoys life as she watches her peers strive for more. There is a university nested in the town, where university events swirl around like shirts in a washing machine. And there is a royal palace on the outskirts of town where a patient and grateful sun is setting on four friends sharing a wooden deck in silence. Inside the structure many more friends come and go, as friends will always do. The four on the deck share the scars and trophies that come with being alive. For they will live, and they will continue, and because they continue, the world will continue around them, its very existence dependent on those from whom it has taken, and will take, so much.